Sign up for our newsletter to hear
about new and upcoming releases.

www.ylva-publishing.com

Other Books by Lee Winter

On the Record series
The Red Files
Under Your Skin

The Superheroine Collection
Shattered

Standalone
The Brutal Truth
Requiem for Immortals

Breaking Character

LEE WINTER

Acknowledgments

Since my knowledge of both Hollywood and medicine could fit on the back of a paper napkin before I started writing this book, I have a lot of people to whom I owe large marble statues in their honor and merry bushels of cash and chocolate.

A massive thanks goes to awesome LA film and television actress Kay Aston, who was one of my beta readers. She explained everything from the little stuff, such as the roles of personal vs set assistants and ins and outs of trailers vs dressing rooms, to the big concepts, such as what really motivates actors, and how they face challenging scenes. My book would be much poorer without Kay's excellent insights.

Thanks to my medically trained mates who helped me with the blood and gore side of things, but especially to doctor and fellow author Chris Zett. She was excellent to brainstorm with, and offered serious treatments for all of my dramatically ridiculous TV injuries.

As always, I'd be lost without my main beta reader, Charlotte. Thank you for being an enthusiastic supporter of my books and ice queens.

To my editors, Astrid, Alissa, and Alex—what a triple-A team! Your encouragement and advice really kept me going.

To the love of my life, sorry for making you a writing widow yet again. I promise to introduce myself to you again *really* soon.

And for my readers, thanks for all the support and kind words over the years. You make it all worthwhile.

Dedication

I dedicate this book to all the actresses who put themselves out there, over and over, for their craft.

I had no idea how exposing and confronting the job was until I dug beneath the superficial crust and began to research what acting really is. To be so vulnerable, and open oneself up to constant scrutiny, demands, and critique is staggering. To be expected, often, to bare one's bodies as well as one's emotions and souls, and somehow remain unaffected, is staggering. That takes such courage.

If all someone sees when looking at an actress is just someone famous or pretty or rich or "perfect", then they really aren't looking.

All my respect.

Chapter 1

JOEY CARTER RAN WITH BRUISING pace to the main exit doors of Martina Hope Memorial Hospital and flung herself into chaos. Rain was cascading down, far colder than it had a right to be for LA. Dodging a rolling crash cart, followed by a gurney, she juggled the precious cargo in her arms.

"Dr. Carter!" someone shouted.

She didn't react at first.

"Carter!" the person tried again. "Joey Carter?"

She spun toward the voice. "Y-yes?" Water pelted her face, splashing into her eyes as she angled toward the light, and the figure silhouetted within it. She blinked away the rain. Her blond ponytail felt like a sodden lump, and water had caught inside her collar. Her hands were too full to adjust her shirt.

A tall, handsome man with pinched features, wearing a white coat, shouted to her over the roar of the rain, his finger pointing wildly behind him. "Get those blood packs to Dr. Mendez, ASAP. He needs at least three units."

"Who?" She gave him an uncertain look.

"Ah crap, that's right. It's your first week, isn't it?" Without waiting, he added, "You know the chief?"

Her eyes widened at mention of the notorious Iris Hunt. She swallowed and gave a nervous nod.

"Okay, she's over there, in front of that crashed ambulance. Dr. Mendez is inside, stabilizing a trapped patient with a severed femoral artery. The man's lost a lot of blood." He pointed at her bundle. "So get that to him fast!"

Joey flew off again, leaping over a puddle as she reached the impossible scene: three mangled ambulances had somehow collided.

She spied the hospital's chief of surgery immediately. Dr. Hunt was on her knees, under the glare of lights, compressing a wound on the man's stomach. Her beautiful brown hair, now soaked, fell just over a starched white collar. Her features, narrow and aloof, seemed even more distant in the bleakness of night. Hunt's intense gray eyes were fixed on her patient.

"Stay with me," she was saying in a commanding voice.

Joey ran in front of the pair, clutching her precious pile of O-neg blood packs. Her left foot hit a piece of gaffer tape on the ground. She fumbled, and her cargo bounced from her hands. Plastic blood packs cartwheeled away, skidding in every direction.

With a gasp, Joey turned, scrabbling to catch at least a few. As she twisted, her heel stomped hard on one pack. A gruesome arc of red shot up in a shower that exploded all over Hunt's face and chest.

Joey let out a pained moan. *Oh shit!* Could it get any worse? *Shit, shit, shit.*

Hunt's disbelieving gaze dropped to her own red-spattered chest, then shifted to outrage as she glared at Joey. "Just wonderful," she growled.

"Oh God! S-sorry... I..." She stopped, taking in the other woman's warning look. Hunt gave her the most minute of head shakes. *And* she was still applying compression to her patient. Joey's eyes flew wide at the realization of what that meant. "Chief Hunt... I'm so sorry. The blood packs were... it's the rain... they slipped."

"Obviously," she snarled. "Get it together. There's no room for clumsiness in this job." Hunt pressed a bit harder on the man's wound, causing him to groan. "What are you standing around for? Get that blood to Dr. Mendez immediately."

"Yeah...of-of course." Joey scooped up the remaining blood packs as fast as she could. It seemed to take far too long.

Red goop was dripping from Hunt's coat and hair and onto her patient. The condescension was dripping along with it when she added, "Sometime before Mendez's patient dies?"

Joey bolted off, around the rear of the crumpled ambulance, disappearing from camera view.

"CUT!"

The fire hoses raining on them stopped and the set broke into laughs. The Steadicam operator who'd been tracking her was almost on his knees, wheezing with laughter.

Geez. Had everyone been holding that back?

Summer Hayes was pretty sure she was feeling about the same degree of humiliation as her character, Joey Carter, a plucky second-year resident on the TV medical drama *Choosing Hope*. She was only supposed to drop the fake blood packs, not coat the imposing hospital chief in them. Stepping nervously back into view of the set, Summer was glad for the darkness that covered the blush creeping up her face.

The booming laugh of director Bob Ravitz filled the air—and normally, a surlier man had never existed.

"Christ," Elizabeth Thornton, aka Chief Hunt, muttered as she made to rise from her bloodied puddle. She darted a cold look at Summer. "Was there any part of my skin you missed?" She glanced around and lifted her voice. "Can I have a towel please?" Her tone turned dry. "Or a fire hose?"

The extra sat up. "Um, hey, me too?" He waved at his gory shirt.

"I'm so sorry—" Summer inched forward.

An assistant ran toward them, holding a thick towel, but before Elizabeth could grab it, the director waved her back down. "Don't move!" That earned him a dark glower. "Sorry, Ms. Thornton, but continuity on blood spatters is a bitch. We'll need to do close-ups right now or nothing will match. So let's all get it right the first time." He looked at his director of photography. "Steve, set up. Let's get this blocked *now*."

"But—" Elizabeth waved at herself. "We're keeping this? It wasn't scripted. I look ridiculous."

Summer was firmly of the view there was no way Elizabeth Thornton could ever look anything less than perfectly put together.

The comment earned her a long look from Ravitz. "Yes, we're keeping it. It gives Iris Hunt more reason to hate the new girl, which was in the script anyway." He glanced at Summer and smiled. "And the new girl *will* want Attila the Hunt all up in her face. Nothing makes fans love someone more than when a villain turns on them. Win-win. Right?" He snapped his fingers at his second assistant and muttered some technical notes.

Elizabeth looked murderous, and Summer wondered what that was about. Maybe she hated the nickname?

LEE WINTER

"What about me?" the extra asked. "Do I just lie here?"

Ravitz ignored him.

Summer glanced at the man. He was soaked to the skin, his shirt ripped open. His chest was red from where Chief Hunt had been applying compression. He shivered.

Elizabeth arched an eyebrow. "If I have to bleed all over you, you have to lie there and take it. Sorry." The tiniest edges of her lips quirked up before she hissed to a lurking assistant director, "How about a hot water bottle for our drowned rat, hmm?"

The AD shrugged and disappeared. Summer wasn't sure if that meant yes or fat chance.

The extra's gaze was entirely on Summer. He gave her a sheepish grin. "I guess this is showbiz, huh?"

"Yeah," Summer murmured as the lighting techs moved in closer to surround them. But her focus remained on the austere star of *Choosing Hope*.

This was the woman dubbed as "difficult" by the industry? Elizabeth Thornton was positively sedate compared with some of the asshole personalities Summer had worked with. And the woman actually seemed to care about the wellbeing of an extra, even if the man himself hadn't noticed.

She glanced around. They were at the VA West Los Angeles Medical Center, using its glass and steel exterior to double as Martina Hope Memorial's facade. Interior shots were done in the studio five miles away. It was a little weird out here at this time of night, devoid of the usual traffic and filled with an acre of cast and crew trailers.

The wind picked up, knocking over a lighting stand. Ravitz cursed. "Would someone secure that before it fuckin' costs us an insurance claim?"

The continuity woman ... Jill? Jan? ... began taking photos of Elizabeth's spattered face and shirt, before moving to the extra.

Then the first few drops of rain hit. The real stuff, not the hoses.

"Fuck!" one of the lighting techs grumbled. "D'ya think we'll be stuck here till midnight again?"

Elizabeth slid her gaze to Summer, saying absolutely nothing as she stared.

"It was an accident," Summer pleaded.

4

"It was just what the scene needed to really pop." Ravitz turned and gave her an approving smile that bordered on something else. "You can't script something like this. We got real lucky."

"Oh yes," Elizabeth murmured, "*that's* the word I was searching for." She smiled blandly and Ravitz nodded, grunted, and turned away.

Summer wondered at the man's missing sarcasm detector.

The extra sneezed. "Shit. I'm frozen."

"I'm *so* sorry," Summer whispered to him and, by extension, the woman still kneeling over him in the dirt. Elizabeth's knees had to be killing her.

Raif Benson, who played the rakishly handsome Dr. Mendez, sauntered over with a charming smile, looking clean, warm, and very dry under a large black umbrella.

Lucky bastard.

He sized up the scene with a smirk, then rocked on his heels, barely containing a laugh as he looked at Summer. "Welcome to TV, kid."

Summer gritted her teeth into something approaching a smile, not bothering to correct him. It was no use. At twenty-eight she was only a few years his junior, but she'd always looked much younger than her age. It had kept her in teenage roles for far too long, and led to frequent condescension from colleagues. At least Joey Carter, aged twenty-three, was an adult role for once.

Out of the corner of her eye, she could see Elizabeth staring at her, and Summer tried very hard not to look at the only person she really wanted to like her on this whole damned show.

Elizabeth Thornton's twisted parody of a smile was not friendly in the least.

"I mean it!" Elizabeth hissed down the phone. She stalked around her trailer, feeling better for the warm shower, a thin blue robe clinging to her body. "Four hours under hoses, not to mention fake blood running into my eyes thanks to some empty-headed newbie screwing up her scene. If I have to do one more season of this mind-numbing drivel, I'll implode."

Despite representing some of the leading lights in Tinseltown, Rachel Cho wasn't particularly good at diplomacy, but she was usually good at saying what Elizabeth *needed* to hear.

Elizabeth waited impatiently.

"Darling, I'm sure you weren't hating on your show quite so much when they turned you into one of the highest-paid women on TV last season. And that 'drivel' got you the pretty mansion you adore so much. Plus, you went from an unemployed, anonymous Brit to a star whose name is on everyone's lips."

Elizabeth glowered. "As the most-hated villain in America. And we both know how that came about. So now they've turned me into the star of *Carrie* so Ravitz and that ego-stunted showrunner can get their kicks at seeing me humiliated. That's not okay, Rachel."

"I thought you said it was an accident?"

"Yes, but they kept it! As if they'd miss the chance of cutting me down to size, making me look like a bedraggled stray. The worst thing is, they're still spreading those rumors that *I'm* the difficult one."

"You know why. That's how this place works. You don't play ball, they remind you who's boss."

"Oh, I know. So I've had it. Find me something else. Something serious. Find something to stretch me in hiatus or I'll walk off this putrid petri dish right now and I don't care how much we have to pay to get me out of my contract."

There was a soft sigh. "You can't walk, Bess, or they'll spin it as proof that you really are the British Bitch, and then see how much work you get around here. Look, just keep reminding yourself there's only one season left. Now I've been talking to Delvine about some offers that have come up and we agree there's one that seems right for you. And it fits with your schedule."

That sparked Elizabeth's interest. Her manager, Delvine Rothery, was one of the best at taking careers from middling to spectacular. "I'm listening." She grabbed a towel off the back of the chair and ran it through her hair again, as if it might wipe from her brain that creepy sensation of blood trickling down her face.

"Ever heard of Jean-Claude Badour?"

"That weird French director?"

"Not weird, darling, *creative*. Artsy. After his last Palme d'Or he decided he's done Europe now and wants to dip his toe into Hollywood. He apparently has a remarkable script, according to the buzz. It's the hottest property in town; everyone wants in."

"*He* won a Palme d'Or? Wait, more than one?" Elizabeth couldn't picture it. But then, she'd only seen one of his shorts—something oddball about butterflies.

"He won Cannes' top prize for *Quand Pleurent les Clowns—When Clowns Cry.*" Cho paused. "I highly recommend you take this one. It's going to elevate you far beyond TV. And, look, you should know he's asked for you specifically to star. He must want you very badly since he's lined up filming for your hiatus."

A sliver of distaste shot through Elizabeth. "Me? Please tell me he's not a fan of *Choosing Hope*? Is that why he wants me?"

"Don't be so cynical. He's French, not American. Of course he hates *Hope*. His actual quote was that you need 'freeing from rancid dribble'."

Elizabeth smiled. Well, he had some taste then.

"He followed your theater days in London. He adored *Shakespeare's Women* as well as *Lucifer's Curse* and *The Righteous Miss Hamilton.*"

Elizabeth stared at her phone.

"Still there? Or are you in shock that someone appreciates you for your acting instead of your *sizzling* chemistry with Raif?"

Sizzling? More like manufactured. It was still a sore point what had happened with her character—more petty revenge from the showrunner.

"Hilarious," she growled. "Fine. I'll watch his sad little clown flick and let you know. When can I see the script?"

"Soon. I've asked; it's not quite ready yet. Filming starts in two months. It's about a reclusive writer in a mountain shack in the middle of nowhere who gets eight visitors. *Eight Little Pieces*, it's called. I'm sure there's some beautiful, artistic metaphor involved. Anyway he wants to do lunch with you and Delvine soon to hammer out the details."

"I haven't said yes yet."

Rachel laughed as though it was a foregone conclusion. She probably wasn't wrong.

Elizabeth said her goodbyes and hung up, feeling optimistic. Even so, she reminded herself, Badour had done a short film about sentient butterflies.

She glanced at her sodden, stained Chief Hunt outfit where it hung on a rail. The reminder of what had transpired this evening—for hours—soured her mood. Anything she signed on for outside of this show had to be an improvement on the dreck they'd been dishing up in recent seasons. *Three* ambulances all crashed into each other? Right outside the hospital's entrance? That made *so* much sense. Was she the only one who noticed this nonsense?

A knock sounded on her trailer door.

"Yes?" Tension flood back into her shoulders. Right about now was when the director would have reviewed the rushes and decided they needed reshoots. She wrenched open the door, pitying the minion with the job of passing along that news to the cast.

"Um, hi?" A twenty-something woman with damp blond hair stood before her. She wore jeans, a T-shirt, and a strained look. "It's Summer. Summer Hayes?"

Was she asking or telling? Elizabeth peered at the young woman, waiting for something more. There was nothing forthcoming. Her eye fell to the hands clutching a steaming paper cup. The girl gazed at her with wide, innocent, regretful eyes.

Recognition dawned. She did look slightly different with her hair out of its drenched ponytail.

"We meet again." Elizabeth arched her brow. "Here to douse me again? Round two? You know, usually it's the newbie who gets hazed, not the veteran."

That came out a little snippier than she'd intended. It was hardly this girl's fault how ageist this town could be. Thirty-seven years old and she was starting to feel the subtle shifts in attitude. It was grating on her. Back home, she'd be seen as just entering her prime. Here, it felt like they were almost ready to hand her her hat.

"No, you're safe this time," Summer said with a bright grin. "May I come in? I bear gifts. And an apology." She waggled the cup.

"I don't drink coffee, much less the American swill they serve on this set. So, if that's all?" She began shutting the door in Summer's face, too tired to go through the charade of civility.

"Actually, it's, um, tea. From England. I think you might like it."

Elizabeth frowned. "You can't get what I like here."

"Oh, it's possible." Summer smiled, wide and radiant.

Elizabeth pursed her lips and held out a hand for the cup, willing to test Summer's claim out of curiosity if nothing else.

Their fingers brushed as the cup exchanged custody, and Summer snatched her hand back as if bitten.

Great. Was her reputation so awful that new cast members believed she was Attila the Hunt off screen, too?

Then the tea's heavenly scent reached her nose. *Oh...* there was no faking this aroma. It was utterly sinful. This wasn't some random English tea the girl had plucked from the international aisle of Target.

It was *exactly* Elizabeth's brand and variety—an organic guayusa cacao blend with hints of mint and cinnamon, and several other sweet-smelling, exotic spices. It was a special mix from the small tea and art cafe around the corner from Cambridge University. Only Blackie's Tea House made and sold this blend. How on earth was it here? Or maybe her nose was deceiving her?

She drew the cup to her lips. Paused. And then sipped.

Her taste buds exploded. The wash of flavors flowed through the perfectly hot tea—none of that lukewarm, overly sweet milk water the Americans rightly sneered at. She could have wept at the rush that filled her. Forcing herself to lower the intoxicating drink, Elizabeth looked at her expectant colleague in astonishment. It had been years since she'd been home to taste this. The thought that she could have it here, somehow, on hand, was overwhelming.

"What *is* this? Where did you get it? I need the name of your local supplier."

The woman tilted her head back and laughed. "You make me sound like a crack dealer."

Elizabeth's fingers tightened on the container and she sipped again. Which turned into a richly satisfying gulp.

"Will you tell me?" She arranged her features to encouraging. "Since this *is* your big apology?" She gave a smile then, a genuine one she rarely bestowed on strangers—but desperate times called for desperate measures.

It had anything but the desired effect. Summer's gaze dropped to her feet as red crept up her neck and ears.

How...odd. And that didn't seem like fear. More like...self-consciousness?

9

Summer looked up from under her lashes. "Um, my family lived in England for a few years. I found this odd little cafe one day, part art gallery, part tea house, and this was its signature blend. I loved it. Now I have my friends in London send it to me." She shrugged. "I thought the odds were good you might like a taste of tea from home. Seems I was right."

Elizabeth blinked. It had never occurred to her to get her friends to supply her tea. Even now it seemed rude to impose—a national crime for the English, she noted ruefully. After draining the cup with one last, gratified sigh, Elizabeth tossed it in the trash. "Well, apology accepted."

She still felt out of sorts, and the beginning of a tiredness headache was threatening the edges of her temples. The young woman had given her a thoughtful gift and seemed genuine enough. Her eye fell to Summer's generous chest, honeyed LA tan, and girlish, ever-widening smile. Jesus. She might be nice enough, but it was also clear exactly why she was hired. Ravitz had made no secret of it every time his eyes roamed over her.

Elizabeth's mouth hardened. It might not be Summer Hayes's fault, but she was everything that was wrong with this show and Hollywood as a whole. Style over substance. Looks over depth. This…smiling, bouncy, Central Casting girl-next-door stereotype was the least suitable person to be on *Choosing Hope*, given its original mission statement. Yet, here she stood: shallowness in human form.

"Well, thank you for the gift," Elizabeth said, her voice a few degrees cooler. "But if you wouldn't mind," she looked pointedly at the doorway Summer was still standing in, "I haven't had a chance to get dressed since tonight's blood-spattered debacle."

Summer wilted. "S-sorry," she said again.

Elizabeth had a fierce urge to roll her eyes. The girl apparently had a limited vocabulary, too.

She left much as she'd arrived, with a youthful energy and big, soulful eyes.

Summer threw down her bag when she arrived home, exhausted and miserable. It was close to midnight. Everyone on set had been bitching about the delays, and by the time she'd apologized to the gaffer and all the grips, she'd decided to just suck it up and accept that she'd have to work extra hard to get back into people's good graces. Not a very auspicious start to her time on *Choosing Hope*.

She kicked off her boots and collapsed on the sofa. Staring at the walls of her Silver Lake bungalow seemed a much more manageable pastime than figuring her way to the shower, so she let her gaze slide over her framed black-and-white photos of LA's most architecturally interesting streets. She'd taken them all herself and loved nothing more than finding some undiscovered street with quirky-looking homes from yesteryear.

Footsteps approached. A flash of black hair appeared in her line of sight, followed by the light-brown face and penetrating gaze of Chloe Martin, a towering New Zealand actress she'd met eighteen months ago at a charity event where they'd immediately clicked. Summer loved Chloe's unassuming nature and lack of pretension. She had a wide, toothy grin and a passion for basketball. Chloe was in her *Footrot Flats* cartoon dog pajama bottoms and a tank top.

"Hey Smiley, wondered when you'd crawl in. Dyin' to know how your first week of work panned out." She sat on the wooden coffee table opposite.

Summer stared up at the ceiling and licked her lips. "Okay, let's see. The table read was fine. Everyone seemed friendly. Except Elizabeth Thornton, who didn't look up at me once, so it's no wonder she didn't recognize me later."

"Okay, then what? Why do you look like a constipated possum?"

"Today we shot this really intense trauma scene. Three ambulances crashed in the hospital parking lot..."

"Three! Choice, eh?" Chloe cackled. "That's out there as hell."

Summer shook her head at her friend's Kiwi-isms. "I don't think they care if it's stupid. The show keeps trying to top itself on being twisty."

"Good thing then." Chloe lowered herself to the floor, lying flat on a rug. She began bending her knees up and down and flapping her arms. Dead cockroaches, she called them. Something to keep an old sports injury in check.

"Right, then what?" Chloe asked between whooshing breaths. "Did you have to fall into some stud muffin's lap or something? Cos that show's getting crazy with all the bed-hopping."

"Way worse." Summer screwed her eyes shut. "I was supposed to run past an emergency scene, drop a bunch of blood bags, and get my ear chewed off by Chief Hunt."

"But...?"

"But I stepped on one and it exploded and shot fake blood all up into Thornton's face. I don't mean a little, either. It freaking coated her. It was in her hair, eyes, down her collar. It was so bad."

"Holy fuck."

"I know." Summer opened her eyes and groaned.

Chloe burst out laughing. "Oh, mate. She's so scary. That's, um...well, *shit*."

"Hey! I'm trying for denial here." She frowned. "By the way, she's not that bad...she can't be. I screwed up so much, and she was snide but hardly ripped my head off."

"Uh-huh. Except my agent's heard she's a bitch on wheels."

Summer decided not to argue, but she wasn't buying it. Someone as bad as Elizabeth was rumored to be would have skinned her alive.

"Hell of a first impression, hey?" Chloe added. "You must like her, though, the way you defend her."

"How can I not? She's brilliant. Even if she doesn't seem too impressed with the show, when they call 'Action', she's *on*. She gives it everything."

"Old school pro. I respect that."

"Me too." Summer smiled.

Chloe stopped her dead cockroaches. "So while you were busy provoking your new co-star, I have news."

Summer sat up. "Ooh! Your audition?"

"Yup. Got a call back on the shampoo ad. Only problem is, it's bein' shot in Outer Woop-Woop somewhere. Pays a treat but."

"But what?"

"But nothing. I got the job." She gave the thumbs up.

Oh right. Another Kiwi-ism. Summer leaned over and gave her a side-on hug. "Awesome."

"Thanks! I might even be able to make rent this month." She winked. "But can you tell your mum I won't be here for Sunday lunch?"

"Sure." Summer almost rolled her eyes. Come rain or shine, even when Summer was away, her mother always visited for "family" lunch on Sundays.

"Okay, so you down for a basketball training sesh tomorrow?" Chloe asked. "You're by far our most popular stats keeper— given you're our only one."

Summer smiled. She was often roped into helping Chloe's team on her rare days off work. Not helping in a "throwing the ball while staying upright" sense, of course. As tonight had proven yet again, Summer had exactly two left feet. "Can't. I have to help this sweet, crazy woman."

"Ah. Gotcha. Doing some hippie-la-la thing with your mum?"

She snorted. Suggesting that Skye Storm…her mother's actual name… would be doing 'some hippie-la-la thing' was like suggesting cows mooed. When Skye wasn't exploring her spiritual side, blessing her crystals, or demonstrating sewing techniques in the vlogs Summer helped her make, she was creating stunning costumes for movies. She might be eccentric, but she was also extraordinary, which explained the respect that tinged Chloe's voice.

"Yep. I'm producing Mom's next vlog: *Natural Tie-dying: Heavenly Homemade Dyes*. Should be fun but messy."

"That *is* your forte, right? Blood baths and dye baths."

Summer winced at the reminder.

Chloe prodded her in the ribs. "Hey, I just remembered, there's a new girl on the team. Really cute. Dying to meet you. She loves your TV stuff, especially *Teen Spy Camp*."

Burying her face under a cushion, Summer said, "Another twenty-year-old groupie. Awesome." A frightening thought struck. "At least tell me this one's actually *in* her twenties?"

"Just barely." Chloe gave an evil laugh. "You do attract the young ones."

"Shit. I can't help how young I look."

Chloe just laughed harder. "Stop bitchin', Smiley. You'll be working in Hollywood way longer than everyone else. I mean, right now you are *easily* pulling off a role five years younger than you actually are."

"That's not as good as it sounds. Raif Benson called me 'kid'. I get that all the time. Well, not from Thornton. She didn't call me any name at all. Not even mine."

"Because you're dead to her!" Chloe chuckled. "And that's a *good* thing, remember. They say she had some extra fired for looking her directly in the eyes."

"*They* say a lot of things. Doesn't make them true. It's so easy to tear people down. But at the end of the day, they'll still be jealous, and she'll still have talent." She closed her eyes, losing herself in the memory. "When I was a fifteen, my parents were working on this sci-fi trilogy in London. I'd sneak away from my tutor, catch the Tube, and see the matinees in the West End. The first play I ever saw was Elizabeth's one-woman Shakespeare show. I saw it a dozen times before Dad finally noticed how much money I'd been spending."

"You saw Thornton in London?" Chloe asked quietly. "I heard she was amazing back in the day."

Amazing? That was one word for it.

On a small London stage, Elizabeth Thornton had padded out barefoot in a formless, mid-length white sheath, then sat on a wooden stool. It was the only thing on the stage. She was in her mid-twenties back then, but her bearing was tall, confident, and regal.

With the tone of her voice, the angling of her expressive, classically beautiful face, subtle shifts of the spotlight—highlighting her high cheek bones and full, curving lips—she became someone else.

There were no costume changes. No music. No props. Elizabeth was as naked as an actress could be while still covered.

Her voice was clear, strong, precise, as she twisted and curled herself into Beatrice, Desdemona, Juliet, Cordelia, Lady Macbeth, and more. Her anguish as she washed invisible blood from her hands was chilling.

She looked up, once, just to the left of her audience, and it seemed to Summer that their eyes met. Summer's breath caught and held as she soaked in the details—ivory skin, paler under the white spotlight, brown hair pulled back from her face and turned black by the contrasting shadows.

Her heart bellowed in her ears as her gaze swallowed and pulled apart and reconstructed the elegant woman on stage. Making sense of her. Committing her to memory.

"Will my hands never be clean?" Lady Macbeth's eyes pleaded. Her voice, commanding and desperate, seemed both whisper and shout.

Summer's heart clenched at the aching tone. Her hands balled into fists. Elizabeth Thornton was the most beautiful human she'd ever seen—then or since.

"Yes, she was amazing." Summer her eyes. "Seeing her act made me fall in love with acting."

"So, this is a wicked coincidence you ending up on her show."

"True. My sister's mainly excited I'm a series regular again. And Autumn sees it as vitally important for my career to finally play an adult. But for me, getting to work with the best actress I've ever seen really added to the allure."

"Oh, hon, be careful. You'll get your heart broken." Chloe shook her head slowly. "There is nothing worse than meeting your idol."

"Sure there is." Summer studied her fingers, and pulled a miserable face. "Making them think you're an idiot. That's way worse."

"Ah. Right." Sympathy edged Chloe's eyes. "Well, as bad as you feel right now, just remember it's beautiful that you once had a hero who showed you something you now care about so deeply. Sounds like an incredible experience. I envy you that."

It was. It was a gift, a memory she'd never swap for anything. She could still see the elegant tilt of the head. The eyes, profound and emotional, staring right at her. Into her.

If only Summer hadn't gone and ruined it all.

Chapter 2

AUTUMN HAYES LEANED OVER THE railing at Hollywood Mega Mall, taking position. "You ready?" she asked her sister, pushing her sunglasses onto the top of her head.

"Yep." Summer took a deep breath. She could do this.

"Warmed up? Vocal cords? Know the words?"

"Check, check, check." Summer wiggled her shoulders. "Where's my mark?"

"Down there. Beside the trash can."

Summer laughed. "Upscale show then."

Autumn rolled her eyes. "For maximum effect, you have to be incognito until the big reveal." She pointed to a man in a black jacket, walkie-talkie at his hip, roaming the mall floor. "That's Doug. He's aware of what's about to happen. He'll step in if things get out of hand, and he has more security on standby."

"Okay." Summer squinted at the enormous guard. "Though I hardly think a few teenagers will be much of a match against him."

"Summer, the bulk of your Punky Power fan base is now in their early twenties and many still love you. That affection can get out of control in an instant. Remember Koreatown last year? No such thing as a simple meal. People text their friends and multiply out of nowhere. If we do this right, there'll be two hundred excited, social-media-sharing fans thrilled to see you before it's over. And try to angle your back to that poster as often as you can." Autumn pointed at the colorful sign advertising *Just Like Spies*, the hottest new flick starring singing sensation Jemima Hart.

"Product placement? Seriously?" It seemed so tacky, but Summer could hardly take the high moral ground. She was here to take part in a flash mob performing Jemima's hit song from the *Spies* film, after all. The new movie was a mega-hit, so it was a bit sneaky to use its success for their own ends, with only the most dubious spy connection, but Autumn was adamant that no one would care and everyone worked the angles in Hollywood.

"Actually no, it's not product placement. Look opposite."

Leaning over the railing, Summer looked down. Just behind a plastic palm tree, a camera was being set up discreetly. An overly hairsprayed woman in a navy pant suit was talking to the cameraman.

"Is that who I think it is?" Summer nodded toward the woman. "Katie Rivers?"

"Yes. I called in a favor. By the time you're done, not only will you be hashtagged to all the news sites..." she waggled her own camera, "but also featuring on *Celebrity Entertainment.* I've given Rivers full bio notes about your new role on *Choosing Hope*. From teen spy to junior surgeon. She loved it."

"Joey's not a surgeon, though."

"Semantics. Katie doesn't care. She loves 'whatever happened to child-star X' stories. Right. Get down there, stun the shoppers into a stupor, be your usual friendly self to fans, and remember your number one rule."

"Yeah, yeah." Summer groaned. "Don't fall over."

"Exactly. You'll be great."

<hr />

On Sunday morning, Elizabeth found herself tucked up on the couch with the sad clown movie and one of her oldest friends, Alexandra Levitin. Alex was an indie film director, but they'd come up through Cambridge's Footlights theater club together.

"I can't believe Jean-Claude asked for you," Alex said as the opening credits flickered in the background. She ran her fingers through her cropped red hair. "That man is so big right now. Or about to be."

"Big ego, too, if his interviews are anything to go by. Oh, for God's..." Elizabeth pointed at an artsy special effect. "Weeping watercolor. The man's a genius," she drawled.

"Hush," Alex said. "He's a poet and you know it."

"That rhymes."

"Infidel. I think I liked you better in London. And not just because you were in my bed."

Me too, Elizabeth wanted to say. She didn't. It was a can of worms, their covert six-month fling, and she wasn't planning to reopen it. Still, sometimes she missed the simplicity of being a no one. She could flirt furiously and make love with anyone she wanted. Not that she had back then, but the principle sounded good.

Now she dragged her male friends to red-carpet events to play coy, double-entendre games for the cameras with her. All so the insatiable Hollywood press could become breathless at the thought that Elizabeth Thornton might have found love. She'd have preferred to avoid the events altogether. Unfortunately, her laid-back manager and hard-nosed agent had been in lock-step agreement. Out-and-proud lesbians don't get cast as leads. Neither do anti-social hermits.

Everything had seemed so clear back when she was young and treading the boards in London. She would become a great theater actress. She would take a string of beautiful lovers, be interesting and witty, have a full life. She had not planned on enduring humiliation on the set of a top-rated, B-grade medical drama. Nor on developing an almost reclusive existence, broken up only by shopping-list chats with her elderly housekeeper and occasional catch-ups with the same six British theater friends—including her ex-girlfriend, Alex.

She pursed her lips and reached for the popcorn.

———— ◆◇◆ ————

By the end of the film, Elizabeth had to admit it was beautiful, if a little pretentious, as only French films could be.

"What did you think?" Alex asked, eyes shining.

"False advertising," Elizabeth teased. "No clowns were involved in the making of that production."

"Don't be so literal. What'd you think? Really?"

"I think I'll be doing lunch with Jean-Claude Badour."

"Good. Hell, if I could make films half as well as him, I'd be delirious." Alex glanced at the clock. "Speaking of lunch, when will the rest of the group be around? I've been missing everyone. And I have a desert shoot soon, so I'll be away for a month."

"Soon." Elizabeth pressed *Exit* on Netflix and the TV shifted back to regular programming. She sighed at the upbeat, over-the-top frivolity of *Celebrity Entertainment.*

Which star has run off with his assistant for a Vegas wedding? We'll tell you next! But first! Hollywood Mega Mall patrons were treated to a flash mob yesterday, thrilling crowds when a group of seemingly ordinary shoppers suddenly burst into song. Their musical choice? The catchy Just Like Spies *theme song. And fittingly, there was a famous TV spy singing along with them!*

"Ugh, turn it off," Alex complained. "Too much shallowness and I lose my will to live."

Elizabeth didn't budge, eyes narrowing at the screen. "I believe that's my co-star. The idiot who drenched me in fake blood." She pointed the remote at a young blond woman who'd stepped out from behind a pillar to add her voice to the chorus of singers.

"Her?" Alex squinted. "Huh. Looks sweet. Oh, *ouch*." Summer had bumped into a singer attempting a few dance moves. "She's not very co-ordinated, is she?"

"No, she's not." Elizabeth scowled.

"Aww, look. Good recovery."

Summer laughed and, while still singing, grasped the hands of the woman she'd bumped into, twirled her around, and let go again without missing a beat of the song. The girl could think on her feet. When she could *stay* on her feet, of course.

Summer Hayes, who played Punky Power for three years in Teen Spy Camp, *caused a riot with excited fans in line to see* Just Like Spies.

The camera cut to the hundreds of fans surrounding Summer as she signed autographs on bare arms, posed for selfies, and joked around.

"Look at her, Bess." Alex smirked. "See, *that's* how you interact with fans. Take note—not a scowl in sight."

"I hardly think that's relevant, since my show's fans all hate me." Elizabeth smiled smugly.

"Way to look on the bright side."

"I am. I prefer my existence to *that*. Who'd want to be mobbed every time they shopped?"

"Price of fame."

"No, it's the price of playing the game. That's all this is—it's just a marketing stunt."

Hayes will soon be seen as Joey Carter on the hit show Choosing Hope. *From teen spy to junior surgeon! All the details are on our website. More after this break!"*

"See?" Elizabeth felt a little deflated. But why shouldn't her co-star promote herself? It was just that it all felt so…Hollywood. "And Summer's character isn't a damned surgeon, either."

"*That's* what you're fixating on?" Alex laughed. Her look became speculative. "She's good-looking, you know."

"I hadn't noticed." Elizabeth folded her arms. "She's a public menace." *With good taste in tea.*

"Boy, you sure are testy over a cute LA chick."

Elizabeth just glared.

Brian Fox and Rowan Blagge rolled in first. Eternally wry Brian and his dapper, long-faced boyfriend were discussing the best neck-tie knots as they settled into their favorite armchairs. Elizabeth placed a platter of finger foods in front of them, wondering if they could find a duller topic.

"Windsor knot. Half Windsor in a pinch," Rowan declared, reaching for the peanuts.

"Plattsburgh. Obviously," Brian countered.

Amrit Patel wafted in a little later. Six-foot-four and gorgeous, he was most famous as the one-time international face of Cartier watches. Next came Grace Christie-Oberon, England's national treasure and the queen of English historical dramas—with the BAFTA awards to prove it.

In the US, she'd been dubbed Gracie-O. And yet, despite her astonishing talent, Rowan's sad-sack comedy routines were still more well-known here than she was, and Elizabeth was vastly more successful than all her friends put together.

Grace had far too much class to ever say a word on that topic. Besides, her whole focus at this moment was very much on Amrit. She slid her elegant frame—adorned in a dropped-waist lace dress—onto the couch beside him and offered a sultry smile.

The final member of their group, Zara Ejogo, dashed in late, looking harried. She might have started out in drama at Cambridge like the rest of them, but her talent for creating costumes on the fly had seen her snatched up by Hollywood first.

"Finally," Alex drawled, crunching on a carrot stick about as wide as she was. "I was beginning to fear Rowan would do his Montreal Comedy Festival monologue about living in a basement as we waited."

Rowan gave her a long-suffering look. "I'm only pleased my pain is giving pleasure to others."

Nudging him, Brian said, "What pain, love? You're not living in your parents' basement anymore."

"Scarring lasts a lifetime."

"Didn't said basement have a spa in it, though?" Grace asked. "And wall-to-wall murals of beautiful rainforests?"

"Pain is not a contest," Rowan said, lips ticking up. "I never said mine was the worst."

Grace glanced at Elizabeth. "Bess, could you be a dear and fetch me a nice glass of white to wash down Rowan's manly tears."

Brian cleared his throat. "I have an announcement. I have a new movie role. *Alien Zombie Apocalypse.*"

"Do you play the scientist?" Amrit asked. "Or the villain? Or the villainous scientist who unleashed the plague on us all?"

They all laughed.

"At the risk of sounding typecast," Brian said, injecting his most theatrical voice, "I am indeed the evil scientist who undoes society as we know it."

"So a regular Tuesday for you, then." Grace glanced at Elizabeth again. "Or fetch a tea if the wine's too much trouble."

Elizabeth paused. Grace sometimes forgot she wasn't a national treasure in their little circle. She stood anyway, and glanced around. "Anyone else?"

A smattering of drink orders were called out.

"I'll help." Zara followed her to the kitchen.

As they prepared the drinks, they heard Alex in the background, regaling the rest about her new project, something to do with global warming. And quiver trees, whatever they were.

"This is a bonkers town, isn't it?" Zara added sugar to one of the teas. "Yesterday I was working on a lizard outfit. But when I quote *King Lear*, everyone looks at me like *I'm* the nutter."

"It's what we signed up for." Elizabeth stirred another tea vigorously. "More or less."

"You know, I never really understood why you came here. The rest are obvious. Rowan got his comedy tour, so Brian went with his man. Amrit came for the adventure, and I presume, the pretty young men and women who fawn over him. Grace came because…" She glanced at Elizabeth and hesitated.

"Officially…the next big career step," Elizabeth supplied.

"But we know why she's really here." Zara peeked out the archway at Amrit. "That must have been one hell of a fling if she's still not over him." She put down her spoon. "I know why I'm here, 'Oscar winner for costume designs', just wait! And Alex's indie films were getting her noticed. But you?"

She studied Elizabeth, who shrugged. This again. Zara tried to find out the answer to that burning question at least once every six months, always asking in a slightly different way to try to lure a different answer out of her. Elizabeth had no intention of sharing the real reason.

"I missed my friends. London wasn't the same without you all. One by one, you up and left until there was only me."

"But your theater career was taking off."

"It didn't mean much with no friends to enjoy it with. Besides, the action's in Hollywood, apparently."

"But Bess, you always wanted to be on the stage. You could do Broadway. Why LA?"

"I like the weather. Very…sunny." Elizabeth opened the fridge to get the milk.

"Sure you do." She eyed Elizabeth's pale complexion. "Sun worshipper that you are."

Elizabeth shrugged. "There's plenty of work here, too."

"True. Unless you're Grace. But maybe she's too picky. She could have work if she lowered herself to do American TV."

Elizabeth gave the fridge door a heavier slam than strictly necessary.

Zara's face transformed into mortification. "Oh bollocks. Hon, you know I didn't mean it like that. No offense."

"None taken. It does feel like lowering myself these days. Do you remember the original premise of *Choosing Hope*? A teaching hospital which focuses on minorities? Real, gritty stories? Doctors from all walks of life overcoming the odds? It's why the damned thing was called *Choosing Hope* in the first place. It was supposed to be about giving people hope, no matter where they're from."

"Well, that, and the hospital is *called* Martina Hope Memorial."

Elizabeth poured milk into several of the cups. "My point is, the premise was different and interesting. I was proud of it. Chief Hunt was a mentor to these young doctors. And now..." Her face hardened. "*Attila the Hunt.* If that's not bad enough, you should see the newest cast member—this entitled-looking blond girl who should be doing swimwear ads, not gritty dramas about medical students pulling themselves up by the boot straps."

"Come on, your show went south long before they cast some entitled chick," Zara said. "Are you really annoyed at her or is it that *Hope* is selling out? Because I caught a few eps last season and that show's turned like week-old Chinese leftovers. Everything's about who's shagging who. And let's not start on Hunt's tragic love life."

"Beginning of the end," Elizabeth muttered, arranging the cups on a tray.

"True, but at least it got you this amazing house." Zara nudged her.

Why did everyone keep reminding her of that? She glanced around. Her four-bedroom Los Feliz home was nestled in the hills and had impressive views, the most spectacular of which was from the pool deck that looked out toward Santa Monica Bay. Inside, the surfaces gleamed, from the honeyed hardwood floors to the polished granite countertops. It suited her tactile tastes. She loved to stroke smooth surfaces.

Elizabeth was well aware she was lucky to have this place, and her career. She was grateful for the opportunities Hollywood had afforded her.

It was just that she had a hard time letting go of what the show had been. A show she'd emotionally invested in. Now, it was obvious where it was going.

"Come on, let's forget about work and enjoy what it got you. The views up here still get me orgasmic." Zara strode off to the living room.

Elizabeth's guests turned to look at her as she entered after Zara. She headed for Grace first, giving her the wine.

"Thank you," she said, accepting it. "Now what's all this Alex tells us about you getting a Badour film? That sounds promising. More so, perhaps, than what you've been doing lately?" She smiled to take the sting out.

Elizabeth felt it anyway. She shouldn't. But looking like a failure in the eyes of your mentor cut deep. "It's more a lunch with the hope of a job," she said. "Although he did have me in mind. He saw me in *Shakespeare's Women*."

Grace's perfectly sculpted eyebrows shot up at that.

Elizabeth had pitched the idea of that show to her back in London, hoping Grace might come on board and champion it. Instead, she had frowned. "No props, no costumes? Theatrical suicide," she'd said. "I'm so sorry, Bess, I can't endorse it."

She'd disappeared to LA shortly afterwards, and Elizabeth had raised the funding herself and put the play on with a shoestring budget at a family friend's theater that just barely counted as the West End. It had drawn strong crowds and enough excellent reviews to be dubbed a critical hit, and even made a modest profit. That had been the first time Elizabeth had stepped out on her own. The play meant everything to her.

"Badour liked your little show? Well, for a Frenchman he has some redeeming qualities then." Grace's tone was amused.

A thrill shot through her. That meant Grace had liked it too? When had she seen it? Elizabeth's mind skidded back over the times, dates, days, desperate to remember.

"Anyone who appreciates the Bard is in my good books," Grace clarified.

Oh. Of course. Elizabeth's smile dimmed.

Alex shot her a sympathetic look.

Christ. Am I that transparent?

Elizabeth settled in her armchair, sipping her guayusa cacao tea. It was some generic version, not a patch on the exact variety she adored, but it was the best substitute she could find.

The tea only reminded her of Summer Hayes. So young. Eager to please. Beautiful. Little wonder Ravitz had his eye on her. Funniest thing, though, the girl seemed oblivious. How could any actress who looked like Summer be so unaware? She hadn't noticed the way the boom operator's eyes had slid over her, either. Or how the extra whose chest Elizabeth had been working on had smiled up at her appreciatively when they were re-setting for close-ups. The girl wasn't much of an observer then. Not to mention being too clumsy to function.

That felt churlish. Summer seemed nice enough. Maybe Elizabeth was becoming the bitch they all said she was? Her bad-substitute tea suddenly tasted bitter.

The room was silent. Had she missed a question? "I'm sorry, what?"

"Do you like Badour's movies?" Brian repeated. "Rowan and I saw *Quand Pleurent les Clowns* last year. Divine. It was like an unstable still life."

What did that even mean? "I did appreciate it for what it was," she said. "An ambitious film-maker showcasing his skills. I'm curious to know what Hollywood makes of him when they meet the man, not just his films."

"And what it makes of you," Grace noted. "They'll see you, not your on-screen villain for the first time, as well."

"Um..." Elizabeth frowned. "No, I'd still be playing a role. It's no different."

"It's very different." Grace leaned forward, giving her a close look. "It's a trademark of all Badour films. He reveals the actor as well as their character. It's why his films seem so real. I, for one, will be very intrigued by what he finds under your skin. You've been holding out on us for far too long."

Elizabeth blinked. "What do you mean?"

"You hold your cards so close, dear Bess. Soon we'll get to see all of you. Your secrets. What's behind the mask you always wear. I cannot wait. In fact, an unraveling would do you a world of good." She thrummed delicate fingers against the leather arm rest.

Blood rushed to Elizabeth's face. Her secrets? These were not for anyone's consumption. Certainly not for Grace to pick over. Or the wider cinema-viewing population.

Silence coated the room like ash. Alex's eyes had gone squinty, like she was trying to understand what Grace was getting at.

Brian slid his gaze between Elizabeth and Grace. "Um, Grace, dearest, no one's expected to share anything they don't want to, here or elsewhere. Besides, Bess's a big girl. I'm sure she can handle a demanding Frenchman. She'll be fine at drawing a line in the sand she's most comfortable with."

Thank God for Brian. Elizabeth exhaled. He'd been her first friend when she began her law course at Cambridge. He'd discovered her in the cafeteria one day, hunched over a textbook, and had amused her with an impromptu sketch: *Woman Eating Alone.* He'd invited her to see him and his friends in a play. That had been the start of everything.

Her shift from law to drama had felt like the most natural thing in the world. And then came Grace. A decade older, she'd entered their world as a guest lecturer and decided Elizabeth was a talent to be refined. That was the day Elizabeth's small, safe world tilted on its axis.

Grace laughed suddenly. It was light and pretty, and a complete affectation—Elizabeth had heard her stage laugh often enough to know that. "Sorry, Bess, I was just playing. Ask someone to tell you their secrets and they'll deny they have any. Intimate to someone you *know* their secrets and their horror is palpable." Grace waved carelessly. "I'm sorry, though. I see that wasn't the nicest joke."

"No." Amrit peered at her. "It wasn't."

Her expression shifted to one of actual regret. "Oh dear. I've put my foot in it, haven't I? Can you forgive me?"

Elizabeth eyed her friend. Irritation rose up. But then memories flooded her, of all the times Grace had helped her, taught her tricks for remembering lines or projecting her voice, as well as tips for dealing with handsy producers or star-struck fans. She'd also given Elizabeth the biggest gift of all, when she'd first arrived in LA. Grace was the reason Rachel had agreed to represent her. She smiled. "Of course. Forgiven."

"Excellent," Grace said with a satisfied purr. "I know my sense of humor's always been lousy. I hope you still like me anyway?"

What a fine performance of contrition. Even so, Elizabeth gave her the benefit of the doubt. "Always." Lifting her tea, she tilted it in silent toast toward Grace.

Chapter 3

MAKE-UP DONE, SUMMER STIFLED A yawn while Sylvia, the set's hair stylist, fussed around her. Next to her sat Molly Garcia, who played a second-year medical intern on the run from her handsome, unhinged twin brother.

Fidgeting, Summer stared at her fingers. She had survived four hours with her mother and had the green fingertips to prove it. With any luck, she'd be able to keep her hands in her pockets for her upcoming scenes because Skye Storm's *Heavenly Homemade Dyes* vlog had been more demonic than anything else.

It was barely seven and she was dying for the tea steaming in her cup on the table three feet away. But that would require moving, and Sylvia was lethal with jerking her hair if she so much as twitched.

That tea was the liquid of the gods. She couldn't, of course, confess to Elizabeth exactly how she'd come by her habit. She pursed her lips at the thought.

"No duckface!" Jon, the make-up artist, leaned across and rapped Summer's knuckles with an eyebrow pencil, then resumed listening to Molly's story about some hot new club.

"Sorry." Summer's mind drifted. Her first scene required her to trail around with a group of other residents while the Head of Cardio, Dr. Mendez, explained various patients' conditions. He would ask the residents questions. She had to answer one. She'd been practicing her line.

Could there be a problem with the chordae tendineae, doctor?

It was something to do with a heart valve. She'd looked it up.

Could there be a problem with the chordae tendineae, doctor?

Could there...

"...heard she's a bitch. Guess that's where she got the nickname."

Her brain suddenly tuned into Molly's conversation. Unless there were two women on set nicknamed 'bitch,' it was a safe bet as to who she was insulting.

In the mirror, Summer caught Jon offering one of those neutral nods that sought more juicy gossip, rather than signaling agreement.

Sylvia frowned. "Well, don't believe everything you hear," she said. "Ms. Thornton is a total pro. It's not her fault what they did to her character."

"Pity our social media team, though." Jon waved his eyebrow pencil. "Hunt and Thornton both get a ton of hate on the official fan forum board. Several hundred posts, easy."

"A week?" Molly asked. "Holy fu—"

"A *day*."

Summer's lips pressed together, earning her another sharp look from Jon. How would *that* mess with a person's head? It might explain Elizabeth's bad mood.

"Perfect casting, if you ask me." Molly grinned. "She has resting bitch face."

"She does not!"

Everyone's eyes darted to meet Summer's in the mirror.

Jon snorted. "And here I was thinking you were a mute, darling." He tapped her cheek. "A beautiful mute, of course."

Molly eyed Summer too. She had an attractive face, a buzz cut, and olive skin and played a scared, butch, loner Haitian refugee. She was none of the above in reality, and especially loved dropping the name of her boyfriend into every conversation.

"Well, Rico says..."

Case in point.

"...that Elizabeth Thornton's sour face would leave any man limp for life. Not that he has to worry about that with me around." She smirked.

Ew. Also total BS. The men Elizabeth dated, all manscaped British hunks, were elegant, immaculately dressed, and refined, with names like Brian, Rowan, and, lately, Amrit. They seemed more than happy with Elizabeth's company. And, unlike the infamous Rico, none of those men looked like they'd make tacky comments about any woman's looks.

Sylvia sighed. "It's a shame. Ms. Thornton is nothing like Chief Hunt." She gave Molly a warning look. "She's just reserved. British. And you've got to admit it was a mean thing they did to her character. That'd annoy anyone."

"Good ratings, though." Jon beamed. "My God, we hit top ten."

"Oh come on," Molly shrugged. "It's just drama. The usual stupid TV crap. It went down with Hunt the way it does with everyone."

"Not like this," Sylvia said. "Everyone else on this show gets drama thrown at them but they get to stay likable. Hunt throwing Mendez's engagement ring in his face when he proposed? After he'd just told her he'd finally found love for the first time since his wife died? That wasn't *just drama*." Sylvia touched up Summer's hair then reached for the spray. "They wanted people hating her."

"Why?" Summer asked.

Sylvia gave her a curious look and squirted gunk all over her hair as if readying it to survive cyclonic winds. "Ay-yi. Good question. No idea."

"Maybe she pissed off someone upstairs?" Molly said. "Or all of them. Gah, she's so uptight and boring, who cares? Moving on." She pulled out her phone. "Jon, tell me which Instagram filter brings out my eyes best? I need to look put together and shit, but not too posed or plastic."

Jon's eyes lit up as he launched into an answer.

Sylvia murmured that Summer was done. She made to move her chair back, but was stopped by Sylva's hand on her arm.

"It's good you see past the nonsense," the hair stylist said under her breath. "Don't get sucked into the rumors. It's mostly bull. Especially about her."

"I know."

Sylvia's eyes crinkled. "Well. I like you." She released Summer's arm. "And Ms. Thornton's one class act. She has more talent in her pinkie than most of the rest of the cast. You could do well watching her."

As if I could stop. Summer reached for her tea to avoid saying anything that would give away her unchecked admiration. *Damn. Lukewarm now.*

Sylvia gave an impatient cluck as she glanced at Jon and Molly, deep in conversation on the merits or otherwise of sepia filters. She waved her comb. "We're behind. Too much talk-talk-talk. Not enough work-work-work."

Summer left them to it. She'd have loved to have picked apart Sylvia's words, but business came before curiosity.

Could there be a problem with the chordae tendineae, doctor?

———— ◦◦◦ ————

"Could there be a problem with the tendineae chordae, doctor?" Summer asked.

Raif shook his head and began to reply.

"CUT!"

Crap. Summer blushed. "Sorry. Um, of course I know it's the *chordae tendineae*, and I'll..."

Ravitz was staring at her. "Not that! What the hell's on your fingers?"

Oh no! She'd pulled her hands out of her pocket on the second take. "Um, dye?" Her voice rose an octave. Summer offered an apologetic smile. "From a tie-dying incident gone bad?"

There was a silence. Then a masculine guffaw.

Well, at least Raif found it funny.

Then Molly, right beside her, lost it in a series of squeezed out snorts. Then Steve, Kaylah, Jeremiah, Malek, Tori, and... *Oh hell. There goes everyone.*

Summer rammed her hands back into her pockets, forming fists. Not funny at all.

Dread filled her when she saw that Elizabeth had just arrived, ready for her next scene with Raif.

Still Ravitz hadn't spoken. He simply stared at Summer. His gaze flicked to Elizabeth, and then his eyes positively gleamed.

"I could just put them back in my pocket again," Summer offered, cheeks aflame.

Elizabeth's eyes widened incredulously as she worked out what the issue was.

Okay, great. Now Summer was a laughing stock with *everyone*. Including the one person she really didn't want to appear a fool in front of.

Ravitz was now on his phone, having an intense exchange while waving in her general direction. She caught the name Hugo. The head writer?

She was *so* dead. Maybe literally. Was he working out with Hugo how to kill off Joey? She glared at the green stains on her fingertips. Death by gangrene? On this show, nothing was too crazy.

Ravitz crooked his finger at Elizabeth. She approached him and bent her head to listen.

Finally, she nodded and walked to the edge of the set, her mask firmly in place. This was Chief Hunt's detached expression, one part pure ice, nine parts derisive sneer. All parts intimidating.

"We're going to go again," Ravitz announced. "Ms. Hayes, leave your hands out of your pockets. Say your line—correctly this time—and then Mr. Benson," he turned to Raif, "before you answer, Chief Hunt will enter, interrupt, and say something about the fingers. Ms. Hayes, respond to her line *exactly* as you did to me. And Ms. Thornton will then reply, okay?"

"Um, sure? Why? I mean, could just..." Summer pointedly shoved her hands back in her pockets, appalled to be the cause of a rewrite, even just a short one.

"Because I said so. Any other questions?" His eyes dared her to challenge him again.

The set was silent, and behind her she felt her cast mates stiffen.

"No, I'm good," she said brightly. Far, far too brightly. *Christ. Take it down a notch.*

"Good girl," he nodded, then waved at the camera operator.

Summer winced.

"Positions, people," he called. He looked at Elizabeth, who was on her mark, then glanced around, and called, "Speed. Rolling, and...action."

"Could there be a problem with the *chordae tendineae*, doctor?" Summer asked. Relief flowed through her that at least she'd got that bit right. Her anxiety spiked, though, when Chief Hunt stepped into her field of vision, with a face like soured milk.

"Dr. Mendez," Hunt said, voice clipped, "I need a word about your last report. It's simply not acceptab..." Her gaze drifted to Summer's hands. "What is *that*?" she pointed.

"Um..." Summer actually withered a little under her sneering scrutiny, and hoped they'd chalk it up to brilliant acting. "Dye? From a tie-dying incident gone bad?"

Hunt's gaze turned challenging. "Be careful what you dip your fingers into around here, doctor." She looked bitterly at Mendez. "*Everything* can harm you."

So they're playing up Hunt's bad breakup again? Okay.

Summer found herself saying the first thing that entered her head. "That's okay," she smiled, aiming for unfazed with a hint of brazen, "I can take care of myself."

"Somehow I doubt that," Elizabeth said in an ad-lib of her own, suddenly taking Summer's hand, flipping it over, and examining it, her arched eyebrow mocking.

In spite of all Summer's experience and every ounce of acting skill she had, the only thing in her rapidly emptying mind was the feel of Elizabeth's fingers around hers. She took a step closer, right inside Elizabeth's space, then said words that bypassed her brain entirely. "You don't know me, then. But you will."

Summer had meant it to come out determined, strong, cocky. Instead she sounded wistful. Joey Carter, second-year resident, sounded like Summer's former self, whispering to that ethereal woman on stage in London. Her line also sounded, well, a tiny, little bit like a come on, if you thought about it. She desperately hoped no one would read it that way. It was probably only in her head anyway.

Elizabeth—definitely not Hunt this time—started and inhaled sharply. She dropped Summer's hand instantly. Her eyes darted to Raif. "We'll talk about that report later, Dr. Mendez," she snapped. "See me after rounds." Then she pivoted on her heel and stalked out.

"CUT!"

Everyone was staring at Summer. There was no sound.

She wasn't exactly sure where to look. Ravitz's jaw was hanging open. Maybe he hadn't expected the newbie to toss out a bunch of ad-libs? But if that was it, why hadn't he stopped the scene sooner?

He gave her a slow smile. It reminded her of a snotty kid up to no good. "Thank you, Ms. Hayes. Most...ah...unexpected. Okay, people, let's finish the scene. Mr. Benson, start with: '*All right, back to business. No, Dr. Carter, it's not the chordae tendineae*'. And then resume the scene as written."

Sliding a bowl of salad and a water bottle across an empty table near craft services, Summer slumped into a chair. She dropped her head onto the chipped laminated surface and left it there. She was sooo tired and still in a world of stress over this morning.

"Long day," said a voice near her. Next came the rattle of a tray landing opposite.

She lifted her head. Tori Farmer. The pleasantly rounded African-American actress played a Bronx-born doctor on the show. Funny thing was, her real accent was as broadly Texan as Summer had ever heard. It was kind of cute. Actually, so was she. Tori radiated energy, warmth, and charisma. And, boy, the camera loved her.

Summer attempted a friendly smile and sat up straighter. "I thought children's TV was bad. The pace they set here is pretty full-on."

"Yup." Tori nodded. "You get used to it. I've been here a year and it's like second nature now." She bit into a cheeseburger that looked considerably more interesting than Summer's salad. After swallowing, Tori said, "Saw you had an ad-lib today. Ravitz thinks the fact he allows them every now and then is a sign he's in touch with his creative side." She snorted.

"Ah, okay." *So that's what that was about?*

"It was an interesting scene though. Your take with Thornton."

"Uh, yeah." Summer scratched the label on her water bottle with her thumbnail.

"That was somethin'. I've never seen the British Bitch look shocked before. I actually think you knocked her out of character for a second. Amazing." Tori beamed at her. "No one's *ever* done that."

Summer swallowed, unsure where Tori was going with this. "I just said the first thing that came to mind."

"It was clever. We've all been talking about it."

"You have?" Summer squeaked, then cleared her throat. "Any... conclusions?"

"That it was genius. By throwing down the gauntlet to the Chief, you just guaranteed yourself a ton more scenes with a lead." Tori lifted her coffee and tilted it in salute. "I don't think I'd have thought of something like that in a million years. Or if I did, I don't think I'd have the nerve to try it." She laughed. "I might be a tough Texas kid, but Hunt and Thornton both are scary as shit."

Relief flooded Summer. Everyone thought her line had been a challenge? Some cynical play to get more scenes? Was that how Ravitz saw it too? No wonder he'd smirked.

Tori seemed to be waiting for some sort of response, so Summer gave her a half grin. "Well, it'll be interesting to see what crazy stuff they hurl at us next."

"Oh yep. This show's certifiable. And don't start me on the gobbledegook. Would it be too much for 'internal bleeding' to be just called that?"

"Ha. Tell me about it." Summer's expression faded when, out of the corner of her eye, she saw Elizabeth enter with one of the executive producers, and then line up to collect food from the craft services table. Her posture was painfully erect, yet her movements were graceful and languid.

"Cold fish, isn't she?" Tori followed her gaze. "Doesn't hang out with any of the other actors. Doesn't go for drinks. Doesn't make friends on set. And I'll bet that's a business lunch." She pointed at the producer with her. "I don't think I've ever seen her smile."

I bet she has a gorgeous smile.

"Earth to Summer?"

"Hmm?" She turned back to Tori.

"You checked out." Tori grabbed a fry and dunked it in ketchup.

"Sorry. What were you saying?"

"A bunch of us are going for drinks after work on Friday. Wanna come? Some of the guys asked for you specifically, if you know what I'm sayin'." Tori's eyes twinkled.

"Not this week, sorry," she said with a polite smile. "I'm busy. Maybe next time." She wasn't busy. It was just easier this way. Spending time with cocky men who thought their looks and charms could overcome her lack of interest was exhausting. Maybe she'd go in a month when everyone had paired off.

"Sure." Tori nodded. "Next time."

Elizabeth and the producer headed their way, bearing trays of food. Well, if a small bowl of soup for Elizabeth counted as food. The man she was with was monologuing beside her.

Was Elizabeth even needed in that conversation?

She neared them, and Tori's fingers tensed around her coffee cup, gaze suddenly fixed on the table. However, Elizabeth didn't even falter, continuing past them to a distant, empty table.

"Oh thank God." Tori clapped a hand over her heart. "For a minute there, I thought she was gonna chow down with us."

"Would that have been so bad?" Summer asked, forking a lettuce leaf and inspecting it. It looked as sad close up as it did on her plate.

"You say that now, oh innocent one, but I heard she had an assistant fired for bringing her a coffee instead of a tea." Tori shuddered. "I don't know how the EP does it." She tilted her head at Elizabeth's lunching companion. "How does anyone talk to her?"

"No clue," Summer murmured.

But I'd love to know.

Chapter 4

AFTER SEVEN WEEKS WITH *CHOOSING Hope*, Summer now had a good idea as to who was who. She knew the names of the security guard's twin boys, when the craft services caterers had birthdays and how sarcastic and amusing Elizabeth's on-set assistant was. A round, owlish Scottish woman in her early forties, Finola had large turquoise glasses, shrewd eyes, and an accent few could penetrate. Summer won herself brownie points for easily picking through it.

She occasionally sent tea sachets via the assistant, who was only too pleased to pass them along, telling Summer her gifts had been putting a smile on her mercurial boss's face for the first time in months.

Well, that was good to know, since Elizabeth so far had made no comment to her at all. Then again, their schedules hadn't aligned too often. That was a shame, because Summer had begun to crave seeing the angular face on set, and that slow, watchful gaze that seemed to unglue every bit player with an instant case of forgotten lines.

Summer hadn't meant to share her precious tea stash regularly, but she hadn't been able to get Elizabeth's euphoric look out of her mind.

Tonight she encountered Finola rushing out of Elizabeth's trailer. Glancing at the yellow guayusa cacao box in Summer's hand, she stopped in her tracks.

"Oh, Summer! Just pop it inside, and be sure to close the door when you leave. Sorry, I can't stop and talk. My husband's car has broken down again." She rushed off.

Summer entered the empty trailer, and realized she was alone in the place Elizabeth took solace. It was hard to blame her for hiding in here. Over the past seven weeks, Summer had heard a lot about what people thought of Elizabeth. The most common view was that her lack of friendliness was a sign she thought she was better than everyone else and the show.

Even if that were true, they had no right to judge her. This show *was* beneath Elizabeth Thornton. Hell, if Summer could act that well, she'd also have a hard time hiding her derision for what they churned out here.

Summer slid the tea box onto the small kitchen counter, straightening it so one line of the cube was perfectly parallel with the wall. Immediately she turned to leave, aware of the trust Finola had put in her by granting her this access.

Colors caught her eye, making her pause. A picture of Elizabeth out to dinner with some people was stuck to a wall near the microwave. Summer studied it. She recognized Amrit first. Elizabeth's boyfriend looked his usual suave self. Another man was bending over, his face obscured. Her gaze flitted to a petite redheaded woman with watchful eyes.

Elizabeth's arm was casually around her waist, her other arm looped loosely around the shoulder of a taller, elegant woman with an otherworldly quality about her. This woman was all high cheekbones, elegant nose, and porcelain skin. *Oh wow. Grace Christie-Oberon.*

Back in London, Grace had been like royalty. Summer saw her face on posters and buses everywhere. So she and Elizabeth were friends?

Her eye darted back to Elizabeth, drawn to the happiness radiating from her face. It was nothing Summer had ever witnessed around here, where she kept a stiff, professional mask welded on all day.

A pity. Summer would love to meet this relaxed woman whose eyes sparkled with mirth.

Suddenly it felt like an intrusion to even glimpse a side of Elizabeth that she didn't readily share. Guilt bit into Summer, so she quickly turned to go.

The door opened. Summer almost tripped to a stop.

Elizabeth filled the frame, staring back at her. She was in pure Hunt mode, from her tight, imposing bun to her polished black heels. Her expression of annoyance fell away as she caught sight of the yellow box on the counter. "Ah, my ninja tea deliverer strikes again."

Summer smiled tentatively as she held up her hands in mock surrender. "I guess the gig's up."

"I don't think it'd shock you to know you were my prime suspect." Elizabeth hung up her white doctor's coat on a hook behind the door and released her hair from its bun. Running her fingers through it to straighten it out, she glanced back at a mesmerized Summer. "I did wonder how the tea arrived whenever I wasn't around. Would I be right in thinking you had a short Scottish accomplice?"

"I have no idea what you're talking about." Summer hid her grin. "You have a Scottish assistant?"

"Who mentioned an assistant?"

Oh. Oops.

"You won't win an Emmy with that innocent look." Dry amusement flitted across Elizabeth's face as she seated herself in front of the vanity near one end of her trailer, turning on the lights that ringed the mirror. After reaching for a small bag of supplies, she began to wipe her make-up off with proficiency.

Hunt gradually morphed into Elizabeth, austereness disappearing into softer lines. "Finola must be slipping if I caught you breaking and entering." She met Summer's eye in the mirror. "And thank you, by the way." Her eyes crinkled as she waved toward the tea box. "I should have said it weeks ago, but work's been frantic."

Summer smiled. "I'm glad to do it. I've never met anyone who likes my tea as much as me."

"Now you have." Elizabeth regarded her. "You smile a lot, don't you?"

"I can't help it. I know some people think it's annoying."

"It is."

Summer's expression fell.

"Usually. However, dare I say, it suits you. Besides, girl-next-door types who don't smile don't get jobs, do they?"

"I guess not. Although I don't want to do those roles forever. I'd rather be diverse, like you."

"Me." Elizabeth studied her. "I'd have thought you'd been told by now to avoid me." Her tone slid into playful. "Aren't I supposed to be clubbing seals in my downtime or something? I'm sure I read that somewhere."

Bursting out laughing, Summer said, "Can't picture it. Hunt, maybe... on a bad day."

Elizabeth gave her an inscrutable half-smile. "You laugh a lot, too. Careful. People will think you're a pushover." Her expression darkened. "Although the only thing worse than that is actually *being* pushed over. You don't want that. Trust me."

"Another reason to be more like you."

"Isn't that a risk? You don't know which rumors about me are true. To quote Oscar Wilde, 'It is perfectly monstrous the way people go about nowadays saying things behind one's back that are absolutely and entirely true'." Elizabeth reached for the top button on her blouse and began to unbutton it.

Summer's gaze swan-dived into the rapidly appearing soft, white skin.

Pausing at button four, as though suddenly aware she couldn't complete her ritual with Summer there, Elizabeth gave her a pointed look.

"Oh, sorry! I'll leave you to change." Summer spun around, feeling the tips of her ears burning. As her hand reached the door, she glanced back. "You know, you talk a good game, but I don't believe the rumors about you for a second. To quote Bertrand Russell, 'No one gossips about other people's secret virtues'." She turned back to leave.

Behind her came a soft snort.

Smiling from ear to ear, Summer exited.

Elizabeth lay on her deck chair in the blackness, unwilling to turn on a light and ruin the feeling of being adrift in the stars. Her fingers clasped a clanking glass of ice cubes and Hendrick's gin. An indulgence she'd come to lean on of late.

Her eyes followed the blinking lights of a plane far above, escaping somewhere else, away from the vapidness of this bizarre bubble into which she'd injected herself.

Delvine had yet to confirm a date for lunch with Jean-Claude, who was out of cell-phone reach in Kings Canyon National Park readying his production. The set apparently comprised of one writing shack. That was it. How much prep work did the man need?

Waiting only magnified her dissatisfaction. Little things that she used to ignore or laugh at annoyed her now. She couldn't remember the last time she'd laughed. She ran her thumb over the condensation on her glass. When you got to that stage in a job or a relationship, when nothing's funny and all you see are flaws, it's time to leave. Accepting a new, lower normal was never wise. But that's all she'd been doing lately. Having little say in all of it was enraging. Not to mention a little frightening, given how easily it had happened.

A shiver stole through her. Elizabeth put down her drink and rubbed her arms.

She'd only signed a seven-year option because she'd believed *Choosing Hope* would run three seasons at most. And she'd believed in the show back then.

No one could have predicted its meteoric rise in ratings, largely due to Dr. Mendez and his love life. A love life that had, for two seasons, involved her character. And been followed by the systematic dismantling of every virtue in Iris Hunt, until the chief was a black hole of bitterness that sucked in anything good or decent.

At the thought of good and decent things, Summer Hayes's face drifted into mind. Elizabeth sighed. The woman was like a niceness plague, eating away at her eternally bad mood. Sometimes, like tonight, she just wanted to wallow in her dark thoughts after yet another day of suppressing her emotions. But despite her best efforts...

Since she'd caught Summer in her trailer, the engaging young woman had begun stopping by for a brief word now and then, no longer just leaving her tea with Finola. She'd drop in quotes from philosophers or satirists, which Elizabeth easily parried with her own. Summer was surprisingly well-read. Or well-Googled. Still, she was curious for someone LA born-and-bred, dipped from birth in this shallow puddle of egos and ambitions.

But that was just it: Summer wasn't like the rest. Elizabeth had become used to conversing with two groups of people. There were her friends—acerbic, clever, and convoluted. And then there were the detached, professional interactions she had with colleagues and associates. Having someone who fit neither box, who was so upfront and open, well-read and well-travelled, and who seemed genuinely pleased to see her, was... unsettling. It ran counter to the way she liked things—everyone and everything ordered into boxes of personal and professional.

But nothing—not Summer's blitzkriegs of sunshine and tea, nor her own therapeutic wallowing in bad moods—seemed to make a dent in Elizabeth's overall state. Stress, boredom, tiredness, and irritation infected her daily, given her character had the emotional depth of a cardboard cut-out.

How could she endure one more season if she was so close to throwing in the towel already? At least hiatus was coming up. If she could swing Badour's new film in her break, it might be enough to get her through. Her brain needed the intellectual kick start.

What if she didn't get the part, though? Would she snap one day and tell the egotistical showrunner a few home truths? Would she be blacklisted as "too difficult"?

It was such a first-world, Hollywood problem—detesting the very job that made her rich and successful. But still, unhappiness was unhappiness, no matter how nice the car you drove.

Elizabeth wondered what Grace would say to any of this.

She'd probably simply look at Elizabeth, wait a dramatic beat, and ask what she wanted. *Really* wanted.

She always did that.

Sighing, Elizabeth grabbed her phone, scrolling through the news alerts. She liked to know what the lies were before she could be blindsided by fans on the street.

Hollywood Gossip Zone had been hounding her non-stop since Chief Hunt became a Mendez-hurting villain. Their latest bent was to accuse her of all sorts of onset atrocities, quoting anonymous sources. Apparently she could get extras fired for looking her in the eye. If only that were true—it would imply she actually had some power on set.

She kept scrolling. Alex's global warming film scored a mention in *Variety* as "one to watch". *Good for her.* Elizabeth flicked her an email with the link.

Rowan's new comedy show was getting rave reviews. She smirked at one of the headlines.

"SADDEST MAN IN LA TOO FUNNY TO IGNORE"

No point emailing that to him; he'd have bought twenty copies of the magazine already and be sending Brian out for more in the morning.

"FORMER CHILD STAR BULLIED ON HOSPITAL DRAMA SET"

She froze as she saw an unflattering photo of herself dressed as Hunt, looking mid-rant, and an inset picture of Summer as Joey Carter.

Sighing, she clicked on the story. Something about sources reporting a shocking accident that had disfigured Summer's hands, turning them green, and how Elizabeth had grabbed them and mocked the injuries to the crew.

Of course she had. Because that's what an evil bitch would do. She read on.

Hayes is a popular three-time winner of the Nickelodeon Kids' Choice Award for Favorite Female TV star. She is best known for her role as Punky Power, a junior secret agent in the popular hit Teen Spy Camp.

There was another photo of Summer at the end of the story, looking young and bright. She'd have been about twelve? Impossibly cute.

Elizabeth drained the rest of her gin and finally reached for the latest *Hope* script. She was too wired to sleep so she may as well learn some lines.

Just another day in paradise.

Summer sat in her favorite quiet, out of sight corner of set—she hated feeling closed in by her trailer walls if she could avoid it—and waded through her text messages. Chloe's selfie from the shampoo ad set was hilarious. There were flowers in her hair, a coconut bra, and some sort of jungle backdrop. She was sticking out her tongue and crossing her eyes.

Chloe was due back tomorrow from "Outer Woop Woop," which was good, because the house was way too quiet without her. She kept Summer feeling normal and sociable. Without her, it was easy to get too focused on work, her world shrinking into just *Choosing Hope*. Even her photography hobby had gone by the wayside lately.

As her sister kept reminding her, "This is your first adult role that the whole country will be watching. Don't screw it up. Well, again."

A Google alert popped up for her name and she clicked on it.

Wait, what? Elizabeth was now *bullying* her? She read on. Someone at *Choosing Hope* was leaking this crap. Was Elizabeth really hated *that* much by their colleagues?

Fury rising, she called her sister. "Have you seen HGZ today?" Summer demanded the moment Autumn answered. "I want you to call them up and ream them a new one."

"Well, hello to you, too, little sis," Autumn replied with a snort. "Yes, I've seen it. And America's favorite girl-next-door doesn't ream anything or anyone. Ever."

She had a point, but still. This was wrong. "So we're making no comment at all?" Summer asked incredulously. "What about what Mom always told us? Always do what's right. No excuses. The rest will take care of itself in the end."

"Easy for Mom, who doesn't need her reputation to be kept pure as driven snow."

"But it's so unfair!"

"Yes it's unfair, but not to you."

She desperately tried to think of something to change Autumn's mind. "Okay, how about it makes me sound like some victim?"

"You sound sweet as ever. The rest is for Thornton's people to deal with or not. Let it go."

Gritting her teeth, Summer ended the call. *Damn it.* Autumn was deliberately missing the point. Summer went online, downloaded a photo of a bull, opened Twitter, and copied a link to the HGZ bullying story. She wrote "Complete..." next to the bull picture, then posted it with a grim stab of satisfaction.

Her phone lit up two seconds later. A text from her sister.

DELETE!

Summer chuckled and pocketed the device just as one of the writers' assistants stuck his head around the corner. "Hey, thought you might be here. New scene today. Hot off the presses, Ms. Hayes." He dropped a script in her lap. "Emphasis on hot."

Hot?

She thanked him and flicked through it, searching for her name.

CARTER TURNS HASTILY, HER STEAMING COFFEE
SPILLING DOWN HUNT'S JACKET.

HUNT (FURIOUS): You're useless. I don't know
what Dr. Mendez sees in you.

CARTER: At least he wants me… for my skills,
of course. (FAUX INNOCENT LOOK)

HUNT (SNEERING): Oh, I'm sure that's why.

Oh, hell no. Now they were going to imply her character had caught Mendez's eye? Since when? And Hunt was going to be bitter about it, even though she'd dumped his ass hard? That made zero sense.

But even that absurdity wasn't the problem. Summer wasn't stupid. She knew exactly why she'd been hired, and it wasn't to sell some gritty hard-luck story like the other actors. Her type was cute and lovable, and people rooted for her on sight. Her stomach dropped at what this meant. Nasty Chief Hunt starts a vendetta against the sweetest character on the show? Poor Elizabeth. Her hate mail would double. Looked like the hair stylist was right. Someone was trying to make life a bitch for the show's lead actress.

Summer frowned. She wasn't suicidal enough or powerful enough to suggest a rewrite. Cockroaches had more cachet than she did around here. Maybe she should just let it go. Not every battle was hers to fight. How many times had Autumn told her that?

It didn't make it right, though.

A bold idea hit her. *Oh wow.* Well, that was one option. Did she dare? If she messed this up, she'd lose her job. If she got it right, she'd save Elizabeth from a terrible plot.

What a decision.

Her mother's words floated through her head. *Always* do what's right.

Straightening, she made up her mind.

Elizabeth was in a foul mood. They wanted her to participate in a public, verbal catfight over Mendez? With *Hope*'s sweetest resident? Because, of course, that's exactly what a hospital's chief of surgery would do.

Slamming the script on the table in her trailer, she ran the lines in her head. They were so inane she'd already committed them to memory. Sadly.

Elizabeth headed to the hallway set, fury powering her stride.

Summer was already there, practicing with a stunt co-ordinator the best way to hurl coffee at someone's chest.

Elizabeth ground her teeth.

Glancing over at her, Summer smiled in greeting, but Elizabeth was too angry to contemplate any form of response.

"You need a rehearsal first?" the director called over. "Not your usual scene, is it?"

No it damned well isn't. It was character sabotage and the foul stench of the writing burned her nostrils. Elizabeth glared with such venom that Summer paled and Ravitz muttered, "Never mind then. Just get on your marks."

They took their places. Summer faced away from Elizabeth, ready to deliver a line off-screen before turning to the camera.

"Speed...Rolling...Action!"

Elizabeth approached down the hall as Summer gave her line. Spinning around, Summer smiled, her face lighting up at the sight of Chief Hunt—*what was that about?*—and her coffee flew from her cup.

Elizabeth planted her feet, attempting to look surprised, and waited for the hit of cold, brown liquid. They'd add a steam effect later.

It barely caught her sleeve.

"Oh my God, Chief Hunt, I'm *so* sorry." Summer offered a hangdog expression and wide eyes.

Christ, it was funny how horrified she looked. The worst of Elizabeth's anger evaporated. "You're useless." She tried to inject some acidity into Hunt's voice. Instead, in the face of that whipped-puppy look, Elizabeth's lips...twitched. "I don't know what Dr. Mendez sees in you." *Oh dear.* Hunt almost sounded rueful. *Has my character ever done rueful in her life? Unlikely.*

"At least he wants me," Carter replied, relief thick in her tone. Then she looked aghast, eyes blowing wide open. "For my skills! Of course!"

Amazing. Elizabeth stared in surprise. Summer was a natural comedienne. Her delivery was brilliant.

"Oh, I'm sure that's why." And this time Hunt's lips did curl up into a rare smile that counted as agreement. Like they were two friendly colleagues eye-rolling some unwanted male attention.

Summer practically smirked.

"CUT!"

Everyone burst into laughter, and Summer gave a soft grin, relief shining in her eyes.

Elizabeth's shoulders relaxed. It was nice not being the butt of the joke for once. She glanced around.

Ravitz's face was one long, unimpressed scowl. "That's not the intention of the scene, you two. Can we try it a different way?" He injected heavy-duty sarcasm and added, "As *written*, for example?"

Take two involved another clean, white coat for Elizabeth and an even funnier take from Summer. Her eyes were somehow wider and even more apologetic.

For the life of her, Elizabeth couldn't dredge up any of Hunt's usual attitude. The chief had apparently discovered her funny bone for the first time in her uptight existence.

Takes three through to five weren't much better, earning a stern rebuke from Ravitz to "up the bitchiness ASAP. You two hate each other."

That resulted in take six, where Summer seemed to be satirizing a scheming bitch from *Dynasty*, and it was side-splittingly hilarious. If they ran that parody take, it'd be a viral sensation for years.

"CUT! Jesus H. Christ, Hayes, what the hell was THAT?" Ravitz's entire body was practically vibrating with his frustration.

Summer, blue eyes big and sad, rushed over to his chair. She knelt before him and said, "I'm *so* sorry Mr. Ravitz. I'm trying, but I just can't seem to get Joey to be a bitch. I think she's fighting me."

Elizabeth finally lost it, her hands falling to her knees as she doubled over and laughed until she wheezed. That set off the associate producers—which apparently was official permission—because it set off everyone else again. Except Bob Ravitz.

He glared around the set. "We'll go again. Sometime *soon*, if you don't mind."

After take seven, Ravitz did something Elizabeth had never seen before. He gave up. Flicking his watch a surly glance, he snapped his fingers. "Alright," he growled. "We can't waste more time on this. We'll make use of what we have." He pointed to a lighting tech. "Set up the next scene." Then he stalked over to edge of the set, beckoning Summer to him. "Ms. Hayes, 'trying' won't fly around here. Get your inner bitch ready next time or find a new line of work." His expression, however, seemed doubtful she could muster even the faintest bit of malice.

"Yes, Mr. Ravitz," she replied with a series of nods. "Definitely."

He strode back to his chair. "Ex-fuckin'-child stars," he muttered, loud enough for the two of them to hear. "Far too much damned *cute*."

Elizabeth eyed Summer, wondering if she'd be offended or offer a shrug and a sheepish look. Instead, her eyes contained an odd, resolved look. There was no hint of embarrassment at screwing up.

Oh! Elizabeth's thoughts shot to all sorts of interesting places. So, Summer Hayes was a much better actress than anyone gave her credit for?

How...risky. Certainly the only thing that had saved the young woman's job was the fact that no one else had worked out she hadn't been trying to get the scene right at all.

Elizabeth stepped closer to Summer, bending her head to avoid any prying eyes. "Why?" she whispered.

At first Summer looked startled, before her face became blank. All traces of amusement had vanished, and Elizabeth now doubted any of it had been real to start with.

"That scene was shit as written," Summer murmured. "And I don't mean for me." She gave Elizabeth a pointed look.

"Yes. It was." Elizabeth regarded her in astonishment. *She did this for me?*

Summer's expression was so warm it was almost unnerving.

Elizabeth headed back to her trailer to wait for her next scene, thoughts in chaos. Ravitz might be an asshole, but he had a point. When it came to Summer Hayes, there was way too much damned cute.

Chapter 5

SUMMER SLUNG HER BATTERED VINTAGE canvas bag over one shoulder, trying to focus on what lay ahead. After a hard day's shooting, mentally running through her to-do list helped calm her down.

Gym for an hour, followed by a glass of that evil, cleansing wheatgrass thing Chloe wanted her to try. Great for the skin, apparently. Summer's weekend would be hectic, laying down some voice work for the six-episode *Teen Spy Camp* animated series, plus spin class, and a facial with a friend of her mother's she could never say no to. Then, sign some photos for Autumn for a big fan giveaway...and... *Elizabeth stared at me like I was fascinating.*

Summer stopped walking. She'd taken a huge risk today. People got fired for less than what she'd done. Yes, technically, she'd said every word in the script, but she'd also ignored the intent. The hardest thing had been pushing aside her ego and allowing important people to think she sucked as an actress. That made her itch. She could have hauled out her inner bitch in the blink of an eye if she'd believed in the writing. But that scene was toxic.

Besides, this wasn't just a terrible direction to take Hunt. Summer's own character was smart and capable and shouldn't be trying to flirt her way through her residency program with her handsome boss. How was that a good message?

Even so, she'd been lucky today. Lucky that Ravitz, like so many other people she'd worked with, made assumptions based on her looks. For once it was useful. Somehow she'd pulled it off and no one was any the wiser.

Okay, almost no one.

She'd assumed that Elizabeth would be the first to think her useless. The look on her face, though, when she'd asked why... Her curiosity felt as powerful as a touch.

Why had Summer done it? How could she have answered truthfully?

Because I respect you too much to allow you to face more fan hatred.

Because Hunt being mocked as a caricature is grossly unfair.

Because I want you to be great. Like you were in London, when you changed my life.

Autumn would kill her if she ever got wind of this. Ignoring direction because you disagreed with the writing was the height of stupidity.

Resuming walking, Summer wondered if Elizabeth thought Summer was a fool for putting her job on the line for her. Some might see it as a sign of weakness—possibly to be exploited. But the way Elizabeth had looked at Summer hadn't been mocking or dismissive. She'd seemed taken aback. Grateful.

That felt...*wow*.

Glancing up at the green Exit sign ahead, Summer quickened her pace. Unwinding with pajamas and Netflix slid to the top of her list.

Elizabeth entered the corridor and offered a small nod. Her glossy, dark brown hair was out of its severe bun and flowed softly around her shoulders. Her graceful stride lacked the almost military, clipped walk she used on the show. And her face, usually all angles and derision, was gentler without the lighting designed to emphasize her "character." Code for age and imperfections. Which was insulting all round. Since when was thirty-seven old? And if Elizabeth had any physical flaws, they weren't apparent to Summer.

She sighed at herself. It was embarrassing how much space her brain allocated to the diverting topic of Elizabeth Thornton.

"Summer." Elizabeth murmured.

Summer. Okay, she'd do a little dance later because Elizabeth had never used her first name before. "Heading home?" Summer asked, as they fell into step. *Agh. Stupid question.*

Elizabeth gave her a faint smile. "What gave it away?"

Laughing, Summer mimed shooting herself in the temple. "Yeah. Sorry."

"I've been meaning to offer to pay for your tea. Sorry I keep forgetting. It can't be cheap getting it shipped over from England so regularly."

"It's fine. I do a quid pro quo with some friends who have a Tootsie Roll addiction. It's not that much in the end."

"I see. Well, thank you. Finola claims the tea has been improving my legendary bad mood somewhat." She gave Summer a self-deprecating smile. "Although I'm sure our colleagues would claim they can't tell the difference."

"Our colleagues should stop confusing you with your character." Summer grinned. "And speaking of Hunt, I'm sorry about what they're doing to her. I liked who she was."

"Mm." Elizabeth stopped at the door and waved a pass at the security panel. Its light flashed green as the door unlocked. "I gathered that with your little stunt today. You turned a scene that was beneath us into something almost...fun." An amused smile darted across her lips as she held the door open for Summer. "I appreciate you saving Chief Hunt's honor."

"I didn't do it for Hunt," Summer said without thinking as she stepped outside.

"No? Why—"

Hell! Summer's feet met empty air as she remembered, too late, the two steep steps between the building and the ground. She fell.

Elizabeth's hand flashed out, grabbing her wrist, jerking her upright, her other arm wrapping around Summer's waist, preventing a face-plant onto concrete.

Summer twisted awkwardly to regain her footing and wound up looking straight up into Elizabeth's face. Her exasperated expression said this was about the klutzy idiocy she'd expect.

"Shit!" Summer squirmed away from those soft hands. "Forgot about the steps." She gave an awkward laugh. "Obviously. You may have noticed I'm a little clumsy."

"Once or twice," Elizabeth drawled. "Can you at least attempt to drive home safely?"

"Will do my best." Warmth flooded Summer. It almost sounded like Elizabeth cared whether she lived or died. That had to count for something. Her brain snorted at that merry delusion. But Summer couldn't wipe away the grin splitting her cheeks as she pulled out of the studio lot and headed for home.

⋯⋯⋯

A pointed jab to her ribs woke Summer. She yawned and batted Chloe away. She wasn't in the mood for wake-up prodding, given it was a Saturday. The gloss of her roomie being back home had worn off already.

"Come on, Smiley, you'll want to see this!"

"Mmph?" Summer peeled her eyes open. "It's way too early for enthusiasm."

Chloe shoved a phone screen in her face. "You're the star of HGZ."

What? She sat up. *Since when does Hollywood Gossip Zone touch me?*

"And these pics are everywhere," Chloe said.

Summer squinted at the screen, which showed a grainy photo of herself, held in the arms of...*oh shit*...Elizabeth. Well not *held-held*. But it sure looked that way in this frozen moment. Elizabeth's smirk looked almost affectionate rather than exasperated. Summer's face, tilted toward the camera, seemed surprised, trusting and...ugh...*into it.* "Oh my God."

"Ex-actly." Chloe eyed her.

"Who took this?"

"Does it matter? Obviously some gutter-trawler with a long lens can see the studio's exit from the street. Now, focus. What's the sitch between you two? I thought you exploded blood all over her or something? Now she likes you? Gotta say, hon, flings with your co-stars are a baaaad idea. Even when they're as gorgeous as her—I mean, if you like that whole beautiful, ice-bitch thing." She frowned. "Hey, does this mean Thornton's a lesbian? Or another Hollywood bi? Wait, she has some hot boyfriend, doesn't she?" She glared at Summer. "Jesus, girl, are you the *other woman? You?*"

"Ungh." Summer felt sick. "Of course I'm not the other anything! You know how clumsy I am. I fell, she grabbed me, that's it. Look at my feet... they're pointing in different directions!" Dismay rose in her chest. "Crap. I'm so dead. Elizabeth's going to kill me for fake-outing her as my...um..."

"Lover?" Chloe's eyebrows did a suggestive little jig.

So. Dead. The fans who detested Elizabeth would seize on this. They'd paint her as some closeted, predatory lesbian.

The thought of Elizabeth furious with her was suffocating. They'd only just gotten to the point of having a conversation that lasted longer than a sentence or two.

Summer's phone rang, so she pushed Chloe's cell away and rolled over to reach hers.

"Oh, great. It's Autumn," she muttered. "Hey, Sis. ... No. ... No... definitely *no.* Are you kidding me? As if she'd ever want to... We were leaving work and I fell and she saved my ass from an ER visit. ... Oh *thank you.* I'm *so* glad my balance issues are a source of amusement."

She listened to her sister's commentary for a moment, cutting in when Autumn took a breath. "Are you issuing a statement? Because it's both of us affected this time. Can we say something like 'Elizabeth Thornton has impressive reflexes given she caught me when I tripped at the studio. Sorry to disappoint the gossip hounds but I'm just a klutz'?" She listened to Autumn tweaking her quote into something less idiotic, and then said, "Yep, that's great. Put that one out. Thanks. Bye."

Chloe gave her a speculative look.

"What?" Summer asked.

"You know, even if it's not with Thornton, you're way overdue a bit of lady lovin'. It's been ages."

"I'm too busy."

"Oh please. Half the cast of *Choosing Hope* is married or hooking up, including your *girlfriend*." Chloe snickered and called up a photo of Elizabeth from a red-carpet event. Next to her, dashing Amrit Patel ran his fingers through his swooping, perfect hair. "See? If she can find time for love, so can you."

"I don't have the energy." Summer glumly regarded Amrit. "Aside from the emotional investment, it's hard work sneaking around places. Hollywood's such a fishbowl. I go out with someone new and I'm hyper-vigilant the whole time for smartphones and paparazzi, when I'd rather just enjoy a date like everyone else. It's not fun."

"That'd suck." Chloe's brown eyes radiated sympathy. "I hadn't thought of that."

"Besides, right now I just want to do well at this role. I don't want to be the 'former child star' anymore. I just want to be actress Summer Hayes. And I sure as hell don't want to be renowned for a workplace romance with a world-famous co-star."

"Okay, that's cool. So, you doing basketball with us today?" Chloe's eyebrows slid up.

Summer knew that look. "Did you just mentally disregard everything I just said and plan to hook me up with that fangirl on your team?"

"Who me?" Chloe's innocent look needed work. "Okay, maybe."

Summer snorted as her phone rang again. "Ugh! It's Mom. She'll be so delighted I've 'snagged' myself an A-lister she admires. This is the worst."

"No way, the worst is when your dad calls, eh?"

Summer's stomach dropped. "Oh, God." She squared her shoulders and took the call. "Hey Mom, and before you start, it's not true. No, I mean it!"

Chloe rose from the bed and gave her a wave, leaving Summer to her fate.

Skye Storm's excited tones burbled down the phone as she blew past everything Summer said. So Summer gave up trying to reason with a madwoman and tuned her out, focusing on what was really bothering her. And it wasn't her gruff father's impending lecture on the virtues of discretion, either.

No, it was: *What is Elizabeth thinking right now?*

Sitting up in bed at six in the morning, Elizabeth flicked through email after email, confronted with the same photo her agent, manager, and friends had all sent her in the past hour. Zara had added just one sentence: "Bwahahahahaha. *Cougar!* Too funny."

Grace's short email had made her stomach turn. *"Oh dear. Are we a lesbian now, Elizabeth?"*

The tone was bad enough—the hint of disdain that Elizabeth had been foolish enough to get caught in a scandal. Because despite the words, her censure had nothing to do with lesbians, whom Grace happily counted among her most devoted fans. No, what made Elizabeth's stomach twist most was Grace's ongoing obliviousness about her life.

In all their years of friendship, Grace had never asked why Elizabeth never seemed to date anyone. The rest of her friends had all nudged the question her way a few times, backing off when Elizabeth hadn't engaged them. Alex had been the exception, of course.

The constant silence from Grace was revealing.

Of course, friendship was a difficult thing with someone used to being the center of the universe. Being engaged in a personal conversation with Grace made you feel special and lucky to be included. She'd drop intimate, secret snippets into discussions while twirling a martini glass expansively, her words part confession, part lesson, as she segued from the men she'd loved to those to be avoided. The guru on the mount.

Was that friendship? Grace's version of it? Elizabeth had always liked to think so.

On days like today, though, her imperious, oblivious friend rubbed her up the wrong way—not for what she thought, but for what hadn't even occurred to her to think.

Sighing, Elizabeth returned to the photos. It all looked so strangely sordid, as if Elizabeth was about to fling Summer down and wipe that stunned look off her face. It was bad enough Hunt was hated by fans; now they'd be openly speculating as to whether Elizabeth was a closeted lesbian—a question far too close to home to be safe.

Why did Summer have to look so...what *was* that look, anyway? Amazed? Incredulous?

Did Summer really think I'd let her break her neck and not lift a finger?

Elizabeth's image was desperately needing some rehab if that were true.

Rachel called moments later, while rushing to a breakfast meeting. Amid the sound of her feet pounding up stairs, her agent gasped out, "Say nothing and don't draw attention to it."

"I'm not the one drawing attention to it. Everyone else is," Elizabeth protested.

"Bess, I know. But picture this gossip as beneath you. Then act like it. If anyone asks about it outright, look surprised they would think something so ridiculous. Oh, and do yourself a big favor: Put some distance between yourself and the girl. There's a leak on your set, so don't give them any more grist for the mill."

"What grist? We exited a building together!"

"Well, then don't exit buildings with her anymore." Rachel sounded long-suffering as ever. "Especially not one that fronts a parking lot with wide gaps in the fence, facing a public street. Look, it's not hard: just don't hang out together on set or after work—"

"But we don't—"

"And before long everyone will move on to the next scandal, so you can reconnect later if you want. But for now, give her a wide berth so your sneaky set mole doesn't get fed, and this will blow over. Oh, one last thing, before you give her the flick, get her to talk to her people and make sure they don't get some half-baked idea to give this non-story any oxygen. Make sure they *don't* put out a statement. People will think there must be something to it if they hose it down. Okay? Gotta go." Rachel hung up.

Elizabeth had just finished getting dressed half an hour later when the next round of exasperated emails landed. This time it was Delvine. Her rant included a screen shot of Summer's manager's statement.

Well, that was fast. Rachel would be pissed.

By the time Elizabeth had dried her hair, Delvine was on the phone, somehow sounding both appalled and snide. "They've gone with a denial and are painting you as some hero for saving Summer from injury," her manager said.

"Delvine, *that's* what happened."

"Yes, but people think denials are all fake. It's a rookie error to issue one on something mundane. But I looked up the actress's people and she's only got one, if you can believe it. Worse, it's her sister. So, what can you expect? Oh, and get this, the actress is called Summer, the manager's Autumn, and the mother's Skye Storm. Apparently she's never married her live-in lover of thirty years. It's like a hippie commune, that family."

Elizabeth rolled her eyes. "I dread to ask who the father is. Moon?"

"Oh no," Delvine's voice took on a hint of caution. "Brock Hayes. One of the most respected stunt co-ordinators in the business. Man is a legend—knows everyone, been in everything. From what I gather, he won't like this one little bit, people talking smack about his precious daughter."

"Calling her a lesbian, you mean?" Distaste coated Elizabeth's mouth.

"I have no idea if that's an issue, but I don't think that's what'll have his boxers in a bunch."

"What will?"

"Darling, please don't make me say it."

Elizabeth's lips thinned. "Whatever it is, I'm sure I've heard worse."

"He won't like that his perfect princess has been linked with *you*. Your reputation is not…stellar right now."

"Great." She ground her teeth. "Attila the Hunt strikes again."

"No, any disapproval will be about you. The British Bitch stuff."

"It's a lie spread by Lenton. That showrunner's as thin-skinned as a jellyfish."

"I know, I know. It's all nonsense. You're a doll to work with. No lies, no diva nonsense. You don't run around nightclubs drunk or high or wave your tits about or get on Twitter and abuse the fans who rain shit over you.

And you're obviously discreet as hell with the women you date, because all I hear about is you and Amrit."

"He does appreciate the publicity. Actually I've been thinking of retiring him and tapping Rowan in as the love of my life this year. His comedy act could use the exposure. He's up for it."

"Don't you dare! The bored housewives lap up Amrit's gorgeous British-Indian charms. He's the only thing keeping the women's mags fawning over you at all. They're doing a good job at counterbalancing HGZ's vendetta. Besides, didn't you fake-date Rowan once before?"

"Years ago. And not fake-dated; I don't do that. Just took him as my plus-one. As if anyone would remember that anyway. I was a no one."

"Oh, trust me, they will. Stick with Amrit. In fact, more than that: I want to see the two of you lighting up Twitter within the next twelve hours and reinforcing all that lovely heterosexual sensuality you apparently ooze for each other."

"You know I hate doing that. Taking a friend as a date to a red-carpet event is one thing. Letting people jump to conclusions is fine. But this is actively faking it. I've never done that. Besides, does anyone really care?"

There was a dainty snort. "They care. And this is about what sticks. What you do next after those photos is what people will remember about you. Think of that when you cuddle up to Amrit. Oh, and tell him to wear his burgundy tie. Looks stunning in photos."

Elizabeth groaned. "Fine. Now, say something to keep me sane: Any word on Badour's movie?"

"Yes, actually. Our Frenchman's back in town in a few days. He's going to call me to sort out our lunch date. Which is even more reason to get the *British Bitch* headlines out of circulation by then. You know HGZ is using these photos as an excuse to rehash all the ugly old rumors about you. I don't want him second-guessing himself as to your suitability. Directors get twitchy about difficult actors."

"I thought you said he wanted me, though?"

"He did. I'll make sure he still does. So, are we clear? Amrit in his burgundy tie and dinner somewhere public tonight. Try Casa Vega or Hamasaku. Paparazzi are camped out front most nights. Maybe somewhere else tomorrow. Or a frolic on the beach for fifteen minutes, if your English-rose skin can bear it."

Oh hell no. She was not cavorting on the beach for the public's edification.

"And if you must comment on the story at all, stick to whatever Hayes's statement said so your stories line up," Delvine finished.

"Of course they line up—it's the truth!" This was insane.

"Even better. You won't have to remember any lines."

Elizabeth glared at her phone. "Can I just say how ridiculous this is? I stopped a woman from splitting her head open yet now I have to fake-date a friend to appease fans who *already hate me.*"

"Yes, yes, we're all mad, darling. Okay, Bess, I'll let you know when I hear back from Jean-Claude. Oh and remember, try to smile once in a blue moon, it'll be great for your image."

Her phone went dead.

Elizabeth scowled.

———⊷⬦⬦⊶———

Summer sat in her small on-set trailer, relieved for its solitude. It was about half the size of Elizabeth's, containing only a couch, bathroom, and coffee-making facilities. She didn't care. It was an escape from the stares and whispers.

Unable to help herself, Summer again called up the latest photos on her Twitter feed. Amrit and Elizabeth laughing. Eating at Casa Vega. Holding hands. Elizabeth playfully adjusting his burgundy tie. Well. That was one way to address the rumors.

Summer was no innocent. The timing on Amrit and Elizabeth's date was as fake as most of the boobs in LA. But just because the pair had a sudden, burning urge to be seen in public didn't take away from the obvious warmth they had for each other. His wide, flashing white smile as he gazed into her eyes with pure affection...

Summer didn't know why she was fixating on this. Well, maybe she did.

There was a knock.

"Come in," she said, tucking her phone away.

The door opened. Elizabeth filled the frame, dressed as Hunt, her hair in its starched bun. She closed the door after her and leaned against it. "Well," she said. "I had an interesting weekend. How about you?"

Summer's cheeks burned. "I'm sorry you had to haul your boyfriend around to prove you're not..." she indicated herself. "You know. I am *really* sorry my feet got us into this mess again."

"Amrit loves the publicity. He'll probably send you a thank-you card. I, on the other hand, do not." Her expression became pinched.

"I'm really sor—"

An impatient wave moved the air between them. "Obviously, it's not your fault, but it is...irritating. Not to mention unedifying." Elizabeth hesitated. "I'm here for two reasons. We know someone leaks to HGZ from our set. Until this...situation...with the photos blows over, my people don't think it's a good idea for me to be seen with you in any non-professional capacity that could be misconstrued." Looking skeptical, she added, "Not even to exit buildings with you."

Summer blinked. *Exit buildings together?* They'd done that once! By accident! And beyond a few brief conversations, they had only a professional relationship. So it sounded like Elizabeth was saying that she intended to avoid Summer like rancid milk now and would Summer mind not bothering her again with her inconvenient presence?

In the silence, Elizabeth shifted uneasily, then glanced away.

"And the other thing? You said you had two." Summer prayed her anger and humiliation weren't obvious.

"My manager, Delvine Rothery, has asked that Autumn not issue any more statements on this, and if she has a compulsion to do so, to consult Delvine first. Here's her card. She's one of the best, so..." Elizabeth slid a card onto the table.

The implication was clear. *Your sister is a rank amateur, and my shit-hot professional manager thinks Autumn's screwed up, but she'll stop her from doing that again.*

"What was wrong with Autumn's statement?" Summer gritted her teeth. "It was the truth."

"Yes. But apparently fans don't believe the truth." Elizabeth nudged the card closer when Summer made no move to take it.

A chill went through her. Elizabeth wore the face of the woman who'd made Summer love acting. She sounded like the woman for whom Summer had taken the biggest professional risk.

And Summer had no idea who she really was.

Because here Elizabeth Thornton stood, treating Summer like some flea-bitten dog she didn't want around.

And Elizabeth had done it so casually, as if unaware of the pain she'd just inflicted, or how small she'd just made Summer feel. Maybe there was some truth to the British Bitch rumors after all.

Lips tight, Summer forced out a "Fine." She felt every ounce of warmth, respect, and admiration she'd ever had for this woman drain out of her. "I won't bother you again. I'll only go near you on set when I have no choice. Does that satisfy you?" It sounded more bitter than she'd intended, but to hell with her.

Elizabeth's jaw worked. "I've got a scene in five minutes. I have to go. Please get your sister to call my manager. Goodbye, Summer."

Summer nodded curtly. Her hands balled into fists, the short nails biting into her skin. The fucking audacity of using her name now. Only once the door clicked shut behind Elizabeth did she exhale. And to her horror, she felt the sting of tears in her eyes.

Elizabeth had once likened Summer to a kitten. *Well, that was like killing one*, she thought as she closed the door to Summer's trailer. There was no mistaking how all that softness and glow just seemed to deflate at her words.

Necessary words, Rachel had insisted. And yet...were they? Really?

The humiliation in Summer's eyes at what Elizabeth had accepted as a practical plan had robbed her of speech. She hadn't meant to make Summer feel rejected. And what had Elizabeth said to reassure her?

Nothing.

As Elizabeth strode back to her trailer to fetch her white coat for the next scene, she started rethinking Rachel's strategy. *Strategy?* It was barely even that. Elizabeth should have questioned it, or even thought about it for five minutes before simply following it.

People shot out of her way as she thundered down the corridor.

She should have ignored Rachel and said to hell with what people would think.

And yet...she didn't want to be "out", which was right where those fake rumors would lead if they swirled around long enough. She wasn't ready yet, personally or professionally.

So because of that, without even thinking, she'd done something that made her feel sick.

Reaching her trailer, she slammed the door behind her and reached by rote for a mug. Her other hand fell to the tea box. Empty.

Fuck.

Chapter 6

IN THE WEEKS THAT FOLLOWED, watching Summer became a form of penance for Elizabeth. She glared at her hideous substitute tea, an ongoing reminder of why she couldn't have the one she loved.

The lively, bright young woman she'd first met seemed to have changed before her eyes. Now she was subdued, withdrawn, and measured. She didn't trip, flail, joke, or smile around Elizabeth. Maybe she did these things elsewhere, but for some reason Elizabeth didn't think so.

It wasn't her fault. Whatever was going on with Summer was coincidental.

Oh sure. You inform a woman who has been nothing but good to you that you plan to avoid her to further your own career, and she's going to shrug that off like it's nothing?

She exhaled in annoyance.

The problem was she'd left an apology too late. She should have done it immediately, but now too much time had passed and everything was strained and awkward. It wasn't just the missed apology she regretted. If she could turn back the clock to three weeks ago, she'd take back the whole conversation.

It was startling to notice how much she missed that wash of natural niceness whenever Summer was around. Elizabeth wasn't alone in that. Finola had been bemoaning Summer's absence with an increasing avalanche of sad clucks that made her sound like a disappointed chicken. Of course, she likely just missed the good mood Summer's tea put Elizabeth in.

It was hard to know what to make of this new Summer. Her detached expression was so empty, flat, and indifferent. Elizabeth hated it, and yet couldn't take her eyes off her. She was on a constant, fruitless search to see the woman who'd been there before.

Their scenes together now had a completely different feel to anything else on the show. There was a watchfulness to them. On her part, they noticeably lacked malice or bite. And on Summer's part, they lacked the warmth that seeped into everything she did. All Carter's scenes with Hunt were infused with a contradictory cocktail of wariness, faint teasing, speculative gazes, and a certain, loaded *something else*. There was a weight to the scenes now. And yet there was also the accompanying, slight uptick of lips that proved Joey never minded anything Chief Hunt said. It was baffling and hypnotic.

Often, after Ravitz had called *cut*, Elizabeth froze, eying her co-star in confusion, wondering how much of it had been a deliberate acting choice and what emotion she'd been attempting to convey. Because whatever it was, Elizabeth couldn't decipher it.

Summer's mood shift was so unusual it didn't match the rest of her scenes. Joey Carter was bright and breezy one moment, introspective and subtle the next. And yet Ravitz said nothing. His expression, though, as he watched them, boded no good. Elizabeth wondered, not for the first time, whether Summer's days were numbered.

If that happened, she'd feel the lowest she ever had. Although, if she was being honest, she might feel a bit of relief, too. Scenes with Summer had become far too distracting. Elizabeth hated being distracted at work. It was unprofessional. She had standards, even if *Choosing Hope* didn't. But it was odd. No one had ever shifted her focus from work before.

This was as mystifying as the puzzle of a woman behind it.

———— ⋄⋄⋄ ————

Going about her working day without Elizabeth in it was weird. By consciously removing the other woman from Summer's brain, forcing herself not to wonder about her, what she was doing, thinking, wearing, at any given time, it became alarmingly clear how completely she had been focused on Elizabeth.

Summer knew what that meant, even if it was unpalatable. Oh she'd dressed it up as respect and admiration, but it was pretty obvious she'd been emotionally invested in someone who had tolerated her and now didn't want to know her at all.

She ground her teeth. Not *emotionally invested*. What, was she part of a portfolio? With a sigh, Summer finally admitted the truth: She was in deep. What she felt was far more than just friendship, and the allure went well beyond Elizabeth's acting. The woman was beautiful and smart and kind of funny if you dug a little. And she had those gray eyes that bored into you and seemed to know everything. The way she moved was languid and liquid, like silk. Then there was that voice. Could a voice get you pregnant? Summer was due any day if that were true.

Hell. She really was pathetic.

The worst part was that her inconvenient emotions made a mockery of her strict rules on matters of the heart. Years ago, Summer had decided three things:

1) Never fall for a straight woman.
2) No settling, ever. Never pine for someone who doesn't care as much as you do.
3) Never get involved with a fan, or vice versa, as the hero/fan balance is never equal.

Summer had broken all three rules with Elizabeth...and, worse, she hadn't even been conscious of it. Humiliation burned through her again.

Judging by the indifferent way Elizabeth had dropped her icy little bombshell, there had been no loss on her part. Then again, they hadn't been friends, had they? Aside from the tea deliveries, Summer had been nothing to Elizabeth. Easily discarded.

She glanced about her on-set nook, just around the corner from the scene they were shooting. The tiny slice of peace allowed her to be close when she was needed but prevented her from having to talk to people...or see one in particular.

It was unnecessary though. She wouldn't see Elizabeth again. That is, not the version she'd thought she knew. Turned out that Elizabeth was an illusion. The real woman was like everyone else: flawed, career-hungry, and selfish. Hardly a shock in this town. It just hurt to have thought Elizabeth was better than she really was. But it wasn't Elizabeth's responsibility to live up to the image Summer had built up in her head.

63

Ultimately, Summer was angriest with herself. She should have known better. She'd been immersed in this world from childhood. All of it was illusion. Everything that seemed real was massaged by actors' people to be palatable to the masses. Everyone was out for themselves, and it was naive to pretend otherwise. But the reminder still hurt. She'd been foolish for not realizing sooner that she'd been swept up in a fantasy.

Chloe had been right. *"Oh hon, be careful. You'll get your heart broken. There is nothing worse than meeting your idol."*

Summer had done way worse than that. She straightened. No more of that. All she felt for Elizabeth Thornton now was anger. Would it have killed her to say sorry before slamming the door in Summer's face for good?

It had been three weeks since Elizabeth had discarded her without blinking. At first, rumors had swirled about what that photo had really meant, but things had since died down. Even so, nothing was the same. Summer was watched on set all the time. And she never felt deader inside than when she did a scene with Elizabeth.

The scripts were peppered with snide comments to build up an angry energy between Hunt and Carter. But Summer just did her lines straight: zero sarcasm, often with a small smile as she turned the bitchy lines into teasing. They couldn't have it both ways. Either her character was sweet or she wasn't.

To her surprise, Ravitz seemed to accept that Carter was incapable of being mean to anyone and simply sighed and called for the next scene.

None of this, though, explained Elizabeth's behavior. Despite what the script called for, there was little bite in her delivery. Often she would hold Summer's gaze, a questioning, curious look in her eyes. Sometimes it was hard to know whether Hunt or Thornton was watching her.

Each time they called *cut*, Elizabeth would linger, wearing an inscrutable expression, as though itching to say something to Summer. She never did. After the first few times, Summer stopped giving her the chance and just left the set immediately.

Summer wondered what fans would make of these latest episodes when they aired. Attila the Hunt declawed around sweet Dr. Carter?

"There you are!"

Summer looked up to see Tori wearing an overly dramatic expression. She wasn't quite a friend yet, but Summer appreciated their lunch chats.

"Yes?" she asked.

"Been trying to find you everywhere!" Tori handed her a paper plate. "Here, sustenance. You missed lunch. Again."

A large greasy muffin stared back at her. "I haven't been too hungry lately."

"I've noticed. It's been weeks, girl! It's like you fell off the face of the earth. I thought I'd have to share a table with Thornton or something worse than death." She laughed heartily.

Summer's stomach clenched. "That'd suck." She poked at the muffin, which looked like a failed diet plan on a plate.

"So wassup? Why are you avoiding everyone, not eating, and all moody?" Tori paused. "Oh my God!" She lowered her voice. "Are you pregnant?"

"What? No! I just had some stuff to deal with. But it's almost over now. I hope." She tried for a winning smile.

"Hmm." Tori's look was skeptical. "Tell ya what, Saturday night, we're hitting Residuals Tavern on Ventura. You will mix, mingle, get your ass sociable again. And Mateo's going." She grinned.

"Not interested in Mateo." Summer broke off a tiny corner of muffin and tossed it in her mouth. She chewed gingerly. It didn't entirely suck.

"Okay, that's cool. It'll break his gorgeous Latino heart, but okay."

"I'm sure he won't be short of offers. Just tell him to flash his six-pack again. Or you could date him?"

"Hmm. I think you're trying to divert me. Sneaky." She wagged a finger. "You think I haven't noticed you've been bummed since those photos of you and the Brit came out?"

Summer's head shot up.

"Hey, it's okay. Don't worry. No one thinks you're tapping that. I've seen how you can trip over nothing at all, so I totally buy your story. But I get it. It's a fucked-up rumor and it's hard to think everyone's talking about it."

To avoid replying, Summer shoved more muffin in her mouth.

"So, this here's your intervention. We all miss Happy Summer. So for your own good, I'm hauling you out Saturday and there's nothing you can say about it."

"Pretty sure I can say no."

"But you won't."

Summer lifted her eyebrow. "Why won't I?"

"Because it's me asking. And I'm hella charming."

Summer laughed. "True."

"So how about it? See you at seven? Just you, me, and our fellow fictional medical residents. No brooding allowed."

Sighing, Summer considered the offer. It might be nice to get to know some people.

"As long as you tell Mateo he's got no chance, then I'm in."

"Sold." Tori elbowed her in the ribs. "So if not Mateo, is there anyone you *do* like?"

Summer's heart sank all over again, and her gut squeezed tightly.

"Oh shit!" Tori looked appalled. "Whoever busted your heart into bits, I'm really sorry."

Tears pricked her eyes. So much for being over Elizabeth.

"How's my favorite hospital boss, darling?"

Elizabeth stared at the inky sky from her deck chair and muttered down the phone to Delvine, "Just peachy." It beat the truth. A hated job, guilt over Summer's transformation that had now stretched into a month, no decent tea, zero professional stimulation. She took a sip of gin and tonic.

"Excellent. Notice I'm choosing to accept that answer at face value rather than ponder why you're drowning your sorrows at home alone at ten-thirty on a weeknight."

"What makes you think that?"

"Your ice cubes are clinking. Anyway, I have news for you on our Frenchman."

"Oh?" Elizabeth perked up.

"Well, good news and bad news. First, Rachel's pitching a major fit so leave her alone for now, okay?"

"Um, why?" Her heart plummeted. "Don't tell me Badour got a face full of British Bitch stories and is having second thoughts?"

"Yes and no..." Delvine cleared her throat. "He still wants you, don't worry. We're all on for lunch next Sunday, the 27th, at his hotel suite. I know it's only ten days' notice, but make sure you're free. But, yes, he did see a lot of sensational stories about you. On that note, he'd like you to bring your girlfriend to lunch too."

"My what?" Elizabeth almost dropped her glass. She couldn't possibly mean…

"Summer. Summer Hayes." Delvine managed to make her cough sound both strangled and sheepish. "It was an awkward conversation. He got most indignant when I said there was no girlfriend. And then he got angry with me. I got a rant, something about how people tried to keep him in the closet too when he was starting out, and it's only now that he is open and free that his life is it's full worth. Anyway, I gather he thinks I'm trying to protect you by stuffing you and Summer into the closet and he won't tolerate me doing that to you. He is *adamant* that he saw the pictures and he knows the truth when he sees it. So the bottom line is this: Lunch with Summer or the deal's off. And Summer had better turn up as your girlfriend not your co-star or he'll be furious at all of us for trying to trick him."

Elizabeth's mouth fell open.

"Still there, darling?"

"Let me get this straight: You and Rachel ask me to treat Summer like persona non grata—"

"To be fair, that was your hard-ass agent, not my fabulous, easy-going self—"

"Whatever. So I do that. Now Summer hates me, which isn't entirely unexpected, and yet…somehow…I have to convince her to go to a business lunch as my girlfriend or I don't get a role I really want. Have I got that right?"

"Essentially." Delvine sounded a little strained.

"And he seems to think I'm a closeted lesbian—"

"Which you are, darling."

Ignoring that, Elizabeth gritted her teeth, "…who beds her twenty-three-year-old co-star."

"Twenty-eight."

"What?" Elizabeth frowned.

"Summer is twenty-eight. She's been playing five years younger than she is for ages. Don't you ever Google your co-stars?"

"She can't be."

"Oh, she is. You're only nine years apart, which is hardly too outlandish. So is that your only objection?"

"This is ludicrous. Badour really thinks *she's* my type? Little Miss Sunshine sleeping with someone with my reputation?"

"Ahh, but that's part of the appeal. See, he doesn't understand it and can't wait to witness you two together to figure out how this relationship works. He loves excavating the human condition. Haven't you seen his films? That's his life's work. What makes people tick. You are catnip to him right now. Of course, he also heard the other rumors about you, the ones about how impossible you are on set. So this lunch is his way of seeing if you two can work together."

"You're forgetting that Summer wants nothing to do with me. Why don't I go along to lunch, explain it was a big misunderstanding, and win him over anyway?"

Delvine snorted. "Well, let me tell you exactly how that will go, because I did try that whole misunderstanding angle…at length. He said, and I quote, 'Do not give me such lies. They can be private about their love if they must, I will be the soul of discretion. But no hideous closets. Never lie to me. I cannot stand humanity's deceit'."

For the love of… "Why on earth is he so convinced that your denial is a lie?" Elizabeth flung her hand up at the skies. "Has it ever occurred to the man he might be wrong about something?"

"On reading humans, he is convinced he's always right. Anyway, it's up to you. Do you want me to pass on this or do you want to bring Summer? I'll remind you everyone wants a piece of this. It's the first American production from cinema's latest It-boy. It's sizzling hot."

"What did Rachel say?"

"She thinks you should tread carefully, and remember hotel staff have ears."

"But she thinks I should do it."

"She says she's seen the script and that movie will give you a future far beyond America's worst villain."

Wonderful. She sighed. "Did I mention Summer hates me?" Elizabeth tried again. "She'd never agree to helping me."

"Pay her then. Call it a side acting job."

"You don't know her. I don't think money motivates her. I'm not sure what does, but I doubt it's that."

"Then promise her a meeting with one of the most influential indie producers in film-making. A star on the rise who'd be excellent to network with."

Elizabeth turned that over. "That might work. But the other problem is that I'm not sure she can act romantically interested in me."

"Because she hates you?" Delvine sounded amused.

"That's one factor. But also, from what I've seen of her acting so far, she mainly excels at humor. The rest is sort of a confusing mess, to be honest. I'm not exactly filled with confidence."

"You don't think *Summer Hayes* can act?" Delvine laughed out loud.

"Why's that funny? Her top credit to date is a children's spy show!"

"My kids loved *Teen Spy Camp* and especially Junior Agent Punky Power. Dismiss what you haven't seen at your peril, darling. Summer hides her talent well under that sunny facade. Trust me, though, if she wants to help you, she could pull this off in a heartbeat. The question is whether you can actually get her to do it. That's up to you. I know you've got charm when you decide to use it. Dust it off for five minutes; shock us all. Now I've got to go. Text me if she agrees and I'll confirm with Badour."

The call ended.

———※———

Summer was running lines with one of her colleagues...Tori something...when Elizabeth approached the quiet corner that seemed to be her on-set hiding spot. She'd seen her here before, but given her a wide berth, recognizing the need to be left alone.

"May I have a few moments?" She glanced pointedly at Tori.

Tori snapped her head to Summer, who gave a nod of acceptance, before scampering off.

Elizabeth lowered herself into the vacated canvas chair.

Still studying her script, Summer said, "Why, Ms. Thornton. Aren't you worried people might get ideas if they see you talking to me? Alone, no less?"

"I'm sorry."

There was a silence. Summer lifted her head. "Why now?"

Elizabeth hadn't expected the bitterness. She really should have done this much sooner. "I'm taking a meeting with a French director. Jean-Claude..."

"Badour?"

"You know him?"

"My mother did the costumes for *Quand Pleurent les Clowns,* among some of his other movies. I've met him a few times. There was a karaoke night and pool wrap party for *Clowns*; I got to see a lot of him there."

"Oh." Well, there went Elizabeth's ace card. *How would you like to meet someone you already know far better than I do?* "Your mother's a costume designer?"

Summer gave her an impatient nod. "What does any of this have to do with me?"

"Jean-Claude is making his Hollywood debut. I don't know much about it yet. I don't think anyone does."

"*Eight Little Pieces,*" Summer said. "A writer in a remote shack gets eight visitors after the nearest road is blocked by a rock fall. They knock on her door, seeking help. It's all an allegory. The eight people each represent a different part of her. You know, like loss, shame, lust, regret, power, that sort of thing. The visitors aren't real, they're just facets of her own personality, but she doesn't know it until the end."

That was what it was about? It did sound good. Elizabeth frowned. "How do you know all that?"

"Jean-Claude and Mom stay in touch. They sort of vibrate on the same eccentric frequency. She spitballs designs with him and he talks latest projects with her." Summer leveled a cool look at her. "Why so interested?"

"He wants me to star in his film. I could fit it into hiatus. The thing is...he wants me to bring my girlfriend to lunch before confirming my casting." She held her breath.

"Your *girlfriend.*" A shadow crossed Summer's face. "He saw the photos?"

Elizabeth nodded.

"And you denied it?"

"Delvine spent some time trying to convince him it was a misunderstanding. He believes that the proof is in the photos, therefore any denial is a lie he cannot tolerate. He wants to do lunch next Sunday, the 27th. With both of us. It wasn't really a request."

"Your people told you to avoid me and now they want you to fake-date me over lunch to get this role?" she asked. One hand tightened on her script, fingers whitening.

"I realize I have no right to ask. I know I was unfair to you."

"Unfair." Summer's laugh was brittle. "Is that how you see it? And now you've apologized only because you need something from me."

Elizabeth exhaled. "You have every right to be angry. I understand that."

"So give me one reason why I should do this for you?"

Elizabeth worried her lip with her teeth. She briefly thought of offering money, as Delvine had suggested, but the look in Summer's eye told her that was the worst idea. Time stretched out. "I can't think of a single reason."

"Well, at least you didn't offer me cash."

At least I read one thing right.

"Answer me something." Summer tilted her head. "Did you ever think about how it felt for me, being told I wasn't even worthy of exiting a building with you? Did that cross your mind at any point?"

Elizabeth hesitated. No, she hadn't given it a great deal of thought, beyond that she'd upset Summer.

"I'm worth more than that. I don't care who you are, how good you are, or where you are in this show's hierarchy. No one's disposable."

Shame burned through her. Summer was completely right. "I'm truly sorry. And I see now it was wrong of me to ask this of you." She made to rise.

"Why did you? Knowing how it would end?" Summer watched her closely. "You must want this role badly."

She debated how to answer that. *Great opportunity. Career step. Interesting possibilities.* But under Summer's hard gaze, all the usual tweaking of the truth flew out the window.

"I'm dying here," Elizabeth said in a harsh whisper. "Piece by piece, bit by bit. My character has no humanity left. I count down the days until I'm free. And sometimes I don't know how I'm going to get through it. I'm angry all the time, frustrated, bored, and it leaks out onto people who don't deserve it." She glanced at Summer. "Decent people."

Elizabeth looked at her hands. "I don't want to be like that. This role is fresh and exciting. It'll push me, and keep me sane through one last season on *Hope*. And hopefully it'll propel me to something far beyond TV dramas when my contract expires. Lastly, I don't expect you to understand this as you've only ever played likable characters, but being hated 24/7 is a draining existence. It wears away at you. I'm only human." She rose. "I'd appreciate it if this conversation stayed between us. Sorry again, Summer." She turned to leave.

"I'll do it."

Freezing, Elizabeth said, "What?"

"Tell Delvine to send me the details. I'll play your girlfriend for one lunch. It'll be nice to see Jean-Claude again. Just don't expect me to forget I'm still seriously pissed at how you treated me."

"I…understand." She inhaled. "How about we get our stories straight early next week? Monday or Tuesday? We both have late starts."

"Sure." Summer picked up her script again.

Elizabeth offered a smile. It was not returned. She hesitated. She should take her win and go, but she had to know. "May I ask why you agreed?"

Summer didn't look up. "You were honest. Now if you don't mind, I have a scene to learn. If you see Tori, can you ask her to come back? I mean, if you can manage that without terrifying her?" A hint of a smile threatened Summer's lips. It was tiny, but still…it was there.

"I'll do my best." She couldn't repress a smirk. As she walked away, Elizabeth felt lighter than she had in weeks.

Summer woke abruptly, her tongue feeling twice its normal size and her eyes as if they'd been gouged with sandpaper. Her head felt as though fists were hammering her skull. How did she ever think drinking that much was a great idea? But Tori had been the absolute master of "just one more". And her big brown eyes had seemed so cute at two in the morning. Ugh.

"Finally!" Chloe exclaimed. "I've been trying to wake you for ages. Thought you were gonna snore till noon."

Summer scowled. "Lies. I don't snore."

"Uh-huh. Just like you don't have a hangover. Here." Chloe passed her water and a tablet. "Aspirin."

Summer grimaced but took it, swallowing gingerly before putting the glass down.

Chloe was still eying her, which made Summer grumpier. "What? Sizing up my bed hair?"

"There's a limo outside. Driver says he's here to pick you and Elizabeth Thornton up and whisk you to some hotel. I told him I'd get you. I didn't admit it'd involve waking the dead."

The hell? "That's *next* Sunday, not today! The 27th!" Summer grabbed her phone to check the date. A black screen stared back. *Oh right.* The battery had died somewhere around her third Manhattan. She plugged it in.

"See! Today's the twentieth…" Her comment died in her throat. Her home screen was filled with notifications. A text from Delvine and another from an unknown number. Summer stabbed Delvine's message.

Date change, darling! Lunch with JCB now TOMORROW. Sorry for short notice. If you can't make it, call me ASAP, otherwise a car will be @ your place at 11:30. See you then! Delvine

Summer tapped the unknown number's text.

It's Elizabeth. Re: lunch. Delvine said she'd told you about date change. We must prep for tomorrow. Pls pick up.

God. "Time is it now?" Summer whispered. It was a stupid question because she could clearly see the time in large, mocking letters on her phone.

"Eleven-forty," Chloe said helpfully.

"Crap!" Summer flung back her bedding and sprinted for the bathroom. Chloe padded down the hallway after her and gave the closing bathroom door a nudge to keep it ajar. "Aren't we going to talk about why you're going to a hotel with a certain person you're allegedly not dating?" she called.

Summer flung off her sleepwear and turned the shower on. "It's a business thing. With Elizabeth, her manager, and Jean-Claude Badour."

"Who's that?"

"A producer, writer, and director. Top indie creds. His work's beautiful." Summer tested the water with her fingers. "Lunch is at his suite at the Four Seasons to get Elizabeth some big role. I'm just going with her." She got in.

"But why?" Chloe called out louder to compete with the hiss of water. "You can't be competing for the same role. Or are you friends now? Friends who lunch together?" she added skeptically.

"Definitely not friends. But there *is* a role for me. I'm playing Elizabeth Thornton's girlfriend."

There was a long, long silence then finally, "Girl, we so need to talk."

------◈------

Elizabeth eyed Summer with irritation. They were all in the back of a ludicrously stretched limousine. Delvine sat on the long seat opposite, paperwork fanned out all around her, trying to finish some transatlantic call she'd been on since before Elizabeth slid into the car. And then there was Summer, who had mumbled something about a dead phone, and then wrapped her arms around herself and made no further attempt at conversation.

They were late. Elizabeth hated being late. It might be acceptable to some people, especially certain laid-back Americans, but she was always punctual. She was also always prepared. Even if Summer didn't share the same instincts. Maybe the girl thought she could just wing a fake relationship? Or perhaps she was punishing Elizabeth for the way she'd treated Summer in the past? That didn't seem like Summer, but she didn't know her well. Either way, she didn't appreciate having her fate in someone else's hands.

"Darling, no!" Delvine was saying. "If you check the terms of the contract, it quite clearly stipulates that my client's availability is subject to..."

Summer, on the far end of the long seat she shared with Elizabeth, slumped lower down against the window, a monument to human misery. She wore dark sunglasses, had a greenish tinge to her skin, and her hair bore the look of being frantically brushed. Her clothes comprised a faintly crumpled sunny yellow dress and sandals.

"Would you like a drink?" Elizabeth waved at the car's small fridge.

"God no." Summer swallowed.

So, that confirmed that theory. "I meant water. You look like perhaps you need to rehydrate?"

Summer shook her head, then winced. "Please no," she whispered.

Elizabeth was perplexed. She'd been imagining this scenario over and over, fixating on how lunch would go and what Summer's demeanor would be like, and at no time did it occur to her that her co-star might turn up less than professional.

She retracted that thought immediately. Summer wasn't here in a professional capacity, but rather, as a personal favor. And the change of dates had been on short notice. But still…what if Summer couldn't pull this off?

Peering out the window, Elizabeth watched the blur of palm trees flash against endless blue skies. So California. When she'd first arrived, she'd taken to visiting the beach with a thermos of tea and a good book. It hadn't taken long to realize the fantasy didn't match reality. Sand ended up in her tea, and too much sunscreen was still never quite enough for her skin.

Elizabeth glanced at the miserable woman again. "Are you up for this?"

"Yes," Summer said in a hoarse whisper. "I'm fine."

"You don't look fine."

That earned her a glare, as much as Elizabeth could tell through those glasses. Well. The kitten had claws…at least when hungover.

Silence descended for four more blocks.

"Don't you think we should get our stories straight at some point?" Elizabeth ventured. "Or were you planning to wing it?"

Summer looked like talking pained her. "Sorry I missed your calls last night. I was out."

No kidding.

"But you'd be wrong if you think I haven't done any research," Summer continued. "I'm prepared."

Research? On what? Playing a lesbian girlfriend? Elizabeth's career highlights?

"I meant we should decide our stories about how we met and *fell for each other*," Elizabeth said, unable to resist the sarcasm.

That got Summer's attention. She pulled off her sunglasses and gave Elizabeth a hard, hard look. "You act like falling in love with me would be the most absurd thing imaginable. I'm also starting to doubt the sincerity of your apology. Such as it was." She rammed her sunglasses back on and returned her gaze outside.

"I didn't mean it like that." Elizabeth tried to hide her growing testiness. Even if that's exactly how she'd meant it. It *was* absurd. Badour was clearly some ego-puffed fantasist who refused to see facts. She wondered at what point "Monsieur Human Condition" would notice what a ludicrous couple they were. And when he did, the whole lunch would be an unmitigated disaster and she'd lose this role and go back to hating her life.

Elizabeth had read the *Eight Little Pieces* script that Rachel sent over the day before. It was everything Summer had said, and much more. It was layered and clever, very French of course, and so compelling. Playing the emotionally fractured writer Elspeth would give her career an amazing boost if Badour could pull off even half the brilliance on the page. It had awards written all over it, too. No wonder even her antsy agent was tolerating this charade, if it got Elizabeth the part. But none of this would work if Summer didn't get her act together.

Everything from Summer's shoulders to her fists was bunched up and tight. Her closed-off expression reminded Elizabeth of how she'd looked when Elizabeth first asked her to do this.

Elizabeth already regretted her honesty that day. Baring her soul made her feel vulnerable and embarrassed. For some reason, though, she hadn't been able to keep her mouth shut. Maybe Summer's eyes had gotten to her. Sad and big and lacking the faith and trust they'd once held.

"Summer," she murmured, "I'm grateful you're putting yourself out for me today. I know it must be very hard for you…"

Summer's lips pursed.

Now what had she said?

"Why very hard?" Summer turned to look at her. "I play roles all the time. This is no different. Or are you hinting that I'm not capable of acting well?"

Elizabeth repressed an eye roll. *Was* she capable? Elizabeth had no idea. Summer might be able to pull the wool over Ravitz's eyes, playing a clueless ingénue, but the man wasn't terribly smart, either. Delvine seemed to think Summer was talented, though, so the jury was still out.

"I have no idea what you're capable of," she said honestly. "I just assumed you hadn't played a lesbian before. So I guessed it would be hard for you."

"*Guessed?*" Summer sounded curious. "I've looked up your acting history. You haven't played a lesbian either. So don't you know yourself whether it feels hard or not? Why did you say guessed?"

Oh no. That was a dangerous question. The impish voice in the back of her brain dared her to reply: *Well, Summer, I had to guess because I don't have a clue how heterosexual women feel about playing lesbians.*

Mercifully, Delvine got off the phone just then, tossing it into her glossy shoulder bag before ramming her scattered paperwork in after it. "Sorry about that. Dramas non-stop. Why would I allow my biggest male star to do ads on Japanese TV? It's cheapening his brand." She eyed them both. "Remember that, you two. Never say yes to everything." She hesitated when she glanced at Summer, then added, "Darling, thank you for agreeing to this. It means a lot to Elizabeth."

"I know," Summer replied curtly.

Delvine regarded her, then slid her gaze over to Elizabeth. "And are you two okay? With each other? And what this entails?"

"Fine," Elizabeth replied.

"Great," Summer said.

"It's only one lunch," Delvine said. "Summer, be a dear and try not to look like you want to kill Elizabeth for five minutes?"

Summer snorted. "I'll try."

Delvine smiled. "Excellent." She paused, studying Summer. "You know, my kids loved *Teen Spy Camp*. I watched it with them all the time. We cried great buckets when Punky's best friend almost died. What was her name?"

"Hannah," Summer murmured.

"That was a beautiful scene. What was the line? About needing the two of them? Can you still remember?"

Elizabeth frowned, wondering where Delvine was going with this. Her manager wasn't prone to pointless small talk.

"I remember every word." Summer's face softened. "I loved that scene."

"As you should. But what was the bit, when Punky held Hannah's hand in the hospital?"

With a soft sigh, Summer took off her sunglasses again and tangled them in her fingers in her lap.

"Don't leave me," she said suddenly, her voice hollow and pained. Shock coursed through Elizabeth at the transformation. "Please, you can't. You're my best friend. This life's made for two of us, not one. Remember that time you taught me how to climb Mr. Murphy's tree in ten seconds flat? Or when we went berry picking, and the juice wound up down our shirts? Our moms were so mad."

Summer giggled, sounding so achingly young, then her expression fell. "Or when Marley died. And you told me no one would understand, not really. But that it was okay. That it was a love for just me and him, and I'd always have the memories of wet noses, muddy hugs, and a hundred sneezes." Her eyes filled with tears. "You got me through everything, Hannah Jane Marshall. I need us to be two again. I can't be just one. We've got so many adventures ahead. Oh, please, please, don't go."

Chills shot down her spine, and Elizabeth forced the prick of tears back by sheer force of will.

Remarkable. Why the hell were they wasting talent like this on Joey Carter?

Summer inhaled deeply, and a faint blush crept up her cheeks.

Delvine wiped her eyes and then clapped loudly, earning a wince from Summer. "Oh yes, goosebumps every time. Brilliant." She turned to Elizabeth. "Wouldn't you agree, Bess?"

Oh, so *that's* what this was. Delvine had contrived all this to prove to Elizabeth that Summer could act. She loved being right.

Elizabeth, in turn, loathed being manipulated, and the triumphant gleam in Delvine's eyes set her teeth on edge. She glanced at Summer, who was watching her, breath held.

"Yes," Elizabeth said, her voice neutral. "I would agree."

Summer's shoulders bunched up again, before she put her sunglasses back on and turned from them both, sagging in obvious disappointment.

Delvine lifted a shapely eyebrow at Elizabeth, looking scandalized.

Guilt pierced her. She hadn't realized her opinion mattered so much to Summer.

Had they been alone, Elizabeth would have shared her true thoughts on the performance. She still could, later—assuming her furious co-star was still talking to her at the end of lunch.

Chapter 7

JEAN-CLAUDE BADOUR WAS EXACTLY AS Summer remembered him. Elegant, pretentious, eccentric, and sweet, not to mention devoted to his boyfriend—Marcus, a French-Canadian chef. She greeted them both like old friends. After all, once you've sung Mariah Carey in a Parisian karaoke bar together, there's no going back. Besides, she'd seen them both at her mother's grand Christmas party last year, so it hadn't been that long between drinks.

"Summer! *Mon cherie*, you look the same as ever." Jean-Claude kissed both cheeks with enthusiasm. "Taller maybe?" He winked.

She rolled her eyes, recalling the first time they'd met, on the set of his steampunk romance *La Chute des Pétales de Rose—The Fall of Rose Petals*, which her mother had worked on. Summer, then thirteen, had been bemoaning her shortness to a dapper Frenchman she'd discovered sprawled out behind a box of lighting equipment, nibbling on lunch. Of course, that had been two growth spurts and fifteen years ago. She now knew members of lighting crews never wore bespoke fashion nor indulged in cheese and paté lunch platters.

Summer glanced around. She could smell cooking, so obviously the luxury suite had its own kitchen. Was this all to impress Elizabeth?

"How is your *père*?" Jean-Claude asked. "Still smashing into things?" Before she could answer, he rushed on. "I've spoken to your delightful *mère*, of course. Skye is thrilled you have Elizabeth in your life. She tells me of this powerful *amour* between you that crosses all divides."

Elizabeth's head snapped around to look at Summer. Delvine's eyes became speculative.

Okay, she would definitely have to kill her mother later. No wonder Jean-Claude had been so convinced Delvine was lying. He'd gone directly to his inside source, who'd confirmed the rumors as fact. Because Skye never listened to a damned word Summer said and loved making up her own narratives when the truth didn't suit.

Turning, Jean-Claude greeted Elizabeth with a brush of lips against each cheek as they murmured their hellos.

Delvine's phone rang and she muttered a half-hearted apology, announcing "duty calls" before she scuttled out onto the balcony in a jangle of beads and bangles, closing the French doors behind her.

"Sit, sit," Jean-Claude waved at an overstuffed couch. He took one of the chairs facing it; Marcus, the other.

With a measured look that seemed to say *gird your loins*, Elizabeth took Summer's hand and led her to the couch, where they sat side by side. Their thighs touched; navy pants against Summer's thin yellow dress. The heat of that leg traced up and down her skin like wildfire.

Elizabeth did not let go of her hand. Summer might still be annoyed, but it took every ounce of concentration not to react to that warmth. She cursed her hormones for not yet getting the memo from upstairs. This woman was off limits, because she was unattainable, straight—not to mention rude and selfish and...*still straight*...and...a whole bunch of other things she couldn't remember right now while her hand was being clasped.

Suddenly everyone was staring. Summer started. "Sorry?"

Jean-Claude tilted his head. "I asked what it is that attracted you to your lovely woman."

Summer tried to think of a coherent answer. She needed something romantic, convincing, and heavily censored from her still on-edge hormones. At that thought, she felt her cheeks redden.

Jean-Claude chortled. "*Non, non*, I didn't mean *that*."

Ugh. Summer wanted to kill him for making this tawdry.

"*Pardon*, Summer, I have embarrassed you. I'll give you an easier question. Tell me something she does that amuses you."

"Um." Summer's mind blanked. Funny? Elizabeth didn't appear to have that gene. She was dry and witty and highbrow with her humor, but she didn't really do *funny*.

"It can't be so difficult, can it?" Jean-Claude prodded.

Oh shit. She was screwing this up. Elizabeth's eyebrow lifted in challenge.

"She screams like a little girl whenever she sees a spider," Summer blurted out. "I'm not even talking big ones, just tiny ones. I have to go wade in there with brooms to get it outside or she'll be checking under the bed all night."

The hand holding hers tightened. Hard. "Spiders," Elizabeth drawled. "Oh yes, that's right. Hate 'em."

Frowning, Jean-Claude said, "My film set is in the wilderness. There may be spiders sometimes. Will this be a problem?"

"No problem," Elizabeth said smoothly. "I'm sure I'll cope."

"She will," Summer nodded. "I was exaggerating a little. She doesn't really scream that much. It's more a pained whimper. Or series of them."

Jean-Claude laughed.

Elizabeth's look could have cut glass. "Arachnophobia is quite common," she murmured. "And I do not scream or whimper."

"Of course," Jean-Claude said in a placating tone that only made Elizabeth clench Summer's hand harder.

"And what of Summer?" Jean-Claude asked Elizabeth. "Does she have any amusing foibles?"

Elizabeth's lips puckered as though tasting a lemon. "Not really," she replied. "Her cactus obsession I suppose. Her home is a shrine to them."

"You like..." he squinted at Summer, "the cactus plants? Really?"

"Succulents," Summer corrected instantly, as if this was a common mistake. "Cactuses are just a type of succulent. Some of them are so cute. But I don't like anything with prickles. Well, except Elizabeth of course." She patted Elizabeth's hand with the one not trapped in a vice-like grip.

"Ha!" Marcus brightened. "That is funny."

Elizabeth's face wore the odd, blank expression she used when she was about to turn into Hunt. That never ended well.

"It is good you can tease each other," Jean-Claude said earnestly. "So, Summer, how goes the photography?" He glanced at Elizabeth. "You must know how talented she is, *oui*? Her mother is so proud and sends me her photos on the email."

"Yes, so much talent," Elizabeth said. "She always makes her subjects look so beautiful. It's the way she lights them."

Oh crap.

"Beautiful? Lights them?" Jean-Claude shook his head. "Summer, are you taking photos of people now?"

Elizabeth stiffened. "I meant her landscapes are attractive. She shoots in just the right light."

There was a silence. Okay, Jean-Claude was about two seconds from working out this whole thing was a bust.

"I've been experimenting with landscapes lately," Summer jumped in. "Of course I still love photographing architecture. I take Elizabeth out with me often."

Elizabeth exhaled beside her, grip loosening slightly. "Yes, we're always investigating whatever building has taken Summer's fancy this week."

"Which style has captivated you most? I, too, love architecture. The perspective of lines and the beauty of light, it is not so much different from shooting movies. It's all about angles and flow."

Annnnd the vice grip was back.

"There are so many," Elizabeth murmured. "I really couldn't choose."

"But you must like at least one?" Jean-Claude's eyes never left her face.

"I'm not sure... I..." Elizabeth faded out.

"Carroll Avenue, wasn't it?" Summer suggested. "In Angelino Heights. I'm sure last time we went you said it was such an interesting assortment of Victorian looks."

Elizabeth nodded. "Of course, yes, Carroll Avenue. It's a reminder of home. Victorian style is so familiar."

"Really?" Jean-Claude eyed her curiously. "Except LA's Victorian is not much like London's. It is so pristine; more like a film set."

A twitch of Elizabeth's eyelid was the only sign she was not handling this turn of events well.

"It's the *flavor* of it she appreciates," Summer said. "Plus she's a huge Michael Jackson fan. So..."

Elizabeth's eyebrows shot up.

"She is? Oh. *Oui*, that makes sense then." Jean-Claude nodded.

Marcus leaned forward. "I do not follow. What has a singer to do with this?"

"*Thriller* was shot at 1345 Carroll Avenue," Summer said. "It's the zombie house from the music video. It's really famous."

Marcus gaped. "And Elizabeth, *you* like this house of zombies?"

"Yes," Summer answered for her. "She really does. She made me take photos of it from every angle."

"I do," Elizabeth confirmed. Then she lowered her voice to mutter, "Apparently."

Jean-Claude clapped in delight. "How unexpected. Now tell me, how did you two meet?"

Elizabeth's jaw tightened.

Damn. They really should have gotten their stories worked out. Summer's head started pounding, and only half of it was due to her hangover.

At their pause, Marcus stood. "Gossip later, drinks first! I have something special. Summer, assist me? We'll let Jean-Claude catch up with his leading lady."

More alcohol? Summer winced. She let go of Elizabeth's hand, her fingers almost white from lack of blood flow, and followed Marcus to the kitchen.

⊷⊷⬦⬦⊶⊶

"So," Jean-Claude gave Elizabeth a close look, "I am very fond of Summer. I've known her for years. Her *mère* is a good friend also; supremely talented. I have all the time for Skye."

"Indeed." *Summer certainly left some things out.*

"This lovely girl, when she would come to my set it would be like a ray of sunshine. Always with the happiness. She has not changed even now. Still the same brightness in her. So I understand why it is people are drawn to her. What I do not understand is why you look at her the way you do."

"How do I look at her?" Elizabeth tensed.

"Like she frustrates you. She is to be endured."

"Not at all. Summer's a delight." Her smile felt flat.

Jean-Claude folded his arms. "*Non,* I do not like this. I won't tolerate it if you are using her. Summer does not deserve less than your complete *amour.*"

Oh, fantastic. The pretentious Frenchman really can read human behavior? If he was even remotely good at this, he'd soon realize they weren't in love.

"I don't like to wear my feelings on my sleeve," Elizabeth said.

"Hmm."

"And I'm not here to discuss my girlfriend."

83

"And yet, that is why she's here."

"I don't follow."

"In truth, my backers do not want you for the part, even though you are perfect. They think you are too hated, and audiences won't open their minds to see you as Elspeth. They wanted me to find someone famous, yes, but someone with…humanity."

Oh, ouch.

"I thought, maybe, seeing you with Summer, I would see the essence of who you are," he continued. "Then I would calm my nervous investors, and explain, but of course you can capture Elspeth's complex humanity. Instead, what do I see? Walls. Indifference. And that is how you are with someone you love? How will you be, playing Elspeth's emotions?"

He demanded to see her human side, even though he had no right to it? The arrogance! Still. She lined his words up alongside Grace's impressions. How Badour liked to expose the actors inhabiting his roles. He wanted to see *her*.

"So what am I to think, Elizabeth?" Confusion lined his face. "Either you hide your feelings for Summer so deep they are inaccessible to you— which makes you unsuitable for Elspeth. Or you have no feelings for her— which makes you unsuitable for Summer. Which is it?"

"Option three," Elizabeth countered. "I hide my feelings because I haven't yet shared them with Summer. She should know first, wouldn't you say?" She lifted her chin.

"Ah." He leaned back, eyes gleaming with curiosity. "But these feelings, they *are* there."

It was sort of a question, sort of a statement, strung together with hope. He wanted to believe. That was reassuring, at least.

"I *do* care for her," Elizabeth said, with every ounce of conviction.

He digested that. "Then tell me…make me believe it: What is it about Summer that captivated you?"

How was any of this his business? Elizabeth sighed inwardly. She could do this. She was an actress, after all. She'd interned at the Royal Shakespeare Company, for God's sake. If Elizabeth couldn't even convince one eccentric film-maker that she had a romantic interest in a beautiful, likable co-star, she should give up the game.

"Opposites attract," she told him with conviction. "It's really that simple."

"You feel Summer is your opposite? You don't see how you are alike?"

"Well, we have a shared passion for acting." She considered what little she knew about her. *What else do we share?* "And tea!" *Oh hell.* She'd said that like someone coming up with the winning answer on a game show.

"You share acting and…tea?" Jean-Claude's expression was baffled and withering. "What about the Shakespeare?"

The what? It dawned on her that Jean-Claude knew Summer a *lot* better than she did. And what did he mean? Had Summer dabbled in some high-school Shakespearean productions? Or did she like to see the Bard's plays? Or…wait, hadn't she grown up in London? Did she take in plays at the Royal Shakespeare Theatre, like every would-be actress?

"Of course," she said evenly, "we both love Shakespeare." That seemed to cover all possibilities.

He gave her an odd look. "I meant the other thing, but yes, it is clear she loves the Shakespeare."

The other thing? She desperately tried to think of possibilities and came up blank. Elizabeth shifted uneasily, wondering when they could talk about Elspeth, the tormented writer in her wilderness shack.

"How long have you two been dating?" Jean-Claude asked.

Well, that was too much to hope for. "Since we met at work, four months ago."

"Ahh, an on-set romance. How do you get on with Skye?" Jean-Claude's eyes twinkled. "She is something, *oui?*"

She could hardly lie. He could just check with Skye. "We've been so busy. I haven't had a chance to meet anyone in Summer's life yet. Besides, that's the curse of new love, isn't it? People get so wrapped up in each other."

"But…" he frowned, "surely, you must have at least met Chloe by now? She is *très* amusing. I met her at Skye's Christmas party last year."

Who the hell is Chloe? Wait, maybe she was a pet? Some handbag-sized Pomeranian? "No, I haven't met the famous Chloe yet." She smiled.

His frown deepened. "What is it you see in Summer then? If she is so opposite, what is it that makes you click…" he snapped his fingers, "and say, *ah, there*, she is for me."

With reluctance, she let her thoughts drift to her guiltiest, most private secret. The memory clawed at her. The only woman she'd ever loved—not that the woman knew. How lost she'd felt when Grace moved to LA. Within six months, Elizabeth had given in and followed her. Who gives up their budding career for someone who can't love them back? And, as pathetic as that was, it was no different to what Grace had done first. Elizabeth glimpsed her own pain mirrored in her mentor's eyes every time Grace saw Amrit. How messed up could they get?

The saddest truth about unrequited love was how lonely it was.

Jean-Claude was staring at her impatiently.

Damn him. Elizabeth had promised herself over a year ago that she'd never again willingly think of Grace *that* way. For her own mental health, she'd forced herself to put out of her mind what could never be. But she also needed this role. Jean-Claude had to believe she understood love. So she drew on her most painful emotions.

The softness of Grace's skin. Her perfect, classical features. Even up close, without make-up, she was flawless. Those palest of blue eyes could pierce Elizabeth. Her voice…undulating and sensual, like she was peeling an apple with her tongue. Her lips, pale coral, pliant, ready with a teasing smile or the plumpest of pouts. It was as if she'd been made to order: British Female. Class: Perfection.

Elizabeth let the memories tumble her back to London, so lost in love. She rolled over how that felt, that mindset and heart-set. Then she let the words come.

"I care for her because she's beautiful. I don't just mean outside. Inside, she shines with a charisma and vitality that draws people in. Everyone wants to be close to that, to warm themselves on it. I'm not impervious. I miss her whenever she isn't near."

Elizabeth inhaled, realizing everything she'd said could as easily apply to Summer as Grace. "You know when you hear a song on the radio you love and it just resonates? You want to hum to it long after it's over, because you don't want it to be finished? Summer makes me want to hum. She's my song." A flash of color drew her eye and Elizabeth realized Delvine was standing inside now, her back to the closed balcony doors, mouth slightly agape.

"She makes you hum." Jean-Claude seemed to be turning that over.

"And she also has spirit. She fights for what is right."

"Summer? Sweet Summer?"

"Not so sweet when she sees an injustice she thinks needs correcting. I've seen it. How can I not admire someone who puts what's right ahead of everything? Even themselves?"

Guilt slammed into her at what she'd done—deeply hurt a woman who'd hurled herself on a grenade at work to protect Elizabeth. Until now, Elizabeth had only really considered Summer's anger, not her sense of betrayal. She'd been too focused, too…self-involved to think about anyone else. Shame pricked at her.

What am I becoming?

Shaking her head, Delvine walked over. "Well, Bess, after that little speech, I can see why you're taken with her."

Elizabeth only just resisted an eye-roll. Her manager came across as cynical even when she was attempting to sound genuine.

Jean-Claude, mercifully, ignored her. "Kindness and goodness, it is an aphrodisiac to many. It's why I appreciate my Marcus. So, I think I see why you are together."

Oh thank God.

Elizabeth's relief was only matched by her acute need for alcohol. A nice gin on the rocks should do it. Preferably a double. She wondered if it'd be rude to rush off and make her own.

⁕

Summer joined Marcus in the kitchen, where a soufflé was rising in the oven and he was partway through slicing and dicing a cheese platter. The room smelled like heaven.

She looked around for the "something special" Marcus had alluded to.

"From my *grand-père's* vineyard." He pointed at half a dozen bottles of white wine on the counter. "There's nothing finer than his '98 vintage. It's magical."

Wine? *Oh no.* "Last night," Summer began, hating how idiotic this would sound, "I sort of went out with some colleagues and got…" *Blind drunk? Completely plastered?* "A little tipsy. And I have the headache to match. I'm sorry, but I can't face alcohol right now. I'd love to try your grandfather's wine any other time."

He gave a solemn *tsk*. "I'll give you and Elizabeth a bottle or two to take home. You can have it with a romantic meal." He looked pleased at the idea.

Summer really liked Marcus. He was as cuddly and round as Jean-Claude was tall and angular. The couple had met on a set in Montreal, when the catering company Marcus worked for supplied craft services to a Jean-Claude film. The two men just seemed to fit together.

"We'd love to have a bottle! Thanks."

"Excellent." Marcus pulled out four wine glasses and began to pour. Tilting his head toward the fridge, he added, "There's ice water and juice in there for those of us who cannot handle their alcohol." He winked.

She laughed. "Thanks. So how are things, anyway? Did Alice's surgery go well?"

"Oh *oui*, she is fine. A little grumpy, but she'll live. Old bones and fidgety mothers, not so good a mix."

"No," Summer agreed. "But from what I saw of her at our Christmas party, she'll never let something like a broken hip slow her down. She kept telling the caterers fifty ways to fix their food!"

He slapped a hand over his eyes. "That was so her. Ah! That reminds me." He tapped a black leather folder on the counter with *Menu* embossed on it. "I'm in charge of lunch today, of course. I wanted to check whether I should order something to go with my dishes. If you or Elizabeth have any allergies, I can get room service too."

Allergies? Summer's mind spun. This was like a test. Girlfriends should absolutely know this about each other. "Um, well, she can't eat onions, of course," she said confidently. *Why the hell did I say that?* "And no chocolate. Or cheese. Or..." *Who has just a chocolate and cheese allergy?* She brightened and rushed on. "Because she can't have any dairy, really. So milk's out too. Sadly. A shame."

There. That sounds like girlfriend-level inside info. Her brain suddenly caught up with a shriek. *What are you doing? This isn't something to improv! Get it wrong and people DIE!* Her horrified mind began picturing Elizabeth turning blue from some random allergy that Summer could have prevented. Or bloating up like a puffer fish.

"Hold that thought!" she said, then grabbed a wine glass that Marcus had just poured. "Elizabeth was thirsty. I'll get her fixed up and be right back."

She rushed out, but slowed when she caught the fascinated looks on Delvine and Jean-Claude's faces. What were they were discussing?

"How can I not admire someone who puts what's right ahead of everything? Even themselves?" Elizabeth's back was to Summer, but her voice sounded so admiring, so unlike the cold woman Summer knew at work.

Her heart did a traitorous clench of joy. It was just a good act, a perfectly executed lie, she reminded herself. That much was obvious. When you like someone, you don't kick them aside.

"Well, Bess, after that little speech, I can see why you're taken with her." Delvine's wry words had the sincerity of a politician at a baby shower. She'd never be an actress.

Jean-Claude's eyes were fixed on Elizabeth. *Oh.* It was his *idea* look. He was making a decision. "Kindness and goodness, it is an aphrodisiac to many people. It's why I appreciate my Marcus. So, I think I see why you are together."

An interesting answer, and it boded well for Elizabeth getting her role, but it was unlikely what he'd really been thinking.

Summer came around the side of the couch to Elizabeth. "Sorry to interrupt," she gave Jean-Claude an apologetic look, "but I didn't want Elizabeth to get too parched. Everyone else's drinks are coming in a minute."

Handing the wine to Elizabeth, who looked startled to see her, Summer leaned forward and whispered, "Any allergies? Marcus needs to know whether to order something extra from room service."

"Yes," she murmured. "Histamine. Suffocation is one especially fun side effect."

"Yikes. What contains that?"

Elizabeth gave her glass a wry look. "Wine."

※

Lunch comprised a French onion soup starter, a cheese soufflé main course—with Marcus's grandfather's wine of course—followed by a cheese platter, more wine, and an oozing chocolate lava pudding. Except for the wine, which Summer swapped for water, she enjoyed lunch a great deal.

Elizabeth clearly did not. Summer had the good grace to feel guilty.

In deference to Elizabeth's "allergies", she'd been served a small French salad. No dressing, as it contained traces of onion. A small, pink, hotel-cooked salmon dish that had looked far more appetizing in the menu photo. One bread roll. Sans butter. No dessert. Elizabeth also had to ignore the full wine glass. Marcus did not look happy about that.

Elizabeth had not taken the news of her "allergies" well, either, based on the glower she leveled at Summer for most of the meal. Delvine, on the other hand, looked about three seconds away from snorting with laughter.

Oh yeah, hilarious. Because Delvine didn't have Elizabeth's death-stare in her face. But, really, what were the odds the French liked dairy so much? Who knew?

Apparently it was common knowledge, according to Elizabeth, who hissed that little factoid at Summer on their way to the bathroom. Hauling Summer along to "freshen up", Elizabeth's long fingers held Summer's wrist in a pincer grip.

Jean-Claude and Marcus had exchanged knowing looks, clearly assuming they couldn't keep their hands off each other. Summer, with bruises likely forming, wished rather a lot that Elizabeth *would* keep her hands off.

The moment the door shut on the enormous marble bathroom suite, Summer twisted free. "Do you mind? Jesus."

"I *love* cheese and dairy and chocolate," Elizabeth said, voice tight. "What possessed you?"

"You sure don't look like you do." Seriously, the woman looked like no food group with more than two percent fat content had ever squeezed past her lips.

"That's what my home gym and Pilates instructor are for—so I can indulge on occasion. And your overactive imagination has robbed me of that."

"Hey! I panicked, okay? And you're not much better! Who the hell loves cactuses?"

"It's *cacti*, for the love of God." Elizabeth's eyes flashed. It was irritatingly sexy. "And any self-proclaimed succulent lover would know that. I thought you'd blown it right then."

"As if he'd know that. Besides, I think it can be cactuses sometimes. And, hey, at least my amusing foible for *you* was plausible."

"What? You chasing after spiders for me while I cower under my bed? *That* sounds likely?"

Okay, shit, that was funny. A bubble of laughter escaped.

"Not amusing," Elizabeth warned. "Any more than my love of zombie houses is."

Summer burst out laughing at that. "The look on your face," she wheezed, "when I told them you *loved* it. And I had to take..." *wheeze* "photos from..." *wheeze* "every damned angle."

Elizabeth's lips began to twitch.

"And then you *agreed*." Summer wiped her eyes and laughed harder. "Oh my God! You went with it."

The lip twitching increased until it was almost a smile. "You left me little choice."

Summer elbowed her ribs. "Come on, *girlfriend*, it was hilarious, and you know it." She smiled from ear to ear.

A tiny laugh escaped Elizabeth and she shook her head. "You and your awful ad-libs."

"Yeah, I know. I'm sorry. And I concede I owe you a really good three-course French meal."

"I'll settle just for the pudding. Was it as divine as it looked?" Elizabeth's expression was wistful.

"Better," Summer sighed. "Bliss. I'm really sorry about the no-dairy thing. Wish I could sneak you some cheese cubes or something. The brie is phenomenal too." Summer snorted again, picturing that furtive mission.

"If it's brie, then you'd be smuggling me oozing cheese puddles." Elizabeth's eyes crinkled. "And I don't think you're giving this the gravity it's due."

"Probably not."

Amusement danced between them.

"I'm sorry I didn't get your calls last night," Summer said, becoming serious. "Or that I didn't work with you in the car to get our stories straight today. I was in such a pissy mood."

"You hid it well," Elizabeth deadpanned. "Look, I want to say I'm very sorry for how I treated you before all this. It was a terrible plan to solve any gossip by just avoiding you. It was wrong I didn't fight it."

"I'm sorry too. I missed you." *Well, that just slipped out.* "And it really hurt." *Christ. Do I think anything I don't say?*

Elizabeth inhaled. A troubled expression crossed her face. "Well... I... I know it flies in the face of my reputation, but I didn't entirely enjoy it much when you weren't around. Not just for the tea, either."

"I'm not sure that was a compliment," Summer said, "but I think I'll take it."

"You should." Elizabeth smiled. "I'm so rarely nice."

"Liar. Damn. You're also hard to stay mad at."

"Just wait." Elizabeth glanced at her watch. "You should get the urge again pretty soon."

"Why do you say that?"

"I am the British Bitch." She shrugged. "It's a thing."

Summer sat on the closed toilet seat and gave her a thoughtful look. "Where did that rumor start? Who did it?"

"What makes you so sure it's not based on fact?"

"It's not. You're a complete professional on set. So come on. Spill."

"Lenton."

"Our showrunner? What happened?"

"I objected—strongly—to a terrible storyline involving Hunt. It never happened in the end. But they set out to destroy her character in retaliation. Quite a lesson in who runs the show. And for added fun, rumors suddenly appeared on gossip sites about what a diva I am."

"Assholes."

"Mmm." Elizabeth glanced around. "I won't have to put up with it much longer. If I can get this part, it'll be something to focus on. A fresh direction."

"Well, let's get you that part then." Summer stood and kinked her neck left and right, as though preparing for a boxing bout.

"By the way, who's Chloe?" Elizabeth asked.

"She lives with me."

Hesitating, Elizabeth asked, "A...pet?"

With a laugh, Summer said, "Can I quote you? Nah, she's my roommate and best friend."

"I see. And what's the *Shakespeare thing* you have?"

Summer blushed. "Ah, it's a bit dorky."

"How can Shakespeare ever be a bad thing? Do you watch a lot of plays or study it or…?"

"Yes to all that. But I also have a party trick."

"Don't tell me it's Shakespeare in Klingon?"

"Nope. It's just… I remember every bit of Shakespeare trivia I've ever heard. It's rare anyone can beat me."

An intrigued look crossed Elizabeth's face.

"What's that look for?" Summer asked. "You have an up-to-no-good expression right now."

"Nothing." Elizabeth brushed her pants and moved to the door. She paused. "Have we got our stories straight now?"

"Not really, but no one's actually asked me anything about you beyond your food allergies."

"And look how well that turned out." At least she seemed more amused than enraged now.

"Sorry again," Summer said with a small smile. "The good news is that Jean-Claude looks like he's run out of steam grilling you on the personal stuff. Must be time for the professional by now?"

"*If* he offers me the role."

"He will." Summer had no doubt. "You passed his test."

"How do you know?"

Summer shrugged. "He gets a look when he's made up his mind on something. He got it already. You're in. I mean, as long as we don't mess this up on the home stretch."

"Then let's make sure of it."

"Yeah." Summer rubbed her still smarting arm as she followed Elizabeth out. "Got quite a grip there, lady."

"I need my strength up to flee spiders. Speed is simply not enough."

Summer chuckled. "Okay, I'll accept that as an apology, only because I made you out to be a wimp."

"Excellent." Elizabeth's smile was magnificent as she made her way back to the table.

Summer told herself she did not care in the least.

Elizabeth was a little surprised by how good it felt to have Summer back to her normal self.

"Welcome back, Bess," Delvine said as they rejoined the table. "I trust all's well."

And just like that, the air shifted. Jean-Claude's expression changed from genial to hard. Elizabeth sensed the danger but for the life of her couldn't work out what had just happened.

Jean-Claude scrutinized Summer as she resumed her seat. "Why do you call your girlfriend Elizabeth?"

Summer frowned. "That's her name."

"When I first talked to Elizabeth's agent, Rachel kept saying 'Bess this', 'Bess that'. I asked, 'Did I misunderstand? Is your client actually Bess?' And she replied that Elizabeth is only Bess to the people close to her. Just now Delvine called her Bess. But not you. I hadn't realized what had been biting at me like a flea all lunch until this minute."

Summer's face went completely still. "I call her Bess some days, but always Elizabeth on set." Her brows knitted together. "Sometimes I forget we're not at work."

"You have not once called her Bess today," Jean-Claude's eyes were edged with suspicion.

Oh no. No! Not now, not when she was so close.

"Um, darling," Delvine jumped in, "shall we discuss your masterpiece? I did so love the script."

"*Non.*" Jean-Claude waggled his finger between Summer and Elizabeth. "What is this? You are lying to me?" His brown eyes burned with anger.

Elizabeth's throat went dry.

"Jean-Claude?" Marcus asked. "What is it?"

"Something else has bothered me. New couples in love—what do they all have in common? Eyes—never taken off the other. Hands—always reaching, touching. Voices—softer when they refer to the other. It is universal, *oui*? These two? They do none of these things."

Marcus turned to Summer with a look of betrayal. "This is not real?"

Summer shook her head. "Of course it is." Her vehemence didn't change either man's expression.

Perspiration began to trickle down Elizabeth's neck. She tried, desperately, to think of something to say to fix this, but nothing came to mind. It *was* true. They hadn't done any of the things a couple in love would.

"We have been trying to keep us secret," Elizabeth said quietly. "We thought it would be obvious Summer cares for me if she started calling me a personal name at work. So she calls me Elizabeth."

"She cares for you." Jean-Claude gave her a disbelieving look. "This grand love you share, and I just can't feel it. This is not right. I'm starting to think that—"

Suddenly Summer straightened, a look of resolve on her face. "Did I ever tell you how I met Elizabeth?"

Waving his hand dismissively, Jean-Claude said, "On set. *Oui*, she told me."

"No, that's just when she met *me*."

Elizabeth's mouth parted a little. Where was Summer going with this?

"Oh, I can't wait to hear this." The drip of sarcasm in his voice was impossible to miss.

"It was in London." Summer smiled softly. She shifted her hand to cup Elizabeth's on the table, and left it there. "I was fifteen, stuck in London while my parents worked on the *Andromeda Quest* trilogy. I was good at sneaking away from my tutor to take in the West End matinees. That was the first time I saw Elizabeth, in a one-hander. *Shakespeare's Women*."

Elizabeth went stock still. Had Summer really seen her? Had she been in those darkened crowds while Elizabeth turned herself inside out? Then again, hadn't Summer said she'd done her research? Elizabeth's theater history was easy enough to look up.

Summer closed her eyes. "Elizabeth would come out each day, sit on a wooden stool, under a single spotlight, and become the women of Shakespeare. I was in awe. She was the most beautiful person I had ever seen. I don't mean just physically. I was drawn to the emotions; how she made us feel. Her power to hold us in her hand and toy with us like it was nothing at all." She opened her eyes and looked at Jean-Claude. "I discovered my love of acting that day. So is it any wonder why, when I saw her on set, I fell for her? So what does it matter what I call her? You read people. Look in my eyes—can't you see the truth?"

How convincing she was. Elizabeth could relate to Delvine's look of astonishment. There was no way Summer could have researched that level of detail. She had to have been there. As for the rest? Well, she certainly spun a convincing tale.

Jean-Claude became thoughtful. "I saw her in that play too. I can believe your reaction. Impossible to forget. I always thought one day we'd work together. Perhaps you thought the same? Or maybe you found more than a love of *theater* for your hero that day?" His tone was playful.

Summer bristled at the implication. "No. I was just a kid. Elizabeth Thornton was my idol, out of reach. I read up on her, though, everything I could find. One story talked about a brand of tea she loved." She stared at the tablecloth, her cheeks growing pink. "Elizabeth mentioned there was a tea house near her college that made a delicious blend of guayusa cacao. I caught the bus there the next day and I tried it, imagining I was sharing a cup with her. Discussing Shakespeare together, becoming great friends." Rolling her eyes, she added, "God, I know how lame that sounds, but teenagers do stuff like that. Anyway, the tea was sublime and I developed a taste for it. Now, obviously, it's wonderful I have something I can share with her."

"So you did truly meet on set?" Jean-Claude asked. The suspicion in his eyes had fled.

"We did." Elizabeth gave Summer a small smile. "I wondered who this LA girl was drinking my tea. Hell of a first impression." She leaned over and dropped a kiss on Summer's cheek.

Summer's flinch was subtle, but there.

Great. Does she have to be skittish now? Elizabeth prayed it hadn't been obvious.

"So it was love at first sight?" Marcus asked, sounding hopeful.

"No." Summer's cheeks reddened again. "Actually, it was hard for me at first, meeting her. She's a real woman, not some kid's idealized fantasy." Her eyes met Jean-Claude's. "Usually it's never a good idea to meet your heroes." The last sentence was almost a whisper.

"But it turned out so well." Summer smiled. "I saw her for who she actually is. Under all the make-up, under the fame, under the reputation. Once I really got to know her, I was hooked. I didn't want the lights to come up and for her to disappear once more. And now, here we are. I never want to leave her side again."

Marcus beamed. "That's beautiful."

Summer was still clutching Elizabeth's hand, running her thumb over it. Elizabeth could feel signs of nervousness in her warm fingers. How much of that speech had been real? Summer clearly was an adept actress, but this seemed far too good to be ad-libbed.

"I see I was right about something," Jean-Claude said. "Well, two things really." Without another word, he left the table, returning a few minutes later with three copies of the script.

"First—you are my Elspeth." He slid one to Elizabeth.

Excitement filled her. *Thank God!*

"And two, Summer, I believe you would make an excellent Lucille. She's a mix of naive, naughty, and seductive." He gently tossed copies to Summer and Delvine. "There are a few new scenes that you won't have seen. I'd been contemplating whether to rewrite the script the moment Skye told me it was true about you two. Now I'm convinced I was right. The lovers off-screen shall play lovers on-screen."

"What?" Summer's eyes widened. Her hand squeezed Elizabeth's painfully, then let go.

Delvine blinked, snatched up the script, and flicked through it.

Clearing her throat, Elizabeth said, "Jean-Claude, while I'd love to be your Elspeth, and thank you for that, there was no Lucille in the script I read."

"As I say, this is new."

"You mention on-screen lovers. I thought Elspeth has a one-night stand with Lucas the linesman. He was to represent lust?"

"Lucas is still there but now there is no intimacy. He will play regret. Lucille is lust." Jean-Claude took a sip of wine.

Delvine cleared her throat. "This is quite a change, darling. It isn't some chaste scene, either."

"It will be beautiful." His eyes narrowed. "It is frustrating. Americans so often see sex on screen as something dirty or, what do you say? *In your face.* Like porn. It is used to exploit, even when it is about love. I would never tolerate that. This, I promise, from all my heart, will be sublime. Partial lighting. Soft shadows, gentle focus. Twisted sheets, perfectly draped. Art."

"Be that as it may, we have to talk about this...art," Delvine said. "Negotiate. It's a big thing for any actor to consider. Especially for a couple not wanting their relationship known."

"Wait, 'not chaste'?" Summer muttered, reaching for her copy of the script. "*How* 'not chaste'?"

"Page forty-six," Delvine muttered.

Summer flicked there and they both read.

"Oh," Summer whispered.

Elizabeth stared at the stark words.

Oh.

Chapter 8

"WELL," ELIZABETH SAID AS THEY drove home. "That was…"

"Yes." Summer stared out the window. "Didn't see that coming."

"Me either. I had no idea, obviously."

"No, I know. Of course you didn't."

"What are you going to do?" Elizabeth asked.

Summer turned, her stomach sinking. She'd thought it was obvious. "What do you mean?"

"Well, how are you going to wriggle out of the role? Yet still give Jean-Claude the impression you're my real-life lover?"

How *would* she be able to do this? Summer hadn't even handled Elizabeth's peck on the cheek well earlier. But…and it was a big but… this was a huge acting break. She'd gone straight from sweet little girls to cute girl-next-door. To be offered a mold-shattering role like this was priceless. She'd just have to find a way to make it work. What she really didn't appreciate was how certain Elizabeth seemed that Summer shouldn't take it.

She gave her an even look. "Why would I wriggle out of it? It's time I dropped the ingénue roles. I'm twenty-eight—long overdue to play an adult with actual, God-forbid, human desires."

"You *want* to do this?" Elizabeth stared.

Did she have to look so damned shocked? "Yes."

"The scenes between Elspeth and Lucille…" Elizabeth darted a glance at Delvine, observing them from the seat opposite, "I mean, there's a reason that Lucille is Elspeth's inner manifestation of lust."

"I noticed," Summer said dryly, willing her brain not to skitter around with its hair on fire again. It had taken half an hour just to steady her pulse after the initial shock. "I read it too."

"We can negotiate limits," Delvine spoke for the first time. "How much skin. How far it goes. I'm sure Jean-Claude will be open to some compromises. He hardly strikes me as the prurient type. And Elizabeth's agent has an excellent lawyer for exactly this. But the content of the scene is not the issue here, is it?" She eyed them. "Do I have to spell it out?"

Summer sighed. "I know. It's the gay thing. And the fact it's about us."

"Exactly," Delvine said.

Elizabeth shook her head at Summer. "You're saying you'd be willing to..." she paused.

"Play your lover?" Summer's exasperation rose. Did this really sound so implausible to her? "It's acting, Elizabeth. Sorry, I mean *Bess*. You really didn't think that was an important detail to mention? That almost cost you everything."

"Hell, I know." She ran her hand through her hair. "I didn't think. The meeting happened so fast." She hesitated. "You really don't have a problem with any of this?"

"Why would I? Take the sex scenes out of the equation and the part's brilliant. The layers? The way Lucille asks just the right questions because she knows all Elspeth's weakest spots? Her secrets, her desires, her darkest fears? She's tormenting herself and doesn't even know it. It's a dream role. They never give clever, nuanced, R-rated parts to women like me."

"No, they don't," Elizabeth agreed. "If I were you, I'd want it too."

"So what's the problem? You're sounding really thrown by this. Is it because it's me playing Lucille? Or is it the lesbian sex that has you antsy?"

"I am *not* antsy," Elizabeth's chin lifted. "Or thrown. It's not about me—I assumed you wouldn't like it. I thought it'd make *you* feel awkward."

"Well, here's a terrific idea: Why don't you let me worry about me? There's nothing about Lucille I can't handle, so don't put whatever your fears are on me." Summer's heart was thudding out of her chest. Truth be told, the scene scared the living crap out of her, but Elizabeth didn't need to know that. To hell with anyone who would try to take this role from her.

Elizabeth's eyes tightened, and she opened her mouth.

"Okay, ladies," Delvine cut her off. "This is starting to sound like a pissing contest. Can we agree that you're both more than capable of doing the scene and move on? And then can we talk about the pink elephant in the limo?"

Elizabeth gave a strained nod.

Swallowing, Summer also nodded. She'd been so busy convincing everyone, including herself, that she could do this, that they hadn't even addressed the biggest thing.

"Are you both willing to play gay?" Delvine looked at them. "Virtually everyone who does, no matter who, gets gay rumors around them. It's only brief but it's as regular as taxes. I know it's ridiculous. You play a murderer and no one asks you how many bodies you've buried. You may get asked if you're a lesbian, if you've ever been with women, if you ever wanted to be, how you liked kissing your co-star, and most especially, if you're secretly into each other. That's what's ahead."

Elizabeth's body went a little rigid and her jaw set hard. "Don't we simply laugh it off as being just a role like any other?"

"Yes," Delvine said, "we do. That's exactly how it gets handled. What I'm asking, though, is if you're fine with facing the questions."

"It comes with the role apparently." Elizabeth was viciously flicking lint off her pants. "I want the role. Do the maths."

"Mm." Delvine glanced at Summer. "And you, darling?"

She shrugged. "I'm okay. Autumn will freak at first. But it's time my on-screen self grew up. So yeah, it's fine. Small downside."

Delvine regarded her. "You will have it much harder than Bess. You're still Punky for many people. Some will be angry and say you've ruined Punky for them, or sexualized her somehow by sexualizing yourself. You may get trolled or boycotted, or your old children's shows targeted."

Summer gaped at her. "Why? This is an independent arthouse film. For adults."

"I'm aware. And I need you to understand all the potential fallout. It may be fine. But remember, you're the every-girl parents and kids could both bond with, and suddenly you're kissing America's most-hated villain, who is also somewhat older and female."

Elizabeth cleared her throat. "More than 'kissing'," she murmured. "Don't forget pages fifty to fifty-six."

Oh God. Summer hadn't thought this through at all.

"Look, there's nothing major to worry about," Delvine continued, "but there's always one concerned parents' group claiming to act in the name of morality who will seek to make a name for themselves using this. And you're so damned marketable. The media will eat up a controversy like this."

"Controversy." Summer tried to picture being in anyone's crosshairs.

"You've never been hated," Elizabeth said kindly. "It's manageable, but it helps to be prepared for it. Emotionally."

"*If* it happens," Delvine said. "Maybe society's evolution will amaze us." Her expression said quite the opposite.

"But it's just a role." Summer swallowed and remembered what mattered most. "A great one."

"It is." Delvine agreed. "And I promise that the backlash, if there is any, would be only temporary. However, you should seriously talk this over with your people. I'm not your manager, so it's not for me to say what you should do. Just give the ramifications some thought."

"What if I was your client? Would you advise me to take it?"

"But you're not."

"Imagine I am, for a minute."

Delvine smiled. "Free advice? In this town? Summer, darling, you have quite the nerve."

"Yep," she grinned, offering her most impish look. "I know. But please?"

Elizabeth laughed. "The big guns, Delvine. Now you're done for."

Shaking a finger at Summer, Delvine said, "I've managed Oscar winners who aren't this persuasive. But I am immune."

"Really?" Summer flashed an even cheekier expression. "Should I beg?"

"Oh, I definitely think you should," Elizabeth said, making a *please continue* motion. "I need more amusement in my life. Isn't that what you're always telling me, Delvine?"

Delvine rolled her eyes. "You two can both quit it. Alright, Summer, you must have caught me on a good day. I'll tell you what I think. Take the role and laugh all the way to the awards, because it *will* clean up, and then fling yourself onwards to the next big thing. Don't get tied down on *Choosing Hope* for long. You're too talented for that. And, when this does blow up, if your sister can't swing all that free publicity into making you a household name, then call me and we'll talk. I'd be proud to represent you. Okay?"

Summer grinned. "Thanks, Delvine. I appreciate the advice. I'll stick with Autumn, though. She's worked hard to get me where I am. I trust her."

"Yes, she's done well to take you to where you are now. I'm not trying to poach you. I can see you're loyal. I'm just explaining things. There's only so far even the most dedicated amateur can take someone's career. It's all about connections and contacts, which she won't have."

A small bubble of anger rose up.

"Anyway, I digress." Delvine leaned forward. "If you *do* take this role, and I'm talking to both of you now, can I ask you at least to put in an actual effort next time?"

Oh hell. Just how obvious had they been?

Elizabeth gave her an arch look.

"Don't play innocent," Delvine said. "The deal almost imploded today because you…" she pointed at Elizabeth, "didn't tell Summer your preferred name."

Guilt ran through Summer. She hadn't exactly made it easy for Elizabeth to brief her on anything.

"We can't have that again, or anything similar," Delvine continued. "If you're filming in the middle of nowhere for a month, you'll both need to do a far better job at faking this. And Jean-Claude strikes me as the sort of man who'd fire his leading lady, screw the costs, if he found out she'd been lying to him the whole time. Does that sound about right, Summer?"

She nodded slowly. "He really hates deceit. He'd do that."

"I thought so. Then don't screw it up. Treat these next few weeks as a research period. And I don't want to hear any more asinine ad-libs about cacti, spiders, or zombies. You're lucky you both have enough charm to pull that idiocy off. Take this seriously. Meet each other's friends, family, goldfish, whatever it takes to be convincing. Do it properly."

Elizabeth pursed her lips. "I'm not going to introduce Summer to my friends as someone I'm dating. They'd howl with laughter."

"Lovely." Summer ground her teeth. "Thanks for that."

"I didn't mean it like that." Elizabeth glared back. "I just mean they're smart. They'll know in two seconds it's a con. They know I don't think much of…" She petered out, a guilty look crossing her face.

"Don't stop there." Summer folded her arms. "What don't you think much of? Or who?"

Elizabeth's lips pressed together.

With a groan, Delvine pinched the bridge of her nose. "You two are going to be so much fun."

"Come on," Summer goaded. "Who don't you like? Former child stars? Kids with showbiz parents? Blonds? LA girls?"

Elizabeth twitched.

"LA girls," Summer muttered. "*Right*. Let me guess, we're all vapid, entitled idiots with lap dogs in our handbags?"

"I didn't say that." It came out strangled.

"How can you believe that? After knowing me?" Summer hesitated as a worse thought occurred. "Or do you still think that, even after knowing me?"

"That's just it," Elizabeth protested. "I don't *know* you. Did I know the truth about how you came to like my tea? You seeing me in London? *That* was a surprise, I can tell you. You being some sort of..." she gave a dismissive wave "...devoted fan."

Fury flooded Summer. "Hey! I saved your butt today when I didn't have to. I could see we were losing Jean-Claude. He needed to hear something real. So I told him something honest even though I knew it'd be embarrassing or, worse, you'd judge me for what I did when I was young. And to thank me, you fling my honesty back in my face? Mock me for who I was?"

Elizabeth looked as if she'd been slapped. "Summer..." A faint pink crept up her cheeks. "No. I..."

"All right, stop!" Delvine gave them a long-suffering glare. "You two can figure it out on your own time. Bess, of course I'm not suggesting you try and fool your friends. I've met them. Yes, they'd assume you were joking. So just be honest. Explain what happened and that they need to help Summer research you. And Summer, get your parents to share with Bess a couple of childhood anecdotes or something." She rubbed her temple. "This shouldn't be so hard."

"I can't."

Elizabeth and Delvine looked at her.

"Mom's impossible." She threw up her hands. "You don't understand. She believes the rumors. She gets ideas into her head, like she did when she saw the HGZ photos, and doesn't believe a word of my denial, because she likes the idea of it. Besides, she's friends with Jean-Claude, so I'm not even sure I *should* try to convince her. What if she says the wrong thing to him?"

Delvine frowned. "Okay, new plan. Be honest with Bess's people, and fake it with yours."

"I don't want to lie to Dad." Summer winced. "But he'd tell Mom. Shit. I'll have to lie to both of them." She sighed. "I'll tell Autumn, though. As my manager, she has to know the truth. And then there's Chloe."

"Who?" Delvine asked.

"My roommate."

"Does Chloe have any contact with your parents?" Delvine sounded exhausted.

"All the time. Mom comes for lunch every Sunday, sometimes with the rest of the family in tow." Summer groaned. "And Chloe can't lie to save herself. She'd blurt out we were faking it if my parents just asked her to pass the ketchup."

"I see. Well, think of it like this: It's a test. An...audition. If you can convince Chloe, you'll be ready for your role." Delvine eyed her closely. "Or if you can't bear any of this, just say so now. I can see you'll find it hard. Maybe it's best to pull out before you waste anyone's time and Jean-Claude can find a new Lucille. It's up to you. We'll all understand."

Summer considered that, just as the car reached the top of the driveway outside Elizabeth's home. She stared at it in amazement. She'd been too out of it that morning to take it in. Before her sat a stunning hillside home, walled on one end with glass. Through that glass she glimpsed the shimmer of a beautiful pool, and an incredible view.

Wow. It made Summer's cute bungalow look like a garden shed.

"Okay, this is me." Elizabeth tossed a glance at Summer as she exited the limo. "We'll talk tomorrow at work." She turned back to her manager. "Delvine, I'll call you later and discuss what I want changed. To hell I'm doing a full nude scene. I don't care who's asking."

"No problem," Delvine replied. "I'll handle it with Rachel. Talk soon, darling."

The door closed. The driver steered the limo around the circular gravel drive and soon they were headed back down the hill.

Summer sat in silence, digesting the words "full nude scene" next to the image of the woman who'd uttered them. The reality slammed home.

Elizabeth naked.

Me naked.

In a tiny bed in a cozy writing shack in the wilderness.

How the hell am I going to get through this?

Maybe Delvine would be great at negotiating? Sheets and shadows and low lighting all around? Hope flared. But still...*Elizabeth naked. In my arms.*

"So. Summer Hayes. Everyone's favorite girl next door." Delvine adjusted her bangles and gave her a speculative look. "You're full of surprises."

"I am?"

"You know, I normally have excellent gaydar, but I didn't pick you at all. Don't worry, I think it sailed right over Elizabeth's head."

"W-what? Wait, *what* sailed over her head?"

"Summer, darling, I gather Skye's a little eccentric, but no mother would assume the HGZ photos were real if she also knew her daughter was straight. So she had to know you weren't."

Oh shit. Summer's shoulders slumped. She couldn't muster a lie and Delvine clearly wasn't stupid.

"I only pointed it out so you don't make the same mistake with someone less discreet. I will tell no one. I have a few closeted actors on my books, so I'm attuned at picking up the clues. That's the only reason I noticed."

Summer nodded glumly.

"But on that topic—noticing things—there's something else I can't overlook." Delvine worried her fingers over her bangles.

For some reason, seeing the up-front manager hesitate made Summer's stomach churn.

"Look, it was a good speech," Delvine said. "You had Elizabeth convinced. That's impressive, because she is no one's fool."

Startled, Summer asked, "Convinced about what?"

"About how you're just trying to help her and she shouldn't judge you by who you were at fifteen." Delvine paused. "The thing is, Summer, you hide it well, sweetheart, but it's plain to me you do have some sort of feelings for Bess."

106

Oh. My. God. Denials sprang to her lips but, under Delvine's knowing eyes, none of them made it to her tongue.

"It's okay." Delvine's expression was gentle. "We live in Hollywood. Whose heart doesn't beat that little bit faster for some of the perfect specimens we work with? I don't think anyone's immune from a few secret crushes. And I promise Bess doesn't know."

"But it's not like that. I just want to be her friend."

"Is that so?" Delvine considered that. "I heard you at lunch. Your beautiful story about how you saw the real her and fell for who she really was after years of knowing only her image. I suspect it was quite the opposite, though. I believe you did see the real her. And Bess, being Bess, was her usual aloof self, walls up, dismissive of those around her, not interested in being friendly. That probably hurt like hell, especially since there's probably still a piece of you, deep inside, who remembers how teenage-you looked up to her. It's all a bit confusing. Am I close?"

Summer felt sick. How humiliating.

"You have to understand, Bess is not a bad woman, so don't judge her too harshly. She gets so focused on work, and given the bad mood she's been in these past two seasons, she's not too pleasant to anyone. She forgets the little things, the social lubrication, you'd call it, such as noticing the people around her. It's not personal. Her mindset is just on getting her job done and escaping back home. Add to that she's also cautious because of her fame. It's hard for her to let down her guard at the best of times. But right now, she's at her most impenetrable."

"It's fine. I understand."

"I told Bess you were a good actress and *there*." Delvine offered a wry smile. "You had me almost convinced. It's not fine, though is it? I'm sorry for asking, and normally I wouldn't involve myself, but Bess *is* my business, so…"

She lowered her voice, even though the privacy screen was up between them and the driver. "Are you really going to be okay doing this role? You'll have to pretend to be intimate with a woman you clearly feel something for. She doesn't feel that way for you and never will. Elizabeth's heart is not something she shares often, and never with co-stars."

"I know that." Summer glared, even as her heart sank.

"Then if this is about getting to do that sex scene just so you can be close to her in a way you never can be in reality, it will mess up your head badly. I've seen it. Not to mention it's destructive on both sides. It's not right."

"Oh my God, *no!*" Summer gasped, offended. Didn't Delvine get how awful that scene would be for her? How hard it'd be to have to work past her feelings just to *do* the role? "How could you even…" Her fury rose. "I'd quit this minute if I thought for a moment you were right. I'd never take advantage of the situation for some selfish reason." She shot Delvine an appalled glare. "How can you ever think that? I'm interested in this role *despite*…everything, not because of it."

"Good." Delvine nodded with satisfaction. "Now *that* I believe. Thanks for putting my mind at rest. I didn't seriously entertain the thought, but I like to check. Don't worry, I won't breathe a word of this. Good managers are like priests. Just with better fashion sense."

Summer gave her a relieved smile. Delvine matched it with a wide one of her own.

"There's that smile you're famous for." In a wistful tone, she added, "Bess used to smile a lot too, you know. Back in the day. When she first arrived in LA. She was so happy to be here."

"Really?" That was hard to picture.

"Oh yes. She was with her Cambridge friends again, and the whole world was alive with possibilities. Now work's a grind and it breaks my heart. It's why this role's so important. Why, despite all the baggage, I don't want anything to mess it up for her." Delvine gave her a direct look. "Or any*one*."

"I'd never hurt her." Summer meant it with every fiber of her being.

"You already have," Delvine said. "But don't worry, she'll live. It's probably a good thing for her. A reminder to think about how everyone else fits into her world. To think outside her bubble. It's time she had a bit of a shake-up. It's not just her. Being famous makes some people too inward focused as they try to protect themselves. It's difficult to avoid."

"I don't understand. How did I hurt her?"

"It upset her greatly when you withdrew from her. Funny thing is, she hasn't even realized you were the cause of her even more atrocious mood of late."

"It was *her* damned idea! Well, her people. *You!*"

"Not me, dear. Rachel Cho. Agent extraordinaire. It wasn't the advice I'd have given. The thing Rachel never considers is just how few genuine friends people like Elizabeth have. Everyone wants a piece of the famous. So she socializes with few people. Her social life comprises only the friends she met at college in London twenty years ago."

"Seriously?" Summer had assumed Elizabeth had dozens of friends.

"Yes, well, she's complicated. So consider it high praise that you're the first person I've seen break the mold on her friendships. I think I know why, too. You grew up around famous people, didn't you?"

Summer nodded. "They were always at our parties."

"I'd bet you've never once thought about her fame. That's incredibly rare for her. I think she's picked up on it subconsciously."

Summer stared at her in dismay. "That's all it is? She likes me because I don't treat her like she's famous?" *Great.* A stray dog could have had the same impact.

Delvine laughed. "Of course not. I think she genuinely liked you for however briefly your friendship lasted before Rachel decided it needed torpedoing."

Summer bit her lip. "Liked? Past tense?"

"I should have guessed you'd pick up on that." Delvine smiled sympathetically. The car slowed in front of a gleaming glass apartment building.

"Listen, darling," she said as she gathered her bag, "despite any other complicated matters between you two, I think you're really good for her. She smiles around you more. She's almost like the woman I first met. But you bring out the dragon in her, too, and she'll get as furious with you as I've ever seen. It's been quite a revelation watching you two going at it today. I can't tell you how rare it is you get the full-spectrum Bess. She's usually so damned British and buttoned-up when it comes to her feelings on anything. Still, be careful. Big emotions have a lot of power to hurt if you're on the receiving end. You don't want to immolate under Bess's laser focus. Or, if you must fall apart, can you at least do it *after* you've done *Eight Little Pieces?*" She shot Summer a mercenary grin.

"Got it," Summer drawled. "No self-destructing until after your client's big film role."

"There now, I knew we'd understand each other perfectly." Delvine's smile was positively angelic as she got out of the car.

Chapter 9

ELIZABETH STARED INTO THE MIRROR of her trailer, wondering if the woman looking back was prepared for what lay ahead in the coming weeks. This had disaster written all over it. One small error, one ill-timed flinch, and she'd wind up with no movie and an irate Frenchman on her hands.

She glanced at the wall clock. Summer was supposed to be here any minute. It still made little sense to her how wholeheartedly the young woman had flung herself into wanting to play Lucille—no reservations, doubts, or fear.

Elizabeth had all three. She didn't want the speculation, attention, and prying questions. She hated all that. The role would bring an avalanche of scrutiny, probably requiring her to step up her appearances with Amrit. And lie. Elizabeth sighed. She hadn't come to Hollywood for this. To manufacture a life about as real as the Chief Hunt collectible doll the network had put out at the height of the Mendez romance.

She shuddered at the reminder, picking up a hairbrush and twirling the handle. It was part of a polished wooden set of brushes her mother had given her. Elizabeth wondered if her love of smooth things was all just a balm to the jaggedness of her double life. Straight on the outside, gay on the inside.

Her gray eyes stared back at her, offering no answers. At least they hid her turmoil.

Summer, on the other hand, seemed fearless. Although that might be because this was just some fun acting challenge for her. Something to tick off on her CV. She'd move on without another thought. Summer wouldn't feel bared to the bone and terrified that if someone just looked at her in a certain way, they'd *know*. It was always the hardest thing about being an actor. How much of yourself do you choose to reveal? How much do you expose for the price of admission? How much do you hold back and protect?

Summer had been right, calling Elizabeth out for projecting her fears. These were her own issues to pull apart. So, Elizabeth would throw herself into Elspeth. She'd choke back those fears and twist herself into the soul of a reclusive writer.

A woman who lusts for women.

What would it be like to kiss Summer? Or have her kiss me?

She frowned at the thought. It was unprofessional. This was a job.

There was a soft knock, and Elizabeth turned to the door.

"Come in."

A hand holding a cup of tea appeared first. "Peace offering." Summer stepped inside, toeing the door closed behind her. She was dressed as Joey Carter, in hospital scrubs, her hair in a ponytail.

"Ah. Now that's how to make an entrance." Elizabeth gratefully took the cup and waved at Summer to sit, before taking a long sip. Liquid heaven. She groaned.

Meeting Summer's eyes in the mirror, she noted a small blush. Seriously? *This* was the woman who was supposed to seduce her on-screen in less than a month? It seemed about as likely as Chief Hunt discovering her love for puppies.

"So," Summer's gaze roamed the trailer as Elizabeth drank, "Any thoughts about this 'researching our lives' thing?"

"Mmm, yes." Elizabeth placed the steaming cup on the table. "My friends are due on Friday night for a semi-regular event. We call it 'party night' to give it an air of respectability, but it's just a games night. We eat a little, drink a lot, and every few months, including this Friday, one of the highlights is watching my thespian friends try to best each other with trivia questions. *Shakespearean* trivia. It's also a little interactive, depending on how much alcohol has been consumed and who can remember the lines they're attempting to deliver."

Summer's eyes lit up. "No wonder you got that naughty look when I told you about my party trick. I'll be your ringer."

"If that's like a ring-in, then yes. My friends have a high opinion of their knowledge, and being an American you'll be underestimated immediately. It should be highly amusing to watch."

Summer grinned.

"Somewhere in the middle of all that, you should be able to extract enough information out of them to give the impression to Jean-Claude that you actually know me."

"Sounds good." Summer pulled out her phone. "What time and what do I bring?"

"Eight, assuming filming doesn't run late. And you don't need to bring anything but your wit. You'll need that. My friends will test it. Fresh meat and so on."

Summer eyed her. "Okay, just who's being set up here? Me or them?"

"A little of each. I suspect it'll be educational all round. I admit I'm curious as to how you'll handle them."

"And you'll be the one who laughs either way?"

Elizabeth feigned innocence. "Who can say?"

"Uh-huh. Well, I'll be there. And I see your Shakespeare night and raise you a Sunday pool party."

"What?"

"Mom's doing a thing. Pool, barbecue, drinks, a few friends. She's insisting I bring you. And Autumn wants Delvine to come, too. To strategize on the QT."

"Strategize?"

"So they're both on the same page."

"That makes sense. I'll ask her."

"No need. Autumn did already. Delvine said yes." Summer sighed. "I feel like I should apologize to you in advance for everything Mom'll put you through. I did mention she's offbeat, right?"

Elizabeth hid her smile. How bad could one slightly eccentric woman be?

"Well, she's a force to be reckoned with," Summer continued. "My best advice is to just go with it. Do not fight her on anything. That's how Autumn and I coped growing up."

"And how did Autumn take the news of all this? The film role and fake-dating?"

Summer shuddered. "Ugh, no comment. I didn't even know she knew half those words. But she also read the script. And when she was done freaking out, she admitted to being blown away by the role. She also knows what Jean-Claude's like. She can't see any way around doing what we're doing."

"Neither can I."

"It's only for six weeks, anyway. Two weeks of getting to know each other now before *Hope* wraps for hiatus; a month of filming. We can 'break up' after the movie's shot. Jean-Claude will never be any the wiser."

Six weeks wasn't too terrible. "Yes. But…" Elizabeth hesitated, not sure how to phrase it.

"What is it?"

"I have concerns. About you."

"You don't think I'm up to Lucille?" Hurt flashed across Summer's face.

"My more immediate concern is whether you're up to the role of playing my girlfriend. You flinched when I kissed your cheek yesterday."

Summer sagged. "Yeah. Sorry. I wasn't expecting it."

"Well, expect it, especially at that pool party. If we're going to pull this off, we can't cut corners. I'll expect and provide occasional PDAs. Are you okay with that? If not…" *Then why on earth are you doing a sex scene with me?*

"I know. I wasn't really ready yesterday. The hangover didn't help."

"But you'll be okay on Sunday?"

"Absolutely." Summer snapped straight, as if preparing for war.

Christ. Was that how she saw this? Some unsavory tour of duty? It was exasperating and a little insulting. "Have you ever even…" Elizabeth stopped herself from asking a most inappropriate question. *Have you ever even kissed a woman before?* The answer seemed pretty obvious. "Will you be comfortable with this?" she asked instead.

"About as comfortable as you." Summer offered a small shrug. "But we're both adults. And it's acting."

"It is." Elizabeth reached for her tea and swallowed. It improved her mood another ten percent. "Just be ready is all I'm asking." She leaned over and brushed her lips against Summer's cheek, relieved to see no flinch. *Much better.* "And Summer?" she said, lowering her voice to throaty. "I think you should call me Bess."

Summer had never been so nervous in her life. Somehow she kept her voice steady, announcing her presence into the electronic box beside the bronze gates outside Elizabeth's home. They slid open and she navigated her blue VW up the steep, curling drive. She parked in an area that had five other cars and a souped-up Hog. She wondered whose motorcycle it was.

As she squared her shoulders, Summer realized that this party night mattered more to her than the Badour role. She wasn't here for the research. Summer was doing this for one reason: To impress Elizabeth, whose opinion still mattered to her, no matter how much she'd tried to tell herself it didn't. Tonight, Summer was being allowed inside Elizabeth's private world. She wasn't Elizabeth's friend, of course. But just being invited was overwhelming. So no matter what, she'd make sure Elizabeth wasn't sorry she'd asked her in.

After ringing the door bell, Summer wiped her palms down her forest-green pants. She wondered if her cream halter top was too casual. It flattered her arms, but maybe there was too much skin? She hadn't even thought to ask about a dress code. God, what if she looked completely ridic...

The door opened. Elizabeth was resplendent in a pair of tight, pale-blue jeans that made her legs look spectacular. Four buttons were undone on her white, long-sleeved cotton shirt. Four. *Oh God.* Soft white skin was revealed in cleavage that Summer absolutely, positively shouldn't be staring at. Her head snapped up. "Hey."

"Right on time." Elizabeth smiled. "I hope you don't mind, but we started an hour ago. I wanted to brief everyone on the situation first. That way we'd get all the annoying jokes out of the way." With a long-suffering look, she added, "There were plenty, trust me. Anyway, come in." She stepped aside.

Summer handed her a bottle of wine as she walked past. "From Marcus's grandfather's winery."

"Excellent. I'm sure the others will appreciate it. Come on through and I'll introduce you around." She closed the door and led the way down a hall.

God. Her ass was incredible too.

Elizabeth glanced back. "You look good by the way. Nice top."

"Thanks. Also you. Um. Gorgeous. Like always."

What the actual fuck, brain?

Elizabeth's chuckle only made her feel more stupid.

They moved into a wide, cream-colored living room, with honeyed timber floors, several white sofas and armchairs, and glass walls on three sides.

"Whoa," Summer muttered, gazing outside at the sparkling infinity pool, and the city skyline stretched out beyond. "That's some view."

At the sound of laughter, she turned to find half a dozen pairs of eyes on her. Summer's gaze went from person to person, taking in the people Elizabeth cared about. She recognized three of the faces. Brian, Rowan, and Amrit? All *together*?

"Uh...Eliz...Bess...You've stayed friends with all your exes?"

For some reason, everyone laughed at that—except for a petite redheaded woman whose eyes widened. "Why do you say that?"

"She means my red-carpet posse," Elizabeth told her, sounding almost bored. But her gaze was pointed.

"Oh," the redhead muttered. "*That.*"

Red-carpet posse?

"Summer, meet Alex Levitin," Elizabeth waved to the woman who'd spoken. "She's an indie film director."

"Hi." Recognition hit. "Hey, didn't you do *Heaven's Blood*?"

"I did. So it was you? I heard maybe one person saw that." She offered a wry look.

"Actually my mom worked on it. So we both saw it."

"Your mom?" Alex peered at her. "Oh... yeah, I see a resemblance. You're Skye's kid?"

"Yep."

"Damn LA's a small world. Skye's great. Mad as a cut snake, but great."

Summer wondered what she was supposed to say to that. It was one thing for *her* to call her mother crazy, but for a complete stranger to...

"Hey, hey," Brian suddenly leapt to his feet and came over to her. "Don't mind Alex, I promise she meant it in a good way. She loves people who think outside of the box, like her." He gave Summer's hand a squeeze and shot Alex a reproving look.

"Oh God!" Alex sounded stricken. "Sorry, love. I have complete respect for Skye. After all, anyone who can embody an angel with a demon soul in costume form is a godsend."

"And right there is why no one saw *Heaven's Blood*," Brian teased. He turned back to Summer. "I'm Brian Fox." His smile was as warm as the large hand that captured hers.

She already knew who he was, of course. Elizabeth had dated him back in...

"Over there, looking dashing in red suspenders, is my boyfriend of twenty years, Rowan Blagge," Brian finished.

Shock pierced her. She knew Rowan, too, of course...as another of Elizabeth's old boyfriends. Or so she'd thought.

"Hi, Summer." Rowan waved. "It's good to finally meet someone from Bess's crazy doctor show. We were starting to think she tosses them into the body bags on set at the end of every day so we can never meet them. Such a shame."

"That wouldn't do much, though," Summer said earnestly. "Body bags are quite easy to escape if you know how."

Brian snorted. Rowan gaped at her, looking delighted. "I dread to ask how you know that."

"You think Punky Power, teen spy, sat on her butt all day?" She cocked an eyebrow. "I have mad skills. I can even crack a basic safe. Like for real."

"That could come in handy." Rowan tapped his chin, as though imagining the possibilities.

"You know, I thought so too." Summer gave a disappointed huff. "But it actually hasn't. Not without a criminal inclination."

He laughed. "Ha. Well, maybe one day."

"I live in hope." Summer grinned.

Amusement danced in Elizabeth's eyes. "And this is Amrit Patel." She waved to her stylish boyfriend, arranged on the couch in an artful, aristocratic pose, like something from a magazine shoot. He reminded Summer of a ballet dancer at the peak of his career. He wore an immaculate royal blue silk shirt and designer shoes. When he smiled, his white teeth flashed against his light-brown skin.

Rising to his full, towering height, Amrit tugged his shirt cuffs straight and supplied Summer with an utterly charming smile. He gathered her hand in both of his, turned it over, bowed, and kissed it.

That earned eye rolls and low groans from everyone else.

"Enchanted, Summer," Amrit murmured. The sheer charisma of the man was almost tangible. No wonder Elizabeth loved him. "It's such a *pleasure* to meet you." His smirk was pure rogue.

Okay, what? He was flirting with her. Right in front of his girlfriend. "I...um..." She shot a confused look at Elizabeth, whose eyes crinkled in amusement. "Aren't you," Summer replied, "actually all of you," she pointed at Brian and Rowan, "Elizabeth's exes...or, in Amrit's case, current boyfriend?"

The room burst into laughter.

"Sorry, sweetie," Brian told Rowan as he resumed his seat. "I keep telling you Bess is the one for me. It's the couch for you."

"I'm not dating any of them." Elizabeth headed for a side buffet with empty glasses lined up on it. "Now or ever. It's Delvine and Rachel's idea to keeping the chatter about me going. Handsome men, red-carpet eye candy. The usual. It's good for their careers and mine. Drink?" She tilted an empty wine glass questioningly.

Summer stared at her. "You're not together?" She swished her finger between Amrit and Elizabeth. "And you were never with Brian or Rowan?"

"She's not my type," Rowan said. "I prefer more stubble."

O-kay. Looked like she was the fool. Elizabeth was apparently an even more convincing actress than Summer had given her credit for. "Wine, please," she muttered.

Elizabeth uncorked Marcus's wine and poured.

"Well, that was worth the admission price," came a low, soft purr from the corner of the room. The voice was velvety, soft, and light, but not warm.

Summer turned to see an immaculate forty-something woman sitting like a queen in a butter-soft, cream-colored leather armchair.

"Hello, dear, I'm Grace." She gave Summer a slow, appraising look and tilted her head. Waiting.

No surname. She obviously thought she didn't need one, and her words contained an air of expectation. Summer knew that pause well. Famous people did it, and often didn't even realize. They were waiting for the recognition, the excited acknowledgment that, *yes, I am who you think I am,* and only after the gushing begins and ends can the conversation move on.

Grace Christie-Oberon had been the most famous woman in England when Summer lived there. The actress's perfect face had graced every billboard. Profiles filled newspapers and magazines. She always topped the UK lists of most beautiful women. Little wonder "Gracie-O" expected something approaching an awed gasp from a lowly upstart like Summer.

Except Summer wasn't in the mood to play. Her mind was still reeling from Elizabeth's revelation. "Hi Grace," she said simply. "Nice to meet you, too."

Summer turned to the final unintroduced person in the room, a beautiful, dark-skinned woman with ample curves and warm, brown eyes. She wore a stunning ensemble in crimson that suited her shape and coloring to perfection. Summer's mother would adore this outfit.

"Gosh, I love what you're wearing," she told the woman, and saw a flash of dissatisfaction dart across Grace's elegant features. Grace probably assumed Summer didn't know who she was. "Who's the designer?"

"Me." The woman beamed. "I love you already. I'm Zara Ejogo."

"Zara does costumes." Elizabeth inserted the cork back in the bottle and handed Summer her wine glass. "And there's no one she can't make look amazing, including herself."

"You have so much talent," Summer said sincerely. "I mean, I know we've only just met, but I want to take you home to meet my mom!"

"Well, at least buy me dinner first." Zara's lips curved into a teasing grin.

"Oh God!" Summer laughed heartily. "Yeah, that did come out a little wrong, didn't it?"

"Or right," Brian said. "Since I hear you're taking a walk on the Sapphic wild side soon? And with our dear Bess, no less."

"Yep." Summer took a sip of the wine, and found a seat on an empty couch.

Elizabeth joined her, with a glass of clear spirits in hand. Smelled like gin.

Summer took in the faces watching her. "So I'll need lots of tips on what makes Elizabeth...Bess...tick."

"Good luck on that one," Grace intoned, eyes inscrutable. "Bess Thornton is a vault."

Elizabeth lifted an eyebrow. "Hardly. You all know me better than anyone." A smile followed, but it lacked the warmth she'd shown to Zara.

What an odd dynamic. Summer flicked a glance at Grace. The woman seemed to think she was better than Elizabeth. Or better than everyone in the room? Maybe that was unfair. Her face softened each time she looked at Amrit.

"Oh, we have all the dirt on Bess." Alex smirked. "Ask and find out."

"She has dirt?" Summer found that a little hard to believe.

"Definitely." Alex gave her a nod. "Who among us doesn't?"

"Good point. Okay, give me your funniest Bess story then."

Everyone broke out talking, debating the best answer. It seemed to be a toss-up between The *Howard's End* Incident, whatever that was, and something to do with a case of mistaken identity when she met Ang Lee.

"Are they close to the mark?" Summer whispered to Elizabeth as the debates got more enthusiastic. "Or do you have a funnier one?"

"Wouldn't you like to know?" A hint of smile dusted her lips.

"Actually, I would."

"Hmm." Elizabeth gave her a considering look. "Year Nine," she said quietly. "I was at this posh, uptight, all-girls school and was caught smuggling in books on the banned list and running a library from my school locker. I had it all worked out. Due dates, lists of students involved, even some minimal late fees for the worst offenders."

"You little rebel."

Elizabeth's eyes danced.

"So what sort of books were on the banned list?"

"Oh, the usual ones that hormonal teenagers want to get their hands on. *Lady Chatterley's Lover* was popular; that sort of thing. I had easy access. My father's a playwright with an extensive library of all the classics and many modern titles, too. I decided he wouldn't notice a few books going missing here or there. I always brought them back."

"How enterprising. So what happened?"

"Well, Miss Fletcher, my English teacher, caught me."

"Uh-oh. Did you get in a lot of trouble?"

"Not...exactly. She was a new, younger teacher, on a tight budget, with a voracious reading appetite. She became one of my most frequent borrowers. Sometimes we'd discuss D. H. Lawrence's themes if no one else was around." Elizabeth smiled fondly. "She was my favorite teacher."

"That's…"

"Shocking? Corruption in the English school system?" Elizabeth teased.

"I was going to say amazing. For two reasons: One, that you were so enterprising and shared your love of literature with others. And two, why weren't the girls just Googling racy fan-fiction?"

"Well, that might have been difficult since this happened before Google. But even so, nothing is more alluring to teens than something forbidden. I think that made them enjoy it more."

"What would your parents have said if they'd known?"

"Oh, they knew. I accidentally left my bulging book bag at home one day, along with the list of students' names earmarked for each title, and my father found it. He dropped my bag off at school, telling the office it was "urgent homework" that needed delivering to me."

"Wow. That's so cool."

"It was."

"What about your mother? Would she have freaked out?"

"She's a professor in medieval English literature at Oxford. I suspect she knew as well. They probably had a good laugh about it. Not that I'd ever know. They take the view 'the less said, the better' on most things."

"The polar opposite of my folks. Mom has an opinion on everything. Geese flight paths would probably get her into debate mode as much as Spanx versus girdles."

"I look forward to meeting her."

Summer gave her a skeptical look. "I'll remind you on Sunday you said that."

Across the room, Grace cleared her throat to speak and it was like a flare had gone up. The raucous debate stuttered to a halt. Elizabeth's focus left Summer in an instant. Well. That was a nice reminder about her status in Elizabeth's friendship hierarchy.

"I think you've all forgotten one story." Grace tilted her wine glass at them. "The costume change at Footlights on Bess's debut performance? When *both* curtains went up a little earlier than expected?"

There came a chorus of laughter, mentions of a "costume malfunction", "curtain guy probably did it on purpose", and a grim smile from Elizabeth. Her face had gone rigid and the knuckles around her glass turned white.

Why had Grace felt the need to raise something that was clearly humiliating for Elizabeth? Why do that to a friend? The amused gleam in Grace's eyes said Elizabeth's uncomfortable reaction was exactly what she was aiming for.

That clinched it. Summer didn't want to hear this story—ever. Maybe that made her soft, or lacking a sense of humor, but it felt wrong. Her gaze fell on Alex, whose expression was pinched.

Huh. So Summer wasn't the only one who had reservations about this?

Grace's mouth opened, her smile seductive, inviting, about to lay Elizabeth's most embarrassing dirty laundry out for the room's amusement.

Shut up, Summer wanted to hiss at her. A distraction would be good right about now. Well…there was one thing she could do.

Catching Amrit's eye, Summer offered him a wide, friendly smile. He blinked and reflexively smiled in return, his dazzling white teeth on display. He angled his body toward her, and his gaze became darker and interested… which had the effect of freezing Grace mid-word.

"So tell me, Summer," Amrit said, seizing the opening, "Are you seeing anyone? Do you have some cute boyfriend being driven wild by this subterfuge you've dreamt up with our Bess?"

Grace frowned and drew in a long sip of wine.

"Ooh, good question," Alex nodded approvingly. "And I can see from Bess's surprised look that she forgot to ask."

"That's why we're here, though, isn't it?" Summer said. "To fill in the gaps? And no, I'm not dating anyone."

Amrit brightened enough to pass as a lighthouse beacon.

"But I have no plans to date either," she told him. "This whole thing is complicated enough without adding a real relationship to it."

"Ouch," Rowan chuckled at Amrit. "Crash and burn, my friend."

"Maybe later," Amrit sounded unconcerned. "You are too beautiful to pass by, Summer. I can wait."

Jesus.

Beside her, Elizabeth stiffened. Grace looked ready to crush her glass in her bare hands.

"How about you?" Summer turned to her couchmate. "Anyone real you're dating that I should be aware of? Or avoid?"

Alex chortled. "Yes, do tell, Bess." She leaned forward. "Inquiring minds are *dying* to know."

"No, no one. As you well know." Elizabeth gave Alex a loaded look and then rose. "Let me get the food. And I think the Q&A on me can be postponed until after the usual proceedings."

"The usual proceedings?" Summer asked.

"She means the trivia component of our night," Grace said with an elegant flourish of her hand. "Shakespeare. Don't be too upset if we get all caught up with tricky questions. We don't expect you to know all this. That's quite all right."

A soft snort sounded from behind Summer, courtesy of Elizabeth, on her way to the kitchen.

Summer plastered on her most innocent look. "Well, I *am* American, so you'll have the cultural advantage on me."

"We do," Brian said, eyes kind. "So, as Grace said, please don't worry if you don't know the answers. We grew up with it, so we have a head start on our lad, Will."

"Thanks. I'll try my best. I think I'll help Elizabeth with the food."

She left the room, thinking about Elizabeth's friends. They were a mixed bag. Zara warm and intriguing. Alex sharp, whip-smart, and more protective of Elizabeth than the others. There was an undertone between them that Summer couldn't decipher. Grace, although subtle and oozing class, was a sly one. She obviously didn't like Summer one bit. It probably had a lot to do with Amrit's interest in her. He was as charming as the day was long, but boy, was he ever barking up the wrong tree. And peacemaker Brian and droll Rowan were adorable, funny, and well matched.

"Hey," Summer said as she found the kitchen. Polished wood surfaces gleamed at her. She trailed her fingers across a counter. "Need a hand?"

Elizabeth glanced up. "Sure. Can you help me carry out the trays over there? Take off the plastic film, too. I just need to finish up the platter."

"No problem." Summer eyed the vegetable sticks and dips. "Your friends seem nice." She couldn't help the slightest hint of accusation that slid into her voice.

"But?" Elizabeth paused chopping carrots into sticks.

"You couldn't have given me a head's up about you fake-dating the guys? No wonder you're up for repeating the game with me. You're an old hand at it."

"I am no such thing," Elizabeth said in exasperation. "It's only ever been red-carpet events. That's it."

"I saw the photos of you at the restaurant with Amrit after..." She trailed off. *After I made an idiot of myself and tripped down some steps.*

"Yes. *After.*" Elizabeth said. "That's why he and I played up to the cameras. It was the first time Amrit's ever been my date outside of an official media event. And I had to make an exception because Delvine didn't like the optics of you swooning in my arms."

"Hey, I wasn't swooning, I was falling."

"The reality doesn't matter."

"What happens when you want to date someone in real life? Are they just expected to put up with seeing you and Amrit all over the magazines?"

"The people I date don't care about him."

"They don't?"

"No."

"Why?"

Elizabeth pressed her lips together. A carrot met its fate with an especially loud chop. "Not relevant."

Ouch. She was right. But still. *Ouch.*

"Look, while we're on the topic, you should avoid Amrit," Elizabeth continued. "He's not into relationships. He's more into the chase, and once he snares the pretty obsession of the week, he moves on."

"Is that what happened with Grace?"

"How do you know about that?" Her expression was careful. "Did you read it somewhere?"

"No. I have eyes."

"Oh." Elizabeth opened the fridge and pulled out a large platter. "I suppose she's being a little less subtle tonight. She's normally more discreet."

"Well, she's not made of stone. He's flirting his ass off right in front of her and she's clearly in love with him."

"Maybe."

"She is." That level of jealousy wasn't a friendship kind. "You know, I'd be happy to tell her Amrit's all hers."

"No, don't. It would just embarrass her. Leave it."

And yet she doesn't mind embarrassing you? "Okay."

"She's usually much more removed from all this. Besides, she's the queen of... well, everything." Elizabeth's voice was so wistful.

"Everything?"

"Well, style, class, acting, beauty, you name it. But most especially the illusion. She's normally not so..."

"Human? Obvious?"

"Something like that."

"You sound really impressed by her."

Elizabeth glared at Summer as if she didn't like the sound of that. "She mentored me, years ago. She's remarkable to watch at her craft. And she did something for me that gave me my career. I owe her this house and this life."

"What did she do?"

"I was a complete unknown when I arrived in LA, but she wasn't. She got Delvine to manage me. But then... then she got me an agent. Someone impossible: Rachel Cho."

Summer knew all the industry buzz on Cho. She was famously picky with her client list and rarely took on unknowns. Being signed by her was like winning an Oscar. Which seemed fair, since she had so many Oscar winners on her books. "But how did Grace manage to do that?"

"You have to understand that when Grace first arrived, everyone thought she would take Hollywood by storm. She was being written up as the hottest property in town. Given her awards, theater background, and national prestige back home, it was a given that she'd be snapped up by one of the big-name agents. Even after some months, she hadn't decided who'd do the snapping. Then I told her I was moving to LA, and that's when she made *me* the condition: She'd only sign with someone who took me on too."

"She did?" That was beyond unusual.

"Yes. She's always looked out for my career. Thanks to her actions, I soon won the starring role on *Choosing Hope*. So my career *is* down to Grace." Her expression dared Summer to disagree.

Elizabeth claimed no credit *at all* for her own success? Why? It couldn't be that she lacked self-confidence. She was talented and knew it. And yet, she thought everything was all thanks to perfect, queen-of-everything Grace?

With a nudge of finality, Elizabeth finished with her platter and straightened. "Grace's career hasn't been what it deserves to be. She never complains about it. But we all know the truth: She should be the star, not me. It's almost…" she gave a pained look, "embarrassing that I'm the successful one now. Hollywood is clearly blind and stupid." The last line dripped with venom.

Um, what? Summer had seen an awful lot of Elizabeth's moods by now, but never this one. Embarrassed, appalled, and defensive? She seemed personally offended her mentor wasn't appreciated.

"Well, it's great she helped you," Summer said cautiously. "You deserve every success, by the way. Grace or not, you've done really well. It's not entirely luck."

"Actually, it's almost all luck, since it's clearly not about talent," Elizabeth countered adamantly, picking up the platter. "If talent was the criteria, Grace would be the household name, not me."

Summer avoided that statement like a grenade and simply nodded.

"Tray," Elizabeth reminded her, inclining her head toward the second one. "Let's go out and shake up the Bard lovers. I admit I've been looking forward to this all week." And then, as though nothing out of the ordinary had been discussed, she shot Summer a brilliant smile.

Chapter 10

"Okay," Brian said, between bites of celery stick, "let's get started. Same rules as always. Someone asks a question. Whoever answers correctly first gets one point and to ask the next question. If no one gets it right, the asker gets five points and to ask another question. I have my iPad to adjudicate any tricky stuff. Everyone clear?"

"And what does the winner get?" Summer asked curiously.

"Oh-ho!" Brian chortled. "Love the confidence. The winner gets..." he glanced around, "...a kiss from our lovely host. Okay?"

Elizabeth rolled her eyes. "How exciting for you all."

"I'm keen." Amrit winked.

Summer wondered if the man was born with Flirt Mode set to maximum.

"Such incentive," Grace said with a sarcastic drawl. "All I've ever wanted is Bess's kisses."

Summer darted a look at Elizabeth. Was this some old joke between friends, or was that as mean as it sounded?

Elizabeth's jaw worked. Her eyes fixed on her glass of spirits. No reply.

Summer turned to find Alex's sympathetic gaze burning into Elizabeth. So, she hadn't been imagining that undertone.

"Absolutely." Brian supplied a cheery grin. "Who wouldn't want a kiss from the lovely Bess?" His voice was warm and placating, taking the sting out of Grace's acerbic line.

"Can of worms, this," Rowan muttered, taking a deep gulp of beer. It was black and looked about as appealing as slurping tar. "But we're all agreed on the terms?"

Everyone nodded, including Summer.

"First question," Brian said, "an easy one as a warm-up for everyone." His eyes drifted to Summer, and it was clear it was meant for her, to make her feel welcome.

"Where was Shakespeare born?"

There was a silence, and everyone turned to her. *Subtle.*

She puckered her brow and drenched her voice in doubt. "Um, Stratford-upon-Avon?"

"Well done," Brian beamed. "Excellent. Now can you think of a question for us?"

"Hmm." Summer scrunched up her face. "How about, which of Shakespeare's plays was the shortest?"

A brief hubbub started as answers were debated. Rowan cocked his head. "*Comedy of Errors*, isn't it?"

Summer nodded. "Yes. Although I would have also accepted *Double Falsehood*, which is shorter, although whether it's truly a lost Shakespeare play is still in dispute. Personally, I think it is."

Rowan gave her a measuring look, which prompted a soft laugh from Elizabeth.

Clearing his throat, Rowan said, "I see our American friend might know a little more about the Bard than she first let on. Next question. Name this play..." His voice suddenly filled the room, becoming a deep, authoritarian boom. "'*Let me wipe it first, it smells of mortality*'."

"*King Lear*." Summer answered before anyone else had even opened their mouths. "It's an interesting line. The King's response to a commoner asking to shake his hand." She didn't wait for Rowan's agreement because she knew she was right. "Gee, okay another one. I think maybe we should try something harder, don't you?" Her eyebrows lifted. "How many Shakespearean plays contain a character dying solely due to grief? And I'm not counting the thirteen people killing themselves as a result of their emotional state. I mean the grief itself causing death, usually from loss of a loved one."

And that was the moment it dawned on everyone what was going on.

"Elizabeth, you sly old cat!" Zara laughed, waving a finger at her. "You've brought us a ring-in."

"I have no idea what you mean," Elizabeth reached for a carrot stick, sticking it into the dip. "And *old*? Thirty-seven is hardly old. You've gone

127

native—absorbed the dark souls of Hollywood." She looked around. "Does anyone know? I'll guess six."

"Four," Grace said.

"Three," Alex tried.

"People don't die from grief." Rowan gave Summer a suspicious stare. "It's a trick question. None."

"In Shakespeare's time they did," Brian countered, "or playwrights thought they did. One."

"Zara?" Summer asked.

"It can happen in real life." Zara shook a finger at Rowan. "I've heard stories of old people losing their spouses of fifty or sixty years and dying a day or a week later from a broken heart. You're far too cynical, mate. Five."

Summer shook her head. "No, ten."

Brian grabbed his iPad and began searching. "You're right. Someone's actually done their thesis on it." His eyes brightened in challenge. "Another five points for Summer Hayes, Shakespeare Shark."

"Next question." Summer grinned. "When Shakespeare died, he left almost everything he owned to his daughter. But what did he leave to his wife?"

"Oh my God." Grace stared at her in astonishment. "Where *did* you come from?"

Elizabeth's answering bright, full smile filled Summer with pleasure.

Summer won, as she'd known she would. But what made it all worthwhile was how Elizabeth looked as the evening progressed. She seemed...well, proud wasn't quite the right word, but satisfied. Summer was just relieved she hadn't disgraced herself in front of Elizabeth's friends.

"It wasn't even close." Brian shook his head, then slapped his notepad down on the table. "For the record, Summer ninety-five, Grace thirty-nine, everyone else, never mind and have another drink."

"How much did you study for this?" Grace asked, eyes sharp, as she drummed her fingers on her chair's arm. "Because it's just a casual thing among friends for us."

Irritation flashed through Summer but before she could answer, Elizabeth interrupted. "She didn't study at all. I sprung this on her. It's true I knew she had a Shakespeare bent, but I didn't know it extended to Shakespeare giving his wife his second-best bed and his bedclothes."

Summer gave a sheepish shrug. "Shakespeare trivia's always just stuck in my brain. I couldn't shake it if I tried."

"Well, bravo," Brian said. "It's a change for us."

"That an American knows Shakespeare well?"

"No," he grinned. "That someone finally beat Grace. I'm not sure if you're aware, but she's England's darling when it comes to all things Bard-ish."

"Oh, I know. I lived there for a few years as a teenager. I saw the billboards and the buses."

Grace's eyes were hooded. Summer interpreted her expression as: *So the American knew all along who I was and didn't bow and scrape? The infidel.*

"By the way," Alex broke the silence, "have you forgotten the little matter of the prize?" She waved at Elizabeth.

"It's fine," Summer said, her heart suddenly pounding. She'd hoped everyone had forgotten by now. It had been two hours ago.

"Nonsense, dear." Grace's mischievous gleam was back. "If you're to play her lover, you'd better get some practice in."

Ah. So embarrassing Summer was her new objective? Shocker.

Elizabeth shook her head. "I'm not sure I agreed to it anyway."

"Oh, I'm sure we know why you didn't," Grace purred.

And there it was again. That haughty tone with the faint, fine edge. Grace might as well have just declared: *Why would anyone want to lower themselves to kiss the common American?*

She glanced around, wondering who else had realized it. Brian and Amrit were both frowning. Rowan was discussing something else with Zara. And Alex was staring at Grace as if she had two heads. Elizabeth's expression was painfully neutral.

"Grace," she started and then stopped, sighing. "I have no problem with giving Summer her prize." Elizabeth glanced at her. "Assuming she wants it?"

Summer could say no—she desperately wanted to, because how awkward would this be? But then Elizabeth, who was trying to save her from feeling rejected, would be the rejected one. *Damn it, Grace.*

"Of course," Summer said lightly, like this wasn't the most momentous thing and her heart wasn't doing the fandango at triple speed. "Practice, practice, practice." She turned to Elizabeth, who smiled, leaned forward, and dropped a kiss on Summer's lips.

Summer slid her hand to the back of Elizabeth's head and pulled her in for a longer kiss, just to show Grace she didn't mind one damn bit. That she wasn't embarrassed, uncomfortable, or... *Oh hell.* Suddenly, they were kissing for real. Elizabeth's soft lips pressed to hers, yielding and delicious.

Arousal flooded Summer, shortly followed by her heart pounding like stampeding horses. She pulled away, giving the others a sheepish grin.

Brian whistled. "There we go, the champion is rewarded."

"Not just the champion." Zara winked at Elizabeth.

"Yes, you're all hilarious." Elizabeth sounded completely unmoved. She rose.

By contrast, Summer wasn't sure her breathing would ever be normal again. *Don't meet your idol,* Chloe had told her. Oh, no, she'd just kissed her senseless instead.

"Summer, could I have a hand in the kitchen?" Elizabeth asked.

"I'll help." Grace stood as well.

That earned incredulous stares.

"What?" Grace asked them. "I do know the fine art of washing dishes. Or stacking them. Or...whatever." Her hand swished about.

"Sure you do." Alex's eyes sparkled with amusement. "From when you last had to do them yourself. In the eighties."

Summer busied herself in cleaning-up tasks and tried not to be too aware of the woman she'd just kissed. Whatever Elizabeth had intended to say to her had been thwarted by Grace joining them. From the moment they'd entered the kitchen, Grace had held forth with a series of entertaining anecdotes, many of which made Elizabeth smile, and did exactly what they were no doubt intended to do: Make Summer feel like a third wheel. Remind Summer of her place—that she was not Elizabeth's close friend like Grace was.

She'd met Graces before. Stars who hated *not* being the center of attention and didn't like sharing even when they had the spotlight.

Summer neatly stacked a pile of dishes, tuning into the raucous bursts of conversation from the living room. The boys appeared to have started an argument about soccer. Which team had the most stylish uniform.

"And then you remember," Grace was saying, claiming Elizabeth's wrist with her milky-white hand, "we managed to escape before the theater manager's brother caught up with us."

"I remember." Elizabeth smiled, glanced at Summer, set her dish cloth on the counter, and said, "If you'll both excuse me one moment." She headed down the hallway to where Summer presumed the bathroom was.

Grace turned and studied Summer. "So, Summer Hayes. *Choosing Hope*'s newest cast member. I've heard all about you. Exploding blood packs. Green fingers."

Great. "Not my best weeks."

"I suspect not. Quite the mess you and Bess have gotten yourselves into now, too. I'm not sure I'd be so amenable to going through such a farce for a role."

Maybe that's why you're always unemployed. "It's only for six weeks."

That seemed to perk the other woman up. "Is that all? Oh, well, that's good."

Summer shifted the dishes to one side. Clearly Grace was counting down the minutes until she would disappear back out of Elizabeth's life.

"I've known her for almost twenty years," Grace said out of the blue. "There's nothing about Bess I don't know."

"Good," Summer said, conversationally. "That's why I'm here. To learn from her friends."

"I'm more than just a friend. Did she explain? I mentored her for years. Taught her everything she knows."

Not this again. Summer highly doubted Grace was Elizabeth's sole imparter of acting knowledge.

"I know it's hard getting a handle on her," Grace said. "She doesn't share often with outsiders. You're actually the first…acquaintance…of hers we've met from LA."

And they were back to this. Yes, yes, old-friend Grace was in the inner circle and Summer was a no one; not even a friend. Why didn't Grace just cut to the chase? *Don't you understand I'm better than you?*

It suddenly struck Summer that Grace was trying too hard. If she believed what she was saying about the depth of her friendship with Elizabeth, it didn't need to be said. Actually, why was Grace even bothering with Summer at all?

"I do have one question." Summer leaned back against the counter. "Since you know your friend so well."

"Of course."

"What's her favorite tea? I hear she loves tea."

"It changes," Grace said after a pause. "Often."

Like hell it does. Still, Summer decided to give her the benefit of the doubt. "Does Elizabeth have any allergies?" she asked innocently. "You know, in case craft services ask me?"

"Why would they ask *you*?"

"I'm supposed to be her girlfriend, remember. So does she?"

Grace hesitated before drawing in a breath. "If that happens, get craft services to ask her."

Oh wow. She had no clue at all, did she? How could someone go out to dinner with a friend for two decades and not know why they didn't drink wine? *Bess is such a good friend. We're oh-so close.* What a faker.

Was Grace really that oblivious? Was she too self-absorbed, perhaps? If something didn't affect her, then it wasn't worth remembering? Was *that* her deal?

"Did Bess tell you how I got her her start in Hollywood?" Grace asked.

"Yes," Summer kept her tone bland. "It's good you did that for her."

Grace frowned at her underwhelmed reaction. "I held some of the biggest names in Hollywood over a barrel. All those puffed-up power brokers, flinging offers at me. They would have done anything to sign me. So I signed with a female agent just to annoy them. That was priceless."

"Mm-hmm."

"But I only chose Rachel Cho because she agreed to sign Bess. And, fortunately, now Bess's career has taken off."

Because of me, was the implication. Well, Grace might convince Bess of her bullshit, but Summer didn't have to buy into it. "Actually I think she's famous because of her talent," she said politely. "If she was awful, she'd never have been re-signed on *Hope* after the first season. But she was so interesting to watch that they extended her contract, increased her part, and that's what made her a national name. Ultimately, *she* made herself great."

"She's not great," Grace said with a dismissive wave. "Greatness is a word thrown around far too often by young people with no understanding of what it is. Greatness should be reserved for legends. Elizabeth has a long way to go to get to those heights."

Your heights, you mean. Summer said nothing.

"Now I worry that your sad little TV show is ruining all her training. So many bad habits she's picking up. And my God, the drivel they have her saying. I'm embarrassed for her. She's better than that. Better than any artistic eccentricities Jean-Claude Badour flings at her as well. If only I could retrain her, turn her back into something worthy of..."

The air shifted, and they turned to find Elizabeth standing in the doorway.

Surprise and guilt crossed Grace's features. "Oh." She hesitated. "Bess. I..."

"No, it's fine," Elizabeth said. "I suppose, for someone like you, my job *is* embarrassing."

"Wait, no," Summer cut in. "You're the best part of the show. You always make more of what they give you. And, of course, it used to be so much better."

"Used to be?" Grace laughed. "Sure it was. Bess, tell her about the plot you got killed off in season four."

"No." Elizabeth folded her arms across her chest, leaning against the door frame.

"No? Well, I will. They wanted Hunt, the head of the hospital, to get drunk at work and fuck an intern in the supply closet. The boy didn't even have cheek fuzz he was so young. Hunt was old enough to be his mother. Given how lowbrow the writing is, maybe that's exactly the kink they were going for."

Elizabeth sighed. "I had it stopped. Yes, it was a disturbing abuse of power for Hunt. I wouldn't have done it."

"Jesus," Summer said. "That's terrible. No wonder you fought it."

A muscle in Elizabeth's jaw twitched. "What's done is done. And Grace, I appreciate all your career advice, but we don't always have a say in how our career unfolds, do we? We make the best of it."

Grace inclined her head. "Never forget your roots is all I'm saying. Don't let what you were fade away. I'm here to help. Always."

"Thank you. Now, I thought I heard Amrit asking for you."

With a nod, Grace headed back to the others.

"Amrit wasn't asking for her," Summer murmured.

"I know." Sighing, Elizabeth said, "Sometimes she gets a bit intense about my career. She means well, but it's hard to hear when I've disappointed her."

"You shouldn't feel bad about your choices. You're so great at what you do."

"Not like her."

"Is she always so... 'Listen up, children, here's the lesson for today'?"

"She has earned the right to give us advice. Although most of the time she's a lot less overt. Get a few drinks into her and she gets a bit..."

"Mean?"

"I was going to say direct."

"No, she's mean."

"Don't judge her, Summer. You don't know her. And she's brilliant at what she does. I owe her a lot."

The warning was clear. "Yes, you're right. Sorry. I'm sure she's lovely."

"She is. And if she was a little too..."

Belittling? Condescending?

"Edgy...with you, maybe her ego is smarting. It's not every day she loses at Shakespeare." Elizabeth's eyes brightened. "Now *that* was impressive. You certainly didn't disappoint."

"I did enjoy that," Summer grinned, thrilled at the praise. "And the..." She stuttered to a halt, realizing she was about to say "prize". There was no way she was admitting to enjoying that. "...rest of it."

Elizabeth's expression was inscrutable. "You have hidden talents."

Okay, did she mean the kiss or the trivia? No, Summer was fairly sure she wasn't talking about the kiss. This was *Elizabeth Thornton*. She glanced at the oven's clock. "I better go. I have an early start tomorrow."

"Oh?"

"Basketball practice."

"You?" Elizabeth eyed her in amazement. "Summer, I may not know you well, and I hope you're not offended by this, but I have never met someone clumsier."

"Ah, yeah." Summer laughed. "I don't mean I play. I keep the stats for Chloe's team, keep everyone hydrated, and hang out with them later. They're a great bunch. I'd introduce you except you'd get mobbed. They're huge Dr. Hunt fans."

"Good God, why?"

Summer shrugged. "Some people just love a good villain."

"Ah. So there are a few misguided souls who don't want my scalp. Anyway, thanks for coming over. Did you learn enough about me?"

Yes. Your beautiful fake boyfriend is a huge flirt, which drives Grace crazy because she's madly in love with him. Plus, I don't think Grace is a real friend, but you're too blind to see it. Oh, and PS, your kiss made my ovaries explode. They're still on life support. Thanks for that.

"Bits and pieces. It's a start," Summer said. "So I'll see you Sunday? Any time after eleven. I'll text you my parents' address."

"Thanks. I'm curious to meet Skye." Her eyes crinkled.

"Oh, I'll bet." Summer leaned over to...what? Kiss her cheek? Hug her? She ended up doing a bit of each. *Awkward.*

Elizabeth sighed. "We really have to get a lot better at this."

"Yeah," Summer said, glumly. "We do. And hopefully by Sunday."

"I love her," Brian announced when Elizabeth returned from seeing Summer out, reaching for a handful of peanuts. "She's so sweet I just want to take her home in my pocket."

"Again?" Rowan countered. "Isn't your pocket full of that other ingénue you fell in platonic bliss with last week?"

"You make me sound so fickle. But Summer's adorable. Seriously. I didn't know Hollywood made anyone like her. The sweet ones on screen are usually bitches off it. She's the real deal."

"That figures," Alex said. "Her mum's mad as hell but really sweet. I'd be shocked if she'd raised a stuck-up kid. I liked Summer too. And she certainly seems fond of our Bess," she added with a teasing tone.

All eyes swung to Elizabeth.

And <u>this</u> is why you shouldn't kiss someone for a silly dare. Not to mention kissing for her friends' amusement was just juvenile—right up Brian's alley of course, which was why he'd chosen it as a prize. Usually no one indulged him, and Elizabeth would have refused this time as well. But then Grace just had to intervene and put her and Summer in an awkward position.

Elizabeth refused to bite on Alex's innuendo. Besides, if they'd seen Summer last weekend, hungover and furious, they might not categorize the woman's feelings as particularly fond at all.

"She seems to kiss well," Zara observed dryly. "That's important if you're going to be doing a fair bit of it, wouldn't you say?"

Heat crept into Elizabeth's cheeks as memories of the kiss flooded back. She shot her friend a dark look. "I suppose."

Now Elizabeth knew exactly what kissing Summer Hayes felt like. Gone had been the eternally awkward creature who smiled at everything and acted like it'd be impolite to even cast a shadow. When she'd pulled Elizabeth down for a real kiss, Summer had been confident and assured. Elizabeth had been drawn deeper in spite of herself, and a pleasurable little buzz had fizzed along her nerve endings like an approving *mmmm*. The woman certainly knew how to kiss.

Should she revise her assumption that Summer had never kissed a woman before? It was hard to tell. The kiss hadn't seemed to faze her at all. Maybe there was hope for Elspeth and Lucille's sex life after all.

"Blushing, Bess?" Grace intoned. "Over a wandering-lipped LA girl? My, my, what *did* she do to you?"

And just like that, Elizabeth felt humiliated and ridiculous. Folding her arms, she wished, not for the first time this evening, that Grace's idea of amusing herself didn't involve humiliating her quite so often.

"Hey now," Amrit said with a gentle smile, "I have no doubt Summer's beautiful lips could make anyone blush."

Ugh, no. He'd only make things worse.

Sure enough, Grace's face turned into a sneer—an elegant one of course, because Grace's features would allow nothing less. "Amrit, you can't seriously hope to slum it with some American starlet?" Grace twirled a ring around her finger. "And what sort of name is Summer Hayes? Summer *Haze*? It has to be her dotty mother's idea of a joke. Really, darling, I thought you had taste?"

He chuckled. "Beauty is beauty. And Brian's right: She's adorable. Not to mention smart. I've never seen you outfoxed on Shakespeare before. And, um, *hello*, that girl can act!"

Everyone nodded vigorously at the reminder of Summer's impromptu performances. Well, almost everyone. Grace's expression was fixed like a statue.

Throughout the evening, Summer had joined in acting out scenes with Brian, Zara, and Rowan. Astonishingly, she knew by heart every line from the passages they'd randomly picked. It was sublime watching Alex and Grace's expressions most of all. They were snobs when it came to English plays, claiming that Americans attempting the classics grated.

Summer made them forget their biases. Her friends looked enthralled as Summer dipped into Viola's ring soliloquy from *Twelfth Night*. She'd slipped in gentle humor next to fierceness, and it was captivating. Grace even gave her the smallest nod at the end, doubtlessly unaware she'd even done it. Alex's mouth was hanging open for most of the scene.

And then, to everyone's surprise, Grace rose from her armchair and offered a "different take" on the scene. Summer returned to her seat. Grace waited a few beats, closed her eyes briefly, and then became Viola. She did the same scene for full dramatic pathos.

Shivers skittered down Elizabeth's spine as the words spun their web around her. Grace was seductive with that silky tone, caressing every ounce of emotion from the scene.

Summer wore an expression of astonishment. *Relatable.* Elizabeth still remembered the first time she'd seen Grace in full-on legendary actress mode. She could barely breathe.

When it was over, Elizabeth's mouth was dry as desert sand; her heart flying. She wanted to pound her hands bloody with applause but didn't dare give so much away.

Grace resumed her seat with a tiny smile. As though it had been nothing.

She always did that. Tore everyone's equilibrium to shreds, shattered everything actors thought they knew about the craft, and then flicked the lint off her pants.

"Well," Grace said now, giving a cynical, but still elegant, snort as she stood and snatched up her bag. "It's been an educational evening, but I must away. Bess, dear, I'll leave you to your entertaining and somewhat delusional friends." With an imperious look, she added, "Well?" when Elizabeth didn't move.

"Oh, right. Sorry." Elizabeth rose to see her out, tracing the same path she had with Summer not twenty minutes earlier. A flash of memory of them standing at the door, Summer's head tilted a little as she said goodbye, reminded her again of those soft lips.

How could someone who looked like that, so innocent, kiss so beautifully? So wickedly? So downright *deliciously*?

"Your focus is shot to hell," Grace said sharply, as she reached the front door and spun around to face Elizabeth. "It has been ever since that perky cheerleader started on your show. Have you not noticed?"

What? Her attention swung to Grace.

"Case in point," she continued. "Look, I know it's amusing having someone follow you around and hang off your every word, but don't let it distract you. Not even if Hayes can help get you that Frenchman's role you want. Head in the game, Bess." Grace tapped her temple. "Stay focused. *Always.*" After a warning look, she brushed Elizabeth's cheek with her lips, and left.

That simple motion, done so carelessly, burned as always. Elizabeth felt the familiar visceral reaction. A coil of desire, sharp and needy, swirled through her. It didn't matter how often she told her body that Grace was not hers and never would be. It didn't care. Grace was Grace. And that was all there was to it.

After she heard Grace's Jaguar start, her words filtered back into Elizabeth's brain.

I know it's amusing having someone follow you around and hang off your every word...

<u>*I know.*</u>

Distaste and dismay churned in her stomach. Was *that* how Grace saw her? Or did she just mean in general? After all, a whole nation adored Grace Christie-Oberon back home. Who was Elizabeth to Grace? That simple question had tortured her for years.

"Hey, ducky—still with us?"

Elizabeth turned to find Alex leaning against the hallway wall, giving her a quizzical look. How long had she been standing there? "Of course." Elizabeth smiled.

"Everyone's having a smoke and chat out by the pool. Come on, let me help you clean up."

"I don't think there's much left to do. Summer did most of it earlier."

"Not Grace, huh? Color me shocked."

That deserved a chuckle. "Well, she was more the entertainment value than the muscle."

"I'll bet."

They fell into a wordless routine in the kitchen, having done this many times before.

"Sooo…" Alex handed her a pair of wine glasses, "shall we talk about it?"

Elizabeth slid the stemware into the dishwasher with a sigh. It wouldn't be a party night without Alex prodding over its entrails like a pathologist.

"Talk about what?"

"Grace's OTT-ness."

Grace? Not Summer? That earned her attention. "How do you mean?"

"Way over the top for her. Possessive as hell over Amrit. Full velvet bitch mode on Summer."

"She wasn't exactly bitchy. That's just her idea of amusing herself."

"Bess, I know you can't see it, but she was being a sneaky snake tonight. All the sly games she usually reserves for you."

It was an old argument. Alex had some outlandish notion that Grace didn't treat her right. It was absurd. She could handle Grace.

"She has a different sense of humor than most people," Elizabeth said. "I think it's probably hard for her, trying to connect with people when she feels so disappointed with what's happened with her career. I think she's feeling sad."

"Hard trying to connect? What, on account of her being a god?" Alex stopped and waited until she had Elizabeth's eye. "You think I don't know? How you feel about her? Why do you think you and I broke up? It wasn't the distance, or my schedule. Bess, I felt like the other woman."

Elizabeth went rigid. "What? Grace would never…"

"No, she wouldn't. But you would, right? Given half the chance, you'd fling her perfect ass down on the bed so hard, her nose would hit the ceiling."

It wasn't fair. Elizabeth couldn't even keep this one pathetic secret to herself. "Is it written on my face?" With cheeks on fire, she demanded, "So does everyone know? Do you all laugh at me? Oh my God, is *that* why Brian chose a kiss as a prize? He assumed Grace would win like always? Was this some sick joke?"

"No, love, no! Brian was just being his usual random self. Like that time he challenged us to only say words backwards for an hour? Or do a John Cleese silly walk every time we swore? I promise I'm the only one who's figured out your feelings for her. I know you better than anyone else. Of course I notice the little things. Like… how much you enjoyed that kiss?"

"I didn't." Elizabeth glared.

"Come on," Alex said with a tut. "Don't lie to either of us. You enjoyed it. But then, regular as clockwork, Grace ruined it by embarrassing you. Again. Yes, I know she was joking. Your mentor is charming and entertaining to the whole damned world. But she's also controlling about the things she owns. Why do you think Amrit sprinted out the door after that fling with her?"

"She doesn't own me."

"Doesn't she? Okay, just for shits and giggles, next time you see her, I want you to tell her how wonderful Summer is. How amazing and fun, and you're just *loving* spending time with her, and she's the best thing ever. If I'm wrong, she'll say 'how nice', sound bored, and turn the conversation back to herself. But if I'm right, watch her shred the girl."

"You're wrong." Why couldn't Alex see this? "I matter to Grace. She's hard on me at times, but it's for my own good, to keep me focused. She wants me to succeed. She's invested a lot of time in me, so that makes sense. You know what she did for me when I got here. You know how she got me my agent. You don't do that for just anyone."

"No, you don't. It's interesting she did that, though, isn't it?" Alex's smile didn't touch her eyes. "Why did she?"

Elizabeth slid the dishwasher closed and pushed the power button. "She was looking out for me. Don't be so dismissive of her. I wouldn't be half as good as I am if not for her lessons. You saw her perform tonight. She was incredible. It's an outrage she's not a legend in LA."

"So you keep telling us." Alex sighed. "And who told you that?"

Scowling at Alex, she headed back to the living room.

"Want to know what else I think?" Alex asked as she followed.

"As if I could stop you." Elizabeth settled on the couch. Through the glass doors, she could see the boys outside, leaning over the pool fencing, smoking, chatting, and laughing with Zara.

Alex flopped at the far end of the couch, lifting her feet onto Elizabeth's lap. Old habits.

"Okay, let's hear it," Elizabeth said with a sigh.

"Grace put on that little acting tour de force to put Summer in her place because she'd impressed us. Grace was virtually saying, *Yes, American, you might have talent, but I am a legend.*"

"Grace *is* a legend."

"Agreed. And now your new friend has been fully briefed. That was the purpose of the demonstration."

It had been a little out of the blue, Elizabeth had to admit.

"Think: when was the last time Grace performed just for our amusement?" Alex asked, gaze sharp.

It had been a while. "Years?"

"Exactly. So it had to mean something, don't you think?"

"Sometimes a cigar is just a cigar."

"Uh-huh," Alex said skeptically. "Know what else I think? Summer Hayes is going to crack the world right open for you. She's a catalyst."

"Be serious. She's a twenty-eight-year-old ex-child star from LA. Her biggest claim to fame is being a teen spy. What you see is what you get. She's just...a girl."

"Who can kiss your socks off."

Elizabeth's light snort came out of nowhere, surprising her.

Alex joined in with a laugh.

"Okay, fine, yes," Elizabeth conceded. "She can kiss. But still."

"All I'm saying is, the woman doesn't even know it, but she's pushing Grace's buttons, Amrit's buttons, your buttons—or *button*, given I suspect it's a different one entirely—" she waggled her eyebrows, "and when this all starts to go thermonuclear, the sexy Badour film, Grace's passive-aggressive games, your batshit crazy TV show, all of it, it'll be fun as hell to see who and what's left standing."

"You have a vivid imagination."

"Wait and see," Alex pointed at her. "Once the dust settles, you'll be happier for it."

"You think my world will blow apart and that will make me happy?"

"Yes." Beaming widely, Alex nudged her. "Sometimes ya just gotta blow shit up in order to rebuild it better than ever."

"How violent," Elizabeth drawled. "And you, a tree-hugging, film-making pacifist."

"It's a metaphor, love. Mark my words. Summer Hayes is the beginning of the end of the beginning. And me? Hell, I'm booking a front-row seat."

Chapter 11

"I can't believe I'm going along with this," Autumn grumbled, as she and Summer carried out spare chairs to the pool area. "Faking a relationship is bad enough. Trying to con our parents is insane." She arranged the canvas pair she was hauling into a line.

"Keep your voice down," Summer hissed. "Mom's just in the kitchen."

Autumn dropped into one of the chairs. "God, just when I thought you were over your old fixation on her…now *this*? You have to play her lover? I want to throttle Jean-Claude."

Summer sat beside her and glanced at the sea-shell clock on the wall. Almost eleven. Her pulse sped up at the thought of Elizabeth being here soon, in her childhood home. That felt so weird. "Jean-Claude thinks I'll be perfect."

"Only because you've convinced him she's your lover. He told me he wanted a couple with *the fierce fire*. And let's face it, sex scenes, especially lesbian ones, can be boring as hell if the chemistry's off or the actresses are uncomfortable. So I get it. But are you seriously thinking you can pull this off?"

"You're asking me whether *I* can look like I'm into Elizabeth Thornton?"

Autumn closed her eyes for a moment. "*I mean*, how are you going to cope emotionally with this? How are you going to separate yourself from the role?"

This again? First Delvine, now her own sister? "I'm a professional," Summer said tersely, "and that's what actors do."

"I know you are. But are you over her? At least tell me that."

"Of course." Summer folded her arms and glared.

"I want to believe you."

"Then do."

"It's fucked up, you know. This whole thing."

"It's Mom's fault. She whispered her crazy fantasies into Jean-Claude's ear. Now there's no walking it back."

"I know." Autumn sighed. "God. Just… Summer, don't get hurt. I know you. Please be careful with that big heart of yours."

"I will." Of course she'd be careful. Careful wasn't the problem. It was the rest of it. On the one hand, Elizabeth had been selfish and rude, cutting her off without a second thought. On the other hand, she'd also apologized and sounded like she meant it. And she'd opened up her home. That meant something, right? She didn't have to invite Summer into her private sanctuary. Summer's fingers played with the fraying edges of her cut-off denim shorts. "It's good you'll get to meet her manager today. What'd you want to discuss with Delvine, anyway?"

"It's not about me, it's about her." Autumn's jaw tightened. "In all our interactions, she treats me like some slow learner who doesn't know a damned thing about talent management. As though I spend all day signing autographed photos of you and working out cheesy mall-opening appearances. She thinks I don't understand strategy. If you and Thornton are going to be working closely together, I need her to respect me. I also want to know what her plans are for after *Eight Little Pieces*. The publicity approach and so on."

"I'm sure you'll figure it out. I like Delvine. She's a straight shooter. She's also really smart." Summer hesitated. "Um, she also figured out I was gay from next to no clues. I swear she has like crazy mind-reading powers or something."

Autumn winced. "Damn. I'd tell you to be more careful but you always are."

"Yeah." Summer bit her thumbnail. "I'm getting tired of creeping around though. It feels like by hiding, I'm saying being gay's bad or something. What year is it?" At her sister's widening eyes, Summer added quickly, "Although, I get it. Not right now. Not while I still need the girl-next-door roles. And being hit with the fallout from those photos cured me of wanting to come out too soon. The crap people were saying. That it was a publicity stunt? I'm a fame whore? A gold digger? And it was absolutely revolting what they said about Bess."

"People do love to live down to my expectations," Autumn agreed. "Maybe that's why I'm always single." She looked over at a new arrival and Summer followed her gaze.

"Ah, she's here." Summer watched Delvine air kiss a handful of guests their mother introduced her to. "And you're single because deep down no one will ever be as good as Andrew. Sorry he got that job in London. I really liked him."

"Yeah." Autumn's jaw tightened again. "Me too."

They watched as their mother led the manager around the pool area, Delvine's clinking bangles punctuating Skye's running commentary.

"They seem to be getting on okay," Autumn observed. "Huh. Delvine doesn't look as if we're all beneath her, which was how I'd imagined her."

"Autumn," Summer said quietly, "promise me you'll be extra sweet to her and Elizabeth?"

"I'm always sweet."

"No, you're always *right*. Big difference. You're sort of polite, but it's not always nice-polite. Sometimes you say things like, 'Well, to be accurate...' or 'No, actually, that's incorrect...'. I know people underestimate you, and I get it—you like to show that you know your stuff. But please? Be good? For me?"

Autumn regarded her for a moment. "Hell," she muttered. "Fine. I'll put on my charming face."

Beaming, Summer squeezed her hand. "Thanks."

"But don't think I don't know what your request means." Her warning look made Summer's heart sink.

"I have no idea what you're talking about."

"Yes you do." Autumn squinted at her. "I am praying to whatever deity is listening that this film cures you for good. That working up close and personal with Thornton will get her out of your system once and for all."

"I'm sure it will." Summer said more firmly than she felt. "Absolutely."

Autumn sighed. "Shit. I knew it. You didn't even deny it this time." She put her head in her hands and snorted. "God help us all if you ever turn Thornton's pretty head too."

"You're safe. The only people she finds worth noticing are British acting legends called Grace."

145

Elizabeth checked the address after she pulled up in front of the Hayes family home in Granada Hills. It was on a street lined with towering white oak trees, quite beautiful for suburban LA. But that's not what caught her eye. Summer had left something out when she'd texted her the address. You'd think it might be worth mentioning.

Skye and Brock lived in an obscenely yellow house that was a little hard to miss. It came with a cream, peaked roof, a gas lamp post, and a...she did a double-take...bronze wishing well out front.

Exiting her car, she clicked her remote and pivoted to walk up the garden path to the door.

"Ms. Thornton?"

She turned to find an older, brunette version of Summer standing on the curb, holding a lightweight blue sweater.

"I'm Autumn. Summer's sister and manager." Her smile lacked Summer's warmth. "I just had to get something from my car and I saw you." With a heft of her sweater, she shrugged. "I thought I should say hi."

"Of course. Hello." Elizabeth waited for Autumn to join her. As the woman neared, she could make out more than a few differences. A rounder, fuller face, a lop-sided, smirking mouth that seemed more cynical, and a smattering of freckles. It hadn't occurred to Elizabeth how symmetrically perfect Summer's face was until she saw someone, well...normal, with similar attributes. "Is Delvine here yet?"

"Yes. Mom and her seem to be bonding over a hatred of pastels."

"That sounds like Delvine. I've yet to see her wear anything from a neutral palette."

Autumn tilted her head, regarding Elizabeth silently.

"What is it?" Elizabeth asked as they walked toward the house.

"It's just, I'm having a hard time picturing it. My sister and you in *Eight Little Pieces*." She groaned. "And by picturing it, I mean the *concept*. In general. You know. Not the rest."

Elizabeth gave her a curious look. There was some sort of tension here, but she couldn't place it. "Are you opposed to her playing Lucille? Summer seems keen to stretch herself."

"She usually does such sweet roles." Autumn gave a pained sigh. "Truthfully, yes, I wish she wasn't actually stretching herself in *that* way."

"You have an issue with her playing a lesbian? Or is it that you have an issue with homosexuality in general?" Her voice came out far chillier than she'd intended. It wasn't really a fair question. Much of Hollywood still held Rachel Cho's view that playing gay made an actor less marketable in the eyes of the public. It was accepted as fact, even though no one had any proof. Rachel couldn't be shifted on her stance even the smallest bit—and Rachel *was* gay. Autumn's expression held the same pinched look as Rachel's did on the topic.

"Of course I'm not homophobic!" Autumn glared. "How could you even ask? That'd be pretty hypocritical, all things considered."

All things? Wait, was Autumn gay? Elizabeth sneaked a glimpse at her. Maybe her gaydar was faulty because she couldn't see it. Not that that meant anything. Hollywood was about as straight as ramen noodles. "Sorry," she said. "So your issue is your squeaky-clean sister having her image shattered by a lesbian role?"

"No, it's my squeaky-clean sister playing *lust*. You have no idea how controversial that is for her. Sexy roles in American cinema? Go for it. Beloved child icons in sexy roles? Not so much."

She led Elizabeth around the left side of the house, past a garden bed bursting with vines that were heavy with scarlet flowers and thorns, then into a side door.

Inside was airy and bright, an indigo-painted living room dotted with unexpected knick-knacks, from feathered masks to intricate, embellished candlesticks. The centerpiece was a six-foot-wide set of white angel wings stuck on one wall.

"Don't they catch fire?" Elizabeth pointed below the wings to the ornate fireplace embedded with thousands of colorful glass pieces.

"Mom doesn't use the fireplace. She built it just for the look of it."

They headed into the kitchen next, which looked out over the pool area. The room was a generous size, filled with modern appliances—probably every cook's dream. Except...it was a retina-searing teal blue.

"I know, I know," Autumn said, with that ever-present smirk. "Mom loves eye-catching things, be it colors or people or ideas. Which explains you and Summer. She's totally convinced you're a thing. I can't think of any couple less convincing, personally. But she's sold."

"Why not us?"

"Come on! You're you. And she's…um…the opposite."

Elizabeth wondered at the way she parsed her words. "Please don't censor yourself on my account. Just say what's on your mind."

"You may be sorry you said that." Autumn gave her a rueful grin. "But, okay. Look, you're all tightly buttoned up and measured, and Summer's as laid-back as a pair of flip-flops. If you want to pull this off, you have to look like you know how to chill or people will wonder how Summer and you ever get along."

Elizabeth's nostrils flared. *Lovely.* Yet another stranger making assumptions about her based on nothing. Story of her life. "You know, I'm not Chief Hunt."

"Well, obviously not, or Summer wouldn't like you one bit. I'm talking about your rep. Anyway, at least the faking-it job's half done here. Mom's a true believer. She looks at what she decides *feels* right, not what is. Don't ask her about auras, ever, or you'll be stuck here for a week. Dad's a different thing entirely."

"Should I be concerned about him?"

"Always." Autumn folded her arms and stared out the window at the pool. "It's like this: Summer is Daddy's little girl. She can do no wrong. And if you hurt her, you won't soon forget it."

What did that mean? Elizabeth frowned. "This is a business deal. What hurt am I supposed to be inflicting here?"

Autumn gave her a guarded look. "Don't forget that Dad doesn't know that. And he has this terrifying look that goes with his 'treat Summer right or else' speech." She flung open the kitchen door. "Everyone's outside. Right this way."

They stepped out into a bright pool area. Surprisingly, given Summer had indicated pool parties were this family's thing, the pool itself was quite small. However, the surrounding area made up for it, with a barbecue, a ceiling-mounted speaker system, and outdoor sofas drowning in colorful, tasseled cushions—all gathered under a rustic wooden pergola.

It made sense, Elizabeth decided. Pool parties were usually about the party more than getting wet. Who cared about the pool size?

Speaking of getting wet, a barrel-chested man was breast-stroking his way through the water, his bright red trunks flashing in his shimmering wake.

"That's Dad," Autumn said. "So, golden rule, don't piss him off, okay? And please try and look like you don't think Summer's a special kind of stupid? It'll do wonders in selling your story."

"I don't think that." Elizabeth shot her a baffled look.

"Sure you do. I heard all about the exploding blood pack thing and how mad you were. You know, that could have happened to anyone." Her expression was considering. "So, Ms. Thornton—"

"Elizabeth."

"—I'm going to introduce myself to your manager and work out our strategies, and you…" she glanced over her shoulder at a blond blur, closing fast, "have a showy list of PDAs to get through and make my eyeballs bleed."

"Bess!" Summer came flying at her from one side, a wide grin on her face. "Thanks for coming!" Dropping a quick kiss on Elizabeth's lips, she flung her arms around her in a loose hug.

Autumn snorted. Her eyebrows hiked up as if to say *see?* before she spun on her heel, leaving them to their "showy PDAs".

Elizabeth couldn't quite work out whether she liked Autumn or not. She was shrewd and sharp, but sort of charming in her own smirk-filled way.

"What's your poison?" Summer asked.

"My…?"

Summer waved at an ice-filled tub under the pergola bursting with beer, wine, and soft drinks. "There are lots of cold options. I also brought around your tea if you'd like me to make some."

"Tea always improves my mood. Perhaps we should start there." Elizabeth's smile was softer than usual for the benefit of the half a dozen gazes roaming over them. It had nothing to do with the way Summer was almost vibrating with excitement. Or how nice it felt having her arm slung around Elizabeth's waist like it had always belonged there.

"Tea it is! Be right back." Summer disappeared into the house.

Elizabeth watched her go, and only then registered the tiny cut-off denim shorts and generously filled out white bikini top. Hmm. Summer's hospital scrubs didn't do her justice. Throw in the toned legs and California tan, and Summer was, by any definition, gorgeous.

How hadn't she noticed before? A curl of desire slithered through her, and Elizabeth almost choked in surprise. She turned quickly to get that shapely ass out of her line of sight and found herself in someone else's.

Watching her was a small, attractive woman in her late fifties, weighed down by an enormous floppy purple hat, upon which was affixed plastic flowers. It should look ridiculous, but somehow she pulled it off. Tendrils of wild gray-blond hair curled out from under it.

Well. If this wasn't the infamous Skye Storm, Elizabeth would eat her own wide-brimmed straw hat. Summer's mother made her way over with a grace her daughter lacked.

Funny how genetics worked.

Skye pulled her green caftan wrap around an apricot-colored swimsuit. When she peered up at Elizabeth—she couldn't have been much more than five feet, despite the heels on her tan sandals—her eyes crinkled with delight.

"Well, hello, my dear. You must be the Bess that has my daughter in raptures. I'm Skye." She craned her neck. "Goodness. You're way taller than I thought."

Skye's warmth was infectious, and Elizabeth couldn't help her own lazy smile in return. "And you're pretty much what I expected." She was, too. Charismatic, beautiful, and colorful.

"Ha! So tell me, what did you imagine? Two heads? Flowers in my hair? Oh! I suppose I've almost done that." She tapped the gargantuan plastic constructs darting out of her hat, lowering her voice to conspiratorial when she added, "I have heard I'm *eclectic*."

"I think it's eccentric. So far that's all I've been told about you."

"Eccentric? Hmm. I like that. Who wants to be ordinary? How boring! Right? You don't look boring at all."

"I like to *think* I'm not boring," Elizabeth replied, a smile edging her lips. "But doesn't everyone?"

"True. So tell me, when did you know you liked Summer?" Her blue eyes, so much like Summer's, were bright and keen.

"She brought me tea." Okay, that didn't sound like the most romantic thing. Elizabeth dug around for something better. "You have to understand

I'd crawl over broken glass for my brand of tea, which isn't available here, and somehow Summer magicked it up out of thin air. It was like discovering a piece of home. I was impressed. That's when I first noticed her."

Soft, thin fingers latched onto her wrist, and Skye drew Elizabeth close, staring into her eyes. "I think I should tell you that I've known about you for years," she said softly. "I will always keep your secret. I did then; I told no one." She waved her hand around the pool area. "We all know to be discreet, you mustn't worry. It's quite all right. You're safe here."

"What?" The hairs on the back of Elizabeth's neck stood up.

"Your ex-girlfriend, Alex Levitin? I did the costumes on *Heaven's Blood*."

Panic flooded her at the thought that Alex—*Alex of all people*—had been indiscreet. How many others had she gossiped with?

"Oh, she didn't tell me," Skye said, divining her anxiety. "I worked it out. She left a book on her seat one day and I was curious about what she was reading and picked it up. A photo of the two of you was her bookmark and it fell out. I saw the look in her eyes in that picture, the way she was touching your cheek, and I knew. So when this rumor happened with my daughter? Well, I realized it wasn't as outlandish as Summer kept claiming. Besides, she was protesting far too much." She smiled, warmth and acceptance filling her face.

Exhaling slowly, Elizabeth nodded. Okay, she wouldn't kill Alex.

"I don't say any of this to embarrass you," Skye added. "I just want you to understand that I'm well aware how hard it is to pretend to be someone you're not. And to do it for years can be exhausting. I have seen the harm it does when people take it too far." Skye's expression became intense. "You know, there's a famous gay actor, I won't name names, but he used to bring his lover into the studio in the trunk of his car, then smuggle him into his dressing room. The lover left him over it eventually. I don't want my girl to be treated like someone's dirty little secret. She's too sweet for that. You will not put Summer in the trunk in any sense. Treat her well. With respect. Do we understand each other?" The fingers on her wrist tightened.

"Of course." Elizabeth swallowed. "I won't disrespect her."

"Good. She's special. I know every mother thinks that, but it's true for her. She doesn't have a cynical bone in her body. Her heart is enormous. She means well in all things. She hates cruelty to others more than anything. So, you understand, I just want her appreciated."

"I do. She has a good heart." It was true. Summer did seem just as her mother described. She'd never heard Summer run anyone down, and the only anger she'd ever witnessed had come when Elizabeth had hurt her…and, mystifyingly, also when Grace had tried to tell that traumatic Footlights story. She winced and pushed the memory away. "You should be proud of the woman she is."

"Me?" Skye gave her an odd look. "What have I got to do with anything? Goodness me, parents create the child, but they're their own person pretty young. I don't take credit for who my daughters are. Neither does Brock." She waved to the man in the pool. "Credit where it's due. She's Summer because she's Summer, not because we're her parents. That's all there is to it."

Splash.

Elizabeth glanced over to see Summer's dad hefting himself over the pool's edge without the ladder. His muscled arms bulged, but he seemed to do it easily. Once he was standing, she could see an angry scar running down his chest, almost to his waist.

"A stunt gone wrong." Skye followed her gaze. "A window was supposed to shatter into a thousand pieces. Instead it broke off into three, and one jagged piece snagged him square. He almost died it was so close to the heart."

Elizabeth gasped. "That's terrible."

Brock ambled over, gave Skye a peck on the cheek, and slung his towel over one shoulder. "It wasn't that bad." His voice was a low drawl. "And I have a high threshold for pain."

He sized Elizabeth up with a thousand-yard stare. "So, you're dating my little girl now?" His pale blue eyes grew harder.

"I am." She met his gaze evenly. It had been years since she'd had to do a meet-the-parents thing. It didn't get any easier, even if it was just for show.

"So, how old are you anyway?"

"Brock!" Skye slapped his chest. "She's about the same age you were when you asked me out."

"We're both old enough," Elizabeth said genially.

Brock gave a gruff bark. "All right, all right," he said. "Fair enough. Okay, so I'll give you the abbreviated speech. Don't hurt my girl. She's the apple of my eye. Precious to me. Got it?"

"Got it."

"Good." He ran the towel through his shaggy, graying hair then turned to Skye. "I suppose it could be worse. Remember that moody musician Summer brought around last year? Thank Christ that didn't last."

"No talking about exes," Skye told him firmly. "It's rude."

Actually, Elizabeth would have dearly loved to talk about exes. For some reason, she was having a hard time picturing what kind of man Summer would find appealing. So far all she knew was that Amrit wasn't her type. "If you want to talk about the men she dated before, I don't care."

Brock stared at her. Squinted. Then tossed a baffled look at Skye before turning back to Elizabeth. "Y'know, I'm guessing you two haven't done a whole lot of real talking yet, have you?"

"Why do you say that?" A sliver of anxiety shot through her. What had she said wrong?

"You don't know my girl that well, do you?" His brow furrowed, which, on Brock, looked like she'd pissed off Wolverine. "I think maybe you should talk to her about something more substantial than whatever you've been doing. Okay, I'm gonna get dried off and changed. Back soon." He shot Elizabeth a warning look and left.

"Don't mind him," Skye said. "He's protective of Summer. He'd like her to date someone who sees how smart she is, not just how pretty. So that means getting to know her, not just having fun with her."

"Oh, she's smart. We had a Shakespeare trivia night on Friday. You should have seen my friends. Theatrically trained, Cambridge drama school grads, and Summer wiped the floor with all of them. It was remarkable."

Skye beamed. "That's Summer for you. She always did love her Shakespeare. I presume you know that's all your fault? Seeing you in London when she was fifteen. She got into acting and Shakespeare because of you."

"I understand I inspired her a bit…"

"Inspired? Oh yes, that too. Oh, how she adored you. She wouldn't stop talking about you for three years. Got so bad her sister put a ban on your name being mentioned in her presence." Skye cackled.

Adored? That was a strong word. Still, she remembered how it had felt when Grace arrived in Cambridge for a semester as a guest speaker. Elizabeth had been drawn to her instantly. Talent was a powerful lure. She could hardly judge Summer for having the same reaction she'd had herself.

The difference was that Summer clearly no longer felt that way about her. And while Elizabeth wasn't sure what she felt for Grace now, it was still intense.

That familiar scent of the gods tickled her nose. Summer appeared at her side, pecked Elizabeth's cheek, and passed her a cup of tea.

"Thanks, darling," Elizabeth murmured.

With a nod, Summer slid her arm back around Elizabeth's waist. "So, how are you two getting along?"

Skye nodded. "Fabulously. I'm filling her in on how long your adoration for her goes back. And she's looking all shocked."

Summer's arm stiffened behind Elizabeth's back. "*Mom*—"

"Do you two really not talk at all? About anything important?" Skye interrupted, sounding exasperated. "What *do* you do together anyway? Please tell me it's more than just sex."

With a low groan, Summer rubbed her temple. "Must you?"

"Don't get so prudish on me now. I didn't raise you that way. Where's my free-spirited daughter, hmm?" She glanced at Elizabeth. "Listen to her. You'd think I didn't see her at Jean-Claude's after-party at the hotel pool running around with everyone stark naked. Well, it was the night for it."

Stark naked?

"Of course you saw that, Mom." Summer glared at her. "Because the whole crew got drunk and went skinny dipping. You included."

What? The? Hell?

"Precisely my point. You never used to be uptight. *Now* you get squeamish?" She turned back to Elizabeth. "I just don't understand young people these days. At least tell me my girl is not some prude in bed?"

"Um." Elizabeth wondered what parallel universe she'd stepped into. Her own mother would sooner die than ask such a question. Her father would definitely prefer to die than hear it.

"Mom!" Summer squeaked.

"What? I'm just asking. Not for specifics." She rolled her eyes. "A 'yes' or 'no' will do fine."

"Well, quit it. That's our private business."

"Hmm. All right then. My point is, and it's the same as your father was getting at, a good relationship is founded on more than rumpled sheets and swinging from the chandeliers. Get to know each other. *Properly*. Be each other's best friend. Talk. All right, my darlings?"

"So, ah," Elizabeth began, her brain now fritzing. "Can I ask something... in the interests of clarity?"

Summer looked pained.

"Why did everyone get naked again?"

Chapter 12

SUMMER STRETCHED OUT ON A deck chair in her white bikini, having shed her shorts, watching her parents in the pool with a few family friends she'd known for years. Discreet friends, of course, or this fake relationship would be all over HGZ in no time.

In the deck chair on her left, Delvine was murmuring to Autumn, who was perched in a canvas chair beside her, head bent, listening intently. At least her sister wasn't being a smart ass or combative, which was progress. Summer picked up occasional key words. Market share. Targeted demographics. *Yawn.*

"This seems to be going well," Elizabeth murmured.

Summer rolled to her other side. Elizabeth had changed into a stunning royal blue one-piece, with a white, long-sleeved shirt to protect her arms. Her smooth, long legs gleamed from sunscreen. In the face of all that skin, Summer could only say, "Yeah." Glancing back at the pool, she added, "My parents aren't really the issue though."

"Who is?" Elizabeth sipped the fruity yellow drink she was holding. Combined with her killer sunglasses—large and fashionable, with white frames—and a designer wide-brimmed hat, she looked like she'd just strolled onto the Lido deck of a cruise liner. "This is an excellent punch, by the way."

"Autumn made it. She did a cocktail-making course once, so it should be good. And Chloe is our potential Death Star."

"Death Star?"

That made Summer sit up. "Tell me you did not just admit to ignorance of *Star Wars*?"

Elizabeth slid her sunglasses an inch down her nose. "I was joking." She smiled. "Are you a nerd, then, *darling*? Is the Force strong in you?"

Every damned time Elizabeth said that word, even with that faintly mocking tone, it gave Summer's heart a delighted little quiver. Not just her heart, either. Fake-dating Elizabeth was ruining her ability to relax.

The side gate opened, sparing Summer from having to think of some witty comeback. "Here comes Sith Lord Chloe Martin, right now."

"Chloe's the roommate, correct?" Elizabeth asked, sliding her sunglasses back up. "What does she know about any of this?"

"I didn't have a chance to tell her we were supposedly dating. I left a note about the pool party on the fridge. Last time we talked, she thinks I'm interested in you but I've been strenuously denying it."

Elizabeth frowned. Then frowned some more. "Why would she think that?"

Oh hell! Summer's brain caught up to her words. *Shit!*

"Because of the photos?" Elizabeth asked.

Oh thank God. "Yes, exactly."

"But, still, it's a big leap. She suddenly thinks her straight roommate is gay? For me? Because of a few photos? What am I missing?"

That I'm not straight? Doubt streaked through her. Summer had been debating this for a while now. To tell Elizabeth or not to tell. Would outing herself make this uncomfortable? And what of the sex scene? Did straight actresses want to know if they're kissing a woman who's into women? Is that a fear they have? Or is it all just business? Wasn't it all business when it was a straight sex scene, too, though? Why did anyone have to know anything? Still, the doubts tumbled through her.

Chloe sauntered over, looking her usual magazine-shoot-perfect self. She sat on the edge of Summer's deck chair, near her ankles, and reached into her bag.

"Hey. Sorry I wasn't here earlier. An appointment ran late." She slid a glance between them. "Well, this is a surprise, eh? Look at you two." Her eyebrows lifted.

"Chloe, meet Elizabeth…uh, Bess. Bess, this is Chloe."

"*Bess* now is it?" Chloe regarded Summer as she began to slather her arms in the lotion she'd pulled out. "So were the rumors true all along?"

"Yes," Elizabeth said, voice dry. "I have been bullying Summer for her green-fingered abnormality. And what's more, I *like* it."

"Ha!" Chloe laughed. "Yeah, that was a corker, that one."

"You're a New Zealander? Which island?"

"North. Wanganui."

"Really? I've been there. It has the most beautiful lake I've ever seen."

Chloe beamed at her. "You know Lake Virginia? I cycled all around it, every chance I could, after school. I think half my childhood photos are mapping my height next to the Peter Pan statue."

"I saw him, too. When I was eighteen I hiked all over New Zealand for my gap year. It's gorgeous."

"Awesome." Chloe grinned.

"Yes. I saw Australia, too. But New Zealand suited my genetics a little better." She waved at her pale skin. "I react badly to sunlight."

"Ooh, a vampire, eh?"

"Something like that." Elizabeth looked amused.

"And now you've latched your teeth onto Summer?" Her eyebrows gave a suggestive wiggle.

"Ugh," Summer groaned. "No. That's the worst joke."

"So it's not true about you two?" Chloe sagged.

"Oh, it is," Elizabeth said. "But we're keeping it quiet, okay?"

"Oh!" Chloe darted a look around the pool area. "Does Skye know? Is she planning a party in your honor?"

"Probably." Summer snickered. "I'm sure it's on the drawing board."

"Hey Smiley, shove over." Chloe elbowed her. "Room for two on these things."

Summer slid to one side and Chloe made herself at home beside her on the wide deck chair.

"Okay," Chloe said earnestly. "I want dibs on being a bridesmaid."

"Good one," Summer said. "You hate weddings."

"Yeah straight ones. Lesbian ones are choice. So many extra wardrobe options. You should see me rock a tux. So Dietrich."

"How many lesbian weddings have you been to?" Elizabeth asked curiously.

"Plenty around this town." Chloe crossed her legs at the ankles and straightened her mid-thigh shorts. "Models are so queer in LA. It's all about the 'body beautiful' and exploring your options. Sexual fluidity and all that. There's way fewer barriers in modelling than elsewhere, if you're into that, which I'm not. But, hey, more power to those who are. Since I jumped over into acting, I can see there's a huge difference."

"There is?" Elizabeth asked, looking fascinated.

"Of course. It's the fantasy aspect. Acting's about selling the idea you might be available to the audience as someone they could potentially hook up with. Models don't have that baggage. We're just coat hangers. People don't even see *us* at all. Actors are super visible but."

"But what?" Elizabeth asked curiously.

Chloe frowned. "Huh?" Then shook her head. "So wedding jokes aside, are you two serious or is this just a bit of fun?"

"Serious," Summer said.

"Fun." Elizabeth said at the same time.

They eyed each other sheepishly. *Damn it.*

"Uh-oh." Chloe winced. "Shit. You two should probably talk."

"Yeah. We've been hearing that a lot," Summer grumbled.

"You know, you are an unusual pair." Chloe squinted at them. "I mean, Elizabeth, didn't you go all nuclear winter on Summer? Ghost her and shit?"

"I..." Elizabeth hesitated. "Yes, I did." She sighed. "I regret it."

"Why did you then?"

"I received some bad advice, which I took without thinking about the consequences."

"Hmm." Chloe's brows knitted together. "SSS, huh?"

"What?"

"Self-absorbed Star Syndrome. Your people made you do it." She lifted an eyebrow. "Right?"

The edge and disappointment lacing Chloe's tone came as a shock. How much must Summer's emotional state have been leaking for Chloe to be so fierce in defending her? "Chloe, it's fine; it's in the past," she broke in. "And Bess did apologize."

"No, she's right." Elizabeth sat up and slid her glasses off. "I exercised bad judgment. It was self-serving, self-absorbed, and an awful thing to do to someone. I often wished I could turn back time. I missed Summer a great deal."

"You missed her," Chloe said. "Which bothered *you*. But do you get how much you hurt Summer? That it wasn't your feelings that mattered here?"

"Chloe." Summer felt her cheeks flame in embarrassment.

Elizabeth pressed her lips together. "Yes. I know. And I don't plan on repeating that mistake. In future, I will weigh up any suggestions first before blindly following recommendations."

"Okay." Chloe's grin returned. "Oh, and last question. Very important one. Are you prepared to stand by Summer despite her awful affliction?"

"Her what?" Elizabeth turned to Summer, who lifted her hands in bafflement.

"Her two left feet. It's a miracle Smiley can walk *and* talk. I've seen her trip over a light breeze."

"Ah. Yes. It's a sacrifice I'm willing to make," Elizabeth replied.

"Hey, I'm right here!" Summer protested.

"Yes, you are." Elizabeth reached for her hand, eyes warm and soft.

Swallowing, Summer gave her a not-entirely-fake fond look as their fingers entwined.

"Ugh." Chloe rolled her eyes. "All right, you pass, Thornton. Just ax the mush. You're driving me to drink." Her eyes brightened. "Actually that's a great idea. I'll get some booze and get this party kicking on. You two right for a top-up?"

"I'm good." Summer pointed at her Diet Coke.

Elizabeth tilted her nearly full punch at Chloe in answer.

"Choice. And when I get back I'll be dishing the dirt on embarrassing Summer stories. Watch this space."

"Can't wait," Elizabeth purred.

"You'd better not," Summer warned, "or I'll hold your worldly goods hostage."

"But it's good to know all I can about you, darling." Elizabeth looked at her pointedly.

Damn it. She had a point. "Fine," Summer ground out. As Chloe headed for the drinks area, Summer called out: "But I'm gonna track down the Men in Black, and insist they mind-wipe you both afterwards."

"Seems fair," Elizabeth said. "Besides, how bad could the dirt actually be?"

Summer didn't answer. She was too busy registering the fact Elizabeth hadn't let go of her hand. And how much she liked it.

———————◆◇◆————————

Chloe was still dishing dirt to Elizabeth an hour later, despite Summer intervening often to make sure she didn't stray into territory involving Summer's exes or anything too revealing or even slightly gay. Now that her roomie had moved on to discussing the thrill of hot mud geysers around Rotorua, Summer decided it was safe enough to leave them and head for the drinks tub. A squat, wide shadow fell over her as she yanked the Diet Coke bottle out of the ice. Floral perfume hit her nostrils.

"Thanks for inviting me," Delvine said. "It's been valuable. I'm impressed with your sister. I can't say that's a common reaction after dealing with relatives managing family members. Most are terrible at it." She shuddered. "Business should be all business."

"Well, we sorted out most of our sibling issues really young," Summer said. "Now we're pretty good at separating business from family."

"I suppose that's why it works. She is dedicated to you to a fault, by the way. My God, *loyalty*. Such a rare thing in LA. It's almost shocking. People are usually out for something. Not you two, though. Maybe because you're sisters?"

"Oh, I don't know. What about Elizabeth's friend, Grace Christie-Oberon?"

Delvine stiffened. "What about her?"

Was her tone suddenly ten degrees cooler? "Don't you manage Grace?"

"Not anymore."

"So you did, once?"

"Yes, when she first came to LA. She was considered quite the prize."

Okay, there was definitely something off about the tone. "Why don't you do it now?"

"That's confidential. But it was a mutual parting of the ways."

"Didn't you take on Elizabeth at Grace's request?"

"No. It's true Grace introduced Bess to me at a party. But even if she hadn't, I'd have noticed her. I keep an eye out for new talent. Her CV carried its own weight. It's not just me who thought that. Same goes for

Rachel. We're good friends, even if she drives me crazy at times. And I know for a fact that she was impressed as hell by Bess's talent."

Whoa. What? "So, wait, Rachel *didn't* sign Elizabeth only because it was a condition of getting Grace as a client?"

"Of course not." Delvine frowned. "Where'd you get that idea?"

Summer gave her a long look.

"Ah. I see." Delvine's lips flattened into a thin line. "Well, consider who we're talking about here. It's *Rachel Cho*. She has a reputation for excellence. Can you imagine what a shortcut to mediocrity it would be if she allowed friends of the famous on her books? Yes, Grace mentioned Bess to her as someone to consider. Rachel said no, she didn't work like that. But when Rachel was in London a little while later, she happened to catch a play Bess was doing. It obviously made an impression, because when Rachel returned home, she told Grace that if Bess ever came to Hollywood, she'd be happy to sign her."

"That's quite a different story from what I've heard. Bess thinks Grace is the sole reason Rachel Cho represents her."

"She has been misinformed."

"Delvine..." Summer hesitated. "I don't know what to do with this information. Grace is Bess's mentor. Bess respects her. Actually, she thinks Grace is the queen of perfection."

"Do nothing. Don't kick over anthills, Summer. We all find out the truth in our own time. It's hard, but unless we're ready to hear it, it's useless. Closed ears never listen."

"But Bess doesn't think *any* of her success is her own doing. Don't you think she deserves to know?"

"Of course." Delvine regarded her. "But, darling, you seem to think she doesn't suspect the truth already."

"What?"

"Elizabeth's smart. Very smart. She may come to that conclusion when she's ready on her own. And if not, well, secrets and lies have a way of coming out."

"Oh." It didn't seem right, though.

"I know it's hard. I know you care. But try. Back off for now. You have more than enough on your plate now without telling someone their hero is a controlling narcissist."

Holy...

"Shit." Delvine muttered. "Can we just pretend I never said that? It was very unprofessional. I normally don't slip like that."

Summer nodded. "If it helps, I don't like her much. Grace deliberately hurts people."

Delvine smiled. "I knew I liked you for a reason." She glanced over at the deck chairs, where Elizabeth was listening to Chloe holding forth with a story that involved a lot of arm waving. "So tell me, darling, how goes the grand romance?"

With a shrug, Summer popped some ice cubes into the bottom of a glass and topped up her drink. "It goes. Elizabeth's somehow survived Mom being her usual random self. And as for me, well, I don't think she'll ever entirely see me as a friend. I mean, I've met her friends. Sophisticated doesn't even touch the sides of how different they are from me." She sagged at the thought. "But I think she's been doing a great job of tolerating me so far."

"Ah," Delvine offered a mysterious smile and poured herself a wine. "You may be surprised. And as for your parents? I love Skye to bits."

"You do?"

"Oh yes. I wish your mom did interior decorating. I love what she's done with the place."

Four hours ago, it had been stressful even thinking about Elizabeth meeting her family, Summer mused as they stood ready to part ways at the front door.

Elizabeth curled an arm around her waist, as though expecting to be burst in on any second. Good plan. The Hayes clan did a lot of that.

"Thanks for inviting me," Elizabeth said. "I learned a lot from Chloe."

"I'll bet." Summer gave her a dark look, earning a throaty laugh that caused a tingle to shoot all the way down her spine.

Footsteps approached, and Summer wasn't sure who moved first but suddenly they were kissing. It was meant as a showy farewell kiss, but all Summer could feel was Elizabeth's questing lips.

"Give it a rest, you two," a bored voice drawled. "It's only me."

They broke up and were met with Autumn's inscrutable look.

"Should probably save it for the screen, hmm? I don't think the burbs deserve such an Oscar-worthy performance."

"Is that your way of saying we were believable?" Summer joked.

"I guess." Autumn juggled her car keys and sweater. "I'm heading off. I'll call you later, Summer. Ms. Thornton, nice meeting you. And thanks for connecting me with Delvine. She's terrific."

"She is." Elizabeth nodded. "Goodbye, Autumn."

"Seeya," Summer said.

They watched her go.

"Well, I should get home too," Elizabeth said. "I have some lines to learn. Hunt has more wicked schemes to enact."

"Uh-oh, poor Joey."

"I think Dr. Carter will be fine. It's Mendez who'll find his tires slashed, I'm sure."

"Hunt's such a bunny boiler," Summer said. "Controlling, hard-assed, and occasionally super charming. Quite a piece of work."

"She is. No wonder people hate me."

"If only they knew how little you're like her in real life."

"Are you saying I'm not super charming?"

"Oh, you're plenty charming when you want to be." With a grin, Summer leaned forward to peck Elizabeth's cheek. Their exits were improving, she thought, as Elizabeth swayed in, appearing to expect it. "See you at work tomorrow. *Darling.*"

"Of course." Elizabeth's smile was pure amusement.

Summer's heart squeezed. That woman wore adorable far too well.

Chapter 13

KINGS CANYON NATIONAL PARK, THE backdrop for *Eight Little Pieces*, was beautiful. Serene and soul-rejuvenating, Elizabeth decided, staring at the horizon. Majestic pines and the mist-covered, purple mountain behind them bookended her day. Even after two weeks she still wasn't used to it.

After so long unconsciously shutting out all the sounds of the city, the stillness here was almost unnerving.

At night, it was the opposite. Owl hoots, distant coyote howls, and the buzz of cicadas filled the air. The thrum of nature, for some reason, reminded her of a theater ovation. It vibrated through her, jolting her with the realization of how disconnected she'd been lately from the earth. It was so easy to forget what the real world felt like. Gossip and headlines and followers and fans were so meaningless next to grassy clods of soil, rich with living things.

Elizabeth brushed her jeans and pulled close the knee-length, padded navy coat on loan from Wardrobe. She'd thought London was cold, but the air out here—thin, clean, and fresh—bit through everything and turned her cheeks ruddy. She settled onto the top step of her trailer, not yet ready to face the circus of catering trucks, lighting rigs, and trailers. Sipping a mug of tea—not the good stuff, of course; Summer wasn't here yet—Elizabeth studied the wall of wilderness before her.

People left her alone out here, which suited her introverted streak. It was a welcome change from American sets where everyone was pumped up and felt the urge to be friendly. English productions could be even worse. That old theater troupe mentality of group inclusion usually put her in a bad mood, because she couldn't exactly wave a sign that said, "Please ignore me and we'll get on just fine".

Grace used to laugh at her hatred of group bonding and suggest she play the role of "the gregarious actress who gets on famously with her co-stars." How exhausting that sounded.

Jean-Claude's hand-picked team went about its business with the minimum of fuss or interaction with her. They'd all been working long hours to get Elspeth's scenes wrapped before Elizabeth's hiatus was over. The work everyone was putting in to meet her deadline kept her focused to do her best. Not that it was in her DNA to offer anything less.

"Ah, you are here," Jean-Claude strode up in black jeans, a black turtleneck, and a fat coat that matched hers. A beatnik poet came to mind. He edged his narrow backside next to her on the trailer step. "Not long now, *oui*?"

Ah yes. She was supposed to be climbing the walls, missing her girlfriend after two long weeks apart. Well, if Elizabeth was being entirely honest, she *had* noticed Summer's absence. There was something oddly addictive about her. Her warmth could shake Elizabeth out of even the worst moods. Summer was also one of the few people whose presence she didn't find draining.

"Today's the day." Elizabeth mustered some enthusiasm.

"*Oui*. She called me last night on the satellite phone to say she must stop for the junked food essentials but she'll be here as soon as she can."

Elizabeth laughed. "Fortifications? That sounds like her."

"I am sorry there is no reception out here and you have not been able to call her as you must have desired. The satellite phone is for business calls and emails only, you see." His eyes filled with regret. "If I made an exception for you… mutiny! Everyone would be demanding this access."

"It's fine." Truthfully, she hadn't minded being off the grid a few weeks. "I notice some people make a mad dash for the ridge quite often."

The ridge—God only knew what it was actually called—rose up halfway between distant Fresno and their valley set, and was the only place for miles you could pick up even one bar of reception. Cast or crew with a spare ninety minutes and a burning need to check in on the outside world would shout "Ridge Run" and then disappear off in that direction.

Elizabeth had made the trek just once, needing to hear Grace's voice again. She still regretted the call a great deal.

Grace hadn't wasted any time, demanding to know Elizabeth's approach to her character, her mental preparedness, what notes she'd written. It was like being back at college, Grace correcting her technique and dicing her suggestions. For some reason, rather than feeling her usual excitement that Grace cared enough to ask, this time she resented it. Elizabeth was no longer a twenty-year-old ingénue needing guidance. And so…

She hadn't meant to say it. The words had just slithered out, as though Alex were sitting on her shoulder, whispering comments like a cartoon devil.

"Summer's been the best," she'd said. "It's wonderful having her here. She's so supportive, and we're working together so well." The lie had felt rebellious and she'd smiled.

Well, until Grace hissed in a breath. Then came the silence. And then… and *then*.

Elizabeth gulped her tea, her stomach churning at what had followed. The awful things Grace had said. She'd had no idea Grace was capable of such viciousness, especially to a woman she barely knew. Shock had hit her. Then dismay. Then confusion. And then…she'd hung up.

Elizabeth had hung up on Grace Christie-Oberon and driven back to set in a foul mood.

After that, it hadn't been hard at all to play opposite the beefy actor representing *Fury* in her next scene. Elizabeth's snarling intensity had been both a weapon and a release until all she'd wanted to do was wring her co-star's neck.

Poor man. He'd quailed from her when the director had finally called "cut".

Jean-Claude had rushed over to her, beside himself with giddy glee. "Oh *oui*," he kept saying, hand fluttering against his chest. "Oh my. *Oui*."

His enthusiasm hadn't erased the bitter after-taste of Grace's insults.

"Elizabeth?" Jean-Claude's voice shook her back to the present.

"Sorry?"

"I said we have the little girl, Julia, this morning. In to play Elspeth's *Hope*."

She knew. Elizabeth had met the child and her mother yesterday. Precocious *and* perky. And that was just the mother.

"But after we finish and your Summer is here, we will map out how your two roles intersect." He interlocked his fingers in demonstration. "Are you nervous?"

Taking a sip of tea to stall, Elizabeth thought about that. "The only sex scenes I've done have been on my TV show and they weren't that revealing. Physically or emotionally. But I'm sure the same principle applies. It's all just well-planned technical work."

"I'll take that answer as '*Oui*, Jean-Claude, I am somewhat nervous'." He patted her hand. "It shall be fine. We will banish from the set all those who do not need to be there. Louise has a remote-head camera, so she will not be hovering over you, ruining your mood. And, of course, you have your Summer. Just trust in her. We will make this work."

"Yes," she murmured.

He jumped to his feet and began barking out orders in a mix of English and French to anyone within earshot as he disappeared toward Elspeth's shack.

The compact, 350-square-foot building had been built just for the film and would be taken down when they wrapped. The national park's supervisor had agreed the environmental impact was negligible, especially after Jean-Claude passionately cited the film's "global tourism impact" and other marketing doublespeak that sounded entirely plausible when spoken with a French accent.

The wooden construct had been deliberately aged and looked rustic on the inside. One wall was removable to allow a variety of camera angles on the interior. Depending on where in the shack they filmed—near the insulated, weatherproofed three sides, or the removable front one—it was either hot or freezing.

Elizabeth's wardrobe comprised of jeans, a white tank top, and a blue and gray flannel shirt rolled up at the sleeves. It only kept out some of the creeping fingers of wind, despite all sorts of tarpaulins strung up at the front to keep any icy gusts or rain at bay.

Elizabeth found herself impatient to see Summer's blue VW screech up, and have the woman's happy laugh shatter all this silence. Silence was far too effective at giving a person space to think. And Elizabeth didn't particularly want to dwell on what was really bothering her.

She sighed. Why did everything always come back to Grace? That rant had been so bizarre. She had no right to speak that way about a warm, decent, talented actress who was a…a friend.

Friend?

How had they gone from blood packs and cacti stories to this? Making new friends was not Elizabeth's strength. Besides, she was fine with the six she had. They were comfortable, like old, fuzzy pairs of bed socks. Making new friends meant having to talk to people she wasn't settled with. Not that she minded talking with Summer. It was painless. The more she twisted it about in her head, 'friend' felt like a good fit.

Tossing the tea dregs to the ground, she returned inside her trailer and washed her cup in the small sink. As she did so, one thought tumbled through her mind on repeat, as she scrubbed the white ceramic harder and harder.

What is Grace's problem?

The moment Summer pulled up on location, she felt at home. It was the weirdest feeling. She didn't even like camping, and this place had killed her cell phone reception an hour ago, so that was another strike against it. Yet, here she was, feeling like she belonged. Maybe Elizabeth's small, pleased smile as she leaned against a tree, waiting for her, might have a little to do with it.

Best welcome ever.

"Hey, you!" Summer grinned. "Wanna give me a hand? I promise there're naughty carbs in it for you if you play your cards right."

Elizabeth ambled over. "Does that line work on anyone?"

"Only hot actresses." They met by the trunk and Summer whispered, "Jean-Claude's watching," before pressing her lips to Elizabeth's.

The familiar rush of warmth and endorphins and that sexy scent that was all Elizabeth washed over Summer once more. Her stomach gave a merry clench. *Damn it!*

"So I heard the bad news," Summer said. "Marcus is doing catering? I know he's a good chef but I'm *so* sorry."

"You should be," Elizabeth offered a soft groan. "I've been doing stealthy runs to craft services at ridiculous hours to avoid him or Jean-Claude so

I can get real food. You couldn't have given me an allergy to turnips or something?" She looked imperious as hell, but a glint in her eye suggested she wasn't entirely serious.

"Okay, I've got your back." Summer hefted her shopping haul from her trunk. "I presume your trailer has a fridge? I bought every conceivable cheese they had in Fresno. And any other dairy snacks I thought you might be deprived because of your 'allergy'. You can't blame me for any osteoporosis after this."

"*Our* trailer."

"Hmm?" Summer stopped. "What?"

"I gather Jean-Claude assumed he was doing us a favor. He decided we'd want to share a trailer."

Summer blanched. "Seriously?"

"Don't worry, it's not as bad as you think. We're not in the same compartment. Our Winnebago's a double banger. A door at each end, a partition down the middle, matching facilities in each half. But it gives us *easy access*."

Easy access? "Um. Well…lead on," Summer squeaked. *Oh yeah. Smooth.*

The trailer was large, long, sleek, and split in half, as Elizabeth had said. Each half had its own double bed, fridge, kitchenette and bathroom facilities, couch, table, and wall TV. Jean-Claude was looking after his star, all right.

"Comfy." Summer gazed around her new digs, dropping her bags near the double bed. "But then, anything would be after what I was in on *Choosing Hope*. I mean, I know you're used to the star-issue fancy trailer, but this is a big step up for me."

"You've clearly made it," Elizabeth drawled. "Jean-Claude didn't just toss you a sleeping bag for the backseat of your car."

"Ha-ha. Although, I am a little surprised any indie flick has a budget for something like this."

"They aren't that expensive to hire, and Jean-Claude has only a tiny cast and crew. Plus it'd be low overheads out here. Don't forget, Jean-Claude has some pretty substantial investors backing his US debut."

"Oh right. Guess that explains the fancy hotel suite he wined and dined us at." Summer sat on her bed. "Okay, this'll be cool. I assume you don't snore loud enough that I'll hear it in here?" she teased.

"No one can snore that loud."

"I didn't hear a denial."

Elizabeth rolled her eyes. "Come around to my side. We can file away the essentials you brought." She waved at Summer's bags of food.

Ten minutes later, after they'd stuffed the non-perishables into an assortment of cupboards, Elizabeth poked through the bag of cheeses. "I thought I knew every variety. But what on earth is Humboldt Fog?"

"Goat cheese. From Humboldt County."

"That's some high-end contraband." Elizabeth ordered it in her small fridge.

"Oh, I know." Summer laughed, and then stared when she saw what else was in there. "You drink Diet Coke?"

"No. That stuff'll rot your insides. It's for you. I assumed you'd wind up in here sooner or later to run lines or whatnot."

Warmth spread through her. "Thanks."

Elizabeth shrugged and continued squeezing cheese into her fridge.

"I also got you enough tea to get you through to the next millennium," Summer said. "Or at least the end of this shoot, the speed you drink it." She set another bulging bag on the table.

"*Summer.*" Elizabeth's almost-smile grew full and wide. Her voice dipped lower. "I knew I liked you for a reason."

Summer inhaled. Elizabeth *liked* her? Of course, she probably liked Summer's gifts more. But still, try telling that to her pathetic heart.

"Oh, before I forget, Jean-Claude wants to talk to us at two about our scenes." Elizabeth closed the fridge. "They're setting up lighting right now for *Lust*. Lots of reds and oranges. Looks like the fiery pit of hell in Elspeth's shack. They'll probably need an exorcism in there after our sex scene."

Our sex scene. Two o'clock was only half an hour away. Well. That seemed a whole heap of real, now didn't it?

Chapter 14

IN THE LARGE PRODUCTION TRAILER, Jean-Claude pointed Elizabeth and Summer to seats in front of a monitor. "Welcome, Summer. It's good to see you again."

"Thanks. Great to be here. I missed a certain someone a lot." She smirked.

"I'm quite positive you do not mean me." He snorted. "All right, to business. I knew we would not have much time with both of you, so I made something to show exactly what I want from you tomorrow." He hit a button on the keyboard in front of him. "I shot this on my phone, so no comments about the amateur cameraman, *oui*? This is your scene, planned, step by step."

The bed from the writer's shack filled the screen. Elizabeth's brunette body double was being pushed backward by a second, blond, body double.

He hit *Pause*. "Hold there three beats. See how they're turned? Now, here is my trick to perfection. Pay attention to the music." Jean-Claude hit *Play* again. "I have choreographed this scene to be like an intricate dance. Listen for the changes that signal when you shift. Do just as your doubles do. This music will play on set, so it will be as if it is me whispering the directions in your ear."

A thin overlay of music began as "Lucille" pushed "Elspeth" back on the bed and climbed on top of her, pinning her wrists above her head with one hand, pressing her lips to Elspeth's with all the grim determination of someone facing an execution. Both women had the fluidity of quick-drying cement.

Jean-Claude tapped the side of the monitor. "I expect Elspeth to look like she has never been kissed so well right there."

The scene continued. "Here is where the clothing will come off." He hit *Pause* again. "I don't care how the clothing comes off but make it fast. You are both eager, excited. This is thrilling. This is *Lust*. All right…" He waved at the frozen stunt doubles on the bed. "Now at this point let's assume everyone is naked. This next key change, and the first scene we will shoot, starts in bed, the moment Lucille captures Elspeth's wrists. Watch closely how they move their bodies after."

Elizabeth saw what he meant about this being a dance. The turns and twists were elegant, or would be, if not for the doubles' businesslike approach. After plenty of awkwardly mimed kissing, rocking, and rubbing, the scene finally ended.

Jean-Claude looked to them. "So, obviously you two will do this much better. But now you see what is required, the angles I need, and so on. Questions?"

When the scene was perfectly lit and she and Summer were in place, Elizabeth could see how it would look. Sensuous and liquid. Beautiful. She was impressed in spite of her reservations. Even so, her nerves rose again. This was a lot for her to overcome.

Her people had negotiated an excellent contract, including specifying how much nudity was allowed and for how long. A nude thong had to be worn at all times, to be digitally removed later. Summer's sister had obviously negotiated something similar given Rachel's subsequent wry phone call.

"We've confused the poor man terribly, Bess," her agent had declared with a laugh. "Jean-Claude wants to know why two lovers are protecting their modesty from each other. He said he'd save a lot of money on digital editing if you could be 'more French' about the whole thing. Don't worry, I convinced him it's a standard clause in American productions. Just trot that line out if he asks."

As if reading her mind, Jean-Claude said, "Now, we must discuss the nudity." He glanced at them. "It's all a sleight of hand. Indeed, so much sleight of hand, I suspect you have not seen what I did. Let's watch the scene again. This time, look at the sheets, how they are carefully placed across the hips. Summer, it is your job to ensure Elizabeth is covered the same way your double does it here."

"Okay," Summer nodded. "Protect Bess's dignity. Got it."

"Yes, do try and get that one right," Elizabeth drawled.

"No pressure." Summer's grin seemed nervous.

Elizabeth didn't blame her. This was stressful and difficult, no matter how it was veiled in professionalism and technicality.

They watched again, and Elizabeth was amazed she hadn't noticed before how cleverly the doubles manipulated their bodies or the sheet to always shield the other. Teasing but not revealing. Impressive.

"You see?" he asked.

They both nodded.

Jean-Claude reached into a drawer and pulled out a pair of tablets. "There are copies on these for you to study in detail. Learn this until you know it frontwards and backwards. Understand?"

"It's like a dance," Summer said, taking one. "So we learn it like that. Sure."

"Exactly. You two are my primas, locked in a partnership and a duel. I need you to make us believe. That's why I chose lovers. Relationships always have layers, like Lucille and Elspeth. There is love. There is war. Fear and confidence. Above all, longing. Learn your moves. Learn the music changes. Learn the sheets. So tomorrow, when we shoot, the music will be my voice and you will simply... dance."

They spent the next three hours, side by side, flopped on Elizabeth's bed, watching the video on repeat.

"Why does the music change there?" Summer asked. "What's different? What's the transition he's marking? They're still kissing." Well, not *kissing*. They were mashing lips together until the music changed again.

"Yes, they're still kissing," Elizabeth replied, "if you could call it that, but for the first time, Elspeth initiates a kiss with Lucille, not the other way around. The music shift is hanging a lantern on the fact that Elspeth is worn down and turns the tables on her lover."

"Worn down? That sounds like she's just tired of fighting and is giving in to pressure."

"She is." Elizabeth took a sip of tea. "But it's her own internal pressure, remember. Lucille is *her*, too. Elspeth wants this but hates admitting it. So here's the moment she admits it to herself and finally reaches for her lover."

"So she'd look frustrated with herself there?" Summer mulled it over. "Or even relieved that she finally knows what she wants?"

"A bit of both. Either way, I think Lucille would milk that and look triumphant she's won."

"Yeah." *Good point.* Summer made a mental note to play it that way. "Still, though...winners and losers. It sounds like a war."

"Because it is." Elizabeth dragged the video slider backwards. "Listen to the music here. It's building up the scene like a battle charge. And *here,* when it changes? It's saying, 'And now it begins'."

"Wow." Summer rested her chin on her hand. "How do you know so much about deconstructing scenes like that?"

"At Cambridge we examined the subtext and layers."

Cambridge? Not Grace? So Elizabeth's glorious mentor didn't teach her everything she knows after all?

Elizabeth was looking at her strangely.

"What?"

"I sometimes think you have something else you'd rather say."

"No. Nothing at all." Summer arranged her features to innocent.

A doubtful look crossed Elizabeth's face. "Hmm. So how are you feeling about all this?" She flicked her wrist toward the screen, showing two women frozen mid-clench.

"Musical transitions are locked," Summer said. "I can remember the sheet positioning now too. So that's the when and the where sorted out."

Just not the how. If I act my heart out, will it be obvious? And will I be taking advantage of Elizabeth somehow? It was a conundrum she still hadn't figured out. She needed to, soon.

"But?" Elizabeth said.

"But what?"

"Again, it feels like you're not saying everything." Elizabeth frowned. "Look, I know it's hard for you..."

She had no idea.

"Sex scenes always are," Elizabeth continued.

No kidding.

"I hated my first sex scene too," she finished.

"When was that?"

"Hunt and Mendez. It was so unnatural. I hated being touched intimately by someone I don't know that well. I survived, obviously. But, still, I know it's not easy. You just have to push through. Although many actors like to get a little drunk, too, if all else fails."

"No thanks." Summer wanted her head clear.

"Anyway, I think Jean-Claude's analogy is excellent. This is a dance. We just have to learn the moves. So, do you want to try for a physical rehearsal?"

"Uh..." Summer really didn't. But they should try this a few times before facing the crew. That'd be so much worse. "I guess."

"Here's a blanket we can use to practice protecting my dignity." She arched an eyebrow. "We must get that right at least."

Summer gave a tight laugh. "Okay." Practical stuff. Right, she could do this. How hard could it be to move at a given time, twist at another beat, and so on? She nodded. It'd be fine.

Chapter 15

MAKE-UP WAS QUITE AN...EXPERIENCE. ELIZABETH was presently being examined, top to bottom, in a barely there beige thong, by an elderly Brazilian woman with a perpetual scowl and some sort of bronzing sponge clutched in her hand.

What was she looking for anyway? A treasure map?

"Tan lines," the heavily accented woman finally muttered, half to herself. She waggled a finger at Elizabeth as though the mere thought of such lines was a personal slight. "Terrible on film. I erase. Also freckles and scars." She finally put down the sponge without using it. "No tan marks. Good." Her expression was grim. "Not like your co-star."

For a pleasing moment Elizabeth imagined, in detail, Summer's tan lines. Did she get to the beach often? Or was it all those pool parties at her parents' house?

After being waved out the door, Elizabeth soon found herself on set in nothing more than a thong and a cotton-weave robe. *Thank God for heaters.* She looked around, cinching her robe tightly around her waist. Perched on the edge of the bed, also in a robe, script in hand, was Summer.

She glanced up at Elizabeth's arrival. Her still expression didn't look natural in the least.

Before Elizabeth could approach, Jean-Claude dropped onto the bed beside her, whispering something. He pulled a face and made her laugh. Patting her shoulder, he rose, reaching for the script in her hand as he did, stealing it. "*Non, non,* you already know this. It is not needed."

Summer's expression was now approaching terror.

Hell. Was this going to be a train wreck like last night? Every time they'd practiced the transition scene, where Elspeth takes the sexual initiative from

Lucille, everything had gone wrong. Summer would lose her place or freeze or forget her next action or do things in the wrong order. By their sixth attempt, she'd actually started stammering.

Eventually Elizabeth had decided the rehearsals were becoming counterproductive and sent her back to her trailer to spare them both the ordeal, praying it'd be okay on the day.

Now, here they were. Elizabeth wondered, as she had most of last night, what was up with Summer?

———————————————

Summer's eyes adjusted to the warm orange and red lighting in Elspeth's shack, which didn't actually look like a hellscape, despite Elizabeth's warning. It was soft and enticing. Music played from some hidden CD player, something French and daring to set the mood.

Elizabeth arrived, somehow managing to make a waffle-weave robe look chic. *How does she do that?* And moments later, Jean-Claude appeared at Summer's side, cracked a joke, then stole her security blanket. She watched in horror as her script left her white-knuckled grip. Summer considered protesting, but the man didn't look in the negotiating mood.

He turned to Elizabeth. "And how are you? Did you rehearse well? How did it go?"

Summer sneaked a look at Elizabeth, whose face gave nothing away. They'd spent hours in rehearsal hell last night, with Summer's body draped all over Elizabeth's, and every time, *every single damned time*, her thudding heart and tingling skin had reminded her just how attracted she was to the woman. Her hyper-awareness kept making her forget what she was doing.

Every time Elizabeth had tried to practice the power shift from Lucille to Elspeth, she had actually kissed Summer. *With lips.* Nothing spectacular— just a brush against Summer's mouth to signify the turning point. But the softness and warmth of those lips was so overwhelming that Summer couldn't think. So she froze or flinched or stammered out her lines.

Elizabeth had finally thrown up her hands and called it a night. It had all been terribly British and polite, but she'd effectively kicked Summer out.

Humiliating.

"We did a lot of rehearsing," Summer said, aware Jean-Claude needed some sort of answer.

Elizabeth's lips twitched. "That we did."

Summer couldn't work out whether she was being made fun of or not.

"Good." Jean-Claude rose. "We'll do a rehearsal so you can show me. Then if that's fine, we'll go straight to shooting."

He headed for the small music player on a table out of camera view, stopped what was playing, and hit another button.

The music from their rehearsal video began.

Summer took a deep breath and threw herself into the scene. Relief burned through her when she said her lines correctly, hit all the right beats, sliding and turning when she was meant to, taunting with just the right amount of cockiness, and then...

Elizabeth kissed her. And it wasn't just a brush of lips this time. It was strong, demanding, and needy. Elizabeth's aroused look and soft mouth undid her, just as they had last night.

Summer flinched.

Shit!

Elizabeth ignored it and kept going, and they somehow got through the rest of the scene.

Jean-Claude stopped the music and came back to stand in front of them.

Sliding a look at Elizabeth's face, Summer was impressed at the woman's neutral mask, as though she'd seen nothing amiss.

Jean-Claude, however, was frowning. He didn't comment, though, and Summer appreciated him not making a big deal about her messing up.

"Let's...try it once more, hmm?"

They did it again. This time, instead of flinching, she turned away just before the kiss, so Elizabeth's lips ended up chastely plastered on her cheek.

Jean-Claude stopped the scene immediately and studied her for a painfully long moment. "Maybe you are over-rehearsed, hmm?" he suggested. "Forget rehearsals. You know the moves. You know the lines. So let's just do it. Prepare. We'll shoot in a moment."

Over-rehearsed? Over-stimulated, more like. All Summer's nerves jangled with tension as the lighting techs busied themselves and the hair and make-up women made final touch-ups.

Elizabeth met her gaze. "You feeling any better?"

With a sharp look, Summer replied, "We'll get it done."

Elizabeth nodded and shot her an encouraging smile. "We will."

"We're ready." Jean-Claude glanced behind him and gave a signal.

A shout went up to clear the set. Before long, almost everyone had traipsed out.

Summer looked up. A crane arched its neck into the room, over the bed, a remote-head camera twirling on the end.

"Places everyone. Robes off." Jean-Claude retreated out of sight.

Elizabeth slid under the sheet and removed her robe quickly, handing it to the waiting wardrobe woman. Summer copied her, then began draping the sheet as they'd rehearsed. Her mood grew grimmer as the seconds counted down. Jean-Claude scampered over, changed the position of the sheet slightly, nodded to himself, and disappeared again.

Elizabeth lay on her back, her hands above her head. Immediately Summer scuttled forward, straddled her hips, and leaned forward, clasping her wrists with her hands. It had the effect of covering Elizabeth, allowing her some measure of privacy from the mechanical eye watching them from above.

Protect the queen.

What a random saying. Trust her to think of it now. Summer swallowed back hysterical laughter. *Okay, don't lose it. I can do this. Just don't look down. Don't notice how warm and soft Bess feels.*

Summer glanced down in spite of herself, and immediately regretted it as her mind blanked at the sight of Elizabeth's bare breasts. Full, pale, and her rosy-tipped nipples were... *Shit!* She snapped her head back up. *Damn it!*

Out of the corner of her eye, she saw Elizabeth peer up at her, clearly trying to understand what was going on.

"I'm okay," Summer mumbled. "It'll be fine." Her jaw clenched.

Before Elizabeth could reply, Jean-Claude called, "Speed. Rolling, and...*action.*"

The camera moved over. The music began. And everything seemed to disappear.

Summer let her fingers drift to Elizabeth's neck, and Lucille's first line came to her. "How long has it been? How long since warm hands touched your skin? Hands that weren't your own?" Her fingers danced against flesh. *So soft.*

"Not that long." Elizabeth stared mutinously into Summer's eyes.

"Liar," Summer retorted. "It's been four years. Nine months. Twelve days. Three hours." She tapped each time period out on the delicate skin where base of neck met shoulder.

Elizabeth gasped. "How can you know that?"

"You still have to ask?" She tilted her head, meeting Elizabeth's eye. "You must know. Suspect?"

"No." Confusion crossed her face.

"Then I'll have to make you understand." Summer flung herself forward and kissed Elizabeth hard, pressing their bodies together.

———— ◈ ————

The smoothness of Summer's skin, the heat, and the press of her bare breasts against Elizabeth's own burned into her. It was pleasant, extremely so, a detached part of her brain noted. Why wouldn't it be? Summer was beautiful, after all. But the longer it went on, it was hard not to notice something else. How it was all very...well...mechanical?

Maybe Elizabeth was being too harsh. That's what any film's sex scenes were when you broke them down. Action followed by action until the director shouted "Cut". This was normal, right?

What wasn't normal, though, was the tension emanating from her co-star. The tightness at Summer's mouth, in her eyes, in the vice-like grip of her hands around Elizabeth's wrists. Summer rolled when she was meant to, arched on cue, turned at the right moment, shifted the sheet perfectly to protect Elizabeth. But the whole time she looked thoroughly wretched.

Elizabeth did her best to inject something more into the scene to compensate. She gave Elspeth a pissed-off heat and responded with fervent kisses to show her attraction, but it was like trying to make out with a piece of marble.

"Cut!"

Jean-Claude strode across the room and crouched by the bed near Summer, who immediately flung the sheet over them both.

He shook his head. "You are too tight, Summer, dear. Too..." he clenched his arm muscles in demonstration. "*That*. The camera, it sees. You will fix it?" He waited for her curt nod and retreated again.

Summer slowly readjusted the sheet back to the start position, waited for Elizabeth to stretch her arms out again, then aligned herself over her and waited.

"Speed. Rolling."

Staring up into Summer's detached, distant, hooded eyes, Elizabeth saw nothing familiar. Someone on autopilot. Where was her friend? The woman whose humanity was infectious? A chill skittered through her as she studied those empty eyes.

"Action!"

The music began again. The camera returned to its starting position.

It was even worse this time. Having an acutely self-conscious Summer visibly forcing herself to gyrate against Elizabeth made her feel like the worst monster. Elspeth was supposed to experience a well of pent-up lust, but the best Elizabeth could do was desperately push down her pity.

This had to be so obvious. Even the body doubles' wooden version of the scene was looking more authentic at this point. She slid her hand through Summer's hair and nuzzled her neck. *Such a nice neck.* A shame the cords were jutting out taut as violin strings.

"Cut!"

Impatience crossed Jean-Claude's features. "What is going on?" he asked, coming over to them. "Tell me what's happening?"

A redness crawled up Summer's neck. She didn't speak.

"I think maybe we're just not relaxed yet," Elizabeth suggested in the soothing tone she reserved for unpredictable directors.

"Hmm." Jean-Claude rubbed his chin. "We'll go again. Maybe this time, you don't look like you're off to a firing squad? This is supposed to be hot, exciting. *Oui?* Focus on each other, forget the characters. Maybe act that heat you feel?"

Summer tried for a smile, but it didn't even come close.

Elizabeth nodded.

The next half dozen takes were worse than miserable. Elizabeth gritted her teeth each time Summer gathered her wrists into that iron grip, and exhaled only when "Cut" was called. After every take, Summer's face immediately crumpled into anxiety and frustration. She seemed close to tears.

Finally Jean-Claude swore in French, then in English, and told everyone else to leave the set.

His hands were on his hips when he slowly turned and addressed them. "You know why I chose you both," he began. "Authenticity. And yet on screen, it's like you've never touched each other in your life. It is so flat." He gave them a suspicious look. "Why is that?"

Oh hell. Is he about to work it out?

"Jean-Claude," Summer began.

"*Non.*" His eyes narrowed, and Elizabeth could almost see the cogs whirring. "Do you remember that French lesbian film that won the Palme d'Or a few years back? The *Blue* color thing?" He tutted. "Personally, not to my tastes. The sex scene? Too long, boring, like watching robots grinding. The director cast two straight women in it. This can work if you find women with chemistry, who can overcome being outside their comfort zone. But in that movie, the actresses admitted later they felt vulnerable and exploited. And the director? He had not known. He declared his film forever sullied by their words."

Jean-Claude glared up at the ceiling and shook his head. "*Why* was he not aware of their experience? They didn't tell him? He didn't understand what he was putting them through? It was a lesson. An important one for all of us. I decided always, *always*, if I could, I will cast lovers. Then, even if my intimate scenes are hard to shoot, they will still not be a *hardship* for the stars. My lovers will *want* to touch each other. They will not feel vulnerable or exploited. Their love will be obvious. Authentic. But you two? I cannot see it."

He scowled at them. "I hear that sometimes real couples have no chemistry on screen, but it happens when couples are too familiar, have been together for a long time. But you two, you are just now together, only, what? A few months? So it is not that."

Elizabeth held her breath.

Jean-Claude tapped his lip, eying Summer. "My dear, you look afraid to touch your own girlfriend. Your eyes seek approval for everything that you do, as though you fear her harsh rebuke. How can that be? She won't break." He glanced at Elizabeth. "Will you?"

"No," Elizabeth murmured.

"No. Well." He blew out a breath. "I do not understand this at all." He gave them a close, hard look, "but I suspect *you* do." He waved a finger between them. "We are taking a break. Go back to your trailer. Take…" he looked at his watch, "thirty minutes. Do what you must to figure this out, I do not care. Then come back. Ready. Prepared. And then we do the scene and it will be perfect. Okay? Go. Now. Fix this."

Chapter 16

"Shit," Summer said, closing the door behind her on Elizabeth's side of the trailer. She paced, hands balling and unballing. "Oh my God. That was…Oh. My. God."

"He's right." Elizabeth said gently, only too aware that if she ratcheted up the tension any more, Summer might have a full meltdown. As it was, she already seemed about as brittle as old bones.

"I know he's right! You think I don't know that? Christ. That was a nightmare." Summer ran her fingers through her hair.

Elizabeth decided it was probably not a good idea to point out that she'd get hell from the hair stylist for that. Instead she reached into her fridge and pulled out a gin bottle. "Want some?"

"No."

"Might help your tension."

"I said no." Summer's jaw hardened and she began pacing up and down the trailer. It was dizzying watching her.

"Fine. I will." Elizabeth reached for a glass and poured herself a double, returning the bottle to the fridge. "Jean-Claude thinks we know what's going on." She took a sip. "So…do you?"

Summer paused her stalking. "I'm not screwing up on purpose."

"I know."

"This isn't like on *Choosing Hope* where I'm being subversive to get around a toxic plot. This is a good plot. I want to do well. I do!" Summer folded her arms. "I want this over as soon as possible. Because despite how it looks, I'm really trying."

Was she? Obviously these weren't regular nerves. Summer's acting was as wooden as a tree stump, each scene worse than the last. After two dozen takes, some sort of unconscious self-sabotage had to be going on. Elizabeth placed her glass on the table, adjusting it perfectly center. Right. Time to stop dancing all around this and get to the root of things.

"Summer," she began, trying to phrase it delicately, "you look like you're in physical pain when you touch me. You're so tense, I don't even recognize you. When I kiss you, you flinch or turn away. And you touch me like I'll shatter."

The stalking resumed.

"Come on, talk to me. What's going on?" Elizabeth tried again. "In your head, I mean. We can figure out a way past this."

"Unlikely."

"You told me you could do this. You made me believe it." Elizabeth met her eye. "What's changed?"

Summer paused mid-stride. "This is…harder than I thought."

"What is? Which part?"

Summer stared up at the ceiling and didn't answer.

"For me, the nudity is difficult," Elizabeth admitted, hoping that by giving a little, she might get something back. "I'm not comfortable at all with it, no matter how perfectly the sheets are draped. I really don't want another two days of rolling around in next to nothing in front of strangers. It flies in the face of my acute sense of modesty." She smiled. Perhaps humor would defuse the growing tension? "So if that's what's bothering you, I can relate."

"Sorry you're feeling uncomfortable. But my issue isn't with nudity," Summer said flatly. "Obviously not, or I wouldn't have gone skinny dipping at the *Quand Pleurent Les Clowns* wrap party."

"Okay." Good point. "Is it that you've never done a sex scene before?" Elizabeth really hoped it wasn't that. Summer was playing *Lust,* for God's sake. Failure to get her head around the role itself would mean she'd have to leave. Elizabeth gripped her glass and tried not to think about how bad that would be. Would Jean-Claude re-cast both of them? Find a new couple?

"No, not that." Summer lifted her chin. "Sex scenes in general are just acting, aren't they?"

In general? So there was something specific about this one then? Inhaling, Elizabeth plunged on, hoping third time was the charm. "Perhaps it's the *nature* of the sex scene? Two women?"

"No." Summer's glare intensified. "And before you ask, no, I also don't think people will think I'm gay for doing this." She rolled her eyes. "It's not the nineties anymore. Audiences are smarter now."

Scratch her next question then. Elizabeth opened her mouth, when Summer stopped in front of her.

"Stop it," Summer said. "I have a lot to process and you're not making it easier with the third degree."

"I *was* trying to help."

"I get that it's hard for you. I'm sorry. And maybe you're worried Jean-Claude will replace us. I have that fear, too. But you can't just talk this away. God, if you only knew why—" Summer abruptly stopped speaking, then sank down in a chair opposite Elizabeth with a defeated expression. She buried her head in her hands.

"So you *do* know why." It was a start. "Are you sure I can't help?"

Summer gave her a miserable glance. "You can't."

"You don't know that." Elizabeth gentled her voice. "Please tell me."

"You feel uncomfortable now over showing some skin? That's nothing. I'd ruin everything if I told you."

Elizabeth wasn't sure how Summer could ruin things more, given production had just been shut down over this, but she held her tongue.

Glancing around, Summer let her gaze fall to the empty glass. She walked to the fridge, extracted the gin bottle, and held it up, eying the level on it. Only a shot or two left. "Do you have any more?"

"Yes." Surely she wasn't planning on needing another whole bottle?

"Good. Just had to check." Summer emptied the gin into her glass, then picked it up and eyed Elizabeth over the lip. "Why do you keep your gin in the fridge? My parents don't."

"A master gin distiller told me once that it softens the taste of alcohol, making it easier to drink. Smoother."

"Okay." Summer gave the small glass a swirl then drank the liquid in two swallows. Her eyes watered. "Ugh. I hate gin."

Startled, Elizabeth said, "What's going on, Summer?"

Instead of answering, she clunked the now empty glass on the table and returned to her seat, slouching down. For a moment, she looked just like the awkward young woman Elizabeth had first met in the rain. Hapless, miserable, and unaccountably endearing.

Summer nudged her glass with a finger. "So…I *have* had to kiss people in front of cameras before. Hollywood decides no child over age eleven can possibly be without a love interest. My first ever kiss was on screen. How messed up is that? It was…not fun."

Elizabeth inhaled. Oh. That was truly sad.

"But it was just a job. I mean, that's how I convinced myself not to get freaked out. What made it worse was that Tom…my co-star…had a huge crush on me and everyone knew it. That was a world of awkward, right on top of the awkward of being twelve and having my first kiss in front of forty adults. What I'm saying is, having a sex scene as an adult, in front of only a handful of people who are respectful, is nothing compared to that earlier experience. Jean-Claude's been exceptional at protecting our dignity."

"He has."

"So you have to understand, it's not about the scene itself." Summer's eyes were still fixed on the gin label. "I promise it's not that. I can do that."

"Then, is it…" Elizabeth hesitated. "Me?"

Summer's eyebrows shot up. "What?"

"You are finding it difficult to pretend you're interested in me," Elizabeth clarified. "You don't want to touch me, and you recoil when I touch you. I mean, I have to wonder. Attraction is innate, not something anyone can control, and it might be why it's so hard for you to hide how unappealing you find this. Well, me."

"Hell, this is so hard."

Firming her jaw, Elizabeth told herself it shouldn't hurt. Summer was simply a straight woman unable to fake her sexual interest in a woman. It wasn't personal. "I see." Except it felt pretty damned personal. Elizabeth frowned, and a surge of irritation flooded her that Summer's distaste for touching her was apparently so deep she had to fight to overcome it. "Well, all the more reason for us to get this out of the way as fast as possible, so you don't have to go through the agony of having to look like you want me."

Summer's head snapped around at the sarcasm in her tone.

"What?" Her look was incredulous. "You think…that I don't want to… You idiot. That's not it. I've been *protecting* you."

"From what?" Elizabeth peered at her in confusion.

"Me! Don't you see? I'm attracted to you. So damned much. I'm in hell having to kiss a woman I regard as a friend, who I don't want to feel taken advantage of. It's killing me that I'm torn in half between wanting to touch you and not wanting to take liberties. I'm terrified that if I let myself off the leash, and do the scene the way it's written, it'll be obvious from another planet how much *I* want you."

Attracted. To. You. Suddenly a great many light bulbs went off.

"Now you see why?" Summer's groan was pained. "I thought if you knew I liked you that way, it'd freak you out when I touched you. I remember how I felt with Tom. It was uncomfortable…a violation almost…because I couldn't say no. And our scene today is so much worse than that, because it's not just a kiss, is it?"

Summer's face fell, and tears glistened in her eyes. She rubbed them away. "I didn't want you to think I was getting some cheap thrill out of this. But if I didn't tell you and went for it anyway, well, it's not like you could give consent. So that felt wrong too. It's been messing with my head so badly."

"You're gay?" The question slipped out, though Elizabeth had no right to ask. She hated how incredulous her tone was, and the wary look she received in return.

Fear darted into Summer's eyes. "Yes."

Well. Elizabeth was an imbecile for not seeing the rather enormous clues dropped by Summer's family members.

"I understand if you're opposed to me being Lucille now." Summer picked at her sleeve. "It's one thing to have a professional co-star pretend they're into you. It's a whole other level of uncomfortable when you know they really are. I still have Tom's excited face as he kissed me burned into my head. It's not right."

Summer had certainly hidden her interest well. The poor woman had been tormenting herself over a simple attraction. Although, really, there never was anything "simple" about desire when it seemed unrequited. How well Elizabeth understood that curse. God, how would she have coped doing a sex scene with Grace? Especially when she was in her twenties and intoxicated by her? Empathy almost choked her. It was a struggle to keep her voice neutral when she finally replied, "Now I see."

"Is that all you have to say?" Summer seemed astounded.

189

Offering a reassuring smile, Elizabeth said, "How about if I promise I won't feel taken advantage of? I give you permission to play Lucille as written. All-in. In fact, I insist."

"Won't you feel weird?" Her eyes clouded with worry.

"No. I know you're honorable, Summer, or this wouldn't have been so hard for you."

Summer still looked stricken. "I just don't want you feeling how I did with Tom. I'd rather quit first."

"I know. And I don't. But a little advice?" Elizabeth picked up her glass again and whirled it. "In the best acting there lies a grain of truth. If liking me is yours, then use it. The more you push your attraction away, fight it, the worse your acting gets." Over her glass, Elizabeth eyed Summer, whose cheeks wore a faint blush. "I see now that you've been trying to save my honor all this time. It's sweet, really it is, but I don't need you to. All it's doing is prolonging things and not doing you any favors. Instead, use it. Kiss me like you mean it, fling me on that bed, whatever it takes. Let's get this finished." She smiled. "All right?"

Wonder edged Summer's eyes. "Seriously?"

"Yes. I promise whatever you do, I'll be okay. I'm a big girl. I trust you. And no judgment later either. Just go for it."

"Okay." Summer stared at her, then a resolve seemed to settle through her. "Okay." She smiled, bright and relieved. "Thanks."

<hr />

Summer's heart thundered as they repositioned themselves on the bed. Elizabeth arched her back and settled her arms above her head, just beyond the pillow, waiting for Summer to take position. Her breasts were bare like Summer's, and Elizabeth met her eyes with a direct, confident gaze.

This time, Summer allowed herself to look, really look, to take in Elizabeth's skin—smooth, beautiful, pale—and the faint bumps of her rib cage. Her breasts were beautiful—soft and ample. Summer had been trying so hard not to see any of this before, to be a professional, to give Elizabeth her space. Most especially, she'd been trying to prove that she wasn't interested.

She was, though. And so was Lucille. Time to start acting like it.

Elizabeth's eyes met hers, daring Summer to take her in, daring her to own this moment.

Challenge accepted.

Their eyes stayed locked, the background murmurs receding around them. Summer gathered Elizabeth's wrists in her hand, waiting. Gone was the iron-grip. Now she cradled the flesh and bone, savoring the feel of it. To her surprise, Elizabeth's pulse was pounding under her fingers.

"Action."

Summer lunged, her kisses hot, fevered, and desperate, anxious to find all the ways that made Elspeth...or Elizabeth...moan. Her fingers traced the curve of Elizabeth's cheek, under her chin, tilting her face up for another kiss that she lavished with lips and tongue. Because, fuck it, Lucille *would* use her damned tongue. And Summer was done pretending otherwise.

Her fingernails raked Elizabeth's ribs and her lips followed their path. Summer took a pebbling nipple in her mouth, and the clench of desire she'd been repressing for twenty takes flared sharp inside her.

Summer pushed aside any doubts. Screw it. Lucille would feel desire.

Sensing the camera head pivot, searching for her expression, she gave Elizabeth a burning look. Summer held the pose for a moment, devouring the sight of her on-screen lover before returning to that wet nipple, teasing it with her tongue.

Elizabeth gasped and arched hard against her, eyes darkening.

The music shifted and that was their cue: the moment Summer hadn't nailed even once. She held her breath as Elizabeth reached for her and kissed her hard, taking control.

Falling into the kiss, having permission to do so, was everything. The kiss itself was sublime, there was no denying it. There was no hesitation this time. Nothing but a sensation of sinking into something powerful.

Summer brushed the sides of Elizabeth's breasts with the pads of her fingers. *So smooth, so soft.* A moan wrenched from her throat.

The music changed again. Elizabeth's eyes were half lidded and *interested.* That look. *Oh God.*

Summer slid her hand down, and when Elizabeth spread her legs, Summer began to clench and unclench her fingers against the soft skin of the nearest inner thigh. To the camera at the side, focusing on the subtle muscles shifting in Summer's forearm, it would look like thrusting.

Elizabeth's breathing became harsher.

Summer eased herself further down those beautiful legs, then dropped a kiss on Elizabeth's nude thong. She almost gasped as the scent of arousal reached her.

Continuing to kiss Elizabeth's body, she tried to order her thoughts. Well, it wasn't entirely unexpected, was it? There'd been all sorts of rubbing and friction. Anyone would get a little turned on, right? Summer was certainly in no condition to judge—the moisture between her own legs was copious, bordering on embarrassing.

Refocusing, Summer redoubled her efforts, trying not to notice the darkening patch growing on the cotton between Elizabeth's legs as she waited for Elizabeth to play out her climax.

Why does this have to feel so real?

Elizabeth arched against her, legs tangling with the sheets as her fingers clenched and unclenched against Summer's back. Her moans were throaty and low. So damned convincing.

Just as the music changed, she finished and turned to Summer with a predatory look.

Oh shit. In about five seconds, Elizabeth's hand would float between her legs and discover exactly how much Summer appreciated her.

Maybe this was normal? She'd heard stories. Men being…indisposed. Women getting wet. It could happen to anyone. Right?

Never breaking eye contact, Elizabeth slid her fingers between Summer's thighs.

Summer fought not to tremble at the sensuous touch before remembering that's exactly what she was supposed to do.

For a split second, Elizabeth hesitated, telling Summer exactly when her questing fingers found Summer's wetness.

She tensed with embarrassment. The gaze that met hers, though, was without censure. It was so smoky, so convincing, that Summer simply arched her back, fluttered her eyes closed, and faked an orgasm.

Curling herself around Elizabeth's deliciously bare body, she whispered Lucille's line with fierceness. "You're mine, Bess. I'm yours. We're one and the same."

There was a silence.

Then shaky breathing. Then a strange sort of hiss from Elizabeth.

Then…

"Cut!"

When Summer flung Elizabeth onto the bed with abandon, before kissing her like she was the most gorgeous woman on earth, Elizabeth realized two things rather quickly. One, Summer had overcome her anxiety, so they wouldn't be getting fired anytime soon. And two, she'd unleashed a monster. A seriously alluring one.

All Elizabeth had done was given her permission. Permission to be the best Lucille she could be. To do whatever was needed. Summer had embraced the challenge with an unanticipated fierceness.

Elizabeth was taken aback at just how effective Summer's mouth and hands were at conveying all that molten lust. As her fevered fingers mapped out Elizabeth's tender points, it became harder and harder to divorce the sensations from reality. It didn't feel exactly like acting, but it wasn't real either. Perhaps something surreal floating in the chasm between.

Desire rippled inside her like a drop of ink on papyrus, spreading wider, blurring her lines and edges until all she felt was loose-limbed, warm, and aroused. That had never happened to her before at work. When faking it with Raif Benson, she'd felt like a sack of flour, pulled about for the best angles to flatter his chiseled profile. Their sex scene had been an anatomy of power and dominance, to show Dr. Mendez putting his icy boss in her place.

Not so with Summer. Elizabeth's character here was also being dominated, but Elspeth was adored, too, wrapped in affection.

How captivating Summer was. How skilled that naughty, playful mouth. How teasing her dancing eyes that promised so much. Had Elizabeth's breasts ever been so completely lavished before? Hell. That was a dangerous thought.

Summer's desire-filled eyes were fixed on her again.

Who does she see? Elizabeth wondered. *Me or Elspeth?*

And which answer would I prefer?

Her nerve endings thrummed with excitement. Summer's lithe body was exquisite and enticing in a way Elizabeth had never expected. She'd never before felt desire as such an insatiable hunger, something that burned. In the past, desire meant a delicate, teasing pleasure, playful and evocative. It was shocking to discover—with a co-star in front of cameras, no less—that desire could be a heady, overwhelming rush, a thing to be *craved*.

The music changed; this was the moment for Elspeth to assert herself. Elizabeth took over, relieved when the transition went seamlessly at last.

She feasted on Summer's breasts, and it was no hardship to worship them. The woman was beautiful. Elizabeth's hand fell between Summer's legs. *Oh.* So wet. *For me?*

Does it matter?

An embarrassed hue crept across Summer's cheeks and Elizabeth almost tsked in dismay. No. She wouldn't stand for it. Fixing Summer with a look of pure hunger, she made sure the woman writhing beneath her felt no shame for her body's reaction.

It seemed to work. Summer faked her orgasm with a cry of delight that made Elizabeth squirm in the most pleasant way.

"You're mine, Bess," Summer said heatedly, locking eyes with her. "I'm yours. We're the same."

Perfect delivery. So real.

Wait...*Bess?*

She made a strangled noise.

"Cut!"

Summer exhaled in obvious relief.

Elizabeth gave her a reassuring smile, brushing a lock of hair out of Summer's eyes. "Lovely," she whispered, sensing Jean-Claude drawing near.

"I am?"

She'd meant the performance, but Elizabeth couldn't leave that vulnerable expression unchecked. "Yes, of course."

A dazzling smile split Summer's face. "So are you." Her hand slid down Elizabeth's back, leaving a trail of goosebumps in its wake before coming to rest on her arm. This touch felt very different from Lucille's.

As Jean-Claude stepped up beside the bed, Elizabeth pulled the sheet over her and Summer. Protecting their dignity was more reflexive than practical now.

"Perfect." Jean-Claude beamed. "I *felt* the love. Oh, and don't worry about saying 'Bess'," he told Summer. "We can loop that to 'Elspeth' easily enough. Similar sounds, you see."

Blanching, Summer shot Elizabeth a startled look as Jean-Claude retreated again, a lighting tech calling him over.

"It's fine," Elizabeth said, as though name mix-ups were common in sex scenes. She had no idea whether that was true, but Summer looked appalled. "The main thing is we survived."

Bit by bit, Summer relaxed. "Yeah." She exhaled. "Thank God. No secrets left between us now, I suppose." She shot Elizabeth a sheepish look. "Well, you know all mine."

A stab of guilt hit Elizabeth that she hadn't admitted her own secret. She wasn't ready yet. She couldn't help her guarded personality, how hard this was for her to admit to anyone. And what if Summer was indiscreet and told someone? Dread dove into her brain and began swimming laps.

This wasn't just a secret; it had power. The power to hurt her. Elizabeth didn't want the attention in her safe, ordered world. She didn't want her private life picked apart by vultures, given her public life was already subject to derision on a daily basis.

But what if...she did tell Summer? Put her faith in those trusting eyes and that guileless smile? Would such an admission make Summer more or less anxious? Would she feel betrayed? Or maybe emboldened to ask Elizabeth out?

Would that be so bad? a little voice at the back of her brain asked. Besides, when was the last time she'd been kissed like *that*?

She pushed the irritating questions aside. Irrelevant, anyway, given the facts: She wasn't open about her private life and she didn't get involved with co-stars.

"So, are *you* okay?" Summer whispered. "I didn't... um." She bit her lip. "Make you uncomfortable?"

"What? No. All fine." She flashed a quick smile.

"Okay!" Jean-Claude called over to them. "Ladies? We'll go again. That was excellent, but we'll do another shot for safety before we do close-ups."

The make-up artist reappeared and began touching up Elizabeth, a frown of concentration between her eyes. Elizabeth glanced to her left to find Summer waiting her turn, her expression distant. The sheet had fallen to her waist. Elizabeth's pulse quickened. Summer had amazing breasts, her lower brain noted merrily.

Well, that was unprofessional. However accurate.

Elizabeth forced herself to look only at Jean-Claude, now in conversation with an assistant. But the more she focused on him, the more her thoughts wandered back to Summer's shapely body. She had been rather delightful to touch.

Pursing her lips, Elizabeth tried to recall her lines for tomorrow, when they'd shoot Lucille's first scene, arriving at Elspeth's shack. Dressed in her national park ranger outfit and boots, all cocky and confident, oozing charm.

She'd look *so* hot in that outfit.

If in the next take Elizabeth was a little more heated than before, using her teeth to scrape her way across Summer's body, her tongue to lavish those plump, slippery nipples with extra attention, she chose not to dwell on what that meant.

Summer's flared nostrils and darkened eyes told Elizabeth she had no complaints. They both surged and undulated, and pressed fingertips hard into each other's skin, leaving crescent moon shapes down both their backs.

This time Elizabeth forgot this was a mere technical dance. She forgot everything but the emotions of the scene. She buried herself in the touch, the taste, the smell of Summer, meeting the swell of Summer's body with her own. She shared of herself in a way she rarely did in reality.

And to her surprise, for the first time in years, she felt alive.

Chapter 17

IT WAS PAST NINE BY the time they tumbled off set and headed back to the trailer. Elizabeth felt as if she'd been pummeled. Exhaustion was seeping in, but she was too wired to think of sleep.

Summer didn't look much better. She'd really stepped up today. Parts of Elizabeth's body still ached from all the ways Summer had made her feel like she'd been fucked by *Lust* herself.

Elizabeth was desperately looking forward to some alone time; a long shower, and probably an early night with a little…self-help…to take the edge off the arousal that had been burning between her thighs for hours.

"Gonna drown in some music," Summer declared. "Best way to unwind after so much stress."

"Stress?" Elizabeth teased lightly.

"You know exactly what I mean." Summer grinned, and an adorable pinkness feathered her cheeks. "Thanks by the way. I mean it."

They reached their trailer, pausing by Elizabeth's door, which was closest.

"What for?" Elizabeth asked.

"Making it okay. If you hadn't, I'd still be tied up in knots, fretting about freaking you out if I was too…convincing." She rolled her eyes and leaned back against the trailer's side. "You were as good as your word. You didn't get weirded out at all."

Elizabeth opened her door. It wasn't locked; no one bothered to lock anything out here. Her shower awaited. And bed, with its more base pleasures. She took in Summer's wide, sincere eyes and suddenly felt the need to extend their conversation. "Did I really strike you as such a prude that I'd react badly to you doing your role convincingly?"

Summer snorted. "Oh no, I'm not touching that. There's no safe answer. All I'll say is you kiss really well and leave it at that." She froze. "Um, *Elspeth* does."

Elizabeth hid her smile. How could Summer be an ingénue one moment and Lucille the next? Before she could stop herself, Elizabeth had moved off the stairs and into Summer's personal space. With a mischievous smile, she asked, "Only Elspeth?"

This was dangerous. Co-stars? Off limits. She shouldn't be looking at Summer's lips. Remembering the taste of them was the next step to ruin. And she really shouldn't be taking another step so they were only a breath apart.

Desire flared again, intense and sharp. Her body still scorched from being teased by those arousing lips. Just once today she'd like to know what it felt like to be kissed as herself, not some character.

Elizabeth should put a stop to this right now: the sway of her body, the way she was raking Summer with her gaze.

"Bess?" The desire-soaked roughness in Summer's voice was all it took.

Elizabeth grabbed fistfuls of Summer's denim jacket, pulling her forward, and fused their lips together. Then, with her mouth and tongue, feverish and desperate, she showed Summer just how much she'd been affected by today.

After a surprised gasp, Summer kissed her back with an urgency far more powerful than Lucille had displayed.

Dear God, she's been holding back. In what other ways? The thought was like tumbling over a ravine. It tossed up erotic images that made Elizabeth tremble. Pressing Summer against the trailer, Elizabeth pushed a thigh between her legs and leaned in.

Summer gave a pained moan and arched into her. "*Bess.* Yes."

Heaven.

Summer's hands slid up Elizabeth's rib cage, cupping her breasts through her clothes. The warmth of them woke up her nipples, sending flares of arousal through her. Exhilarating. She should haul Summer inside right now and have this out once and for all. The idea thrilled her. Although at this rate she'd be lucky to even get her co-star to the bed.

Co-star. The word was a splash of cold water.

They'd be back to the grindstone together soon. They had another season ahead on *Choosing Hope* as colleagues. Mess up that dynamic and it could be hell.

This had to stop. She broke the kiss with regret, and stepped back, head dipping. "I'm sorry."

Confusion filled Summer's expression, along with desire and disappointment.

With a steadying breath, Elizabeth said, "I shouldn't have done that. We have to work together and this would complicate things. I'm sorry I overstepped. Scenes like ours today are powerful. You get…worked up. That's what happened. I'm…really, I'm sorry." She straightened her shirt.

"You needed an outlet and I was here," Summer guessed. The brightness she always exuded dimmed. "I guess it helped that you knew I was willing." Bitterness edged her words.

Was that how it had seemed? Like she'd used her? *No!* What a thought! Elizabeth was usually so much better at controlling herself and staying focused on the big picture. She'd never made an undisciplined lapse like this, being caught up in her own desires. She took a measured step back, appalled at herself. "This is all my fault. I didn't think. I'm sorry I got carried away. As I said, it's been an intense day. The rush of everything caught me off guard."

"So you're not…" Summer paused, the furrow in her brow deepening, "not interested in women? You're saying you'd have kissed *anyone* just now if you'd been in a sex scene with them all day?"

Elizabeth sucked in a breath as the reminder of her scene with Raif hit her like an express train. She'd avoided him for two days afterward.

"Not just anyone," she admitted. "But I-I didn't mean to lead you on here. Nothing can come of this. It was just a kiss… and we're colleagues, so…that's all there can be." She scrabbled around for something positive to say. "But thank you for today. You were wonderful to work with."

Work with? Christ, could she make this any worse?

Unable to bear Summer's disappointed face, or the fact that the young woman's mouth had fallen open at her last line, Elizabeth muttered a hasty "goodnight", and fled inside her trailer, her libido now as deflated as her sinking mood.

Summer stared at the wall inside her trailer for twenty minutes, trying to work out what had just happened.

Elizabeth Thornton had kissed her. Seriously, kissed her. No one had forced her to, no script had demanded it, and she'd just...grabbed Summer and devoured her lips. *So damned hot.*

But why?

She hadn't answered Summer's question about whether she was interested in women, either. She'd weaved all around it and finally just said she couldn't be with Summer. That her kiss was just a kiss. Was it, though? Who kisses someone like that if they have no interest in them?

What *had* that kiss been about? An experiment? A little trip to Girls Town to see if she'd like it off-set as well as on? Well, if that were true, Elizabeth certainly seemed to like what she'd found, that was for sure. Summer knew desire when she saw it. And Elizabeth had kissed Summer like she'd been turned on enough to take her on the spot. Summer knew the feeling.

But...maybe it really was just a residue from their earlier calisthenics. Today had been arousing as hell. And yet, it couldn't be all there was to it. Elizabeth's horrified look when Summer had asked whether she'd have kissed just anyone like that answered that question. No, those heated, toe-curling kisses had been just for Summer.

So...what did it mean?

Further intense wall staring provided no answers.

There was only one way to find out.

⸺⊷⟡⊶⸺

Elizabeth sank into her shower, mentally reviewing the professional part of her day...mainly to avoid the confusing end to it. Jean-Claude had been pleased. He'd also spoken at length about tomorrow's scene. In it, Elspeth would begin unraveling and start to see all the characters she'd "met" flashing in and out of existence.

At one point, Lucille would appear beside Elspeth in bed, fully dressed in her ranger outfit, talking about bear season and orgasms, while simultaneously making a coffee with Lucas the linesman in the kitchen.

Elizabeth would have to convey Elspeth's moment of realization that, since seeing two Lucilles at once was impossible, these friends, lovers, and acquaintances she'd been clinging to couldn't be real.

It'd be shocking, she decided, as she turned off the shower. Powerful. Unnerving.

Like the way Summer looked at you after you kissed her so thoroughly.

Sighing, Elizabeth towel dried her hair and put on a robe. As much as she regretted the kiss, she couldn't deny it had been astonishing. She pushed that thought away in annoyance. No playing where she worked.

Even though it'd be exceptionally fun to play there.

She rolled her eyes. *Infuriating brain.*

Summer's interest in Elizabeth was undeniably flattering. A smile darted to her lips at the thought before she tamped it down. Summer's affections were another reason it had been so wrong to tease her. That kiss—that burning, exquisite, delightful kiss she'd never wanted to end—had promised more than Elizabeth was prepared to deliver. At least she'd shut it down immediately. She hoped Summer wasn't too upset by her momentary lapse.

Exiting the bathroom, wrapped in her thin silk robe, the last thing she expected to see was clear blue eyes watching her curiously. She let out a small, startled gasp.

"Bess, dear. I do apologize," Grace said from where she sat regally at the table.

Elizabeth couldn't believe what she was seeing. "Grace? How did you get in here?"

The other woman's smile was amused. "Quite easily. When I explained who I was to your production manager—she loved me in *Hanover Square* by the way—and that I was your acting coach, she pointed out your trailer. When you didn't answer my knock just now, I let myself in. I heard the shower and knew you wouldn't mind if I waited."

"I...see." Elizabeth hesitated, not quite sure whether to join her or find clothes first. "This is a surprise. You don't do random set visits. And you haven't been my acting coach for some time. More of a mentor, wasn't it?"

"Past tense now?" Grace offered an inscrutable look. "Have we fallen so far?" She glanced around. "Before we get into that, do you have any wine?"

"I don't drink wine." Elizabeth sighed. *How many times have I told her this?* "I'm allergic, remember? I have some gin. I think Summer drank the last of the old bottle," she added to herself as she rummaged about for her stash. She opened a cupboard above her head.

"Summer's your drinking buddy now?"

"Just once." She snagged her other bottle and closed the cupboard. "So, Grace, to what do I owe the visit?"

"I missed you. And after our last chat, I became concerned. You sounded so stressed. Then the call ended abruptly and I couldn't reach you because of the poor reception. I was worried. I had to make sure you were all right."

Elizabeth located a pair of drinking glasses. "The call ended abruptly because I hung up on you." Which Grace had to have known. "So are you here because you wanted to continue berating my co-star?"

Grace eyed Elizabeth serenely and folded her hands in her lap. "I do apologize for that. You caught me on a dreadful day. Summer's perfectly delightful, of course, and so much talent; you're quite right about that. I'm sorry if I ever suggested otherwise."

Suggested? Elizabeth poured them both a gin. "What's changed? Because I'm fairly sure you called Summer a 'talentless blond bimbo who used her parents' influence to get her jobs and her pert, youthful body to keep them'. Did I leave anything out?"

Waving her hand, Grace said breezily, "Oh, just ignore me. You know how I get. Amrit was being a bit on the beastly side this week, flaunting his new…well, I'm not sure what that boy of his is. He *mixes drinks*, for goodness sake. Not exactly an intellectual giant. I was distracted. But I promise, I didn't mean a word of it. It was beneath me. Your little friend's a delight. She's so…*sunny*, isn't she?"

Pushing a Hendrick's over the table to Grace, Elizabeth studied her. She sounded sincere, but the woman was a first-class actress. On the other hand, Grace was right about one thing. She did get into foul moods at times, usually when Amrit's eye was roaming to some new man or woman of the hour, and no one could do anything right.

"So why the visit? We're wrapping up at the end of next week. You could have said all of this to me back home."

"Why wait?" Grace examined the clear liquid in her glass. "No ice?"

Elizabeth shrugged. She hadn't gotten around to filling the tray. And she wasn't Grace's bartender.

"Look, darling, you've never hung up on me before." Grace's expression was pained. "So naturally I assumed the worst, that I must have upset you greatly. I can't have that, Bess. You mean the world to me. You do." She reached over and clasped Elizabeth's hand. "I should say it more often."

Elizabeth's heart gave a little quiver. How often had she wished Grace would acknowledge her value? However, Elizabeth was no longer twenty and craving her mentor's attention like air.

Grace took a sip of her drink. "Ahh, Hendrick's," she said with a sigh. "It's a constant in a world that's coming apart, isn't it? Yet another thing I like about you." She smiled, and it was as though Elizabeth was the only person who'd ever existed for her. "Lovely to share it with someone who appreciates it. Hmm?"

Nice dig at Summer. Elizabeth studied her friend. She wore a starched, high-collared shirt—Elizabeth's weakness—a tight charcoal pencil skirt, nude stockings, and four-inch designer heels. Elegance in spades. Enough to trip up any poor sap who didn't see all that charisma coming. Grace could bend anyone to her will when it suited her. Well, anyone, except Amrit. Sometimes Elizabeth wondered if that was his allure.

"Now then, tell me, how goes filming?" Grace said.

"We got through the hardest scene today. Another challenging one tomorrow. The rest is smooth sailing."

"Oh yes, today's racy sex scene." Grace's tinkle of laughter filled the room. "Your production manager told me about it on the walk over here. Those scenes can be difficult—all that nudity and swinging from the chandeliers. I'm sure you're handling it well."

"I'm fine. It was over before I knew it."

"Excellent." Grace adjusted the strap of her gold watch. "Must have been hard for Summer, though. She's young. And it's especially challenging for former child stars, trying to play sexual for the first time. Did the poor girl survive?"

"Summer rose to the challenge. Jean-Claude was impressed. But she's an excellent actress, as you know." Elizabeth couldn't resist the jab.

Grace said nothing for a moment, then shifted her glass from one hand to the other before placing it squarely on the table. "Well, that's good to hear. I'm only looking out for you. You know that, don't you?" Her gaze intensified.

"Yes," Elizabeth replied by rote, wondering how certain she was of that answer.

Grace squeezed her hand with finality and let go.

"And Summer is a good person." Why had she added that? It wasn't relevant.

Grace paused. "Of course. She's quite lovely, isn't she? I suppose she reminds you of your younger self."

"I'm sorry?" Elizabeth stared in astonishment.

"Don't you see it? So full of life, ambition, and youthful exuberance? That *is* why you're her friend. She makes you feel young. There's no shame in that. Especially living where we do. This town makes women feel old long before their time. It's only natural to be drawn to the young things who remind us there's plenty of life left."

Elizabeth gasped, as the obvious smacked her in the face. All their mutual friends were younger than Grace. "*That's* why you hang out with us?"

"Well, I can't deny it. There. You know my secret." Grace laughed. "Your Cambridge friends make me feel young. They're all still so enthusiastic, aren't they?"

Your friends. After all these years, did Grace see none of the people she'd wined, dined, and partied with for seventeen years as her own friends? How was that even possible?

Regardless of Grace's views, her charge was untrue. Elizabeth didn't use Summer to feel young. In fact, she liked to think she didn't use Summer at all.

Shame streaked through her at the memory of disappointed eyes staring into hers not even an hour ago. *Damn it.* Elizabeth was too old to kiss a pretty girl, then try to take it back. Her lips burned with the memory.

"Now then," Grace straightened, "I just needed to check in on you, but you seem fine. So I should really get back."

"What?" Elizabeth looked at the wall clock. "It's late. There's probably a spare trailer around here. I could ask—"

"Oh, I'm not going all the way back tonight. I'll stay over at Fresno till morning. I have a hotel that's five-star and fabulous. I've stayed there before."

Elizabeth sighed inwardly. "But..." *Why come all this way and then leave?* "Are you sure you don't want me to ask about a trailer?"

"No, it's fine. Don't worry about me. You have a movie to make, and I'll only distract you. I won't have that. Career first. Always!"

Suddenly it was like old times, her mentor drilling lessons into her. Elizabeth nodded, wondering if her confusion showed.

"Bye, dearest. I look forward to seeing you in a few weeks. We'll catch up properly then. Come home soon." She dropped a kiss beside Elizabeth's mouth and gave her a dazzling smile, one of the knockout ones that got her on the covers of magazines.

After opening the door to the trailer, she paused, then suddenly turned back. "Oh and take pity on the girl. It can be extra...tricky...when your co-star's so clearly interested in something she can never have." Her pointed gaze made her meaning clear. "Poor Summer."

"What makes you think she's interested in me?"

"At your party night? The way her eyes never left you. She looked lost whenever you left the room. Telling, if you recognize the signs. I know silly crushes can make things difficult. But I'm sure you're across all that. As I keep saying, stay focused on work, and it'll be over soon. Bye, dear."

<hr/>

Fifteen minutes and one shower later, juggling an MP3 player, speaker set, and serious snacks, Summer made her way outside.

She rehearsed her little speech. *"Hope you don't mind some company. Want to hear what sort of music I like? I promise it'll make you laugh. Also, I bear gifts of popcorn and snacks. And let's talk about your wandering lips."*

Okay, scratch that last bit. She'd work up to it.

As she approached Elizabeth's door, it flung open, and a tall, elegant woman came briefly into view before disappearing again. Summer stopped, feeling she should know her. Was it some actress who needed to run lines or something? But that was odd. She'd thought Elizabeth had already finished all her scenes with other actresses, apart from Summer herself.

The woman's sensuous voice drifted down the steps. "At your party night? The way her eyes never left you. She looked lost whenever you left the room. Telling, if you recognize the signs. I know silly crushes can make things difficult. But I'm sure you're across all that. As I keep saying, stay focused on work, and it'll be over soon. Bye, dear."

Grace. No doubting that voice, even before she slapped the door closed and turned, catching sight of Summer. Those cruel words cut through to the bone.

They both froze, taking in each other's measure.

What on earth is she doing all the way out here?

With a long look at Summer's armful of snacks and electronics, followed by a knowing smile, Grace leaned against the trailer door, folding her arms. The move blocked Summer's path and claimed ownership over the trailer in one fell swoop. Her smile turned mocking.

Summer could only stare back as a number of things clicked into place. Elizabeth's kiss. The refusal to offer more while not denying she was gay. The blindly devoted way Elizabeth always stood up for her mentor. The way Grace had divined Summer's romantic interest in Elizabeth.

Her arms went numb, and her armful of booty dropped to the ground in a tangled mess. As she clambered to pick everything up, Summer's cheeks burned. She peered back up at the territorial woman guarding the door.

Brain short circuiting, Summer scrambled back to her own trailer. *Christ. I'm such a blind idiot.* How had she never seen it before?

Elizabeth and Grace.

Chapter 18

THE CAMERA SANK INTO THE room. The boom mic slid lower. Standing beside the bed, Elizabeth inhaled, centering her thoughts on the uniform-clad form of Lucille twisted in sheets before her. And then it began.

"You're not real," she whispered. "You don't love me. You don't want me. Or my touch. Because you're *me*. You're not even here. Are you?"

A mocking, cold smile crossed Summer's face. "It's only you," she confirmed. "Alone. Again."

A tear slid down Elizabeth's cheek. "But you matter to me." She dropped onto the bed, taking Summer's hand. The fingers lay limp in her own. "You mean everything to me. What will I do now?"

Summer lifted her fingers to trace Elizabeth's tears, eyes cold and empty. "What you've always done."

"What's that?" Fear laced her voice.

"You know."

"I don't."

"Yes. You do." Certainty filled Summer's face.

Elizabeth bowed her head and tears splashed down her cheeks. She willed herself to stop. She wasn't supposed to be crying so openly, but somehow Summer's coldness always brought emotions out in her. Seeing her so detached, even if it was just superb acting, broke Elizabeth's heart.

"I need you," she whispered. A tear splashed on her lap.

"Oh, Elspeth. No. You don't."

—❊—

On a flat rock, between two scraggly gray-green bushes, Summer sat, gazing into the black pools of a nearby creek. She hugged the front of her bent legs, chin propped on her jeans-clad knees. It wasn't far from the set, but it was far enough that all she could hear were crickets and distant birds. She closed her eyes to soak in the last warmth of the setting sun.

She'd survived another day of filming. Today had required stop-start shooting from multiple angles to show Lucille jumping in and out of Elspeth's mind. Lucille was symbolic of the writer's mental decay. How apt, given Elizabeth was symbolic of Summer's.

This morning, the other woman had unraveled in front of Summer, clutched her hand, and told her she needed her. Irony of ironies. The longer the scene had dragged on, the more desperate Summer had become for it to end, because she could barely meet her co-star's tear-stained eyes.

Having Elizabeth Thornton gaze at you like you really mattered when the opposite was true was cruelty upon cruelty.

She hoped Lucille's cold mask had been strong enough, powerful enough to hide her feelings. All night she'd tossed and turned over Grace's cruel words, her staking her claim over Elizabeth, mocking Summer's feelings with a single, knowing glance. Followed by Summer's humiliating scramble to safety.

Today, three things seemed crystal clear: Elizabeth Thornton was gay as hell. She was in love with Grace. And she'd kissed Summer as if her soul needed it. Yet those three things couldn't all co-exist. Something had to give. And that something was Summer. She'd be the one hurt.

She was hurting plenty already.

"May I join you?"

Summer's eyes flew open. She nodded, heart thudding furiously, shocked to have not heard the footsteps.

Elizabeth settled beside her on the rock, hair falling over the flannel collar of her shirt. *Still in costume?* She must've come straight from set.

For long minutes, neither spoke as they watched the view.

"How'd you find me out here?" Summer closed her eyes again.

"I had a fifty-fifty bet which way you went. Up or down the road. I asked one of the local guys which was more scenic."

"Okay." Summer tried to sound indifferent.

"You were amazing today. I felt everything. A lot more coldness from Lucille than I'd expected but it was an interesting choice. You seemed to surprise Jean-Claude."

"He liked it." Summer had seen the approval in his eyes.

"Yes. But your animosity toward Elspeth seemed more...personal?" Elizabeth hesitated. "Or did I imagine that?"

"I had good motivation."

A bird squawked overhead, and Summer opened her eyes to seek it out.

"You mean me? Have I...angered you?"

Summer didn't reply immediately. She cast her gaze across the setting sun. It was so beautiful out here. Or it would be if she didn't feel so fractured, like trying to trace an Escher puzzle in her head. "When were you going to tell me?" The words fell out, dull and flat.

"About what?"

"You liking women?"

Elizabeth frowned. "I did explain how charged it was on set yesterday. How emotions...leaked. I was wrong to kiss you. I shouldn't have put you in that position. It was unprofessional."

Summer gave her an incredulous look. Yet again Elizabeth had dodged the question with a non-answer. Summer regarded her. Was this woman ever without her careful, precise mask that kept her true face from the world? Did she allow anyone in? Did anyone really know her? Anyone other than perfect Grace?

Tentatively, Elizabeth asked, "*Is* this about the kiss? Or something else?"

"When were you going to tell me?" Summer repeated, even flatter this time. She waited for another denial. It would fit, wouldn't it? How little Summer rated on Elizabeth's friendship scale? Not worthy of trust, even after she'd emptied her heart out to her? Was it fair to expect the truth, though? They hadn't known each other long. Was Summer being unreasonable here?

"Where's this coming from?"

Another non-answer. "Grace."

"What?" The shock that flooded Elizabeth's face was almost comical.

"I saw her outside your trailer last night. Our paths crossed." Pain seared through her at the thought. "Piece of work, your *friend*." Her teeth gritted.

"Summer..." Elizabeth looked confused. "What did she say?"

"That's just it." Summer spread her hands. "Not a single damned word. She didn't have to. But she looked me up and down, inside and out, and she knew. Everything. I know she did. She knew why I was there, what I felt.

And I looked at her. And…suddenly I knew, too. I knew her thoughts. And that was all either of us needed. So I left."

"How…" Elizabeth's shoulders bunched up. "How did she look at you?"

"Like you were hers. And I was trespassing on what's hers."

Elizabeth's shoulders sagged. "Oh, that. She's my *mentor*. She has, I'm aware, a certain feeling of ownership of my career and it manifests itself as—"

"Stop." With an exasperated look, Summer shook her head. "For God's sake, just be honest with me. She's not *just* a mentor to you. Is she?"

"She's straight." Elizabeth ground out the two words. "One hundred percent. I promise you that. She's never shown even the faintest interest in another woman. Besides, Grace has been in love with Amrit for years. You saw how she was with him. You even mentioned it."

"I know. But even so, you're still *hers*, aren't you? Hell, it kills me I'm so slow on the uptake that I didn't realize what I was seeing at your party. The way you study her? The way you defend her? I thought it was respect. But it's much more. Bess, you're in love with her. And I'd really appreciate it if you wouldn't lie to me right now. I'd like to think I deserve more than that. Don't you trust me?"

Elizabeth rubbed her face. "It's not about trust or you. With Grace… it's complicated."

"Really." Summer's eyebrows hit her hairline. "Next you'll say I'm just imagining everything. And while I do agree Grace might not want you sexually, there's more than one way to desire someone. Because it's plain as day that Grace craves you a great deal."

Frowning, Elizabeth said, "She doesn't want me at all."

"No? The way she defines your view of your career and makes comments about you with these weird undertones? It's possessive. It's an old, old tale: Beautiful woman falls for her mentor. Mentor lives for the attention, feels special. And she protects that relationship at all costs. Grace is worried that your friendship with someone new—me—might divide your loyalties. Maybe you'll forget all about her? Well, no way will she put up with that. Especially since Grace's days of adoration and fame aren't what they used to be, are they?"

"Grace *deserves* to be feted," Elizabeth said with an aggrieved look. "It's an outrage people here can't see what's so obvious."

"Bess," Summer sighed, "this isn't about Grace's abilities. Anyone can see she has incredible talent. This is about how she uses your interest in her, your...*love*...to feel good about herself."

"She doesn't." Elizabeth's expression was grim. "That's not possible."

No denial about the love then? Sadness filled Summer at the confirmation. Well, at least she hadn't pretended it wasn't true. "How can you be so certain?"

Elizabeth appeared to be debating whether to answer.

"Please?"

"I know because Grace has no idea how I feel about..." She stopped, looking pained.

"Her?"

"Women. She doesn't know I..." Elizabeth shook her head. "We've been friends for seventeen years and she doesn't even know I'm a lesbian."

"But how's that possible?" Summer asked gently. "You're so close."

"I've been extremely careful." She lifted her chin. "And I'm a fairly decent actress when I set my mind to it. You may have noticed Grace can be a little...distracted on matters unrelated to herself? That's been useful."

It was a fair point. The more Summer thought about it, the more it made sense. Grace didn't seem to care about anything that didn't directly affect her. She probably absorbed Elizabeth's love as a mentor worship that was her due, and never thought about what else it might mean. How...sad.

"I'm sorry she doesn't really see you," Summer said delicately.

"She does, most of the time." Elizabeth examined her fingernails. "Just on this one issue, she doesn't seem...she can be oblivious."

Summer nodded.

"And she *does* care about me. She drove all the way out here to see me yesterday to make sure I was okay."

Oh, sure, that's why. For the briefest second, Summer saw doubt flicker into Elizabeth's eyes. "Do your friends know?" she asked, searching for a new topic. "About you?"

Elizabeth shot her a disgruntled look. "How I feel about Grace is *no one's* concern. It's bad enough that you... that—"

"I don't mean about your feelings for Grace. I meant you and women in general."

Elizabeth exhaled. "They might have guessed."

"You've never told them?"

"Well, Alex. We dated briefly. Years ago."

That explained some things. "Apart from her?"

Elizabeth clenched her jaw and didn't reply.

"Bess, your friends are great. They're warm and welcoming and obviously wouldn't judge you, since half of them are gay too. What are you afraid of?"

Eyes narrowing, Elizabeth's tone turned ice cold. "I came to find you because we're friends, and I thought I might have hurt you last night. I would hate that. But you do not get to pick over my life choices and judge me."

"Don't get to…" Summer gaped. "Well, I'm sorry if you think I've strayed into your enormous conversational no-fly zone, but exactly what rights do I have in this friendship? You set all the terms. And if I ask one awkward question, I get snapped at like I'm a creepy reporter wanting to dig out all your secrets, even though you already know all mine. Yet when *you* forget yourself, when you kiss me like it counts for something, well, that's nothing to get upset about. Just one little mistake. Moving on."

"I already explained about that."

"No, you lied about that. You kissed me because you're attracted to me." Summer's tone dared her to argue.

Elizabeth's mouth opened, then closed.

"And that's okay; it happens. I mean, hell, you already know I'm attracted to you."

"Summer—"

"The problem isn't that. It's how you made me feel. It's like the old saying, if you can't be with the one you want, be with the one you're with. You were worked up and you knew I wouldn't say no, so you decided to have some fun with the one you were with."

Elizabeth looked appalled by the charge. Hurt crossed her eyes. "You feel that I'm so calculating? That I think so little of you? Is that really what you believe about me?"

Summer studied her outrage. *Was it?* She thought about that. There'd been nothing premeditated about Elizabeth last night. She'd seemed almost giddy. Excited. And she'd just…

"No," Summer finally admitted. "No, I don't think that."

"Thank you." Elizabeth exhaled. "I had no business kissing you like that. Especially given...everything else. It was a foolish moment that I didn't think through. I'm not...prone to them."

"You're not, are you? You're very self-contained."

"I like to be professional."

"Yes." Summer hesitated. "Can you just tell me one thing? I understand now that you keep secrets from everyone. All your friends. You keep all of us at arm's length, don't you?"

Silence. Elizabeth twitched. "Is that your question?"

"Do you even know why?"

Elizabeth's face closed over. Her jaw hardened.

"Okay. It's fine." Summer smoothed her hands down her jeans. "You don't have to say. I just thought maybe you'd like to talk about it sometime. We do have a lot in common."

It was a little insulting how incredulous Elizabeth's snort of laughter was. "We do?"

"Sure. We're both closeted actresses in LA, working on a Jean-Claude film *and* on the same TV show. We enjoy Shakespeare, London, guayusa cacao tea from Blackie's Tea House in Cambridge but nowhere else, and we happen to adore all your friends, give or take one." Summer grinned. "Come on, that's a huge amount in common."

Elizabeth's smile warmed. "Perhaps." Her face opened up a little. "I concede that point."

"Mmm." Summer rested her chin on her fist and stared out over the vista below. "I wish you weren't so hard to get to know." *Oh geez.* "Um...I didn't mean to say that out loud."

Elizabeth fidgeted. "Why do you care?" She seemed genuinely confused.

"I've never met anyone like you before. I'd really like to understand you better. I already think you're interesting. But I'd love to know all of you. The pieces you don't often share with people. The little things that make you *you*."

The smile fell away. Elizabeth exhaled. "It's not that easy."

"Sorry. I know it's not." Well, it'd been a long-shot.

"I meant, I'm not sure *how*. People think I'm aloof and cold and I get labeled 'uptight Brit' quite often. But the truth is, I'm reserved even among reserved people." She hesitated.

"You're shy," Summer guessed.

Elizabeth conceded a tiny nod. "To the point of introverted. And I'm aware that is ridiculous for a performer."

"No, a fair few actors are, actually. It's not that strange. It's why they escape into other people."

"I find it helps to live another life on stage. It's the only time I feel truly free. I felt it yesterday in our scene. I was alive. I love that feeling. I can disappear under the spotlight and be anyone. When I did *Shakespeare's Women*, it was exhilarating. Everything felt possible." Her eyes took on a faraway look. "But then...I always come crashing back to earth. The lights come up and I'm reminded of reality. And my emotional situation, regarding Grace, has been challenging."

Elizabeth didn't elaborate, so Summer turned that over. "Because you've been protecting yourself so carefully so she'd never know how you feel?"

She didn't answer for a few minutes. "It's become a habit of so long, drawing my feelings tight inside myself so that all anyone sees is walls. And somewhere along the line, I think it became a habit to never let myself be spontaneous or open. I weigh up every word, every emotion, before daring to express it. It's become a protective skin I can't shed at whim. This is who I am now." She looked at Summer closely. "Do you understand how out of character it was for me to do what I did last night? Having a spontaneous moment...a bold one at that...is an aberration that astonishes me."

Summer blinked. "I guess so."

"You say you've never met anyone like me? Well, I can't even fathom you. I sometimes wonder what it's like to be you. So open about everything and everyone. Doing things on a whim. Like that day you decided Hunt's reputation needed saving? You just jumped in without thought."

"Oh, I gave it plenty of thought, trust me."

"Fine, but you took the risk anyway. How did you know it'd work out? How do you just say what you think and feel? Don't you worry it'll be used against you? To hurt you?"

It hadn't really occurred to her. "No?"

"No." Elizabeth gave a faintly amazed laugh. "And I'm guessing everyone in your life knows you're gay?"

"Definitely. I'd like to be out officially one day, for all the other little gays kids who need some extra courage. We're just figuring out timing."

"I see." Elizabeth's knuckles whitened as her hands formed fists. "Even the thought of being out fills me with dread. To be so exposed? Open to abuse?"

"Because you'd feel too vulnerable?"

"Of course. But that's not all of it. I've been loathed for years by so many people who don't even know me, and coming out would just be adding more vitriol to my pyre. I can imagine the hate mail then. God, it's wearying."

"You might be surprised. People aren't always their worst selves. I have hope it's changing."

"You're not a villain, Summer. Our coming out stories would be met with very different reactions."

"Maybe you're right. I'm sorry if you are. But I'd like to point out not *everyone* hates you." Summer tossed her a bright smile. "I may have mentioned before that the entire LA Goldstars basketball team loves you. Or, they love Dr. Hunt, at least."

"*That's* the name of Chloe's team?" Elizabeth made a choking noise, somewhere between a laugh and a wheeze. "Could they be a little gay by any chance?"

"What gave it away?" Summer laughed. "Yeah, everyone is except for Chloe. She jokes she's the token straight."

"So, basically, you're saying I'm universally despised by all except a handful of lesbian basketballers?" Elizabeth drawled. "How reassuring."

"It's not just them. For some reason, I like you a lot, too. Even though you confuse the hell out of me at times. You're talented, interesting, and really funny when you choose to be. I think maybe you're stuck in my head like a Madonna song." Summer stood, offering her hand to Elizabeth. "Don't worry, only one of the good ones. Like *Vogue*."

Elizabeth took her hand and rose. "I never know how to respond when you blurt out random things like that. Were you always like this? Forthright to a fault?"

They began walking back to the set.

"Oh no," Summer said. "Only when I got older. When I was Punky, I was this skinny, wide-eyed kid who found fame overwhelming. I was recognized everywhere and I just wanted to crawl away and hide. Then my parents got that trilogy in London. Usually Autumn and I stayed with our grandparents when our parents did long-term location stuff. But this time, while Autumn stayed home to finish high school, Mom insisted I come with them, so I could spend my awkward teenage years somewhere normal as an unknown. It saved my sanity."

"Wise."

"Even Mom has her moments."

"I liked your mother. She was amusing, warm, and compassionate. I... appreciated her."

"Of course you did. She kept embarrassing me for your amusement."

"Just a little." Elizabeth huffed out a tiny laugh. "You have her eyes, by the way. And smile. You do look quite alike. She's beautiful."

Summer's stride stuttered.

"What?" Elizabeth glanced at her.

"You realize you just called me beautiful."

Elizabeth's cheeks took on a slightly pink tinge. "I did no such thing."

"Yeah, you did," Summer teased.

"Oh, for God's... *Fine.*" The tinge on Elizabeth's cheeks reddened. "I'm obviously not blind. You are attractive."

"And..."

"And what?"

"*That's* why you kissed me."

"Must we?" Elizabeth looked pained.

"Yep." Grinning, Summer added, "So...did you enjoy kissing me?"

Elizabeth rolled her eyes. "It was...enjoyable. As if you couldn't tell." Her expression became rueful. "Even though I'm very sorry I took leave of my senses and didn't think it through in the least. I'm sorry if you felt used."

"I believe you." Summer sobered. She gave the tiniest half grin, feeling both sheepish and sad. "Just...please don't do it again, okay? I'm serious. I don't care how much it blew the top of my head off."

Elizabeth's eyebrows lifted in surprise.

"No, don't get cocky," Summer said. "I loved the kiss. But I'm a real person with real feelings and just because you're in the mood to...whatever that was...you can't do that to me again. It hurts later when you explain how it was nothing. If you ever kiss me again, you have to mean it with every fiber of your being. Do you understand? Because I'm not strong enough for this. You can't play with me. Okay?"

Elizabeth's eyes widened. "I promise. And I'm sor—"

"I know you are." Summer waved her hand. "Let's just forget it. Move on. Be...friends."

"Of course."

Summer's jaw firmed. "God. What a day. Or week, really."

"And the rest. This has been an absurd couple of months, pretending to be in love with you to get a role while being secretly closeted to the world."

Summer laughed. "It'd make a good British farce."

"Oh, I'm sure." They approached their trailer. "Can I offer you a reparations dinner?" Elizabeth asked. "I somehow ended up with lots and lots of cheese. Plus there's Diet Coke. And bad eighties music. I found someone's mix CD behind the microwave. And, at the risk of invoking Madonna again, the first track is *Holiday*, so you just know it's going to be diabolical."

"Wow, black fizz *and* high art. You know how to woo a girl." Summer grinned briefly before the smile fell away. There'd be no wooing by Elizabeth. If nothing else, she'd learned that today. The woman's heart was set on Grace.

Elizabeth's expression became regretful. "Summer, if things were different, if I didn't have someone else I...someone I can't quite shake, no matter how often I try, then this would be a whole different conversation. I think you're beautiful, inside and out."

Summer's cheeks warmed at the compliment. *Wait. Someone I can't quite shake?* She'd been trying? Hope surged, and Summer hated herself for it. This was hard enough as it was.

"I have gin," Elizabeth upped the ante. "I hear that makes everything better. Although I may just be quoting myself."

"Almost as good as beer."

At Elizabeth's shocked look, Summer elbowed her lightly in the ribs. "God, you English are easy to mess with. At least I didn't suggest microwaving tea."

"Oh. My. God." Elizabeth glared at her. "Infidel."

"Yeah, I know. But I think I'll leave you to your Hendrick's and Madonna, okay? I need a time out. There's a lot for me to think about."

"I understand. Until tomorrow then," Elizabeth smiled. "Post-Madonna."

"If such a world exists."

That earned a relaxed laugh and a wave, before the click of Elizabeth's trailer door closing shut.

Summer stared at the door for a few moments, amazed at how much had changed in a day.

Chapter 19

SUMMER HAD STAYED ON FOR a few days after the filming of her scenes ended. She was debating whether to stay the full week, having a mini vacation, as Jean-Claude had offered. If nothing else she could enjoy the wrap party; God knew the Frenchman threw good ones. It was tempting, especially given how things were with Elizabeth.

They'd fallen into a habit of relaxing together after Elizabeth wrapped each day. Summer would ply her with cups of tea and silly stories, while Elizabeth kicked off her shoes, peeled off her flannel shirt, and collapsed on the couch. As Elizabeth sipped the tea, she'd always shoot Summer such a profoundly grateful look that it made her insides squeeze.

Elizabeth gradually started sharing snippets about herself. Not a lot, but more than before. Often it was about her childhood and home. She quoted literature a lot, and finally admitted the habit had been picked up at her mother's knee.

"Live with a literature professor and I dare you to come away not knowing how to cite your sources," she teased one night, leaning back on the couch, eyes half lidded, a genial smile on her face.

It was the most relaxed Summer had ever seen her. She wished she could freeze-frame the image forever.

Summer, in turn, told her about growing up with her crazy, chaotic family. "You have to love awkwardness, that's rule number one; color, that's rule number two; and not question the absurd, rule number three."

"The absurd?"

"Vibes, feelings, and so on. Doing or believing things because they *feel* right, not for any logical reason."

"And does your father go along with this too?" Elizabeth asked, leaning forward. "Brock doesn't seem an illogical man."

"We all go along with it. Mom is too hard to argue with. You have no idea. It's exhausting. Don't even start me on the year she decided we would embrace feathers as fashion."

"Feathers?"

Summer sighed. "It was way worse than it sounds."

"Oh I doubt that. It sounds dire. So what influences did your father have on you? I'm suspecting it's not your co-ordination."

"Ha-ha. Yes, Dad worked out pretty early on I was useless at martial arts and all the other physical things he tried to teach me. He says I have the balance of a day-old fawn."

"Imagine that." Elizabeth didn't hide her smile.

"So he did the next best thing: taught me how to fall correctly, so I wouldn't hurt myself on landing. Boy, has that come in handy."

Elizabeth burst into laughter. It was the sweetest sound—high, light, and unexpected. She herself seemed stunned by it. "Oh my God. I haven't laughed like that in…" Her face fell. "Years?"

"Tales of my parents do have that effect on people."

"Oh, I'm quite sure it's not your parents. It's more…" she drew her finger in a circle in the air around Summer's face. "The Summer effect."

"There's a 'me' effect?"

Quirking her lips, Elizabeth said, "There certainly is. I'm not sure how to quantify it. You probably defy science. I'm certain of it."

"I do?" Summer looked at her, lost. "Um, what science?"

"The statistically improbable ability of lowering my defenses to the point you make me laugh like that." She looked bemused. "I'm not sure what to make of it. You're certainly my favorite scientific anomaly right now." She smiled and took another swallow of tea.

Oh. Wow. Summer felt warm, pleased, and all sorts of gooey. Sadness washed over her so abruptly that she almost gasped. Confused, she pushed it away and grinned, topped up their tea, and continued regaling Elizabeth with more absurd tales from her childhood.

When she went to bed that night, Summer turned over her sudden sadness, unable to pinpoint its source. About two in the morning she sat up as the stark truth hit her.

Elizabeth was like being shown a precious gem, and being told she could get as close as she liked to admire it but could never touch. That it wasn't for her, and never would be. As their relationship deepened, the knowledge that Summer would never have all of her hurt more each day. Now it was a constant, low-level ache.

She couldn't stay here. It was too easy in this wilderness, alone with Bess, for the world to dissolve, to get lost in the messy, inconvenient feelings that were becoming too powerful.

The next morning, Summer packed up and offered her excuses—lame ones that made Elizabeth's eyes cloud with confusion and her lips open with unasked questions. Summer was glad she didn't ask them; she couldn't bear the lies she'd have had to tell.

In front of Jean-Claude and a few of the yawning production crew, they shared a rather awkward, brief farewell kiss and a soft, tingly hug, before Summer retreated to her car and floored it out of Kings Canyon National Park.

When she got home, Summer crawled into bed for a few days, not in the mood for human interaction. Wallowing felt like an appropriate life goal.

Around day three, Chloe threw a pillow at her and told her to stop brooding.

It wasn't brooding if she had a legitimate broken heart, was it? Well, not broken-broken. More like dented. Slightly bruised? The worst part was, that heated kiss still filled her dreams, and left her body burning each morning.

Autumn's unannounced arrival the next day interrupted Summer's steady new diet of ice cream and daytime soaps. She answered the door in her PJs at eleven and shuffled back to the sofa. "There's Diet Coke in the fridge," she told her sister, who'd followed her.

"You know I don't touch black death. You shouldn't either."

"You sound like Bess." *Damn it.* She'd been trying not to think of her every five minutes. She tried to focus on a soap star's impossibly handsome head instead. He had an odd tic of licking his lips before delivering each line.

Autumn snatched the remote from her hands and switched off the TV. "We have to talk."

"Hey! How'll I find out who's the father of Crystal's baby?"

"Summer? It's about work."

That got her attention. "*Choosing Hope?*"

"Yes."

"They've finally fired me, huh?" She slumped. "Well, Ravitz did have his beady little eye on me. Like he was figuring out where to bury my body." Wouldn't this top off her month perfectly? Heart squished (a little). Pay check axed. Back to the auditions rat race.

"Not fired," Autumn said cautiously. "It's something else." She slid her gaze upwards and flared her nose.

Uh-oh. Bad juju ahead. "Shit, what is it?" Summer sat up, worried.

"Look, while you were off in the middle of the wilds, your final *Hope* episodes aired—the ones where you and Thornton had that weird vibe around each other? What on earth were you trying to play, anyway?"

Summer shrugged. "No idea. We never did figure it out."

"Apparently that was a common reaction."

"Huh?"

"Fans noticed. Along with thousands of new fans they recruited to try and figure it out with them."

"I don't get it."

"You're being 'shipped' together by viewers. Hunt and Carter now have the portmanteau of 'Hunter'. I hear the lesbian fan fiction and artwork is melting the internet. Hunter's *the* fastest growing fandom in the world right now."

"Lesbi...fan fiction? The hell?" Summer struggled to make sense of the words. It sounded an awful lot like people wanted her and Elizabeth's characters getting it on.

Autumn exhaled. "You heard me. Now Ravitz and Lenton have called in you and your accomplice for an urgent meeting. It's next Tuesday at ten. Dress smart. Be polite. Don't try to be funny."

A meeting? So they *did* want to fire her? She hadn't thought her acting had been *that* out there. Sure she'd been in a dark place for most of those weeks. How awful *had* she been? "Ah, crap."

"Exactly."

"But why are they hauling Elizabeth in too? She only ever reacted to what I did. She didn't contribute." Had Chief Hunt been acting differently too? Maybe a tiny bit less mean? Summer wracked her brain trying to remember, but that time for her was clouded in a swirl of misery. "Anyway, they can't fire her for what *I* did. Besides there's no point firing someone they're already planning on writing out in the upcoming season."

"Maybe they're bringing her exit forward?" Autumn suggested. "As in rapidly forward? I get the impression they're not fond of her."

"They're not. It's not her fault, either. They had some shitty plot lined up for Hunt to have a drunken one-night stand with a barely legal intern, and she refused to do it. In retaliation they deliberately fucked up her character. They gave Hunt Mendez, only for her to break his heart in the cruelest way to turn the fans against her."

Autumn regarded her. "Summer, listen to me really close. Whatever they do to her on Tuesday is not your concern, okay? If they decide to punish her, fire her, or make her character join the circus and juggle skunks, don't react. That's for her to work out. Say nothing that doesn't relate to you. I know you care for her..." She paused, then lifted her eyebrows.

Summer waited for her to finish.

"Oh, we're not going to do this anymore?" Autumn asked. "Your automatic denial that it's not what I think, and that was only when you were young?"

"You can leave at any time." Summer scowled.

"Damn it, damn it, damn it. *Fuck!*" Autumn burrowed the heels of her hands into her eyes. "This...is not helpful. That shoot was supposed to cure you, not make it worse. And now we have Hunter to contend with, too? What is it with you two that you keep attracting the gay? Especially the gay with each other?"

If only she knew. "Autumn," she tried for her most conciliatory tone, "I'll behave at the meeting. Anything else?"

"No." She sighed. "Summer, are you okay? You haven't seemed yourself since you got back. Did anything happen out there?"

"Not a thing. Unless you count a few mosquito bites."

"And did you cope okay with the sex scenes? Was it hard or did you get over it?"

"Both. But I'm fine." Summer reached for the remote. "I think Javier's the baby daddy. He was always around when Crystal was dating that media mogul."

Autumn took the hint. "You can always talk to me, you know. And I do get just wanting to lounge around, but *pajamas* in the middle of the day, Summer? Seriously?"

"It's my vacation." She glared.

"Okay, okay." Autumn held up her hands. "I'll see you Sunday for lunch like always. But remember, next Tuesday at ten."

Summer stabbed the *On* button and her soap resumed.

It had been nine days since Summer had last seen Elizabeth. She *was* counting and didn't even bother denying otherwise.

Summer was in two minds about seeing her again. On the one hand, they'd left things as friends. On the other, Summer's growing feelings couldn't be switched off like a faucet. The memory of the kiss taunted her often. Just as strong was the memory of their talks each night.

Of course, the triple threat was that Elizabeth still looked...gah. Amazing. Her hair tumbled loose over her shoulders. Did she have to wear a navy vest over that crisp white shirt? *Is she trying to kill me?*

Summer slid into a chair beside Elizabeth, opposite director Bob Ravitz, showrunner Stanley Lenton, chief writer Hugo Pollard, and the son of the network president whose name she could never remember. He never visited the set. These were the big guns. Her anxiously thudding pulse calmed down a little. Surely they wouldn't invite him or Hugo to a firing?

Elizabeth glanced over, giving Summer a polite nod.

How had she taken the news of their "Hunter" fandom? Were her people feverishly working on strategies to hose it all down into a lovely sheen of vanilla heterosexuality? Probably.

"Ms. Hayes, at last, thanks for joining us," Lenton said.

Ass. Summer wasn't late. She murmured something suitably polite back.

"I appreciate you and Ms. Thornton coming in on your time off before we're officially back for season seven," the showrunner continued, his gaze flickering between them. "As you know, during hiatus, the final episodes of last season aired. It was...quite an eye-opener seeing the reaction."

Elizabeth darted a glance at Summer.

"*Hunter*," Ravitz took over. "That's what they're calling you two now. You thought we didn't know what you were up to?" The director pinned his dark eyes on Summer. "I discussed it with Stanley when you put the first lesbian subtext in…that episode with the dyed fingers?"

Summer's heart rate nearly tripled. *Shit, he noticed that?*

"God, everyone's trying to find a way to get noticed on TV. So that was your play? I get it. I'm only surprised you talked *her* into going along with it." He pointed at Elizabeth, who didn't react at all. "I talked it over with Stanley, and we decided not to stop it and see what the fans did with it. See if they even noticed."

"They fuckin' noticed all right," the network man said. "This lesbian crap's *everywhere*. Memes, art, social media, all of it. People are writing damned theses on what emotional state you two were playing." He snorted. "Christ almighty, viewers must be bored."

"Yes, Jason." Lenton gave him a shiny, alligator smile. "They certainly must be. So, well done, Ms. Hayes. You did what you set out to, and got yourself noticed in a big way."

Summer stared at him, unable to think of anything to say.

"We had been trying to understand what was in it for Ms. Thornton, but now we know." The showrunner turned to Elizabeth. "You thought we wouldn't figure it out?"

"What would that be?" Elizabeth's shoulders tensed, although her tone sounded relaxed.

"Damned sneaky. First adding the subtext. Then the snaps from the paparazzi—who you obviously tipped off to be waiting."

Summer shook her head to interrupt but he held up his hand.

"Don't bother. Look, Hollywood's a small town. We know everyone's secrets. So I happen to know that you two spent your hiatus doing some artsy queer flick playing lovers for Jean-Claude Badour. So all this earlier stuff's been a covert publicity stunt, using our show. You probably figured by the time those episodes aired, people would be talking about your chemistry and the gay rumors. Then word would be put out that there's an actual sex scene in that indie flick, and they'd all rush out and see it. Clever. Stealth fuckin' marketing at its finest."

Mouth falling open, Summer made to object again. Elizabeth's hand pressing urgently on her thigh made her clang her jaw shut.

"Well, I suppose the gig's up," Elizabeth said smoothly with a tiny shrug. "So you've caught us. Now what?"

Lenton laughed. "I knew it. Sly as hell." He didn't seem too annoyed. Actually, he looked pretty pleased at being right.

Elizabeth's hand disappeared off Summer's thigh. The warm buzz remained. *Traitorous leg.*

"We've discussed it and we're getting in first," he said. "We're gazumping that French flick and using your stealth marketing for our own ends. The network's behind it. Not surprising when you see the ratings we've been getting since you two started your Hunter stunts. We've got all these new queer fans tuning in, and they've told their friends, and straight viewers are all 'What's the damned fuss about?' And now…" He held up a page with a list of numbers. "*Choosing Hope*'s officially the number one non-sport show in the US right now. Not just our network. Not just dramas. All of it. All shows. All channels. We're it."

Holy shit! Summer gaped at him.

Elizabeth's mouth had dropped slightly open. "How exactly are you planning on working this to your advantage?" she asked Lenton, voice silky.

"For starters, we've decided we're supporting Hunter's fans. More than that, we'll make it real for them."

What. The. Hell?

Elizabeth stiffened beside her.

"This'll give our diversity quota for the network a boost, too," the network man cut in. "We're going to milk the hell out of this. A sizzling lesbian romance by fan demand."

"Dr. Hunt's the *villain*." Caution edged Elizabeth's tone. "Why do I think there's more to this than a romance?"

"Perceptive." Lenton's smile turned mean. "Let's just say that plot you objected to so vigorously? It's been rewritten. There're no drunken escapades this time. And your love interest's obviously older than some wet-behind-the-ears intern, so your precious character's integrity is intact. But all the rest stays."

"Hunt is still Carter's boss."

"I'm well aware."

"There's a power-balance issue."

"But not an age or an alcohol one. You got two out of three. I'd take that as a win. Right?" His gaze sharpened.

Elizabeth hesitated. "And Dr. Hunt is now bisexual?"

"Fuck no." He chortled. "We'll discover the reason she was such a bitch to Mendez was because she's been hiding her inner gay all this time. Hundred percent homo."

"Um," Summer said, "sorry, but isn't Joey straight? Hasn't she been flirting with Mendez? Well, more *him* flirting with her, really, but still, I thought, she was written as—"

"She *was* straight," Lenton said. "Hunt's going to turn her queer as a three-dollar bill."

Turn her?

Turn. Her?

"That's not how it works." Elizabeth's eyes narrowed.

"It is now." Lenton gave her a withering look. "Do you think I give a fuck about the laws of sexuality? Hunter fans want *action*. Ratings speak. So that's what's happening."

"But, Mr. Lenton," Summer said carefully, "won't this come across as predatory? Innocent, sweet Joey being seduced by her wicked boss?"

"Yes." He all but beamed. "It will. Hunt's the villain for a reason."

Elizabeth frowned.

"Okay, so won't that, ah, piss off your lesbian viewers?" Summer tried again. "If you're suggesting she's some sort of scheming, predatory dyke?"

"Well, I'm sure Ms. Thornton can walk the line delicately, so we keep the queer-loving liberal fans as well as the edgy plot." He swung his gaze to Elizabeth, challenging her with a stare. "I was under the impression you're a brilliant actress. Shakespeare and so forth? Was I misinformed, Ms. Thornton?"

Elizabeth didn't react. "And if we say no?" she asked quietly.

"We wouldn't fire you, if that's what you're wondering. Or were you hoping we would?" He gave her a knowing look. "Your contract's too expensive to pay out. Hers isn't." Lenton pointed at Summer, who flinched. "We'd fire Ms. Hayes as surplus to requirements for starting this mess, and your last season will be about as much fun as lancing boils. And when the

Hunter fans complain about sweet Joey leaving the show, it'll be made clear why she really left."

"And why would that be?" Elizabeth's even, dry tone barely lifted above a whisper.

"Oh, I don't know. I hear all sorts of rumors about the British Bitch. It's hard to know what to believe. Did the delightful Ms. Hayes flee the show because of your jealous fits of rage over her youth and beauty? Who knows what HGZ will take it into their heads to report?"

Blackmail? Summer's nostrils flared. *That bastard.* Wait, did that mean *he* was the leak?

"So?" Ravitz finally spoke again, an amused gleam in his eye. "I presume we have an exciting new plot that you'll both be happy to take part in?"

No one spoke.

"Well, Ms. Hayes?" Lenton prodded.

Autumn's words rang in Summer's head. *Speak only for yourself.* Okay, was this good for her career? Definitely. A publicity blitz about her on the number one show in the *whole of the US?* She affixed a smile. "I'm sure Joey can find her inner bisexual. Or inner gay. Whatever you'd like, Mr. Lenton."

"Excellent." He turned his measuring look to Elizabeth. "And Ms. Thornton?" Lenton's tone dared her to challenge him.

Elizabeth met it with an unfazed look. "You know, since *Choosing Hope*'s number one, it would be exceptionally foolish to break up the reason you got there. And I believe you know that." Her gaze drifted from face to face. She smiled serenely.

Lenton and Ravitz's jaws clenched in stereo.

"However, mystifyingly, I have seen men in this business put their own egos ahead of success, just to prove a point to someone who has angered them," she said. "The fact is, Summer is too talented to fire. It's a shame you don't understand that yet. So, I'll do this, and then you'll see. She will be impressive in this storyline."

"Bess, you don't have to do this for me," Summer said under her breath.

"I only have a season left. You could have many more." She looked back to the men. "I'll get my people to contact you with my conditions. No sex scenes, for instance. Sorry to disappoint." Her eyes hardened. "A fade to black is the most I'll agree to. I won't have either of us exploited for ratings. And don't try and tell me you wouldn't do that. We all know better."

The men shot looks at each other but didn't speak, as though afraid she'd say no outright.

"And I get creative freedom in precisely how I portray Chief Hunt's shift into lesbianism." She narrowed her eyes. "She will *not* be a predator. At least, not on this subject. Make her as dark as you like in any other area, but on this, she's not playing games. Whatever she feels for Carter or her own coming out, they mean something to her. Something real."

The showrunner exchanged looks with the chief writer. Hugo licked his lips thoughtfully and nodded, scribbling a note. "I can make that fly," he muttered to Lenton. "No problem."

Lenton regarded Elizabeth for a long beat. "All right. I'm sure we can work something out." He smiled another oily smile, then shuffled his papers. "Good meeting. My people will be in touch with yours." His gaze shifted to take in Summer. "See you both back at work next week."

The meeting wrapped up and everyone else strode out, leaving Summer looking wide-eyed at Elizabeth. "That was... you were amazing."

"Know your own power, Summer," she said. "They were always going ahead with that plot. We wouldn't have been able to get out of it without a mess involving lawyers. But I wanted some control, so I negotiated where I had wiggle room."

"Incredible. And I loved how you called him out on putting ego before success."

"Hardly a newsflash." Her smile bordered on mischievous. "But I admit the opportunity was too great to resist, given he was trying so desperately to get me to agree and not cause a fuss over the plot like last time."

"It was priceless. And can you believe how they thought this whole thing had been some big plot? Stealth marketing!"

"Of course they did." Elizabeth picked up her bag. "They see the world through their own eyes. Schemes everywhere. On that note, it's always better to let them believe you're playing the game than being duped by it. Gives you more leverage. They don't underestimate you then. That's why I stopped you telling them the truth before."

"Makes sense."

Elizabeth gave her a wry smile. "It looks like our lives are about to get complicated again."

"We seem to have a skill for it. Autumn will probably cry when I tell her."

"I think I'll have to get Delvine to tell Rachel. Although I'd quite like to watch." Elizabeth sounded amused. "Are you doing well, Summer? I only just returned to civilization or I'd have called. I must say it was odd not having you around on set for the last week. It seemed much emptier. Even Jean-Claude noticed. He commented he missed you too."

Too? Elizabeth had missed her? "Oh, I've been vacationing hard. Catching up on my soaps, denting my ice cream collection, bemoaning the fact I haven't taken my camera out in weeks. What about you? How are you doing?"

They headed for the door together. "I... have had..." She paused. "I was going to lie and say everything's fine. It isn't though. Filming wrapped. I headed home, did a few chores, caught up with Alex and Zara. But Grace is being mystifying and out of contact. I'm not sure what to make of it."

Summer felt a burn of pleasure in her chest. "Thanks."

"For what?"

"Not lying. I love that you shared that with me. I-I love all the things you've shared with me lately. It means a lot."

Elizabeth's lips gave the tiniest of upticks. "Would you like to get a tea with me? Joe's is on the corner. Doesn't do a bad brew for an American establishment."

"I agree. But I don't think I can."

"You're busy?"

"A little," Summer hedged. She wasn't quite ready for being in close quarters with the woman who made her hormones hum. "Maybe another time?"

Elizabeth nodded. "I'd like that. Call me if the mood strikes."

Her hopeful look undid Summer. She sighed. *So damned weak.* "Actually, I think I can shift a thing. I'd love to get a tea with you."

"Great." Elizabeth's eyes crinkled in an adorable way.

God. Summer was nuts to put herself through more heartache. She heard herself saying, "Cool. Let's go."

So weak. She was so, so weak.

"Let me order," Summer said the moment they arrived at the cafe, which was bursting with cakes, crusty bread, and the smells of tea and coffee. "I know what you like. Besides, I owe you something."

"What?"

"Wait and see."

Summer shooed her in the direction of the square wooden tables, where Elizabeth found a spot with a nice view out the window, away from other patrons. She glanced at her watch. Eleven-thirty. She'd call Delvine after this and break the news that she was yet again going to have to deal with The Gay and Summer in the same sentence. She smirked until she remembered what that meant—more scenes that were a little too close to home. How long before people started to genuinely suspect that she had certain leanings? She really wasn't up for the scrutiny it would bring; she craved her privacy. And she certainly couldn't face being anyone's poster girl for a particular group.

Five minutes later Summer returned from the counter, a teasing smile on her face.

God she'd missed that cheeky expression. Nothing had been the same since Summer had left *Eight Little Pieces* out of the blue. When was the last time she'd craved anyone's company? Even Grace she preferred in small doses. Not Summer though.

"I've owed you this since our meeting with Jean-Claude," Summer was saying. "Promises were made."

"I have no idea what you..." Elizabeth paused as a waitress brought over two steaming cups of tea and then returned with a gooey-looking chocolate lava pudding. "Oh!" It was sin on a plate. Her mouth watered. "It's not even lunchtime. Let alone time for..." She waved at the oozing, cocoa-rich concoction.

"It's lunchtime somewhere and it'll go with the tea, which is a special blend with chocolate in it. Not as good as our favorite, but I think you'll like it."

"I suspect I'll need a few hours on the treadmill to make up for all this." Elizabeth's fingers tingled as she stared at the dessert. It looked as heavenly as Marcus's pudding.

"No problem, I thought of that too." Summer moved her hand around the side of the plate and extracted cutlery. "Two forks. We can share if you need some rationalization."

"Ah. You're an expert."

"I have known a lot of actresses in my day." Summer grinned. "Come on, give it a go. Tea's getting cold. And the dessert has to be eaten warm."

Fifteen minutes later, Summer stared back at her over the remnants of a very enjoyable dessert. Sharing food had been a bit unsettling. It wasn't something Elizabeth did. Not even with Alex, even when they were dating. It just seemed too intimate. But Summer had a way of sweeping her up into things, be they kisses or chocolate treats.

All right, not fair. She had, after all, been the one to sweep Summer into that kiss. But Summer's response had been intoxicating.

"What are you thinking about?" Summer asked.

Oh no. They weren't going there. "How Delvine's going to take the latest news. And—"

"Excuse me? You're Summer Hayes, aren't you?"

A well-dressed woman in her thirties pinned Summer with an excited look.

"I am." Summer quietly put down her fork.

"Oh my God, I'm such a big Punky Power fan!"

"Really? Which episode did you like most?"

"I loved them all. I can't pick a favorite!"

Summer smiled. "I see."

"Can I have your autograph?" The woman slapped an 8x10 on the table. It was a black and white photo of a teenaged Summer as Punky, looking particularly adorable.

How convenient she should happen to have it with her. Elizabeth's jaw tightened. Professional "fans" kept photos of dozens of stars in their trunks and whipped them out to be signed if they saw one. Then they'd turn around and sell them on eBay. If it was her, Elizabeth would send this liar on her way with a snarl. She wondered how Summer would handle it.

"I'm afraid I can't. You see you're interrupting lunch with my friend."

"I'm so sorry, but please? It'd mean *everything*."

"What's your name?" Summer asked.

"Summer," Elizabeth leaned in to warn her that this was no fan. "I don't think—"

"Clarice." The woman cut her off with a sharp look, then put a fat, black pen on the table and looked at Summer expectantly.

Summer made no move toward it. "And how do you spell that, Clarice?" She took a sip of tea.

"Oh, you don't have to write my name. Just sign it. I can see you're busy." Clarice's eyes passed over Elizabeth briefly, dismissing her.

"No, I don't mind," Summer returned her tea to the saucer and reached for the pen. "I can personalize it and everything. In fact, I insist."

"No," Clarice said quickly. "It's okay. I just really want your autograph."

Summer took the pen, wrote for a few moments, then handed the photo back.

The woman's expression changed in a furious instant. "Screw you!"

"Have a lovely day." Summer waved as she stomped out.

Elizabeth shook her head. "What did you write?"

"'Dear Clarice, it's rude to pretend to be a fan to solicit autographs from stars for photos you intend to sell. It makes actors feel used and insulted. Kindness always. Summer'. Then I added 'xox'."

"That was a nice touch. So you're not nearly as sweet as you pretend?" Elizabeth snickered. "The scandal!"

"Hey, I'm sweet. To real fans. I just hate con-artists. She was so obvious. She didn't want a personalized autograph. She couldn't name a single episode she liked. She's too old to be in my fanbase, but didn't say she was a mother, which parents always point out because they're embarrassed to admit they've watched the show. And she had a publicity photo on her."

It was cute the way she reeled the evidence off, a determined little line between her brows. "Aren't you a regular Sherlock," Elizabeth drawled.

"Hardly. Besides, we're also at Joe's."

"What do you mean?"

"We're so close to the studio that autograph hunters often hit this place, hoping to find someone famous. Surely you've been ambushed here before?"

"Never. And I've been here dozens of times."

"Oh, Bess." Summer's expression was filled with regret. "I hate that they hate you. It's so unfair."

Elizabeth shrugged. "It means I get to take my tea in peace," she said lightly. "And oozing puddles of chocolate."

Summer smiled at their dessert debris. "So you enjoyed this?"

"Very much. Not to mention the person I was sharing it with."

Summer lost a little of her composure and looked away, cheeks reddening.

Oh. Elizabeth cursed herself. She hadn't meant to flirt. She'd truly meant what she'd said, and it had come out seductive. Desperately, Elizabeth searched for a fresh topic.

Summer beat her to it. "So, since I'm apparently Sherlock, maybe I can help you with your other mystery?"

"My what?"

"Grace? She's missing? What do you know?"

"Ah. Grace always tells me if she's going away. Not this time. I went over to her place when my calls rang out. Her neighbor says she left in a cab a few days ago."

Summer frowned. "Did you try texting? If she's away from a good reception area, texts sometimes get through if calls don't."

"I did. Nothing." Elizabeth finished the last of her tea. "It's out of character. She loves to go over my recent acting experiences with me. Discuss the choices I made and so on." *Lecture me, tell me where I went wrong...* Elizabeth pushed that from her mind.

"Well, it sounds like she's left on a spur-of-the-moment decision."

"Agreed. But why hasn't she contacted any of us?"

"You know, I don't think Grace is that hard to work out. Mystifying isn't really a word I'd apply to her."

Elizabeth stared at her in surprise. Grace was impossible to fathom at the best of times. "Oh?"

"Just ask yourself: What matters most to Grace? And that's where she is and what she's doing."

Elizabeth eyed her. "And what do you think that is?"

Shooting her an apologetic look, Summer said gently, "I'd guess that, right now, as always, Grace is focused on Grace."

The sentence robbed Elizabeth of words. For the next few hours—long after they'd changed topics, briefly discussed Hunter, laughed over some memories from Jean-Claude's film, then waved goodbye—it was all she could think about.

Was Summer right?

The odd, unsettled sensation in her gut told her the insight was eerily accurate.

Chapter 20

DELVINE TOOK THE NEWS OF *Choosing Hope*'s plans for Hunter with a sort of strangled gurgle, followed by a hefty sigh. "I suppose I shouldn't be so surprised they're actually going there," she said. "I mean that ridiculous Hunter hashtag assails me everywhere I go. It's huge."

That was true. Even Elizabeth, who actively avoided social media most of the time, couldn't escape it.

After Delvine had choked back her surprise, she told Elizabeth to go with the flow. "Say you're honored fans like your character, and aren't the writers so interesting, and you never know where they're going next. Then move on."

Rachel's rant was considerably more colorful. She moaned and huffed and said a few things about how damned inconvenient it was that all the buzz around Elizabeth involved lesbian projects. But then she'd startled her at the very end of the call.

"By the way, that Hunter pairing? Professionally, I'm a bit pissed. But personally? Oh hell, Bess, it's great," Rachel confided. "My wife and I have been watching it. Can't tear our eyes off the screen. You two are superb together. The chemistry's electric. It oozes on screen. Try to keep a cork in it though off-screen, would you?"

They had electric chemistry? Oozing electric chemistry? What drugs were people on? Elizabeth hit YouTube, searching for Hunter, and found about two dozen scenes. She watched them, one after the other. And there it was.

How had she been blind to this? The slow way she dragged her eyes over Summer, watching with an almost wonder to see what she'd do next.

Elizabeth's innate curiosity looked like something else, something far more interested.

When had Hunt ever looked that tenderly at anyone? Certainly not at Mendez. No wonder the gay fans were all over this.

Elizabeth glanced at the comments. Her eyes widened. Three thousand? She read a dozen. There was no denying the enthusiasm of the fans. They were hungry for more, begging producers for a relationship between the pair.

Elizabeth loaded the next video. A compilation of all the Joey/Hunt scenes overlaid with romantic music. It had over a million views. *A million!* She hit *Play*.

Fifteen minutes later, her jaw hurt from hanging open. When played back to back, their scenes were like a love letter between two women. The ache in Summer's expression was unsettling.

At the time she'd thought Summer had been furious with her. How had she never noticed the awareness in the woman's eyes? The contemplation? The curiosity? The clear interest? When had that started?

Scrolling back to the beginning of the video, she watched their first interaction. No. Nothing. What had changed? She moved the slider forward again, to their most recent scene. A frozen image of Carter and Hunt, standing toe to toe, filled the screen. Carter's eyes were on Hunt's lips. *Subtle.*

Her own mouth was curled into an amused, barely there smile. Christ. She was as bad as Summer.

Her phone rang. Elizabeth almost didn't answer until she saw the caller's name.

Then she flung herself at the device. "Grace!"

"Darling! You're back!" Grace's beautifully modulated tones drifted down the receiver making Elizabeth miss her all the more. Then she hated herself for missing someone who'd disappeared without a thought or word.

"Yes, I'm back, but where are you?"

"Somewhere wonderful and surprising. Sweetie, I'm couriering you over a plane ticket for this afternoon. Meet me. You must come and see."

"I can't. I have a new script to read before next week and…"

"Of course you can. You're not back at work for days and days. Bring your script, learn it on the plane. Catch you this afternoon. Soon, darling!"

What? Where? "Grace?"

The phone had gone dead. The buzzer from the security monitor on her driveway gates sounded. She flipped the comm panel on. "Yes?"

"Delivery for Elizabeth Thornton," came a bored voice. "Top priority."

Palm Springs, California, was neither wonderful nor surprising, despite Grace's hard sell, and it was too damned hot for Elizabeth's tastes. All of which Grace had to know, yet she'd dragged her out here anyway. They were beside the pool, stretched out on deck chairs under umbrellas, sipping fruity drinks as fawning waitresses attended them.

"Why am I here?" Elizabeth asked. It sounded existential.

Grace smiled. "Because I like having you with me. Your face always puts me in a good mood. Now, here, tell me what you think before you get too far gone on over-priced mai tais." She tossed a script to Elizabeth.

Oh. She was just here for a script assessment? Elizabeth squelched her disappointment.

After studying the writer's name—an unknown—and the title, TBD, she flicked through the pages. It seemed fairly unspectacular, not much different from the dozens of other scripts Grace had rejected since coming to America. It was a romance with a hint of drama, lots of longing looks set against swaying palm trees.

"A little predictable," she suggested diplomatically, handing the script back. "It's not exactly Merchant Ivory Productions. Not a corset or bonnet in sight."

"I'm breaking my mold, darling," Grace said breezily. "I've decided to take a chance on an up-and-coming film-maker." Her face broke into a smile as a good-looking, deeply tanned man in his early thirties ambled over and kissed her cheek.

"Roger, darling, this is my friend, Bess. Bess, this is Roger Plympton, producer of *Loving Under Palms*."

Dear God, was that its name?

"A working title," he said smoothly, "And it beats *Best Fronds Forever*." He chuckled.

Grace joined in with a high, supercilious laugh.

"Delighted to meet you." Plympton reached for Elizabeth's hand and gave it an ostentatious kiss that set her teeth on edge. "Let me introduce you to Jackie Benton, the director." He waved a woman over, and then, as his phone jangled to life, moved away to take the call.

A squarish woman with cropped ebony hair, in a T-shirt, jeans, and boots, sauntered into view, her eyes wandering Elizabeth's form with interest.

"Jax," she corrected, firmly shaking Elizabeth's hand. "The script's not much yet, but we plan to make it into something wonderful for your friend." She held the handshake a little too long.

Elizabeth murmured something neutral in reply. Her gaze flicked to Grace, who was sipping her mai tai and watching them in amusement.

"I'll let you two catch up. We'll see you both at dinner." Jax's smile lingered before she left.

Wait. Dinner? Elizabeth turned to see that her mentor at least had the good grace to look a little sheepish at having apparently volunteered her for schmoozing duties this evening.

"Anything you want to tell me?" she asked.

"Well, imagine my surprise when I discovered my director-to-be was a huge Hunt fan. Astonishing anyone could like that bitter drop of acid, but there it is."

Bitter drop of acid? Hunt wasn't *that* bad. Especially not lately. Well, not in Carter's vicinity, at least.

Grace prodded the drink with her straw a few times. "I didn't think you'd mind lending me a little support tonight. I want this role."

In all their years, Grace had never asked her for anything. Elizabeth had never been sure whether it was because she didn't need help or hated to ask for it. This was a seismic shift in their relationship, yet all Grace did was poke at her drink, looking bored.

Plympton returned, pocketing his phone. "I have to go. Until dinner tonight, darling." He air-kissed Grace's cheek, and the faintest tip of his finger trailed across her shoulder.

"Yes, bye, Roger."

Elizabeth stared at Grace, mutely asking about the wandering touch as the man departed.

"Goodness, this sun! So much of it." Grace fanned herself with her hand. "Let's head over to my suite. We'll talk properly. Come."

Elizabeth followed Grace back to her suite, which turned out to be an enormous room with a whumping wooden fan churning around the stultifying air. Green potted plants in each corner may or may not have been fake. It was far too luxurious to be delegated to any unsigned lead, despite Grace's name.

"Your producer's suite?"

"He lets me stay, yes," Grace dropped the script on an end table and shrugged off her lightweight white blouse. Underneath was a clingy crimson tank top that did her a great many favors. "He has another one as well."

"You're dating him?"

"Roger's interested in me and I'm letting him think he has a chance. Well, until the ink's dry on my contract. Then? Who knows? You know how it is."

She knew how it was in principle. It was surprising that Grace would lower herself to the flirting game over a lackluster role from a pair of unknowns.

"Will you excuse me while I get changed?" Grace asked. "It's simply too hot out here today. Help yourself to a drink." She waved at the bar. "I've made sure there's Hendrick's." Her smile was so dazzling it was unsettling.

Elizabeth blinked. She'd never been so actively charmed by her friend before, although she'd seen her deliberately bewitch many an unsuspecting soul. And Grace had stocked Elizabeth's brand of gin? That felt uncharacteristically considerate.

Reaching for a glass, Elizabeth added ice cubes, and poured in a finger of her favorite label. She swallowed and relaxed at its familiar, soothing essence. Well, perhaps this trip wasn't a total write-off: Grace was in an expansive mood and the drinks were excellent.

Grabbing the script, she sauntered over to the balcony door, passed through billowing, filmy white curtains, and stepped outside. The heat hit her again, like a stifling, fat wall, but at least there was a little wind this high up.

Leaning on the railing, Elizabeth cast her gaze over this dusty, orange, desert town-turned-oasis. It was a favored haunt of Hollywood executives and, at least once a year, lesbians. Not that she'd dare go to a Dinah Shore weekend. Fastest way to out herself in human history. She shuddered at the thought.

Sipping her drink, Elizabeth focused on what was uppermost on her mind. Why was she really here? Grace didn't need Elizabeth's help to get any role. She was gifted in bending anyone to her will, and that included already-smitten producers and lesbian directors with a taste for TV villains. Besides, didn't Rachel sort out the basic schmoozing required for scoring Grace's roles or auditions? Or, failing Rachel, Grace's manager? All of this was odd.

Elizabeth settled into one of the cane chairs, a weathered construct that squeaked in protest, and turned her attention back to the script. Maybe she'd missed something pivotal on her first flick-through?

Ten minutes later she gave up on finding what wasn't there. The story of a woman in Palm Springs waiting for her divorce to be final was so predictable that Elizabeth flipped to the end. Okay. She finds love at the resort with an equally miserable man. It just lacked the violins and... she turned the page.

CUE: RISING VIOLINS.

Jesus.

Footsteps alerted her to Grace's return. She glanced back to find her friend looking...oh.

Grace was wearing a long, see-through white over-shirt, under which was a sinfully tight, tiny, white bikini. She was stunning. When wasn't she? But Elizabeth had never expected to see quite so much of her. Elizabeth was shocked to discover she even owned a bikini. Grace always protected her blemish-free skin from the elements at all costs.

Her creamy-white long legs were as glorious as Elizabeth had fantasized about for years, her stomach taut and flat. Decades with a daily personal trainer had done wonders. The woman could pass as years younger than forty-four.

With a soft intake of breath, Elizabeth turned back to the view, afraid to be caught staring. Her mind raced. Was this for Roger's benefit later? Had Grace decided that this dinner in her room would be a rewarding experience for him?

Surely Grace wasn't that desperate to get a part? Or was she? And if she was, what had changed? She used to sneer at young starlets thrusting their cleavage forward at producers' meetings.

"Enjoying the view?"

Elizabeth gazed down at the pool. "It's quite nice." *If you like cookie-cutter hotel pools.*

"Hmm." Grace's drink clanged, indicating she'd upgraded to spirits with ice. "Good."

Elizabeth turned to face her. "Why am I here?"

"I already told you. I enjoy your company. I missed you."

"And to secure you a part? I'm here to dazzle Jax?"

Shrugging, Grace said, "A bit of value-adding, yes. Why not? We all network to get ahead, don't we?"

Elizabeth supposed that was true. "What did Rachel think of this part?"

Grace gave an indifferent wave. "Who cares?"

Who cares? Something was very wrong. "Grace—"

"I've let Cho go. She's not been as useful as I thought. I'm making my own way now."

Elizabeth sat up abruptly. "You fired Rachel? Hollywood's top agent?"

"I most certainly did. And I fail to see how she's top at anything. What fabulous parts has she found for me? Where are all the movie leads? I played Queen Victoria five years ago, and since then, virtually nothing!"

"Because you keep turning down everything she sends. And you said a flat no to TV."

"Of course I did. It lowers my brand. TV is the clearing house of acting. Without a reputation, I'm nothing." Grace glowered. "I can't say yes to *that*. I'm not..."

"Me?" *Charming.*

"I didn't say that."

"You thought it."

Grace twirled her drink. "Perhaps," she conceded. "Sorry if it offends, but the truth is, I'm better than American television. So are you."

Her snobbery hadn't changed then, even though film no longer had a monopoly on the best writers. Grace had always refused to see it.

"Why this role then?" Elizabeth asked. "Because I'm afraid I can't see what's special about it."

"The team behind it is special."

"Those two?" *Seriously?*

"Don't let appearances fool you. Yes, I know the role is weak. It'll get fixed. But it's about looking to the future. I'm getting in on the ground floor with Jax and Roger. They might be indie now, but they're going places. And when they break through, they'll want me for bigger projects; projects that *will* be fabulous."

What? Nothing in that script had indicated inspiring minds at work. And since when did Grace back unknowns? "Grace," she asked carefully, "how do you know they're good?"

The *ping ping ping* of Grace's bright red talon sounded against her glass. "They will be." She exhaled. "They have to be." Her lips thinned and she threw back the rest of her drink, clunking the empty glass onto the round cane table in front of them. "Fine. That bitch Cho dumped me."

Ouch. "I'm sorry."

"You're not even going to ask why?" Grace peered at her. "Just...*sorry?* Did you know she was going to?"

"What? Of course not."

"Well, me either." She laughed bitterly. "I'm getting another drink. Want one?"

Elizabeth shook her head and watched Grace go in a swirl of thin cotton and minuscule bikini. This was surreal. All of it.

When Grace reappeared, she pinned Elizabeth with a fierce look. "So after Cho...dispensed with me, Roger and Jax sent me this script. They promised me the world, and said they'd make me a star in America, if not on this project, then definitely the next. They've seen all my UK productions. *Loved them.* I'm not a dime-a-dozen actress to them. It's *me* they want. I'm their muse. Do you hear? They appreciate talent."

"Of course they want you. You're gifted."

"Exactly! Why in the hell can't this backwards place see it?"

Worry filled Elizabeth. Grace's veneer was slipping. To see the epitome of dignity snarling at her overlooked worth was unsettling...and new.

"I didn't start out considering Roger's proposal, you know," Grace said suddenly. "I asked around first. Feelers out, that sort of thing. I even asked Alex for a role. In that climate-change atrocity."

Astonishment coursed through her. Although a respected indie film-maker, Alex had little weight in Hollywood. "What did she say?"

"That the integrity of the project must be her priority. That I wasn't right for it, but that she'd consider me for future projects. *Not right for it?* My God, I can act circles around the mediocre talent she employs. She said she was sorry, but her film comes first."

Oh hell. Elizabeth hunted around for something to say that wouldn't add salt to the wound.

"You wouldn't do that to me, would you?" Grace asked. Her eyes, pale blue and sharp, met Elizabeth's. Grace's hand came over to pat hers and then stayed.

Tingles shot through Elizabeth's fingers at the connection; she hated herself for it. Her constant awareness of this woman was exhausting. She sought desperately for a distraction. "How's Amrit?"

Something indecipherable flashed across Grace's face. "Same as ever," she said. "Although he's still flitting about with that boy. Christopher."

Oh. Right. The bartender. Amrit's latest beautiful person of the minute. Well, month actually. "Is it serious?" Elizabeth asked.

The hand on hers tightened until both sets of their fingers turned white. Grace's thumb tapped Elizabeth's hand. "He seems to think so."

"Really? What did he say?"

"A great many things, but never mind. Forget him. You're here. Loyal, lovely Bess. You wouldn't desert me the way the others have, would you?"

And suddenly it all became clear: Grace was feeling abandoned. First by Rachel, now Alex, and Amrit.

"Haven't I always been around?" Elizabeth asked quietly. "Ever since we met, haven't I been in your corner?"

"You have." She offered Elizabeth another stunning smile and squeezed her hand before letting it go. "It's good you're here now. I can do something for you. You need my guidance."

"Guidance? But I don't need any—"

"*Hunter.*" Grace's lip curled in disdain. "I can be of use with that messy business. One queer film to show you're edgy and open-minded is perfectly fine. But that, followed up by the lesbians claiming your TV character? No, no. Don't allow it. Stop it before it gets out of hand. I'm surprised Cho hasn't shut it down for you already."

"Rachel couldn't if she tried. The producers are making my character an item with Summer's."

Distaste crossed Grace's features. "You...agreed?"

"We didn't have a lot of choice. Saying no would have resulted in Summer being fired. She's far too good to be kicked to the curb."

Grace eyed her. "So you're protecting her. You're allowing this farcical storyline for *her*." She tsked. "Didn't I drill into you, again and again, how to be a success? Don't get used. If anything, *be* the user. Lion not the zebra. Remember that."

Her words set Elizabeth's teeth on edge. "I see you practice what you preach. What producer lets an actress stay in his luxury suite without strings attached?"

"A generous one."

"He wants to sleep with you."

"I'm aware."

"Will you?"

"I haven't decided how much I like him yet. Either way, it's none of your business."

"Yet Summer's yours?"

"*You* are my business. Haven't I always looked out for you? Didn't I get you your start here? Who was beside you on those nights when we talked about the actress you wanted to be? Bess, listen to me when I say this: You are being taken advantage of."

"The network wants—"

"Not the network. Stop being blind. Summer is using you. She's wormed her way into a friendship and now she's using you. Watch out for those young ones. They're ambitious as hell. They'll slither right over your head to get to the top."

"The young ones? Since when do you worry about them?"

Grace eyed her a moment. "They're all anyone values. They have the monopoly on any halfway decent roles. Is it any wonder the rest of us strive, through any means, to stay in that mix for as long as possible? Soon you'll see. It won't be fun being so close to forty when your contract's up."

"Why the sudden fixation on age?"

Grace glowered. "Among the grievances Cho aired when we had our final little *contretemps*, was that I'm far too old for love-interest roles and to stop demanding them. She said I was long overdue to consider scripts for supporting parts about mothers and…" she gave her drink a venomous swirl, "…grandmothers."

Oh damn.

"Naturally, I explained I'd do no such thing! That it was up to *her* to find me scripts without a romantic interest at all if the alternative was too hard, but I absolutely won't be playing supporting roles. I am a lead! And then she called me too difficult and terminated our arrangement." Grace sneered. "Welcome to Hollywood. You're fuckable at twenty, long in the tooth at thirty, and dead after forty." She looked pointedly at Elizabeth. "Tick-tock, Bess. And you'll have given your replacement a leg-up."

"Summer's not my replacement. Besides, she's not like that."

Grace clucked. "She is *exactly* like that. She grew up in this sinkhole, with industry parents, and absorbed it all into her skin. You don't think she knew an easy mark when she saw it?"

Gritting her teeth, Elizabeth said, "You don't know her."

"Really? She's working on that number one rule of Hollywood: Sell your own mother to get ahead. Or in your case, sell the woman old enough to be your own mother."

Elizabeth rolled her eyes. "She's only nine years younger than me, for God's sake."

"Well, she looks much younger. The point is, she's hitched her star to yours. Using this Hunter business and the Badour film? Watch her career soar now, while you'll soon get kicked into the abyss."

Anger crackled along Elizabeth's veins. Summer had put her job on the line to save Elizabeth's character from a terrible plot. But telling Grace that would probably only get Summer mocked for weakness. Grace couldn't appreciate anyone who didn't think exactly like she did.

Catching her dark expression, Grace suddenly smiled. "Goodness, look at us, getting side-tracked by all these depressing topics." She sounded carefree, as though she'd never had a harsh thought in her life. "I only meant to warn you about people in general. Even the sweet ones can hide their true natures. Just be careful. Trust no one."

"Even you?" Elizabeth couldn't resist.

Grace laughed. "Funny. Top up?" She waved her glass.

"I'll sit on this one." *You should too.*

"Come inside. There's something else to discuss and this heat is oppressive."

Elizabeth closed the balcony doors behind them, and turned to see Grace pouring herself another drink. This had to be her sixth at least. "Bad day?"

"Not at all. This deal, well, I'll hammer something out tonight with Roger. And you're here, my loyal one. My rock."

"Of course. Is that why you summoned me? You needed someone loyal?"

"It's not just that. I've been giving something some thought—an idea I've had for a few days, in case this deal doesn't work out. One always needs a back-up plan. Hear me out." She sat on the couch and patted the space beside her. "Sit."

Elizabeth complied after a wary pause.

Plucking Elizabeth's hand into hers, Grace took a deep breath.

Elizabeth's uneasiness turned queasy.

"Now," Grace began, "it occurred to me after an uncharacteristic bout of self-reflection..." she offered a self-deprecating smile, "...how all this time, you'd been right under my nose, and I've never fully appreciated you. I took you and your loyalty for granted. An oversight I'd like to correct."

Elizabeth's mind blanked. "Sorry?"

"My career, of late, is...challenging. Cho was right about one thing: I'm not getting any younger."

"Forty-four is hardly old."

"Fifty-three."

"What?"

"I lied. On my CV, in interviews, everywhere." Grace gave a cavalier wave. "Cho knew; she does background checks on all her clients. Part of our disagreement was that I remain, literally, unwilling to act my age."

Fifty-three? She can't be.

"Another reason I like you is you're so good for my ego." Grace laughed. "The shock on your face that I could possibly be this age is fabulous." She shook her head. "Obviously I'm aware why my offers are drying up. And I'm aware that Roger and Jax may be all hot air. That this film might remain as sad as it looks on paper. I'm not delusional."

That was a relief. "But what does any of that have to do with me?"

"I'm tired of the hamster wheel. This town, these two-faced people, the deals, the shallowness, the fakery. *We'll do lunch*, they tell you, and never call. *You're perfect for the part!* And that's the last you hear from them. It's soul-destroying."

"It can be," Elizabeth murmured.

"No, it *is*. So I asked myself what I'd like to do instead. I'm an independent, intelligent woman of means. There must be more to life than this emptiness. It's not good for me. So why can't I just pick up and go? Travel? See what's out there? And take a good friend with me? Someone who shares the same interests and who likes being around me as much as I do them?"

Elizabeth stared.

"Doesn't that sound divine? What an adventure we'd have! I don't need Amrit and his fair-weather affections. Who needs people who don't appreciate us, anyway? Am I right, darling? So, would you like that? Just you and me?"

Elizabeth's emotions wrestled, soaring from jubilation to a freefall into confusion.

"Why that look?" Grace sounded faintly insulted. "I thought you'd be delighted. I'm rich as blazes if that helps your calculations. Oh, I know, it's dreadful to talk about money, but just so you know, you'd want for nothing. You wouldn't need to go back to that debasing show or any of that nonsense. We could see art, culture, music, go anywhere. Imagine!"

Elizabeth could see it only too well. It sounded like a Faustian deal. Give up her career, her autonomy, to become Grace's constant companion, subject to her moods and whims—and Lord knew she had plenty. It sounded like being a kept woman...minus the bedroom rights. On that note... "And what if you met some charming man who turned your head? Would you deposit me at the nearest airport or keep me around as an amusing third wheel?"

Grace's stunned expression made it clear the thought hadn't occurred to her. "Well, of course a fling on the side would never disrupt our adventures. Who wants the hassle of a man in tow?" She smiled. "You could have fun, too, if you wanted. I don't mind who you take to your bed. Man or woman. Doesn't bother me." She offered the most delicate of shrugs.

For a moment Elizabeth couldn't breathe. She'd been so careful. *For years!* "How long have you known?"

"The day we met. You had your eye on the Footlights' lighting technician. Remember her?"

Barely. Because it hadn't been the tech she'd been staring at, but Grace, standing behind her.

"I've also known that you put your career first, and that's why you're so discreet about these things," Grace continued. "I've always admired how well you took my lessons to heart. It's important, staying focused."

Elizabeth's blood thundered in her ears.

"You really thought I didn't know about you and Alex, either? You were thick as thieves for months." Grace's light laughter tinkled. "Whatever do you think of me? That I don't see what's right under my nose?"

The hairs on the back of Elizabeth's neck stood up.

"Goodness, you look so shocked, Bess. I just assumed you'd have told me if you'd wanted me to know. I thought I was honoring your wishes by discreetly looking the other way."

"Oh." Oblivious, clueless, self-absorbed Grace appeared to be none of those things after all. All this time, she'd known Elizabeth far better than she'd ever imagined.

Grace gave Elizabeth's thigh a light, *that's that* slap and beamed. "Now, it's settled—you could have whatever passing dalliance you wished, and so could I. We'll explore the world together. How does that sound?"

"But only if your film doesn't happen? And while Amrit's with Chris?"

"Of course. Didn't I already say that?"

"So, I really am the backup plan." Elizabeth's jaw clenched.

"Don't be so dramatic. You're important to me. Do you think I'd make this offer to just anyone?" She squeezed their joined hands. "Well? Are you in?"

A few years ago, having Grace promise her one-on-one time for months or more would have been everything she'd dreamed of, and she'd have seriously considered walking away from her career for a second time. All because Grace made her feel like she was special to her. But Elizabeth had worked far too hard to get where she was now.

"Don't think I don't appreciate your...overwhelming...offer," she said carefully, "but I don't think it's a good idea."

"No?" Grace's expression morphed into astonishment. "Why on earth not?"

"My career's about to take off with the Badour film. I can't be wandering the world with you when I could be fielding offers. Even if it does sound..."

Nice? No, not that. Her throat closed over at the thought of being with Grace 24/7 for months on end. Watching her swan off with the hunk of the moment. Being instructed at Grace's knee. Or treated like the help, ordered to fetch bags and make drinks. It was all so claustrophobic. None of this could possibly be healthy. Not to mention her body's reaction to this woman, which was more inconvenient than exciting these days.

"Even if it does sound generous."

Grace regarded her for a long time. "Is this about your little crush?" She arranged herself into the study of patience, looking concerned.

Elizabeth's pulse started thudding double time. "Crush?"

"Bess, there's little that goes on in your life of which I'm not aware."

Surely she can't mean—

"Oh, don't worry, I can continue to look past it. You're doing such an excellent job at dealing with your...situation. I promise it's not an issue for me. All right? Is that all that's worrying you? Are we fine now?"

Oh God. Elizabeth wanted to hide. Grace *knew?* She'd virtually patted Elizabeth on the head for being good at fighting her feelings, and now she wanted to move straight on to trip planning? Grace's ability to compartmentalize was staggering.

"No, we're not fine now."

Grace frowned. "But we've covered every possible issue, haven't we?" She paused and studied her. Considering. "Unless...God, is it *that* important to you?"

"I don't—"

"I mean, it's such a minor thing to stand in our way, if that's all this is." A look of uncertainty crossed Grace's face, as though she were deciding something.

"What *are* you talking about?"

Grace leaned over and kissed her. It was a nose-and-teeth-clashing experience that lacked warmth or subtlety. Everything was furious and frantic. Funny how cold her lips seemed, dry and harsh. The trademark prickle of desire that always spiraled through Elizabeth whenever Grace touched her sparked, but then slowly ebbed away into nothing. All that was left was one thought: *Why the hell is Grace kissing me?*

She pulled away, shocked.

With eyes wide open as though she'd never shut them, Grace studied her with a look that seemed to ask, *Well? Did that work? Are you ready now?*

"What was *that*?" None of Elizabeth's fantasies had ever involved some sort of hit-and-run attack lacking all intimacy. "Was that just your 'tease me till the ink is dry' gambit like with Roger?" Anger stabbed at her. "Oh, and I don't sleep with straight women, in case you planned to sweeten the deal."

Grace glared, wiping her scarlet lips in jerky movements. "Oh, lovely. That's what I get for being considerate. And as if I'd ever sleep with you."

"Really?" Elizabeth cocked her head. "So you weren't just working out whether you could? Or maybe you were figuring out how desperate I was? Whether I could be strung along until my 'no' to traveling with you turned into a 'yes'. Is that how pathetic I seem to you?"

Grace gave her an arch look but denied nothing.

Elizabeth scowled. "What's happened to you?"

"It's the American then?" Grace's gaze sharpened. "That's why you want to stay? That perky blond is who you're into now?"

The viciousness in that drawled statement felt like a slap. Summer's comments about how territorial Grace had been outside the trailer flooded back. She'd thought Summer was reading too much into Grace's proprietorial interest in her career. Now she could picture it only too clearly: Grace really did want Elizabeth to herself.

What am I to Grace? The question had tortured her for years. She'd dissected conversations until her heart was bruised. Now she knew. She was some convenient, faithful lapdog…useful for companionship. Her fury rose. She wasn't Grace's possession or her toy. Oh, she'd put up with the mockery and teasing all these years because her heart had needed to keep forgiving her. But this was too much. Elizabeth folded her arms.

"My decision has nothing to do with Summer. And if you belittle her again, I'll walk out right now."

"Bess!" Shock seared Grace's face.

Elizabeth met her eye. "This is about us. Especially you. I know it's been a hard few months, feeling rejected by your friends, and you don't want to be alone. But no matter my feelings for you in the past, I'm saying no to the travel, as well as to anything else you might dangle to entice me to go."

Feelings for you *in the past*. The impact of her words were as startling as a slap. *Do I really mean that?* Elizabeth turned it over. She'd felt less than nothing during that kiss. Appalled and shocked, perhaps. And now, seeing the lengths Grace was willing to go to avoid being alone, she just felt sad for her. To consider sleeping with Elizabeth when she didn't even like women that way? *Who does that? And what the hell does that say about her views on me?* Anger surged again. *How fucking mercenary of her.*

Grace regarded her expression, her face closing. "Save it. I won't have it. You, pitying me? Screw you. And you can stop acting so damned high and mighty. This is *Hollywood*. It's one big red-light district. People wanting it, people selling it, people finding other people's price. I asked yours, that's all. I hadn't even decided if I wanted to pay. All I did was ask."

"I'm not for sale. I do have some self-respect."

"You're saying that I don't?" Grace's tone was low and dangerous.

Shame filled Elizabeth. "No, I'm sorry. I know you've never screwed your way to the top. But I can see you've gotten to such a point of frustration and cynicism that you've been thinking about it lately." She flicked her hand around the suite. "This is the down payment on another veiled promise you're working out whether to keep. Don't. You're better than this. Grace, just go home."

Grace's lips thinned. "So easy for you. You've no idea what it's been like. Talk to me when people's eyes glide right past you to the pouty young things only famous for being famous. Or when your agent says she doesn't have the time to *hand-hold you* anymore in the hope you'll see the light and agree to age-appropriate roles.

"Hand-hold me? Like I'm some doddery old fool?" Leaping to her feet, Grace paced. "I'm still young in my mind, can't everyone see? I'm still beautiful, interesting, and fucking talented. Yet I'm being shown the exit. And now *you* have the audacity to tell me to throw away the only script I've seen in two years where the director and producer want me to play an attractive, vibrant, romantic lead. The first of many such roles!

"But oh, of course, you, Elizabeth Thornton, star of TV's most infantile and mystifyingly popular drama, diminishes the one damned role I might actually get. And then…when I finally face the fact that this is as good as it gets, that my career might be at sodding rock bottom, you throw even my escape plan back in my face. No, you're far too busy now to travel, no matter how much I beg. No matter what I'm willing to offer to have you with me." Her eyes glistened with fury. "And then you talk to me about self-respect. I appreciated that lovely bit of condescension. I wasn't feeling quite low enough."

"Grace," Elizabeth said, quietly. "When I said go home, I didn't mean back to LA. I meant *home*. Be a legend in the UK again. You're so much better than Roger's script or waiting for Amrit, who you must know, deep down, is never coming back."

Grace's eyes grew stormy.

"I'm sorry about him," Elizabeth continued. "And I'm sorry about Hollywood. But neither one is going to change. So why not admit Hollywood's an experiment that didn't work out—no one's fault. I'm sure your old agent back home will find a role in ten minutes flat that leaves this palm trees nonsense for dead. Just tell everyone you're going back for a role you can't resist."

Grace said nothing for a long moment. She sipped her drink slowly, those beautiful eyes hooded, hurt, watchful.

This could go either way. Occasionally Grace could be persuaded to take advice, *if* she agreed with it. Or, she could lash out when feeling provoked or disrespected.

"Life advice for *me* now, Bess? *You* have all the answers? Everyone's life's so simple. That's funny coming from you."

Option B, then. "Of course I don't know all the answers. But I do know you. You could try a gracious retreat and turn it into a victory, if you decided not to be stubborn."

"Well, if you know me, you know I'm honest about who I am. At least I'm not some late-thirties closet job too scared to even admit it to her closest friends."

Elizabeth sighed. "My private life isn't anyone else's business. I'm not afraid."

"*Sure* you're not." Grace tilted her chin back, looking imperious. "Of all our little circle, you're the most timid. Terrified to risk. That's why you've needed me all these years. I had the strength of my convictions. I pursued what I wanted—be it roles or people."

"Did it never occur to you that you don't get what you pursue because you pursue the wrong things? All you know is obsession. Or possession. That's why Amrit sprinted away from you. God, that was years ago, and you still…" Elizabeth waved her hand.

"Actually, he's been back to warm my bed quite a few times more than you're aware of over the years. And even if he hadn't, the heart wants what it wants. I'd have thought you understood that more than most. Anyway, who Amrit chooses to love isn't the point. What matters is taking chances. At least Amrit and I both stand up for things. Try things. New people, new experiences. We *risk*.

"You're so timid about the big, bad world, aren't you, Bess? You wear so many masks that no one can truly know you. Not your parents. Not your friends. I doubt even Alex came close. You keep everyone out. I did try to get to know you once. You pushed me away too. You prefer to give us all some carefully constructed facade. The silhouette of who you are."

Grace leaned forward, eyes flashing. "Do you know the difference between us?" Her voice became silky. "I know what I want, and go for it. You know what you want, and don't. Never say I don't give you good advice. In fact that's all I seem to do, isn't it? Advise you. Support you. And you throw everything back in my face. You even side with the American over me. Like I'm nothing. There's gratitude for you." Her expression flickered before going blank.

Elizabeth couldn't believe she'd once hung off every word this woman said. "I thank you for your advice over the years," she said stiffly. "But I don't think I need you as a mentor anymore."

"Oh, you need me still," Grace said with conviction. "You always desperately need my courage. You'd be lost without me."

For a moment, doubt flooded Elizabeth. Was this true? She did find it hard to come out of her shell. But would she be lost? Between them, who had the booming career? Who kept an agent? Who put on her own one-woman show, without Grace's support? Her doubts bled away.

"No." Elizabeth said confidently, earning a flicker of surprise from Grace. "In fact, I think it's you who needs me now."

Grace snorted. "Nonsense."

"I've been making you feel special for years. You feed on it. Your friends shouldn't exist just to be stand-ins for adoring fans, to boost your self-esteem. Yet that's what we all are to you."

Grace rolled her eyes. "Oh, listen to you. No one forced any of you to do anything for me, for heaven's sake. You're not being held captive."

"No," Elizabeth admitted. "I played your game when I saw how happy it made you. All I ever wanted was to be the architect of your smile."

"And now? You wish me to be unhappy? After everything I've done! Rushing to your set a few weeks ago, to see if you were okay. Your entire LA career? Your—"

"Oh stop." Elizabeth sighed. "I did have a *little* to do with my career success. And you didn't visit to see if I was okay. I hung up on you and you felt me slipping away. Today has been about shoring up my loyalty. You've been throwing everything at me to keep me at your side." She reached over to Grace's shirt and flicked the barely there material. "And I do mean everything."

"What an idea." The words lacked Grace's usual bravado...or conviction.

Hell. She'd been right. Elizabeth swallowed. How cynical could the woman get?

This was over. They were done. She felt it down to her bones. "As I said, thanks for helping me once. I'm fine now. Let's just move on with our lives...separately. I don't think this friendship's healthy for either of us."

Grace's mouth dropped open.

Taking advantage of the stunned silence, Elizabeth gathered her things quickly, and headed for the door.

"She'll never love you." The voice was low and warning.

Elizabeth paused at the door, annoyed with herself for doing so. "Who?"

"You're a closed book," Grace continued. "An emotional sphinx. I might be all the things that you claim. And you might condemn me for throwing everything I have in order to get what I want. But at least I put myself out there. Sometimes I win, sometimes I don't, but it's never for lack of trying. You hide away, avoid risk, and let no one see all of you. No one's allowed close enough to your heart to hurt you. That's why you'll always be alone."

"Glad to see you think so highly of me." The betrayal stung.

"I don't say this to hurt you. It's just a fact. Now ask yourself: Why would someone who seems so friendly, trusting, open, and warm as Summer want someone so diametrically opposed in her life? Isn't that proof?"

"Proof of what?"

"The girl is definitely using you."

Elizabeth looked at her evenly. "You're right. I've been used. I've been foolish." With sadness, she regarded the woman who had been the center of her universe for years. "But Summer's not the one who's been doing it."

Elizabeth left, resisting the urge to slam the door behind her. She'd been blind for so long. Her biggest regret was that she'd spent far too long in love with a woman who didn't deserve it.

Chapter 21

IN THE PAST FORTY-EIGHT HOURS, Elizabeth had done little else but think. Her mind had been a chaotic mess on the short flight home from Palm Springs. She'd been distracted when reading *Choosing Hope*'s new Hunter-loaded script. Not to mention while standing in front of her empty fridge, vagueing out beside her elderly housekeeper instead of rattling off a shopping list.

For some reason, the fridge light staring back at her hadn't been forthcoming on life advice.

In the end she called for an impromptu party night—well, afternoon. Strangely, no one commented on Grace's absence. Far more incomprehensible was that Elizabeth finally managed to open up a little.

Through fits and starts, she explained that Grace wouldn't be coming around to her parties anymore. That the relationship had become too toxic for her, but the rest of them shouldn't feel the need to take sides. And everyone just said "okay" or "cool". Like they'd been waiting for this to blow up for some time.

And then…*then*, she shocked herself completely by just coming out. She threw it in like a polite, conversational postscript, along the lines of: *Thanks for coming, everyone. Lovely tie, Brian. Did I ever mention I'm a lesbian? Just an FYI. Is everyone all right for drinks? Snacks?* Elizabeth then downed her gin like a woman dying of thirst, trying not to hyperventilate.

Their underwhelmed reaction to that bombshell was even more unexpected than the Grace news. Alex gave her a proud grin and a thumbs-up. The others just nodded. *Nodded!* And that was essentially it. The conversation moved on.

Half an hour later, Zara, Amrit, and Brian retreated outside to kick around a football on the small square of lawn to one side of the pool, while Rowan, un-athletic to a fault, called out unhelpful critiques. Like it was any other day.

"Hey," Alex said quietly, coming to settle beside her on the couch. She flopped her socked feet into Elizabeth's lap and blew out a huge breath. "Wow. What a day, huh?"

"One word for it."

"So, your news, huh? We're so glad you finally told us."

"Uh-huh. I could tell by everyone's *shocked* reactions." Elizabeth rolled her eyes. "Everyone knew, didn't they?"

"Yes, Bess. We're all great at respecting your space, but no one's blind."

Pressing her lips together, Elizabeth stared grimly at her drink. "Ah." She had a disturbing thought. "Do you think Brian's serious about that celebratory rainbow sponge cake?"

"Knowing him? Probably. Don't worry, I'm sure it'll be tasteful." Elizabeth laughed.

"So... wanna talk?" Alex asked. "About why you're opening up to everyone now? Not that I'm complaining. We'd all love to know you better. It's just...this is a bit of a departure."

"I'm not in the mood for an emotional autopsy."

"If that were true, we wouldn't have been invited over."

Damn it.

"Hey, remember when I told you Summer was a catalyst and would blow shit apart for you? That you needed it?"

"Is this your 'I told you so'?"

"Maybe. So spill, what's happened now? Something must have."

Elizabeth glanced at her friend. "Grace kissed me."

"What?" Alex squeaked.

Elizabeth smirked and sipped her drink.

"Why would she do *that?*" Alex tried again. "I mean no offense, you're very kissable—"

"You'd know."

"But she's not even the slightest bit bi. She told me that once. I mean, unless it's some weird power game to keep you at her side..." Her eyes widened. "Oh shit. Seriously?"

"I suspect she was testing how deep my feelings were. Whether I could be manipulated with a kiss, and then she'd change tactics later. She's a master at getting people to do what she wants."

"Devious as fuck, you mean." Alex's face darkened.

"In a sense."

"Bess, do *not* tell me you're still going to defend her?"

"No. But I finally understand her now, what was always behind her games. Yes, Grace is a woman who thrives on attention and adoration. But she's terrified of being alone. She's also afraid of being tossed aside professionally. Now she thinks her friends are all abandoning her, so she's panicking, desperate to hang on, any way she can. I've been feeling hurt, betrayed, and angry for days. Now I just feel pity for her."

"Bess, she made her own bed."

"Perhaps. It's still sad."

"Loyal to the end." Alex shook her head. "Y'know it's crazy *you* get called the British Bitch. You have one of the warmest hearts. You can't even bring yourself to hate a woman who played on your feelings for her in the worst way."

"She's hurting. Hollywood isn't kind to women of a certain age. But don't worry. I can be done with her and still feel awful for her that she felt she had to sink to this."

An impish look crossed Alex's face.

"What?" Elizabeth eyed her suspiciously.

"Soooo, you glossed right over the biggest thing. When she kissed you, what was that like? Did it live up to your dreams?"

"Hardly. It felt like she was conquering a territory. The Battle of Britain came to mind. Cold, wet, and ferocious."

"Oh no!" Alex burst out laughing. "Your glorious Queen Grace turns out to be a useless snogger?"

"I know, I know." It *was* sort of funny, though Elizabeth was still a little bruised.

"So what of Summer?"

"What about her?"

"She's available, isn't she? I've seen the way she looks at you. If that woman isn't into you, then I'm handing in my lesbian card."

"No comment."

"Ah, knew it. I've never seen anyone get you to let your guard down quite so much. Around her, you laugh. You tease. You get frustrated. But you're *more*. I think that's what Grace picked up on—why she saw Summer as such a threat. That girl draws you out of your shell."

Was that true? Elizabeth frowned. "I hardly think we're a good match. She's warm, friendly, and open. I'm not. Don't you think she deserves someone like her?"

"Except she seems to want someone just like *you*. Besides, don't underestimate her. Summer's tougher than she looks—she'd have to be to survive unscathed as a child star. Don't sell her short."

"I'm not. But it's a moot point anyway." Elizabeth pushed the whole idea aside. "I have to work with her. Imagine if I took the risk on a relationship and it blew up? We have a major storyline coming up together on *Hope*. It'd be disastrous working at close quarters with her."

"Isn't your character leaving in a couple of months, though? So…wait."

Elizabeth thought about that. Then thought some more. Surely it was outlandish. Or something. She was sure there should be some logical reason not to consider this.

Alex sat back and grinned like a Cheshire cat. "Well, I think we've exhausted all your 'why I can't possibly date Summer' arguments. I greatly look forward to you bringing your girlfriend around on party night. In fact, make her a regular."

"Oh be quiet." But Elizabeth warmed at her words.

Chapter 22

SUMMER DRUMMED HER FINGERS AGAINST her script. Sitting in her on-set nook, pages in her lap, she tried to focus on what was coming up. Finally, she was back at work, finally, she'd be seeing Bess, and finally... Actually that was all she could focus on.

Beside her, Tori prattled on at a million miles an hour, apparently having just seen the Hunter insertions in the script. "Well, girl, I guess the joke's on us, huh?" Tori said. "You knew what you were doing all along."

"What do you mean?" Summer glanced up.

"When you ad-libbed about Hunt getting to know Joey, you started this whole thing in motion." She gestured at the script. "What a pay-off. Have you seen the ratings? Shit, my agent's in heaven."

"Oh, yep," Summer agreed. It was better if it didn't get around that this hadn't been her big masterplan.

"You nervous? About having to kiss her?"

"Hmm?" Summer focused on Tori properly. Oh, right. It wasn't common knowledge about *Eight Little Pieces* yet. Was she nervous? A little. Not like before. This time she'd be kissing a woman she knew liked women too. A woman who had hinted that Summer might have a chance with her, if her heart didn't belong elsewhere. A woman who knew Summer was attracted to her. That changed their previous dynamic in so many ways.

"I'd be so nervous I'd be tossing my cookies right about now." Tori cackled. "Fuck, I have no idea how you'd be able to even touch the British Bitch let alone lay one on her."

Summer's fingers tightened. "Don't call her that. She's not a bitch."

"What?" Surprise crossed Tori's face. "Everyone does."

"I don't care. Name one bitchy thing she ever personally did to you or anyone around here?"

"Whoa…sorry." Tori lifted her hands. "No offense. I'm just used to that being her nickname. I don't even know her."

"No one does, and yet everyone thinks it's fine to talk crap about her. How's that okay?"

"You're right, it's not." Tori's look became speculative. "So…you guys are friends now?"

Shrugging, Summer turned the page, pretending to give her script attention. "We did a film together on hiatus. I know her a lot better now. She's really nice."

The silence dragged on, and finally Summer met Tori's wide eyes. "*What?* You did a film with her?"

"Yeah. She's a great actress. I learned a lot." *And she kissed me like she was on fire and cracked open my heart. But she didn't mean to, so…* "It was educational."

"Geez, you're a dark horse. Everyone around here's too scared to say boo to her, and you've been making films with her! And now…" She elbowed her. "Kissing Hunt." She shuddered. "Nope, still can't picture doing that."

"Am I interrupting?" Elizabeth's cool voice sliced through the air and Tori almost jumped off her chair.

"No!" Tori scrambled to stand at attention. "We were just rehearsing. Gotta go." She bolted.

"Is she always that skittish?" Elizabeth lowered herself into the vacated canvas seat. "Do I want to know what you were discussing?"

"Depends. How much did you hear?"

"Nothing. Why? Should my ears be burning?"

"Oh, definitely. Apparently I'm brave. She can't imagine the horrors of having to kiss Hunt."

Elizabeth's laugh was low and husky. "Well, I don't imagine that she knows what we got up to on hiatus then."

Summer smirked. "Noooo. I think her head would explode." She glanced at Elizabeth's outfit. Ooh. Hunt wardrobe. Hair in a bun. White coat. Clip-on security ID on her breast pocket. Summer did like Bess in full Hunt regalia.

"Yes?" Elizabeth's eyebrow hiked up at her inspection.

"I've decided I like Hunt."

"You do?" Skepticism edged Elizabeth's tone.

"Turns out I'm fond of misunderstood ice queens." On screen *and* off. "And you do Hunt so well."

"Never an icier queen, I suppose. Until *our* scene, that is."

"When the melting begins. Yep."

"Nervous?" Elizabeth asked, her eyes warm.

"Maybe a little. It doesn't help seeing the crowd of ogling men who've turned up from every department to see us kiss. Pretty much sums up our show—it's not exactly staffed by sensitive Jean-Claudes. And we just know they'll milk Hunter for sensationalism and try to make it look scandalous and dirty."

"We won't allow it. We play it as an authentic love story."

"Yes. Joey's all in. This isn't some fun flirtation for her. She has real feelings for the chief."

"And I think Hunt cares for Carter far more than she wants. It's difficult for her, as she hasn't been vulnerable for a long time. This is no game for her."

"Exactly."

Elizabeth hesitated. "Speaking of games, I'm wondering if you'd like to be included as a regular to my party nights. It's usually monthly but it varies depending on our schedules."

"You all want to be killed at Shakespeare again?" Summer chuckled.

"May as well. And lest you think a bunch of Cambridge drama grads is sorely lacking originality or variety, we do a lot of other things to amuse ourselves as well."

"Sounds intriguing. But, um, won't it be a little awkward? With Grace being…" *Her territorial self.* "…Grace?"

Elizabeth examined her hands. "There will be no more Grace. She's out of my life now." There was pain in that statement, a tinge of regret, and an awful lot of acceptance.

"What's happened?" Summer asked, concern flooding her. "Are you okay?"

"I came to understand who Grace is underneath everything." She slid her eyes skywards. "She doesn't want me. Just my endless…appreciation. Anyone need apply."

"Oh Bess, I'm really sorry." Summer's heart went out to her.

Elizabeth sighed. "Well, it's partly my fault. Alex tried to warn me. Often. I always told myself that Grace gave me my LA career, that she made me who I am. How could that not be affection of some sort? It made me feel special. But it was a means to an end for Grace—to keep me around."

Summer shifted uncertainly.

With a frown, Elizabeth said, "You look like you're trying not to say something."

"I-I didn't want to ruin things with you and Grace. But I have it on good authority that you didn't get your agent because of her. Grace asked Rachel to rep you, but she said no. Later, Rachel saw you perform in London and told Grace if you ever came to LA, to look her up. That's it."

Elizabeth's eyes tightened.

"Was I wrong to tell you?" Summer regarded her with growing alarm. "Did you not want to know?"

"That woman never ceases to amaze me. Why did I ever…" She laughed, but it was thin and empty.

"Because she was someone you looked up to. Idols and mentors… they're hard to let go of. Believe me, I know."

Elizabeth's eyes snapped open. "Please tell me I'm not still some sort of hero to you? Not after everything."

"God, no." Summer shook her head. "I see you as a regular human being. Flawed and all like the rest of us. I do know how it feels, though, finding out someone we thought was special is just as messed up as everyone else."

"You think I'm messed up?"

"Sure." Summer grinned. "So am I. You should see the trail of ice cream tubs in my house to prove it. I get embarrassingly weepy once a month. I bite my nails. I trip over my own shadow. I jump into things without thinking sometimes. It just means I'm human. But Grace is too. It's probably good you know exactly who she is, not what you imagined she was. That's important if you still want a friendship with her later."

"I think we're past that. Some days I feel betrayed. Other days I feel a fool. Either way, it just…hurts. But most of all, I'm surprised to find a big part of me is just relieved it's over. That really isn't a good sign. It's time to move on."

"Okay. But I'm still sorry she hurt you." She reached for Elizabeth's hand and squeezed.

"As am I. Yet, sometimes I wonder if I always knew she didn't really care about me for me. A person who cares treats someone an entirely different way, don't they?" She glanced at Summer and then their conjoined hands.

"Yes. They do." Summer retracted her fingers, embarrassed she'd forgotten herself. She was always a touchy person, even when she didn't mean to be.

"You never answered my question," Elizabeth said quietly. "There'll be a spare seat at party night. I'd love it if you could be the one to fill it. It was Alex's idea."

"Well, I really like your friends, so I'd be honored to crush everyone at Shakespeare on the regular," Summer joked. "Thanks."

"Excellent." Elizabeth smiled. Not one of her half smiles, either. It was full, wide, glorious.

Summer's heart thudded an ovation. *Useless damned thing.*

"Back to work for me." Elizabeth stood, straightening Hunt's coat.

"You look hot." *Oops.* Summer felt her cheeks flame.

"Chief Hunt doubtlessly appreciates the sentiment, Dr. Carter." Elizabeth winked and headed for the set.

Well, that was nice—pretending she'd been talking about their on-screen personas.

She scrambled to get her thoughts together. How could she think straight after Elizabeth had just asked her to hang out with her and her friends regularly? And there'd be no more Grace.

No. More. Grace.

Her mouth went dry as she digested what that meant. Hope flared. *Stop it.* Elizabeth was still hurting, at least a little. Her heart fluttered. *Ugh. Stupid heart.*

Hadn't Elizabeth admitted she found her beautiful? And that if it wasn't for Grace...

And just like that, the whole world seemed a thousand times brighter.

———⊷⊶———

Joey Carter put her clothes into her locker and turned with a start to find Dr. Hunt standing just three feet away. The chief's gaze lingered.

They'd been flirting for weeks now, with Hunt always finding heated reasons to seek out Dr. Carter as the two women edged ever closer toward this moment. The big scene.

"Why, Chief Hunt," Joey drawled. "To what do I owe the—"

"It's unprofessional, flirting with Dr. Mendez. He's your direct superior and I won't have it."

Joey leaned against her locker. "Jealous?" she lifted an eyebrow and saw, just for a second, an amused glint in Hunt's eye that was pure Elizabeth.

The chief glowered. "Dr. Carter, you are out of order. It's insubordinate and I won't hear—"

"I don't mean of me. Of him."

Hunt was a picture of shock. "What?"

"Does it drive you crazy, the thought he might kiss me? When you'd rather be the one doing it?" Joey slid up a cocky eyebrow.

A scowl hardened Hunt's features. *Ooh, Elizabeth. Nice.* It fueled Summer more. Bess's talent was exciting. Suddenly it felt like the air had been sucked from the room. She finished her line: "Do you want me? The same way I want you?"

Without waiting for an answer, her fingers slid across the starched white lapels of Hunt's jacket, pulling her in. "Because I *really* want you." That was an ad-lib. A highly truthful one, though.

Elizabeth's eyes softened.

The kiss was supposed to have been fast and furious, enough to express interest, followed by a bitchy hiss of outrage from Hunt, then cool threats of disciplinary action. Instead, Summer clung to her, moving her lips against Elizabeth's, hoping it wouldn't end quite so soon.

Elizabeth's response began unyielding and cruel but, within moments, her hand slid from Summer's waist to her breast. By the time they parted, Summer's nipple was rock hard, and Elizabeth's breathing was hard and fast.

"I could have you disciplined," Hunt ground out. *Wrong line.* It was supposed to be *I will.*

"I suppose," Joey said softly, unable to resist running her index finger down Hunt's lapel, then shimmying it over her name badge. "Would you like that?" The line had been written as a challenge; meant to be hurled back like a grenade. She'd made it teasing.

"Yes," Hunt said. "I would like that." The triumphalism and threat were absent. Instead, confusion clouded the chief's gray eyes.

Summer paused for the director to call "cut". They'd screwed it all up. She stared into Hunt's eyes as she waited, and found *Elizabeth* watching her back. Her stomach clenched. *So damned beautiful. Seriously, there should be laws.*

A second later it became clear Ravitz wanted them to continue. Maybe he liked the crazy, weird, charged frisson?

"I-I wouldn't like that," Elizabeth said this time, the sentence sounding ripped out of her like the most humiliating of confessions.

Oh my God. That delivery was *perfect*. Elizabeth's look was so…raw. Needy.

Summer's fingers clenched Elizabeth's lapel to stop herself from hugging her. *Brilliant.* With a smile wreathed in relief, she let her fingers trail up Elizabeth's soft cheek. "Good."

After shedding Hunt's layers—first stripping off the coat, then letting down her hair—Elizabeth stared absently at the trailer wall. They'd kept that first take, and done all the two-shots, singles, and close-ups on it. She and Summer had also redone it with the pissed-off version the script originally called for. But she'd heard it was the first take they'd chosen.

Elizabeth aligned her coat on a hanger, then stared at the wall some more. So, Ravitz and Lenton might be idiots, but they were shrewd idiots. That first take had felt startling and nuanced, and completely real. Heaven knew that was in short supply on hospital dramas.

A throat cleared, startling Elizabeth back to the present. She'd forgotten Finola had come in some minutes ago. The Scotswoman's impatient look made her wonder how long she'd been chasing her own thoughts. "Sorry."

With a nod, Finola said, "Quite all right. I hear you had a big day."

"Hmm. Hunt learned how to smile for the first time in years. Apparently, on television, only kissing has the power to unwind uptight women."

"Sad but true." Finola laughed.

There was a knock and Finola, being closest, opened the door. A familiar head leaned in.

"Summer!" The assistant's eyes brightened. "That's timing for you. We were just talking about you. Or, rather, hot romances for uptight Dr. Hunt. Come in, dear."

"Hey, Finola, great to see you again." Summer closed the door behind her with a foot since her hands were full. "And yes, I'm still working on melting the chief. It's a work in progress." She kissed Finola's cheek. "How are Caitlin and Alistair?"

Elizabeth blinked. She knew Finola's kids' names?

"Ach, pains in my bum as ever."

"Ha, of course. And you love them to bits. Look, I'm glad I caught you today. I saw this and thought of you." Summer tossed her a small, pink-and-white-striped bag.

With a thrilled look, Finola dug in and extracted a caramel-colored slab of fudge.

"Goodness. Edinburgh tablet? Oh, I've missed this. Where'd you find this out here?"

"I had it put into my last tea delivery from England. I'm glad you like it."

"I love it. Thank you. Now, I'll leave you two to it." Finola reached for the door handle. She glanced back at Elizabeth and said, tone warning, "Treat this one right, you hear?"

Cheeky. Elizabeth arched an eyebrow at the retreating woman, wondering just how perceptive she actually was.

Summer, however, seemed oblivious, and flopped down on the couch as the door shut. "I bring gifts for you too. Well, one. It's just the usual, but you're pretty easy to buy for." She slid over a steaming cup of tea.

Elizabeth reached for it, delighted. "You do know me. I'm very predictable."

"Oh, I wouldn't go that far. Like today's scene. Chief Hunt? All confusion, angst, and doe eyes? Now that surprised me. Genius!"

Elizabeth sipped her tea, enjoying the flavors. Her acting had been instinctual today, not a choice. But, hell, she'd take the genius label.

"You were amazing," Summer continued. "You're gonna have everyone making 'I Heart Hunt' bumper stickers."

"Well, if so, it's your doing. Everyone loves Joey. So if she likes Hunt, you just made TV's most notorious villain lovable."

"Nah, Hunt's always had something lovable going for her. People just need to remember who she was. She's had her boss mask welded on too long. Time to remind everyone of the real her and expose her vulnerable side."

"It's…scary for her, being vulnerable. Being the aloof chief feels familiar and safe to her. But with the right incentive, I think she'll want to show someone her softer side." Her gaze slid to Summer, willing her to understand they weren't just talking about their characters. "And she does have a reason to now."

Summer's smile was gentle. "She'll be fine," she whispered. "She just needs to trust that she has someone looking out for her who cares about her. She's in safe hands. It'll be okay."

"You have a good point." Elizabeth nudged her tea around the table before lifting her eyes to Summer's. "And thanks, yet again."

After a shrug, she grinned. "Nah, tea's easy. People are hard."

"I didn't just mean the tea."

"I know."

"I had you all wrong, you know." Elizabeth inhaled. "I made a lot of judgmental assumptions about you when we met. Because of where you're from, how you look. And every single one you turned on its ear. You're impressive, Summer."

Summer rested her head on her hand and gave Elizabeth a soft grin. "Thanks. But I think you're the intriguing one. And, sort of on that note— how interesting I think you are—I came by to ask something. Want to come out with me on Saturday? I have to shake the cobwebs off my camera. And I want to show you my world. It'll be fun."

"I'd like that." And Elizabeth found she really meant it. She'd love to watch amateur photographer Summer in action.

"Great. Saturday. I'll pick you up at two."

Can't wait, Elizabeth almost replied. But that sounded far too eager. Instead she allowed a faint twitch of her lips. "Two it is."

Chapter 23

ARCHITECTURE WASN'T SOMETHING ELIZABETH HAD ever thought much about. But Summer's burble of enthusiastic commentary brought it alive. They'd looked at styles from Googie to Art Deco, Mission Revival, and the awful Programmatic.

"Dear God, it's like a *Simpsons* episode," Elizabeth complained as she stared up at the giant, round ode to carbs and fat on top of Randy's Donuts on West Manchester Boulevard.

"I know, right?" Summer grinned as she fired off some shots. "That donut's starred in a few movies, like *Mars Attacks*."

"Why do you like it?"

Summer peered up at it. "It's a statement. Nothing bland about it. It screams consumerism and 'look at me'. It's a metaphor for Hollywood."

"I suppose that's true." Elizabeth snapped a photo with her phone.

"Ooh, I saw that. You're a closet Programmatic fan."

"Fairly sure that's a contradiction in terms. No, I thought Brian and Rowan would assume I'm making things up if I didn't furnish proof." She smiled at the thought, then caught herself. Huh. She was having a lot of fun. When was the last time that had happened? "So, Programmatic's ticked off. Where to next?"

"Glad you asked, because this next location's really cool. Besides, I have to make a truth teller out of you." Summer led them back to the car.

"Isn't the saying 'make a liar out of someone'?"

"Normally. Come on."

A little over half an hour later, Summer pulled up her blue Beetle in Angelino Heights. They got out.

"Okay, why are we here?" Elizabeth looked around at the narrow two-story houses, which all had a Victorian, slightly gothic feel.

"That's 1345 Carroll Avenue," Summer pointed at a rundown-looking building better suited to a Halloween backdrop. "Where they shot *Thriller*. Remember us telling Jean-Claude of your undying love of this place?"

"I remember *you* telling him that." Elizabeth studied the creepy building. "No wonder he looked at me sideways. He must think I have zero taste."

"Pretty much. That was evil of me." Summer laughed. "Come on, I want a few shots before three. That's when the tour bus hits."

"Tour bus?"

"A lot of people are into LA architecture and famous sets. The *Thriller* house is really popular. Don't worry, no one lives there, so the tourists don't bother anyone. Right, I need you standing by the door." She pointed. "Chief Hunt, level ten menace, thanks."

"You want *me* in the photo?"

"Yep." Summer nodded. "Humor me."

Elizabeth rolled her eyes and made her way up the creaky stairs.

Summer's face turned professional as she checked her settings and then looked up. "Ready?"

"What, no 'cheese'?"

"Amateurs." Summer snorted. "But say it if it makes you feel better."

Elizabeth laughed, and heard the shutter snap, then assumed a more Hunt-like expression of intern-crushing superiority.

Summer snapped a few more. "Excellent." She thumbed through the shots at the back of the camera.

"What are they for?" Elizabeth asked when she re-joined her.

"One's for Jean-Claude. Proof. And one's for me." Straightening, Summer put her lens cap on. "I'll let you figure out which one's for who." Her smile was cheeky.

Was Summer flirting with her? Elizabeth wouldn't put it past her. She decided she liked Summer in charming mode.

"Okay, the retro diner's next," Summer announced, waving to the car.

"Is that another style?"

"No. We're going to an actual fifties-themed retro diner. Do you think you can face it?" The sweet, hopeful look on her face also seemed steeled to face rejection

"By all means." Elizabeth had never been to an American diner in her life. After seven years in the States, she was long overdue to further her education. "What does this diner create?"

"Dreams." Summer grinned. "Well, the old American dream, specifically. Think ice-cream floats and burgers and fries. *Happy Days*. But don't worry, there are a few salads for us carb counters, and it's got a great atmosphere."

Elizabeth relaxed as they drove, absorbing the views. She hadn't really seen much at all of LA since she'd been here. That was her own fault. Even when she wasn't busy, she hadn't had much interest in it. Just like with Summer, she'd made assumptions about the omnipresence of LA's shallow, shiny, fakeness. But today she'd discovered it also contained hidden pockets of elegance, quirkiness, charm, and garishness—all intriguing in their own way.

What was it about Summer, forever challenging her assumptions? It'd be weird not seeing her around so often when her contract wrapped up. Picturing never seeing Summer again beyond an occasional party night suddenly seemed the worst thing. Already, just being in the woman's slipstream for half a day, doing what Summer wanted to do, had changed her perspective on LA. What would it be like being with her for a week, a month. A year? What else would she open Elizabeth's eyes to?

How interesting would that be?

———— ⋈ ————

Summer led Elizabeth into the diner with its bright orange spaceship exterior. A red and white checked floor greeted them, with matching cherry-red booths. Summer bit her lip. She loved the warmth and cheesiness, but it could be a little full-on. What if Elizabeth hated it?

A waitress showed them to a table.

"Right," Summer said after they were seated, "I know this might be a little over the top on the Americana, but they do great food and it has a real charm to it." She pointed to the blackboard with specials listed. "And the salads are listed over…"

"A burger." Plucking a laminated menu from the table, Elizabeth smiled at Summer, whose mouth fell open. "When in Rome and so forth. I'd like to try a traditional American burger."

"Right…we're doing the whole experience?"

271

"Yes."

"Okay then," Summer grinned back in delight. "I recommend the Blastoff Burger. Really worth it."

"So after all that salad talk, you're secretly a fan of their burgers?" Elizabeth asked in amusement, then dipped her gaze over Summer's form. "Not that anyone could tell."

"I work out lots, trust me. Otherwise my burger habit would be obvious to everyone."

Elizabeth merely smiled.

Their burgers arrived twenty minutes later, and it was all Summer could do not to blush as she watched the way Elizabeth enjoyed hers. She ate in small bites, delicate and dainty, which was impressive. Juices dribbled down fingers and were licked away by Elizabeth's darting tongue.

"You're not eating?" Elizabeth asked. "It's quite good. You were right."

"Oh. Um… yep." *Too distracted.* Her blush was telling, she was sure, but Elizabeth merely resumed eating in that slow, delicious, appreciative way of hers.

They talked, of anything and everything. Summer was amazed to learn Elizabeth's first career had not been acting at all.

"Law," Elizabeth said as she reached for her chilled water. "I know, I know. I can't picture it either."

"But why? Your parents' choice?"

"Oh no. It just made sense to me. I was good at speaking and thinking on my feet, and could spin a good argument. I quite liked the idea of defending the unjustly accused, and so on. But it wasn't to be." She lowered her voice conspiratorially. "Brian. He induced me into his acting cult with a series of hilarious mimes in the university cafeteria one lunchtime. When I first set foot in the Footlights' theater, it was like coming home." She shook her head. "My parents were in shock for about a year."

"Not fans of you being an actress?"

"No, but then, they thought the idea of putting oneself out there for any reason was deeply troubling. Come to think of it, it's a miracle they were capable of romancing each other. My father especially. He's more of an introvert than me."

"How did they even meet then?"

"At a play. My mother was beside him in the audience, doing a muttered, occasional commentary under her breath. Dad started murmuring retorts back. When the lights came up, they looked at each other. And she said 'Well, I've seen worse'. And he admitted, 'Well, I've written worse'. And that was it."

"God, that's so cute."

"Yes." Elizabeth eyes crinkled. "So, what about you? Were you always destined for acting?"

"Everyone assumes Brock and Skye were evil stage parents. But it wasn't like that. They didn't care what I chose. When I was eleven, I met a director at one of their parties who had been trying to find a young girl for her children's movie. She thought I looked perfect for it. I auditioned and got it. I didn't mind acting. I liked not having to be in school during filming. Being tutored suited my brain, because of how it jumps around so much."

"So you didn't love acting?" Elizabeth asked. "You just fell into it?"

"Pretty much. I probably wouldn't have stayed an actress if I hadn't seen your Shakespeare play. I understood then. The power of it. It could have substance. I don't have enough words for how much you blew me away that first day. Suddenly all I wanted was to know everything about Shakespeare. And..." she reddened, "you."

"I'm sure I made for dull research material. But at least I gave you an appreciation for good tea."

"I don't think 'dull' was ever a word for you," Summer laughed. "Besides, there wasn't much to be found beyond your taste in teas, books, and plays. Anyway, after that I decided I'd be a great Shakespearean actress. I know, I know. The fifteen-year-old American who would reinvent the Bard."

"Ambitious." Elizabeth's eyes twinkled. "So how'd that work out?"

"Oh, about what you'd expect. I contacted all the Shakespearean theater companies that were looking for interns or actors, including the Royal Shakespeare Company."

"Starting at the top," Elizabeth teased. "Impressive."

"Hey! You should talk; you interned there."

"I did. But only after completing my drama degree and doing a number of plays did I dare apply." Her eyes were dancing now. "So what did all these companies say?"

"All but two ignored me entirely. I got a stuffy email back from the RSC, saying a firm thanks but no thanks."

"And the other?"

"The Royal Bard Theatre Troupe. I really liked their shows."

Elizabeth nodded. "The RBTT is very traditional, though. You'd have been hard-pressed to ever get a yes from them."

"I know. But at least my rejection letter was personalized. Handwritten. It told me to try my luck in America. It was snooty, but I thought, 'Okay, well, some interaction is better than none'. I replied that I *could* try that, but America doesn't do Shakespeare like the RBTT does. And this woman, Margaret, replied, 'Thank God they don't; it'd be appalling to watch the language mangling'."

"Oh dear."

"Yeah. After that we got into a pretty blunt but amusing exchange of letters until I headed home three years later. Her farewell letter wished me well in getting work in 'that intellectually shallow American swill that passes as drama'. So, that was the closest I came to my dream—being insulted for my nationality regularly." She laughed.

"So after your vitriolic penpal…was that the end of your Shakespearean dreams?"

"Oh yeah. When you're a kid, you don't know where the limits are. Who the hell did I think I was? I was so arrogant. No experience, qualifications, training, cultural understanding, just wide-eyed optimism and huge ambition. No wonder Margaret laughed at me."

"You, wide-eyed?" Elizabeth's lips quivered with suppressed laughter. "I just can't picture it."

"I know, right?"

"So doing Shakespeare in England isn't anything you want now?"

"Let's just say I'm all grown up and a realist now. I'm better at sticking to my niche."

"What do you see as your niche?"

"Becoming the best American actress I can be. And hopefully not being stuck in girl-next-door roles for too long."

"Well, you're on your way now, thanks to *Eight Little Pieces*."

Their waitress interrupted to ask if they needed anything else.

Summer gave her a bright smile and reached into her bag for her phone, which she unlocked and slid across the table. "Could you take a pic of us?" Then she slid an arm around Elizabeth's shoulder. "This place is the coolest backdrop."

Shooting Summer a faintly surprised look, Elizabeth tensed briefly, but then relaxed into her arm.

The woman took the photo. "Done. You guys look so great, by the way. Hunter rocks. Especially the chief." She winked, slid the phone back to Summer, and moved on to the next table.

"Hunter rocks, huh?" Summer laughed, returning her phone to her bag. "And look at you, finally getting some fan love. About damned time."

Elizabeth regarded her for a moment, then an expression of mischief crossed her face. "I have an idea. Can you send me a copy of that?"

Curiosity piqued, Summer texted over the photo. She was about to ask what the idea was, when Elizabeth interrupted, her voice so soft and sultry it blanked Summer's brain.

"Dessert?" she asked. "Or should we bail now before the calories catch up to us?"

Starting her VW with a playful rev, Summer grinned. "Okay, let me get you home. I'm sure you've had quite enough of the American dream for one day."

"On the contrary, it's been excellent."

As they pulled out into traffic, Elizabeth pulled up the photo the waitress had taken of them on her phone.

"What are you going to do with it?" Summer's gaze flicked to her, then back to the road.

"An insurance policy." Elizabeth tapped a few buttons. "I'm going to post it on Twitter."

Summer made a choking sound.

Elizabeth paused what she was doing and glanced over in surprise. Summer's fingers were curled tight around the steering wheel. "What's wrong?"

"Um, won't Delvine and Rachel have a meltdown?"

"Possibly." Elizabeth tried to remember her Twitter password. *Beatrice? Imogen? Ophelia? Desdemona?* It had been awhile. Delvine's assistants usually posted for her about upcoming projects. "They'll probably all have a meltdown." *Ooh. Rosalind.* Great, she was in!

Hold on. *Twenty-three thousand new followers?* Where on earth had they come from? Surely not all from this Hunter thing?

She glanced up to find Summer had resumed driving at a much slower pace, fingers grimly curled around the steering wheel.

"Look, you heard Lenton blackmailing me," Elizabeth said reasonably. "He implied they'll spread rumors about how much I hate you if we put a foot out of line. I don't like being threatened, so I'd like to get in first. We're friends. Friends post photos when they go out to dinner. Lenton can't spread that lie if we've already established we socialize together."

"Bess, won't some people assume we're more than friends because we're playing a couple? Isn't that what Delvine said after the Jean-Claude lunch? Won't this photo just add fuel to that fire?"

With a frown, Elizabeth hesitated. *It might.*

"Add a hashtag," Summer said.

"What?"

"Write '#Hunter', if you're worried. That'll give the more cynical people, the ones who stir up crap online, a reason to think it's all just a publicity stunt. That we're only promoting our popular new fan ship. They'll be so busy debating whether the friendship's real or not that they'll forget to debate whether we're more than that. And the less cynical fans will take the picture at face value—that we're just hanging out as friends. Lenton is screwed if he tries to pretend anything else later."

Elizabeth gave her an impressed look. "You really are wily when you want to be."

"Just because I'm not climbing over people to get ahead doesn't mean I don't know how the game works. I have seen more marketing stunts than you've had hot teas. You should hear the outrageous crap studios get up to in order to promote a film. One PR stunt involved fake-kidnapping an actor off the street. That went downhill fast when a witness called 9-1-1."

"That's ridiculous."

"Yeah. Most of this stuff is. It's a Pandora's box if you let it go too far."

Elizabeth added #Hunter and hovered her thumb over the post button. "I won't do it if you don't want me to."

Summer eyed her. "I'm not bothered at all. I'm just really surprised *you're* considering it."

Placing her phone in her lap, Elizabeth gazed out the window. "Some days it's harder than others. I do get tired of being the villain. It's nice for once to be seen as normal. Human. Just out, enjoying company with friends, not sacrificing babies or whatever else people think about Hunt."

"You're doing this for Hunt?" Summer asked. "To protect your character?"

"Not Hunt—me. I'm tired of being her off-screen, too. The names I get called on the street... Attila the Hunt, Chief Cunt, the British Bitch... and those aren't even the worst. But I detest being threatened by ego-stuffed bastards like Lenton most of all. I won't tolerate that."

Summer smiled. "Remind me never to cross you."

Elizabeth picked up her phone again. "It is a spectacularly good picture of you, by the way. I should have mentioned that first."

"Really?"

"Mmm."

"Playing on my vanity, huh?" Summer grinned. "You'll go far."

Elizabeth laughed and pressed *Post*. The photo jumped into her Twitter feed. "I hope so. Going far, far from *Choosing Hope* is my big plan."

The smile fell from Summer's face. "I'll really miss you when you leave."

"No you won't," Elizabeth pocketed her phone, "because you'll be joining my party nights, if you recall."

"I hadn't forgotten," Summer said softly. "I'm looking forward to it." She said nothing more until they pulled up at Elizabeth's gates fifteen minutes later. "Back home, safe and sound, ma'am."

Digging through her bag, Elizabeth liberated her gate controller and hit the *Open* button. "Would you like to come in? For a drink? Or even dinner? The view's really something up here at sunset."

Summer didn't answer immediately. As she reached the top of the hill, she pulled to a stop, killed the ignition, and turned to face Elizabeth. "That...depends." She hesitated. "Was this a date?"

Oh. That thought hadn't even entered her mind. She could see how Summer might have thought it was. Showing her around LA, taking Elizabeth to lunch...

"Never mind. Sorry." Summer's cheeks rapidly turned crimson. "I may have assumed a few things. Or hoped. Because it's been ages since you've even mentioned Grace, and I thought maybe you'd moved on and... Never mind, it's totally fine. So, um, I'll catch you at work." Her smile was dazzling, but the disappointment in her eyes was difficult to look at.

"I had a wonderful day," Elizabeth tried, giving her a warm smile, "date or no date." She leaned in to kiss Summer's cheek, but the other woman edged away.

Summer's expression was pained. "Please, remember what I said about you kissing me? That if you ever do it again, you have to really mean it? I'm not strong enough to...Um. Please just don't."

Damn it, Elizabeth had indeed promised that. "Summer, I'm sor—"

"No, it's okay. I understand." Summer's smile lit up, bright and fake. "Have a great night. I'll see you at work Monday."

Elizabeth exited and stared vacantly at her front door. She turned, waving a jangling hand full of keys, to say goodbye, to say something else, but Summer's car was slowly picking its way back around the circular drive.

That evening, Elizabeth lay on her deck chair, staring up at the expanse of stars—well, as much as she could see with the light pollution. It was peaceful. The infinity pool in front of her looked sleek and still, like a liquid blanket. She shivered. After so much warmth today, it was odd to feel so cold and lonely. She usually didn't notice her isolation. The ice cubes clanged as she sipped her gin.

She *had* had an amazing day. Summer was fun and smart, and their time together had been illuminating. She was, Elizabeth had come to realize, a good friend.

Could she be more than that?

Sliding another mouthful of gin down her throat, she mulled over Summer's comment about how she'd stopped talking about Grace. How interesting.

Have I moved on?

Grace had called her just once since they'd parted ways. Elizabeth had let it go to voicemail. In that message, she heard laughter and music tinkling in the background, along with a man's voice. Roger the producer? Grace's apparent point: *I'm happy, not pathetic, no matter what you saw that day.* Grace's subtext: *I don't need you. You have been replaced. Easily.*

She hated knowing that was probably all she'd ever been to Grace, just one admirer among many, interchangeable like a cog. Not really friendship, was it? Friendship meant you were unique and important to someone. Summer, for example, always treated Elizabeth as if she was worth knowing for herself. Summer never expected anything from her and seemed to like Elizabeth just as she was.

Picking up her phone, Elizabeth called up the tweeted photo. Laughter creased their eyes, and their smiles were bright, enjoyment leaking from every pixel.

How long has it been since I've looked that happy?

The post had garnered mainly positive responses and been retweeted thousands of times. One retweeter's name jumped out at her: @Summer_ Hayes. Elizabeth looked at the comment.

Nothing better than catching up with good friends. Love hanging with Bess.

Elizabeth stared at the lack of Hunter hashtag. She re-read the words, turning them over, puzzled. Then the reason hit her.

Oh. Oh hell.

To Summer, the photo hadn't been about politics or a clever way to thwart Lenton's games. She'd made the hashtag suggestion in case *Elizabeth* had been worried, to protect her. But Summer never said she cared herself about any gossip from the photo. Besides, for Summer, today had been a date. A way for Elizabeth to see who Summer was and to share in what she loved most—architecture, photography, LA, food.

And what had Elizabeth done? Turned it into a publicity stunt. And even though Summer had suggested the tag, it didn't mean she agreed with it. That much was now clear.

She dropped the phone to the side table and stared up at the night skies. *What does that woman see in me?*

Her phone rang. She braced herself when she saw the name on her screen. "Hello, Delvine."

"Hashtag Hunter? Oh, and lovely photo, Bess." Delvine sounded amused at least.

"Oh, that." She sighed, hoping she sounded bored. "Lenton threatened me, so I'm firing a few shots across his bow."

"Which threat is it this time?"

"Spreading the word that I hate Summer and am jealous of her and we're enemies on set."

"I see. Who took the photo?"

"A waitress. Are you too annoyed?" Life was always much easier when she was in Delvine's good graces.

"No, darling. I wish you'd cleared it with me first, but what's done is done. Rachel will probably have conniptions yet again but leave her to me. Tell you what, though, next time get the waitress in the photo. Looks less date-like. And, Bess, did you actually take a close look at the photo?"

Her stomach sank. "No. Why?"

Delvine's laugh was soft. "Oh honey, you've got it bad. Night."

The call ended.

Elizabeth quickly pulled the photo back up and zoomed in. What was Delvine talking about? There was nothing really out of the ordinar... Oh. *Oh.*

There was such a softness in her gaze as she looked at Summer. Real affection. Far, far too much of it. Nervously, she slid her eyes over to Summer's face—blue eyes sparkling with laughter, smile curled, and gaze fixed on Elizabeth in quite possibly the sweetest look anyone had ever given her.

Only the most cynical hack would call this a publicity stunt. And Elizabeth might as well have just put a sign on her head saying, *Thornton has the hots for her co-star.*

Or maybe that look said she wanted to love Summer...for a long, long time.

Would that be so bad?

The thought stopped her cold. Well. That went a long way to answering the question about whether she was over Grace.

For the past eighteen months, long before she'd met Summer, she'd been mentally edging away from Grace, painfully aware that giving everything of herself to someone who didn't return her feelings wasn't healthy. Only when Grace had kissed her had Elizabeth realized how effective her emotional distancing had been. The revelation had felt like a bullet whizzing around her head: *I don't love Grace.*

Not just that. Even Elizabeth's attraction for her had shriveled up. Seeing a soul's ugliness was like being doused in cold water. Grace's impact on her couldn't be dismissed so easily, though. The woman had shaped who Elizabeth was. She'd never forget her. She couldn't. But...was it time? Could she file Grace away as an influential figure from her past, and simply turn the page?

Am I ready to move on?

Her gaze fell to the photo again. She was leaning into Summer, eyeing her with so much affection. The answer was right there. She'd been blind not to see what her manager had realized with a single glance.

I already have.

Her phone rang again, and she answered, stabbing the green button, barely looking at the screen. "Delvine, I really don't think..."

"Bess?"

She paused. "Summer?"

"Yeah." The voice was small and soft.

There was silence for a long beat, but Elizabeth waited, brows drawing together.

"Bess, I'm sorry I got a bit weird at the end of our...day out. I wasn't fair on you. I should have explained what I was doing when I invited you."

"No, I should have figured it out. It's been awhile. Sorry I was slow."

"Please, don't take any blame. It's on me. I think...I just wanted to see how you fit into my world. If you *could*, you know?"

"And did I?" Elizabeth held her breath, then wondered why she had.

"Yeah. You really did. I love how you got my architecture thing. How you tried a burger and didn't sneer at my diner. I loved all of it... I just... really wanted it to be a date."

"I know." Elizabeth ran a hand through her hair. "I understand."

"That's all I had to say. Okay?"

"Summer? I think…I wanted it to be a date too." Her heart picked up pace at the admission.

"Oh." A pause. "Oh? *Oh!*"

Elizabeth smiled at Summer's audible excitement. "Yes."

"But…what about Grace?"

"Grace is…dead and buried now. It feels right. Finally."

"Not literally I hope?" There was a smile in Summer's voice. "I mean, I *really* like you and all, but I'm not sure I want to serve fifteen-to-twenty for being an accessory after the fact."

"You really like me?" Pleasure colored her voice.

"A whole lot. God, I tried not to. You were so focused on Grace. And it was complicated. But I couldn't help it. I'd love to date you. Be with you. All of it. Everything."

"Oh, Summer. I wish you were here right now."

"Me too." Summer let out a ragged breath. "I could…come back?"

"I-I don't think that's a good idea."

"Right." She sounded deflated.

"I have a rule. Never with a co-star. Maybe it's a silly, arbitrary code I had drilled into me about keeping things professional. But I can see the sense in it."

"Oh. Okay."

Elizabeth exhaled. "But they're writing Hunt out soon, as you know. After that…"

"After that?" Hope laced Summer's voice.

"I'd love to date you. If you're agreeable."

There was silence.

"Summer?"

"Sorry. Can't you hear me smiling? I'm smiling so loud I can't hear myself think."

"That's a yes then?" Elizabeth's own smile threatened to swamp her.

"It's a big, fat, whopping yes."

There was more silence.

"You're still smiling, aren't you?" Elizabeth guessed.

"Big time."

She laughed. "Good night, Summer."

Chapter 24

As the days slipped into weeks, and Hunt's time on *Hope* drew to an end, Elizabeth's scenes increased. Midnight finishes weren't uncommon; she was starting to forget what daylight felt like. Texts, calls, and emails went unanswered. She hadn't spoken to her friends in weeks.

This is temporary, she reminded herself. Soon, she'd be free. She was itching to be alone with Summer. But not now, when she could barely keep her eyes open.

Anticipation regularly edged their scenes together, the rising sexual tension increasingly palpable. If only people knew that the hungry way Chief Hunt regarded her medical resident didn't require a great deal of acting. Elizabeth found herself longing to touch, a craving that was curiously satisfying. It fed her anticipation, which only made her think of what would happen soon.

Summer, as Carter, responded the way she always did. Clever, subtle deliveries of dialog, laden with desire, paired with longing looks. The line between character and actress was blurring. It was all about the dance, the flirtation, the seduction. Okay, technically their characters were post-seduction now, since their attraction had been consummated two episodes ago in a drawn-out kiss and a tasteful fade-to-black.

What a kiss that had been. Her whole body had quivered from it.

After the director had called "Cut", Summer had given her a pained, pent-up look and hissed in her ear, "You know this waiting thing is *your* idea. I expect you to make it up to me fully, later."

"You have no idea what I want to do to you," she'd murmured back.

That thought had curled her toes. Summer's cheeks had been red for an hour.

It was no secret Hunt was leaving *Choosing Hope*. The only question was how they'd handle her character's exit. Hunter fans were begging for Carter to ride off into the sunset with her. Mendez's fans hoped he'd push his scheming ex off a cliff.

The day her character's final script landed, Elizabeth read it immediately. She couldn't wait for this to be over. No more insane hours. No more five o'clock starts, or enduring the shallow gossip of Jon, waving his weaponized lipstick pencils. No more abusive fans on the street. It'd be over soon.

She turned the page to discover Hunt's method of exit.

Oh. Well. Elizabeth sighed. Of *course* that's what they'd do.

"Have you seen this?" The furious question and sound of her trailer door flinging open were almost simultaneous. Clearly someone was too agitated to knock.

Summer was holding the script out in front of her between a finger and a thumb, as though it were diseased.

"Ah, my savior," Elizabeth drawled, setting her own script aside. "I take it you've just read about Hunt's departure? And fierce Carter's valiant efforts to save her?"

Summer's eyes flashed. "They're killing her off."

"Yes."

"I can't believe they're still doing the dead gay trope. Did they learn nothing from *The 100*?"

"Lenton wants to make certain he sees the back of me. I don't think the gay fans entered his thoughts even once."

"Doubt it." She tossed her script on the table and rammed her hands in her pockets. "I asked Autumn if we could fight it. She told me it's not my show or my place. I know she's right, but still." Summer scowled. "Shit. Our fans are going to hate this."

Huh. Elizabeth looked up in surprise.

"What?" Summer asked.

"It's so weird and new. Having fans who care about *my* character? I'm used to the pitchforks. To think I finally start liking Hunt again and this happens."

"Will you be okay to do it?"

"I'll just be lying there. You're the one who'll be doing all the traumatized acting."

"I guess." Summer looked mutinous. "Why'd they have to do that?"

"It's the three Rs for network wins: revenge, ratings, and riled-up fans." She rolled her eyes. "So, will *you* be okay?"

"Yes." Summer looked down.

"Hey," Elizabeth lifted her chin with a finger. "I'll be right there. Just think of me."

"That's the problem." Her nervous gaze caught Elizabeth's. "I will be."

———————⊹⬦⊹———————

Three days later, they were ready to shoot the death scene, and Summer had an infestation of nerves. The set was crammed—execs in suits, the whole writing team, and every staffer under the sun, all apparently pumped to see *Choosing Hope* dispatch TV's most notorious villain.

Ghouls.

It didn't help Summer's mood that she'd barely slept in the past two days. Glancing around, she took in the gloomy front of the VA hospital where they shot *Hope's* exteriors. The sun had just gone down.

"This is ironic," Elizabeth noted with a lazy smile as she approached. "This is where it all began for us."

"Yeah." Summer rubbed her arms, encased in thin scrubs.

"You'll do fine. Hunt, on the other hand, not so much. The effects team meant business." Elizabeth gestured to the fake head wound partially hidden by her hair.

The injury wouldn't be evident until Summer turned her body over. She shuddered. "No wonder I can't save you."

"Indeed." Elizabeth laughed softly and leaned in. "This really is full circle. Me covered in blood out here, you looking horrified about it."

"It's not quite the same," Summer muttered, feeling strangely empty. "For so many reasons."

Elizabeth didn't answer that. "Come on, it's almost time."

Shivering, Summer nodded, mentally reviewing the scene again. A car would crash into Elizabeth's stunt double in a hit-and-run. Carter would find her badly injured lover by the side of the road. She'd check the neck for a pulse, roll her over, discover the head wound, start to unravel, then suck it up, become all business, and begin a futile series of chest pumps.

Mendez fans would be thrilled. Until they found out their hero was behind the wheel. Christ.

So much bad drama, so little time.

———◆———

"Action!"

Joey Carter skidded to Chief Hunt's side, fear filling her face. Dropping to her knees, she rolled the prone body over and gave a strangled cry. Her eyes filled with tears as she stared into Hunt's slack features. "You won't die!" She said it sternly, like an order.

You won't die.

With trembling hands, she shifted matted, bloodied hair away from Hunt's temple and took a look at her battered face. The effects team had done an incredible job—sickeningly so. For a second, it was as if Elizabeth was lying there, about to leave her.

You won't die.

"Don't die," Summer whispered, forgetting her line. It wasn't a demand at all this time, but a pathetic, gasped plea. "Oh my God, please, no don't die." Her voice did a little wobble as Summer tried to ground herself and remember what was next.

Chest compressions. She knew this. Okay. Closing one flattened hand over the other, Summer placed them on Elizabeth's chest as she'd been instructed, and began. She magnified her elbow movements to make it look as though she were pressing harder than she was. She'd practiced for ages on a dummy, then on Elizabeth's body double, under the medical supervisor's scrutiny.

"Don't die," she said under her breath with each compression. After counting ten compressions, Summer leaned forward and placed her lips on Elizabeth's, puffing out her cheeks to simulate blowing into her mouth. The warmth under those blue-tinged lips was so reassuring that she felt ridiculous for her initial, fearful reaction.

Damn, she'd probably already screwed up the scene by being too emotional. A tear in the corner of Elizabeth's eye slowly leaked down her cheek. That did it. Summer's heart clenched, and without even thinking, she leaned in and whispered, "Damn it, don't die! You won't. I love you. You can't leave me."

"Cut!"

Oh shit.

Summer had no idea where that had come from. Or rather, she had a disturbingly good idea. And it was the exact opposite of what the script called for.

Chaos reigned.

The crew broke into applause. Ravitz, Hugo, and Lenton fell into a furious discussion about whether to keep the ad-lib, shooting dark looks her way.

Elizabeth sat up, her gaze darting between the argument and Summer.

Sitting back on her heels, Summer groaned.

"This could take a while," Elizabeth noted. "I don't think adorable Joey's supposed to be in love with a villain."

Well, Joey might not be, but...shit, shit, shit. "Yeah. Sorry, they'll probably make us do it over. But screw that walking-the-line thing they've been writing for us. Of course Joey loves her girlfriend." Oh sure, that's why you said it.

Elizabeth regarded her with interest. "Well, perhaps they'll keep it. The crew's ovation will give them pause. Either way, I gather you did brilliantly. Although, my eyes were closed so I'm not a reliable witness. You did sound appropriately lovesick though." She smiled.

Embarrassment flooded Summer. Not only had she been unprofessional, apparently she'd sounded lovesick.

This fucking job, though! Seriously—it was insane the anguish she had to put herself through some days. She clambered to her feet. "Look, while everyone argues how badly I messed up, I'm just gonna take a quick break."

Without waiting for an answer, Summer darted toward the trailers, just as Ravitz's bellowed "Take ten, people" reverberated after her.

———⋈———

Worry burned through Elizabeth's chest as she watched Summer run. They'd all forgotten lines or ad-libbed every now and then. It happened. Except Summer looked deeply troubled. After a few minutes, she shot a look at Finola and indicated where she was heading. Her assistant frowned and pointed to the fake wound on her head.

Elizabeth nodded, appreciative of her thoughtfulness, and hid the unsightly scar with her hair. No point freaking Summer out more.

She found Summer sitting on her trailer steps, arms around her legs, looking miserable.

At Elizabeth's approach, she gave a sheepish grin. "I forgot my PIN code to unlock the door. All these months, I never forgot it once, but today? No clue."

Tilting her head toward her own trailer, Elizabeth said, "Let's use mine, okay?"

Without a word, Summer stood, brushed off her scrubs, and followed.

Once they stepped inside and closed the door, Elizabeth gestured her to a seat. "Drink?"

"No thanks." Summer sank to the couch.

"Hey?" Elizabeth waited until Summer met her eye. "We're alone. Be honest: Are you okay?"

Summer's head fell into her hands. "God...it's...I know it's only acting. But still. Hunt and you do have a couple of things in common. It was hard."

"My cheekbones, right? I hear we have that in common," Elizabeth joked.

"And the beautiful hair," Summer said, with a tiny smile. "And gorgeous gray eyes."

"Flatterer." Elizabeth gave her a long look, then sat, facing her. "Want to tell me what happened?"

"I just did. You both look the same. Seeing you lying there, it was hard to separate you. That's never happened before. It's silly, I know. But, for an instant, you *were* her. And seeing you like that, it..." She clenched her fists. "Hurt."

"Oh, Summer." Elizabeth felt a rush of warmth. "I'm fine. And I don't have crazy exes hunting me down either."

That earned a wan smile.

"So that's all it was? I looked near death?"

"Mainly."

Elizabeth's index finger teased the loose blond hairs falling into Summer's eyes, trailing them over to one ear and tucking them behind it. "So what else was it? What were you thinking doing that scene?"

Summer swallowed. "Don't die. Don't leave me. Not now."

The same words she'd spoken. "I'm not going anywhere, Summer."

"You're leaving the show."

"Only the show."

"I know that up here." She tapped her temple. "But it's been ages since we've been alone, and we don't talk that often, and I'm going out of my mind. I really miss you."

Elizabeth gave her a worried look. "I thought I'd explained how long my days were. I miss you too. Please know that. I can't wait to get to know you far better."

Looking down at her hands, Summer said, "It's been a difficult night and it's all come boiling over. Craving you so much, all those charged, teasing scenes together, and now finally there you were in front of me, but you looked...like *that*. Bess, I'm sorry. I didn't mean to say it. It just came out."

"I don't understand. What came out?"

"That line was for *you*. I lost my head for a second. I'm so embarrassed."

Elizabeth blinked. "You love me? Your words were real?"

"Yes?" Summer groaned. "I'm such an idiot. Please, shoot me now."

Wonder washed through Elizabeth. Summer's anguished expression could not be allowed to stand for a second longer. With a gentle smile, she said, "You think *you're* an idiot?"

Summer frowned.

Reaching for her phone, Elizabeth scrolled to the incriminating evidence. Their photo. "Please observe: The very definition of an idiot. And I posted this for the whole world to see." She tapped her face in the picture. "Unmasked affection." Her smile became rueful. "Delvine felt the need to point out how revealing my expression was. Then my father, who I had no idea even knew what Twitter was, asked when I'd be introducing you to him and Mum."

"Really?" Summer's eyes widened.

"So here's what I know. I don't look at anyone else that way. You mean a great deal to me." She shook her head at the image, amazed at what seemed so obvious now. "Clearly." Meeting Summer's eyes, she added, "I hope you know that. There's only you."

"Oh." The word came out like an exhalation.

"So, Summer? I'd really like to kiss you now."

Summer stared at her in surprise.

"And to be clear, so there's absolutely no confusion, I really, *really* mean it." Elizabeth leaned in and let her lips show Summer just how much that was true.

Summer deepened the kiss eagerly, drawing her in.

Elizabeth's breath was ragged and her body tingled when they finally broke. All she wanted was more. Much, much more. She leaned in for a second kiss. Dimly, in the background, she was aware of a knock, but Summer's lips were so soft, so sweet…

A throat cleared.

They jerked apart.

"Oh thank God," Finola said dryly. "I thought I'd have to get out my prying bar. Or a hose."

A chill shot through Elizabeth, realizing they hadn't been alone.

Summer blushed and didn't seem to know where to look. "Uh—"

"No, don't worry." Finola shook her head. "Your secret's safe with me. Anyway, I've known for a while. You two. So oblivious for so long, I wanted to moosh your pretty heads together." She tutted. "Now then, I've been asked to find and get you both back to set. They've worked out they're keeping that take and want to move in for the singles."

"They're keeping it?" Standing, Summer looked bewildered.

"Yes, thank goodness. It was so beautiful." Finola opened the door. "I suspect there'd be a crew mutiny if they didn't."

"See? I knew it was good, even with my eyes shut." Elizabeth followed her as she headed outside.

"No, 'good' would be them not killing Hunt at all," Summer grumbled, closing the door behind her. "More dead gay trope to hurt the queer fans. Not that they care."

As they walked back toward the set, Finola pulled out her tablet and scrolled to a news site. "Well, I think you'll want to see this. It went up about half an hour ago. Perhaps your Hunter fans won't be sad for too long."

Ooh La La! 'Hunter' Actresses Star in Sexy Lesbian Drama—Sizzling Trailer for Upcoming Jean-Claude Badour Film Melts Internet.

Underneath was a red-tinged still shot, with Elizabeth and Summer in a naked clinch, covered artfully with a sheet. Summer's expression was pure mischief, while Elizabeth's heated gaze made her seem like a panther ready to pounce.

Oh…my….

Summer gasped. "Salacious much?"

"Surprising, more like," Finola said. "And great timing. I know how these things go. You two are about to be the hottest property in town."

"Well, I suppose I've done it all now," Elizabeth said. "From America's most-hated villain to melting the internet."

Finola cackled. "I'm going to miss you. You've been the least annoying lead actor I was ever assigned to assist."

"High praise." Elizabeth gave her assistant a fond look.

"Sadly, low praise. The bar's set at rock bottom. A-list stars can be such hard work. Not you. You were a kitten everyone thought was a lion."

Summer laughed. "A kitten? Bess? That's hilarious."

"As for you," Finola glanced at Summer, "you're the sweetest lion tamer that ever existed. I'll miss you both."

"Both?" Summer's step faltered. "I'm not leaving."

"You will." Finola sounded so certain. "I've been in this business a long, long time. And after all that Hunter business, and the fuss about your new movie, you'll be drowning in offers. Good." She lowered her voice. "You're both too talented for this show."

They reached the set and Finola gave them one final, indulgent look, muttered, "you two, *honestly*", and disappeared.

Sylvia and Jon scurried toward them, anxious to touch them up.

"She's right," Elizabeth said softly. "You *are* too good for this."

"Delvine said I shouldn't stay too long on *Choosing Hope*."

"Like I did?"

"She didn't say that."

291

"But it's true. I won't make that mistake again. Sometimes risk is worth it." Her gaze lingered on Summer.

Jon reached them first, took one look at Elizabeth's strategically covered wound, and scowled. "Ms. Thornton, your application is *infested* with hair!" He offered a dramatic gasp. "We'll need Special Effects to look at it." He eyeballed her. "What on *earth* have you been doing? And in only ten minutes?"

Affecting her best po-faced expression, Elizabeth shrugged. She caught Summer's "*oh fuck*" look as she tried to sneak away, trailed doggedly by Sylvia waving a can of hair spray.

Elizabeth hid a snort of laughter by only the barest of margins.

Chapter 25

IT WAS OVER. THE REST of the cast, including Summer, had wrapped up hours ago, and it was down to just Elizabeth, doing some pick-up shots of Hunt arriving at the hospital. The scenes would form part of a montage of her time as chief.

Mercifully, the fake wound was gone, so she no longer looked like she'd lost an argument with Mendez's Lexus.

In her break, earlier, she'd tracked down Finola, survived an unexpected, warm hug, and given her a few bottles of 16-year-old Lagavulin—the top-shelf whisky her assistant loved but would never buy herself.

With finality, Elizabeth hung up Hunt's coat in her trailer and studied it. So much mixed emotion for a rumpled piece of white cloth. She'd almost started liking Iris Hunt at the end. Almost.

A knock startled her out of her daydreams. "It's open."

The door swung open. A figure in a hoodie leaned against the side of the trailer, holding a bag bursting with delightful smells. "Hey sweet lady. Need some company?" Summer's grin was wide as she tilted her hoodie back to show her face.

"Dreadful line." Elizabeth's lips curled at the edges. "Have you really not remembered your trailer's code yet? Surely an AD could help."

"Yeah, I remembered it without bugging anyone. I just thought you should celebrate your first hour of freedom with someone."

"Ah. Come in."

Summer did, toeing the door shut behind her. She put the bag on the table and peeled off her hoodie to reveal a tight, white T-shirt.

"I thought you'd gone home hours ago like everyone else." Elizabeth glanced at the wall clock. Well past ten.

"I did. I had some dinner and came back." Summer pointed at her bags. "I bring offerings. The sort that women starring in a hit TV show couldn't possibly eat. But you're not bound by the laws of calorie-deprived TV actresses right now." She opened the bag and it smelled blissful. "Unless you're too tired?"

Too tired for Summer and delicious-smelling food? Was she mad? Before Elizabeth could answer, Summer continued in a nervous rush as she began plating up the food.

"Been dreaming of this for weeks. Finally able to catch up properly. Hope I'm not overstepping by imposing myself or carbs on you before you've even caught your breath." She waved at her delivery. "It's a Blastoff Burger from that retro diner. You seemed to really enjoy it."

"Lovely. Will you have some too?"

"I'm full. I'll just keep you company."

"I'd like that." Elizabeth seated herself and tried the burger, which was as delicious as it had been several months ago. Chewing slowly, she realized she had an admiring audience. Elizabeth exaggerated her appreciation, adding a soft *mmm*, observing Summer's reaction.

She gulped, looked away, then down at her hands, and finally changed the subject. "So, fess up: What'd you swipe?"

Dabbing her lips with a paper napkin, Elizabeth protested, "I have no idea what—"

"Sure you do. It's tradition: Actors always take a memento from set on their last day."

Tilting her head to indicate behind Summer, Elizabeth said, "In the bag."

Summer rummaged through it then drew out a clean, starched Hunt jacket, complete with name tag. "Oooh! You didn't!"

"I believe I did."

"What a coincidence—me telling you how hot you looked in this, and you keeping one."

"Mmm, yes, such a coincidence." Elizabeth's eyes warmed. Summer's appreciation was as good as she'd hoped.

"Starting to think you might be soft on me."

"Just a little," she smiled faintly. "But don't tell anyone. I have a reputation." She took another delicate bite, as Summer's darkening gaze devoured her.

Watching Elizabeth eat a hamburger was a divine experience, Summer decided. She chewed carefully, juices dripping onto her fingers before she reached quickly for a napkin. Summer was mesmerized.

After eating half, Elizabeth set it aside. "Thank you," she murmured. "I thought I was more tired than hungry, but it turns out you've given me a second wind." Her tongue darted out to lick her lips.

"Ungh." Summer's stomach tightened.

"Am I distracting you?" Elizabeth asked, her tone a few registers lower.

"N-no."

Laughing, Elizabeth bundled up the wrappers, tossing them in the trash. Bending over the tiny sink, she washed her hands, her black Dr. Hunt pants straining across her ass.

Holy Jesus.

"Like a drink?" Elizabeth gestured at her fridge. "There's Diet Coke."

Summer grinned.

"Okay, what's that look for?"

"You know why." Summer grinned wider. "You keep my drink. For me."

"Maybe I'm keeping it for any random stranger who likes the taste of sink cleaner?"

"You keep it for me."

"Do I?" Elizabeth sounded amused as she leaned back against the counter. "Thanks again for dinner, Summer. I appreciated the thought. And the company."

"You're welcome." Summer couldn't resist staring at her lips. So perfectly shaped and the palest pink.

"What's your schedule like tomorrow? Are you at work early, or...?" Elizabeth lifted her eyebrows.

Summer suddenly realized exactly why this was a very important question. "Late call tomorrow." She barely croaked out the words. "Starting at eleven."

Their gazes met and for a moment neither spoke.

"I've never done anything like this before," Elizabeth said quietly, all traces of humor gone. "Until you, I'd never even kissed a co-star off-screen."

"We don't have to do anything tonight. I just wanted to spend time with you," Summer said honestly. "It's been so long."

"It has. That's the thing. I can't deny how you make me feel. This isn't something frivolous, is it?"

"No." Summer gazed up at her, willing her to see. "This really counts."

"It does." Elizabeth hesitated, then walked to the trailer door and locked it. The sound of the lock snapping reverberated throughout the silent room. She glanced back at Summer, desire clear in her eyes.

Oh God.

Returning, Elizabeth tugged Summer to her feet and slid her fingers behind her head.

The teasing of her soft lips took Summer by surprise. Arousal snaked through her like quicksilver, and she responded hungrily. Elizabeth's tongue, seeking admission, was like brushing a flame. Heated, dangerous. They kissed for long, tantalizing minutes until Elizabeth pulled away, earning a disappointed whimper from Summer.

"Patience." Elizabeth smiled and teased open the top button of her Hunt shirt. The garment was sharp, pristine, professional. Another button fell prey to her fingers. Then another. Slowly revealed was a nude satin bra.

Mercy. Summer's fingers itched to be the ones peeling aside the material.

"Do you remember the first time you were ever in here?" Elizabeth murmured. "I started to undo my shirt without thinking."

Oh, Summer remembered that very well.

"I stopped of course, when I realized. But I was most surprised by the way you blushed." A smile tugged at her lips. "Admittedly, I didn't think too much about it. You were baffling enough already. But now, Summer, I have to wonder. What *were* you thinking?"

Summer felt sheepish. "I think you fried my brain. But, yeah, I really wanted to touch you."

"Is that so? Where?" Elizabeth eyed her coolly. "My neck?" Her fingertips trailed to her throat. "Collar bone?" Fingers traced the bones in question.

"Y-yes."

"Anywhere else? Perhaps, a little...lower?" Her fingers slid against the hard knots forming beneath the silky bra.

"You like the idea I wanted you," Summer said, suddenly curious. "What would you have done if I *had* touched you?"

Elizabeth's eyebrows knitted. "I'd have flung you out of my trailer and tossed your tea after you. But that was then." Her fingers lifted to trace Summer's cheek. "I gave you permission once before to touch. On set." Her expression became intense. "But this time, you can have all of me." Elizabeth slid off her shirt, then undid her bra, slowly dropping it to the floor.

Her breasts were as spectacular as ever, but there was something overwhelming about being offered them, in the most erotic way imaginable. "I want," Summer rasped, "all of you."

"Then by all means..." Elizabeth pulled Summer over to the bed and pressed her to the mattress. Her lips curved. "But Summer? Take me *slowly.*"

———— ✦ ————

Having Summer Hayes make love to you was like being dipped in slick, erotic massage oil. Elizabeth's nerve endings lit up in response to those smoldering eyes. Oh, she'd been wanted before. But never like this. Summer's hands worshipped the shape of her, the weight of her, memorizing her body. Her fingers and eyes mapped Elizabeth with the devotion of a cartographer.

With fingertips feather-light, Summer traced Elizabeth's tightening nipples. "You're exquisite." Her voice was worshipful.

Elizabeth shivered. Summer had touched her before—for the cameras. She'd tasted her skin, her lips, even her nipples. But this felt so very different. They were alone, for one, and the look in Summer's eyes was nothing Elizabeth had ever seen. It was hungry. Possessive. Fire and arousal. But more than that. There was love.

All for me.

Under the effect of those searing eyes, arousal rippled through her.

Lips teased Elizabeth from her collar bone down to her nipples, where Summer stayed, indulging herself languidly.

Wetness from the trails of her tongue glistened in the low light. Summer paused, reviewed her work, and with a small, satisfied smile, continued lower.

Her hands came to rest on the waist of Elizabeth's dark pants. She hesitated at the waistband, setting off another round of shivers.

Swallowing, Elizabeth said, "Please." Her desperate voice sounded like grit and honey.

Slowly Summer divested Elizabeth of her tailored black pants, before raking her gaze over Elizabeth's bikini briefs. Her fingers traced the lacy trim of one leg, curling under it, teasing the softer skin beneath.

After a playful moment, Summer peeled off the briefs, then sat back on her haunches. She studied Elizabeth's naked body with a hungry gaze.

Self-consciousness pricked at Elizabeth, as it always did, heat suffusing her cheeks. She'd never been the best at nudity; it made her feel too vulnerable.

"You're gorgeous," Summer assured her.

"I appear to be at a disadvantage." She eyed Summer's still-dressed body.

"Oh. Right." Summer scrambled off the bed, tearing off her T-shirt and bra. She hauled her jeans and panties down with little finesse. Kicking the clothes away, Summer straightened. She stood, bare and delectable, hands dropping to her hips. With a nervous grin, she asked, "Better?"

Elizabeth's gaze scorched her from tip to toe. She'd seen Summer almost nude before, but she'd never soaked her in like this. Now she was free to swallow the shape of her—strong bones, soft, generous breasts, and curving hips. "Delectable," she decided.

Summer grinned and pinned her down again in an instant, her lightly tanned skin sliding over Elizabeth's much paler body. Summer's hand slipped low between them with determination.

"You're so wet," she said in wonder.

"All your fault."

"Can't wait to taste you." Summer didn't wait for a reply, sliding into position. Bending forward, she explored Elizabeth's folds with enthusiastic attention to detail.

Oh God. Elizabeth's hips jerked. Her fingers curled into fists, clutching the bedding. Muscles in her arms turned into writhing ropes. Elizabeth's breath became shorter, deeper, rasping out her pleasure. *Oh yes.* She was close.

Summer suddenly slowed her teasing to a crawl. Her expression turned impish.

No! That taunting little... When she'd told Summer she wanted slow, she'd just meant she didn't want everything over in thirty seconds.

"Faster," Elizabeth growled, earning a small snort of laughter.

Summer began using her tongue like a feather.

"This *is* evil."

Summer licked even more lightly.

"Fas-ter!" She clenched her jaw. Desperately, she tried to chase the ecstasy dancing just out of reach. Her hands burrowed deeper into the bedding, becoming white-knuckled fists. "Summer, *please.*"

Summer gasped against her, and then nearly whined. Her swirling tongue hardened. Two fingers slid inside Elizabeth, curling upwards.

God. Lights seemed to be going off in Elizabeth's head "*Oh. Ohh.*" She couldn't hang on. She couldn't... Her body went rigid. Ecstasy crashed through her. For a moment, between one stuttering heartbeat and the next, it felt as if she'd lost all her walls in the tumbling, chaotic wash of sensations. She was bared. Exposed.

Totally naked.

Elizabeth braced herself for the crush of anxiety that always came with it. Yet her throat continued to freely take in air. Her hands slowly unfurled. Her brain sighed in bliss, offering no fretful doubts. Sagging in relief, she steadied her breath. Trust Summer to somehow breach all her walls, and for Elizabeth's blissed-out mind to just shrug.

Her legs shifted. *Christ, I'm so wet.*

Getting her breath back, Elizabeth gave Summer a dangerous, half-lidded look.

Summer swallowed shakily, eyes wide and dark.

Excellent. Flipping them over, Elizabeth pushed Summer onto her back, and took in the sight of her.

Ghosting her fingers across Summer's throat, down her neck and lower, Elizabeth considered all the ways she could take her. All the delectable choices to make her whimper helplessly, the way Summer had done with her. Her hands drifted up to cup Summer's breast.

Summer watched avidly, breath ragged. Her nostrils flared.

"You've been driving me crazy." Elizabeth gave that plump nipple a tweak. "All the times Hunt got to touch you, I imagined this. Us." *Tweak.* "Alone."

Summer's nipples hardened into points.

"I see I wasn't the only one." Elizabeth gave her a knowing look. "Was I?"

"I...No." Summer gasped. "I wanted you. So much. All the time."

"I've thought rather a lot about what you'd like. What I might do when you're laid out before me, like this. Naked. Needy. So wet for my touch." She trailed a finger down Summer's side, jumping a rib at a time.

Summer's lip caught between her teeth.

"I expended considerably more thought on it than I should have." Elizabeth's voice was mischievous. "All this chemistry everyone keeps talking about? It's apparently *electric. Oozing. Sizzling.*" She slid the back of her fingertips over to Summer's belly button, doing a playful swirl around it. The skin quivered. "It's high time we explored it, don't you think? High time I took advantage of..." Her fingers drifted lower, to the trimmed blonde curls between Summer's thighs. "*our chemistry.*"

Summer trembled.

Settling between Summer's legs, Elizabeth slid her gaze up the length of her to the wide eyes staring back. Her hands flattened to part Summer's strong, tanned thighs. "Is this your fantasy?" She blew against the slick folds spread before her. "You, open for me? Me, having my way with you?"

"N-no."

"No?" Curiosity streaked through her. "It isn't?"

"No," Summer moaned. "It's touching you. This is far beyond my fantasies."

Elizabeth touched her languidly. "You didn't dare to dream?"

"Not like this. Please," Summer pleaded, hips arching up. "Stop teasing. I can't..."

"You can. You made me suffer a little, didn't you?" Elizabeth murmured, her mouth moving closer, gaze pinned on Summer's. "What if I got the Hunt jacket out? Would you enjoy that? All those long looks for the camera and we couldn't do a damn thing? What if we finished it *right now.*" Her finger slid forward, poised at Summer's entrance.

"Oh God, stop it," Summer groaned. "I'm dying."

"Are you sure you want me to stop? Really, *Dr. Carter*?" She hit exactly the right tone.

"Fuck...you're killing me." Summer's voice cracked. Her hips quivered.

Arousal swamped Elizabeth's fingertips. "Well, we can't have that." Elizabeth smiled, then buried herself between her lover's legs, licking and peppering her with kisses, alternating with deep strokes of her fingers.

Summer's whispered sighs soon turned into gasps, finally a cry. She arched and bucked, coming as her fingers clenched hard in Elizabeth's hair.

The sight of her lover in the throes of orgasm was intoxicating. Elizabeth was suddenly on the edge again, almost dizzy with desire. She reached between her own thighs and rubbed her clit, hard. Unfocused and trembling, she shut her eyes, her breath coming in short, heated gasps against Summer's center. It took only moments before she shuddered and peaked again.

When she opened her eyes, her first sight was Summer's smoldering gaze.

"God," Summer breathed, voice reverent. "You...that was so hot."

"Hmm." Elizabeth scribbled her soaked fingers across Summer's thighs, admiring the wet trails. She slid forward, onto her side, to lie beside her lover. "I agree." She gave Summer a teasing look. "So, be honest. I think you like me being Hunt sometimes."

Summer's mouth opened, apparently ready for a denial, before she chuckled. "Maybe. Every now and then. But really, you're my turn-on. I'd happily stay like this forever. They'd have to haul me out of here by my fingernails."

"Forever's a long time." Elizabeth pretended to give the flippant line serious thought. "I might have to rearrange my schedule. I'm sure bedding you 24/7 might give Delvine, Rachel, and Autumn matching ulcers."

"Probably." Summer gently ran her hand through Elizabeth's hair.

"What are you thinking?" Elizabeth asked.

"That I'm a lucky woman. And the other thing. What I said earlier." Summer huffed out a breath. "The most embarrassing ad-lib ever. What Joey said."

"What Joey said," Elizabeth repeated. She might not be quite there yet, but it would be so easy to love Summer. "I'm deeply flattered by what Joey said." She kissed Summer again and sighed. "It's late. Come home with me. Stay the night. I can promise a beautiful view from my bedroom in the morning."

"Mmm. Sounds great...I'd love to see you when I wake."

"I meant the view out my window." Elizabeth's lips curled. "You can see almost as far as the bay. It's magic."

"As if I'll be looking outside in the morning." Summer's smile was wide. "Let's go."

Chapter 26

IT HAD BEEN WEEKS SINCE their first night together. Since then, Summer had burrowed into Elizabeth's bed and showed little sign of ever wanting to leave. Elizabeth approved of this development a great deal.

Summer would reach Elizabeth's front door each night after work and melt into her. They'd come together in a frantic clash of lips and skin and fingers. Mornings involved languid touches and slower kisses; exciting in a different way.

It was Finola who finally forced them out of bed. For some reason, she alone had the power to motivate Summer to crawl out from the sheets and work out where her clothes and car keys were. Elizabeth hadn't even realized the pair had become so close.

Today was Sunday and the date of a party she'd invited Summer to, apparently with instructions to bring "that cynical, charming co-star you keep practicing mouth-to-mouth with". Of course Finola would think that was funny. No doubt further ribbing lay ahead.

They were on their way to Summer's place to pick something up for the party. Elizabeth's eyes slid to her grumbling, monologuing driver.

"If it was anyone else," Summer muttered, "I'd have told them where to jump. Interrupting the best sex of my life…"

Elizabeth decided that preening was somewhat vulgar, but she loved Summer's enlightening speech. *Best sex of her life?* Well, she concurred.

Summer's mood had improved by the time she let herself into her Silver Lake bungalow.

The place was cute, although the Kermit-green painted exterior was an acquired taste. Maybe Skye had helped with the décor? Elizabeth laughed when she saw the garden's succulent patch, and a few prickly specimens in particular. "You *do* grow cacti! I told Jean-Claude no lies."

"It's *cactuses*," Summer teased back. "And the most I ever do is look at them occasionally. There's not much hands-on growing involved. Come inside."

Although it was almost eleven, Chloe was mid-crunch of her cereal, sprawled on the couch, when Elizabeth trailed after Summer into the living room.

"Hey stranger," Chloe greeted her roommate. "Starting to think you'd moved out." She arched her neck to see behind Summer. "Oh, hey. A *Choosing Hope* double header. Awesome."

"Single header," Elizabeth said. "I've left the show now."

"Oh, 'kay." Chloe resumed chewing. "Good timing, but. Summer, your mum's here for lunch. She's in the kitchen so you could probably do a camo-crawl to your room if you don't want to see her." She grinned.

"Skye's here?" Elizabeth asked. "Does she often come for lunch when Summer's out?"

"It's Sunday. She's here every Sunday, with or without me," Summer said. "She's adopted Chloe as a third kid." She turned back to Chloe. "Autumn here too?"

"Nope. She's coming later when the chook's on the table."

"Okay. Well, we'll say a quick hello before we get going. We're here to pick up a present on our way to see Bess's old assistant." She glanced at Elizabeth with a slightly guilty look. "It's, um, a birthday thing."

Elizabeth's eyes widened. "Wait, it's Finola's birthday?" Why hadn't Summer told her? Or Finola for that matter? She didn't have a gift or a—

"No, her son's, don't worry," Summer called over her shoulder. "It's cool. I've got a present for both of us. You're covered. Anyway, back in a sec."

Elizabeth wandered the living room, taking in the nick-knacks under Chloe's watchful gaze.

"Someone got lucky," Chloe observed, putting down her now empty bowl.

Elizabeth shrugged. "I feel lucky." It was the truth.

"Don't worry about the kid birthday thing. Summer does it with everyone. Makes friends with the universe. Remembers the most random people's anniversaries, birthdays, all that jazz. Just go with it."

Elizabeth nodded, but it was still a little unnerving.

Skye appeared, bustling out of the kitchen. "Chicken's in the oven. Should be an hour or so and... Oh, Elizabeth, darling! When did you get here? How lovely to see you! Where's Summer? Are you staying for lunch? You must!"

"Sorry, we can't," Elizabeth said. "There's a birthday party for my former assistant's son this afternoon. We're making an appearance."

"How nice of you! Isn't that nice, Chloe?" Skye turned to her.

"Totally." Chloe grinned at Elizabeth, mischief in her eye.

Elizabeth shot her a narrowed look that earned her a laugh for her trouble. Okay. She officially liked Chloe.

Skye dropped to the couch beside Chloe and patted the spare seat on her other side. "Sit, for a moment, dear. We need to talk."

Wary, Elizabeth slid onto the appointed cushion, giving the woman a quizzical eyebrow lift.

"Darling, where are you?" Skye called.

Summer appeared holding a gift bag festooned with ribbons. "Finding the gift. What's up?"

Turning to Chloe, Skye said, "Would you mind keeping an eye on the chicken? Just for a few minutes."

Chloe took the hint, nodded, and grabbed her bowl, disappearing into the kitchen.

Pointing to the vacated seat, Skye eyed Summer. "Sit, sit."

Summer obeyed, wearing a confused expression.

"So, you two." Skye slid her eyes from one to the other and smiled. "I'm so glad it's worked out."

"Um, of course." Summer glanced at Elizabeth. "Why wouldn't it?"

"I wasn't sure it would," she said, lowering her voice conspiratorially. "I know, I know, I'm a meddling mother but I just couldn't help myself."

Elizabeth peered at her, suddenly getting a very odd feeling. "What did you do?"

"Oh, I knew you two weren't dating. Back when Jean-Claude originally asked me. I thought it was a shame and all, because, oh my goodness, how much Summer used to talk about you. 'Elizabeth Thornton this'. 'Elizabeth Thornton that'."

"Mom! Geez." Summer groaned.

"It's true, dear. Jean-Claude saw the paparazzi photos and called to ask about them. I knew why he was asking. He loves to put couples in film. It's a chemistry thing. So…a little white lie just spilled out. I thought maybe you could get to know each other a little better on set. And the way Summer was so insistent on telling me it wasn't true, I thought she was protesting too much. And maybe, Elizabeth, you could see how wonderful Summer is away from your show, because I know you don't have many scenes together, do you? Well, you didn't used to." Her eyebrows lifted. "That Hunter hashtag is everywhere now."

Summer froze. "Mom? Are you saying you…set us up?"

"Yes, dear, I did." She beamed with pride. "It was enormously funny watching you at the pool party. Goodness me, did you actually know *anything* about each other then? I was biting my cheek not to laugh. Your father was incredulous you were even friends. I told him to give you both time. Oh, he doesn't know the truth. He's terribly indiscreet, not like me. And look at you now." She cupped both their cheeks. "So happy together. Do I know a good match or what?"

"You *knew*." Elizabeth barked out a laugh.

"Well, Chloe didn't, though she probably does now," Skye said. "She's an atrocious eavesdropper."

"Am not!" came an indignant call from the kitchen. "And, oh my God, you fakers!" Her raucous laugh followed. "Fuck me dead!"

"I told you it's rude to eavesdrop," Skye called back. She rolled her eyes.

"I don't understand," Summer said. "How did you know we've really gotten together?"

"That Twitter photo—the one at the diner? It was obvious if you've met either of you. You only had eyes for each other." Her smile widened. "I love being right about this."

"What about Jean-Claude?" Summer frowned. "He'll be furious if he finds out."

"Yes. We'll just be sure he never knows, all right?" She nodded firmly to herself. "Good. On your way now. Don't want to disappoint that birthday boy. And Summer, call me tonight about this." Her finger swirled between Summer and Elizabeth. "I require details."

"Mom!"

"Not *those* kind of details. Good heavens. I swear you make me sound like I raised a prude!"

———◦✦◦———

Outside the front door, Summer and Elizabeth exchanged looks.

"I had no clue." Summer slumped against the shut door. She couldn't believe it.

"I gathered."

"I'm sorry. My family is totally mad." She hoped Elizabeth wouldn't freak out about this. Although, she wouldn't blame her.

"I gather that too." Elizabeth smiled. "It's fine. You tipped me off about them going in, remember? I expected a certain amount of craziness."

"What about your family? Please tell me your folks are a little special, too? Prone to some charming eccentricities? It can't be just mine."

Elizabeth laughed. "Not like yours, sorry. My parents rarely ask me anything personal in case I might offer an embarrassing answer. And I guarantee they'd never try to fix me up with a woman I liked either."

With a groan, Summer banged her head gently against the door. "Great. Normal parents. I don't even know what plane of existence my mom lives on. She's nuts."

Dropping a kiss on her lips, Elizabeth said, "No, she's not. She just wants you happy. And I love that your family is anything but boring. Just like you. Come on. Let's go endure Finola's doubtlessly atrocious teasing. And I'll thank you in advance for whatever gift I'm claiming credit for."

"A Nerf Zombie Blaster." Summer grinned.

Elizabeth snorted. "That's so me." She leaned in and snagged Summer closer. "Hey?"

"Yeah?" Summer wrapped her arms around her, enjoying the sensation of holding her tight.

"I've said it before and I'll say it again. You're beautiful. Inside and out." Elizabeth kissed her.

Summer was too dazed to reply. Then again, she often forgot how to form sentences around this woman.

"Okay," Elizabeth straightened. "Let's go face the maddening Scot."

Epilogue

"WHERE ARE YOU GOING?" ELIZABETH'S dissatisfied voice demanded from under a pile of sheets, as she felt the bed dip.

"Shower."

"Time is it?" They hadn't gotten much sleep last night, something that was entirely Summer's fault. Summer and her delicious wandering lips. "Never mind. Too early."

"Go back to sleep then."

"Well, I can't now. Too many distractions." Elizabeth cracked an eye as Summer disappeared into the en suite, leaving the door open.

A few minutes later, the hiss of water began, and Summer stepped into the shower, becoming a pink shimmer behind the glass.

"My favorite view."

"Liar," Summer called back. "It's the one out your window. I'm sure that's what you told me."

"Nonsense." Elizabeth sat up. "It's definitely you."

It was true. Even after six months, she never tired of this. Summer—bare, warm, beautiful, hers. No matter how busy Summer had been with work, how crazy the publicity for *Choosing Hope* and *Eight Little Pieces* had been lately, she always found time for Elizabeth.

The chief's farewell episode had been nominated for two Emmys—outstanding directing and outstanding supporting actress in a drama. Summer's first nomination.

For weeks, the network had blitzed the airwaves with clips from that episode, milking the nominations for publicity. As much as Elizabeth loved seeing the way Summer looked at her in that tear-jerking, dying Hunt clip they used, Summer always turned off the TV in a huff.

"Too real," she'd always say, followed by "and I can't believe I told you I loved you for the first time in front of the whole of America."

"Whole of the world," she'd dutifully reply. *Choosing Hope* aired in thirty-two countries, after all. Summer never found that argument as funny as Elizabeth did.

She hadn't won the Emmy. Ravitz had, though. He'd even remembered to thank Summer and Elizabeth in his speech, before taking full credit for Hunter. "Our bold vision", he'd called it. "Diversity really matters to us."

Sure it did.

Elizabeth had found commiserating with Summer through kisses and passionate sex to be of mutual benefit. Even though Summer hadn't seemed surprised or bothered by her loss.

As the shower ran, Elizabeth reached for her phone and scrolled through *Variety*'s entertainment alerts. Her eye was drawn to a familiar photo.

Grace. Her heart lurched, but not in the way it used to. She felt only a tinge of sadness at the reminder of their contentious parting.

The story announced she'd left *Loving Under Palms* due to "creative differences" and was returning home to the UK to pursue projects there. So she'd taken Elizabeth's advice after all. Grace already had an historical miniseries lined up called *Queens and Legends*. First up was a story about the warrior queen Boudicca which they were filming on some remote map smudge of an island off Wales.

Well, Grace always said she wanted to travel.

Of course she'd nail it. It didn't matter her age or that she didn't have a warriorly bone in her lissome body. Grace would own it. And by the time she came up for air and returned to civilization, she'd be an adored star once more. Exactly what she needed to thrive.

Elizabeth skipped the *Read More* button and moved on. She bore Grace no ill will, but she was in the past now.

Flicking over to her inbox, Elizabeth snorted softly at the first email. The Hunter fans were on protest number fifty or something, trying to get Chief Hunt resurrected. *Good luck with that.* They were also organizing their own Hunter convention. She and Summer had been invited to make a star appearance.

Hell, maybe they'd do it—if she could feed Rachel enough heart medication before telling her. Actually, given her agent's secret love of Hunter, she'd probably attend in disguise.

It was so surreal. Elizabeth's eyes drifted to the naked shimmer of her lover in the shower. If only fans knew she spent her days and nights doing delightfully unspeakable things to Summer Hayes.

Jean-Claude, of all people, was the most in love with Hunter devotees. He might be artsy, elitist, and hate American television with a passion, but the *Choosing Hope* fans had made his film a glorious hit by indie standards. Somehow Elizabeth doubted they were seeing it for the intricate layered storyline, or Lucas the linesman's take on regret.

Even Jean-Claude hadn't deluded himself into believing that either. He'd taken to tagging his *Eight Little Pieces* film plugs with #Hunter.

The shower's hiss stopped. Summer toweled off and returned to the bedroom, nude and glorious.

Adorable.

"I love you," Elizabeth said. *Oh!* She hadn't intended to say that at all. Well, not yet. She'd had it all planned for dinner on Saturday. There'd even be Marcus's chocolate lava cake. She'd wheedled the recipe out of him. As she'd planned the evening, Elizabeth had been astonished to realize how much this meant to her. She craved Summer constantly now, and not just physically. She was a warm, kind soul who reminded Elizabeth of what was important. Summer made life worth getting out of—and into—bed for.

Summer froze. "You do?"

"Of course I love you. You're you, after all. And I'm only human." She smiled.

Summer bounced on the bed beside her. "You 'Joey' me," she teased.

"I'm rethinking it rapidly if you call it that." Elizabeth attempted to look arch, but knew her amused tone gave her away.

"When did you know?"

Trust Summer to demand all the details. She thought back. *Since you flung me down in my trailer and I couldn't remember my own name afterwards? Since you thrashed my friends at Shakespeare? Since you told Jean-Claude I loved* Thriller *house architecture?*

"Who can say?" Elizabeth side-eyed her. "Are we going to have a big discussion about it, because I might point out I'm British. We don't do that."

"Ha. Okay." Summer slung her arms around Elizabeth's neck. "It was my green fingers, wasn't it?" she joked.

"Sure. Nothing says love like gangrene." Elizabeth laughed.

Summer joined in. "I adore you. But you already knew that." She covered her with kisses and lazily traced her fingers over Elizabeth's skin.

"I should move," Elizabeth said, after the teasing stretched on for long minutes. "Do something. I've got that Jane Campion film coming up. I have to learn my lines."

"That English film? You'll be *so* good in it. My highly-placed sources tell me Campion *loved* you in *Eight Little Pieces*."

"Sources? Who?"

"Mom. She knows people who know people who know Campion's dog walker."

"Well, that sounds credible. But I love your confidence."

"Hey, that's what I'm here for. I'll miss you though."

There was that. Four months off in England, away from Summer, who was still sifting through offers now that her *Choosing Hope* run had finished. Four. Months.

"About that…" Elizabeth pursed her lips, not sure quite which way this would go. "Remember how your dream was to do Shakespeare in England?"

"*Was* being the operative word. I grew up, moved on." Summer plucked at the sheet pooled around her.

"What if you didn't have to?"

Summer looked at her in confusion.

"It's just that after your story of acerbic Margaret at the Royal Bard Theatre Troupe, I suspected I knew her. Margaret Kent was the artistic director at the Royal Shakespeare Company when I interned there, before she moved to RBTT."

"You *know* her?"

"I suspected I did. I contacted her to see if she was the same Margaret. She remembers you, by the way."

"Oh God." Summer covered her face.

"Fondly."

"Uh-huh."

"The 'impertinent, oblivious American'. From her, that's almost an enthusiastic interest."

"Sure it is."

"I asked if she had any internships going. The six-month ones."

Nervous tension snapped Summer's body straight. "What?" she whispered.

"She explained how impossible they are to get. Thousands apply— eminently suitable candidates who've been immersed in British culture and Shakespeare from childhood. 'And they don't sound like brassy American foghorns'. Her words, not mine."

"This again?" Summer sagged. "That's why I gave up. You don't have to tell me all the ways she said no. I've heard them all."

"Actually, Margaret said she'd have said yes to you at least auditioning for her if you'd just said the one thing she was waiting to hear."

Summer's eyes flew wide open.

"She was waiting for you to say 'I love the bard more than breathing'. When you didn't say you adored him, she wondered if you merely saw this as a challenge; something to be checked off before returning home."

"*Shit.*" Summer looked appalled.

"So I took it upon myself to fill her in about your passion. I added that you rendered both myself and Grace Christie-Oberon speechless during a private Shakespearean performance."

Summer had stopped breathing.

"She said she'd seen you act. The direct quote was, 'thank God you both left that hideous hospital show. Waste of talent. Oh, and Miss Hayes was robbed of that Emmy'."

"Margaret said *that*?"

"Dame Margaret now. And she did. Along with a comment that the internship's yours if you want it, plus a spiel about how she'd enjoy whipping you into shape, training you properly, torturing you a little, and making sure you understand that theater is about teamwork, not divas."

"She's...offering me an internship?"

"Six months. You'd be doing wenches, handmaids, and mistresses like any other newcomer. If you're lucky, she says she might let you loose on Emilia in *Othello* later."

"I...need a minute."

Elizabeth bit her lip. It had been no small favor she'd called in, putting herself on the line for Summer. Mercifully, Margaret hadn't been too obnoxious about it, despite having the disposition for it. They'd never been friends, but shared a mutual respect. The sharp-eyed veteran had also worked out a few things on her own.

"Is it because you're soft on her, Elizabeth?"

"Our TV show was amping up the drama," she'd said with a soft snort. "It's *acting*."

"*Elizabeth Thornton*." Margaret's tone had contained so much censure that Elizabeth had felt like an intern again. "I saw *Eight Little Pieces*. That was eye-opening. Clever man, Badour. He strips away the layers of his cast as much as his characters. As soon as I saw the film I understood."

"Understood what?"

"It's addictive, isn't it? Being so close to talent? When I saw the Frenchman's film I realized that's what attracted you to her. Her skill was so raw. Real. Impossible to deny. Her talent seeps from the screen like watercolor. More than that—you came alive together. I couldn't just *see* the way you reacted to each other. I *felt* it. Deny it all you like, but it's there. So forgive me if I don't buy your dismissal of affection for Miss Hayes as something manufactured. Do me the courtesy of honesty."

So Elizabeth had done something she never did: bared herself to someone who had no right to her truth. Difficult as that had been, she didn't regret it. Now Summer could have her dream. It meant they wouldn't be apart for endless months. Assuming Summer still wanted this. Nervously, she studied Summer's thoughtful gaze.

"This is incredible," Summer said. "But I'll have to do some fast-talking with Autumn. She'll kill me if I'm gone from LA for six months."

"Actually, she seemed to think it'd be good for your acting development to take the internship. Although she expects you back in LA straight after it's finished."

"You colluded with my sister! And she *agreed*?"

"I did. Besides, Autumn has some Punky cons for you in London and an ex-boyfriend she wants to visit."

"You two sneaks!" Summer slapped Elizabeth's arm. "Oh my God, this is amazing!"

"You're really quite violent. To think you were so sweet when we first met."

"Sweet? I squirted fake blood all over you and you were furious."

"Do you know some of it went up my nose? In my eyes? Down my bra. I even swallowed it. Tastes foul."

Summer winced. "I'm so sorry."

"And then you looked at me with those big, innocent eyes, as though you could just die from the sheer horror of it all, and it was a struggle to stay enraged. That was when I most wanted to quit, but I never wanted you gone. Maybe part of me knew even then."

"Knew what?"

"That you weren't safe to be around." She pulled Summer closer. "That my lungs might find it harder to breathe, that my lips would desire yours, that my eyes would wander to you, and that you were simply far too adorable to let go."

"Oh," Summer breathed.

"And here we are, over a year later, and I still really don't want to let you go. Be it England or LA, where you go, I go. Let's just...be together. Live together. All of it."

"Bess..." Summer wrapped herself tightly around Elizabeth. "Yes."

"Yes?" Elizabeth's heart felt ready to pound out of her chest.

"It's hard enough going home some nights when all I want is to be with you. I miss you all the time. It's not even a question. I'd love that!"

"Okay. That's...that's good then. Excellent." Elizabeth kissed her, relief swamping her. "It's settled." She slid onto her side, resting her head on her hand, and eyed her lover. "So what do you plan to do today?" she asked, twirling her fingers over Summer's bare belly, enjoying the way she squirmed under her touch. "What has you up so early?"

"I have a hot date."

"Oh?" Elizabeth's eyebrows lifted.

"I'm going to check out some sexy ladies."

"I confess undying love, ask you to move in, and already you're stepping out on me?"

Summer laughed. "There are pair of unusual old buildings down by the pier that will photograph beautifully in the early light. Want to come too? It'll be fun."

That did sound interesting. "Why not? Sexy ladies are my favorite things to admire."

"Yup. Damn." She looked down at herself. "I suppose I have to get some clothes on." Summer made to move.

"No." Elizabeth's arm flashed out to stop her.

"No?"

"No. First I want to play with one particular sexy lady."

"Which one?" Summer asked innocently.

"I think you know." Elizabeth tugged her closer. "Summer," she said, her voice low and throaty, "I'm going to kiss you now. And just so you know? I'm going to mean it."

Summer's lips curled.

About Lee Winter

Lee Winter is an award-winning veteran newspaper journalist who has lived in almost every Australian state, covering courts, crime, news, features and humour writing. Now a full-time author and part-time editor, Lee is also a 2015 and 2016 Lambda Literary Award finalist and has won several Golden Crown Literary Awards. She lives in Western Australia with her long-time girlfriend, where she spends much time ruminating on her garden, US politics, and shiny, new gadgets.

CONNECT WITH LEE

Website: www.leewinterauthor.com

Other Books from Ylva Publishing

www.ylva-publishing.com

The Brutal Truth

Lee Winter

ISBN: 978-3-95533-898-5
Length: 339 pages (108,000 words)

Aussie crime reporter Maddie Grey is out of her depth in New York and secretly drawn to her twice-married, powerful media mogul boss, Elena Bartell, who eats failing newspapers for breakfast. As work takes them to Australia, Maddie is goaded into a brief bet—that they will say only the truth to each other. It backfires catastrophically. A lesbian romance about the lies we tell ourselves.

Departure from the Script
(The Hollywood Series – Book 1)

Jae

ISBN: 978-3-95533-195-5
Length: 240 pages (52,000 words)

Amanda isn't looking for a relationship—and certainly not with Michelle. She has never been attracted to a butch woman before, and Michelle personifies the term butch. Having just landed a role on a TV show, Amanda is determined to focus on her career. But after a date that is not a date and some meddling from her grandmother, she wonders if it's not time for a departure from her dating script.

The Music and the Mirror
Lola Keeley

ISBN: 978-3-96324-014-0
Length: 311 pages (120,000 words)

Anna is the newest member of an elite ballet company. Her first class almost ruins her career before it begins. She must face down jealousy, sabotage, and injury to pour everything into opening night and prove she has what it takes. In the process, Anna discovers that she and the daring, beautiful Victoria have a lot more than ballet in common.

Heartwood
Catherine Lane

ISBN: 978-3-95533-674-5
Length: 311 pages (86,000 words)

When the law firm she works for sends Nikka to the Springs, home of lesbian author Beth Walker, she is determined to prove herself to her boss, Lea.

But nothing is as it seems. Beth is hiding her past with a film star. Lea may be keeping Beth prisoner in her own home. The only person who knows the truth is adorably impulsive Maggie.

Will Nikka dare look into the mystery—and into her own heart?

Breaking Character
© 2018 by Lee Winter

ISBN: 978-3-96324-113-0

Also available as e-book.

Published by Ylva Publishing, legal entity of Ylva Verlag, e.Kfr.

Ylva Verlag, e.Kfr.
Owner: Astrid Ohletz
Am Kirschgarten 2
65830 Kriftel
Germany

www.ylva-publishing.com

First edition: 2018

Credits
Edited by Astrid Ohletz and Alissa McGowan
Cover Design and Print Layout by Streetlight Graphics

Made in the USA
Middletown, DE
07 May 2021